P9-CML-449

PRAISE FOR *CRY PILOT*

"I picked it up, I started reading. I kept reading. This is that kind of book, intense, involving, with intriguing world development. Recommended. Joel Dane is a writer to watch."

—C. J. Cherryh, author of the Foreigner series

"Joel Dane's *Cry Pilot* is a hyperkinetic and unflinching battle narrative that never loses sight of the truth of being a soldier: The squad comes before all else. Told with momentum and immediacy, *Cry Pilot* is authentic, exciting, and excellent."

—Marko Kloos, author of *Terms of Enlistment*

"In *Cry Pilot*, Joel Dane has imagined a fascinating high-tech future Earth where ecological collapse and runaway evolution have conspired to create enemies no army has ever encountered before. Told through the eyes of a young soldier seeking to escape a grim past, the action-packed plot holds tight to a human dimension."

—Linda Nagata, author of the Red Trilogy

"Awesome read! The language takes you into the world of the story. The first-person voice invites you to internalize the world of the character, a time and place strangely prescient. Joel Dane has created a uniquely familiar world reminiscent of the Mesozoic Era of large predators, only in the future. I look forward to seeing what he writes next."

—Nico Lathouris, screenwriter, *Mad Max: Fury Road*

CRY PILOT

JOEL DANE

ACE
NEW YORK

ACE
Published by Berkley
An imprint of Penguin Random House LLC
1745 Broadway, New York, NY 10019

Copyright © 2019 by Joel Dane
Excerpt from *Burn Cycle* copyright © 2019 by Joel Dane
Penguin Random House supports copyright. Copyright fuels creativity,
encourages diverse voices, promotes free speech, and creates a vibrant culture.
Thank you for buying an authorized edition of this book and for complying with
copyright laws by not reproducing, scanning, or distributing any part of it in any
form without permission. You are supporting writers and allowing Penguin
Random House to continue to publish books for every reader.

ACE is a registered trademark and the A colophon is a trademark of Penguin
Random House LLC.

Library of Congress Cataloging-in-Publication Data

Names: Dane, Joel, author.
Title: Cry pilot / Joel Dane.
Description: First edition. | New York : Ace, 2019
Identifiers: LCCN 2018037187| ISBN 9781984802521 (trade pbk.) |
ISBN 9781984802538 (ebook)
Subjects: | GSAFD: Science fiction. | War stories.
Classification: LCC PS3604.A487 C79 2019 | DDC 813/.6—dc23
LC record available at https://lccn.loc.gov/2018037187

First Edition: August 2019

Printed in the United States of America
1   3   5   7   9   10   8   6   4   2

Cover art by Matt Griffin

This is a work of fiction. Names, characters, places, and incidents either are the
product of the author's imagination or are used fictitiously, and any resemblance
to actual persons, living or dead, business establishments, events, or locales is
entirely coincidental.

RICHMOND HILL PUBLIC LIBRARY
3297 2001494527   RH
Cry pilot
Aug. 09, 2019

CRY PILOT

My story starts with an ambush.

A grubby street kid spends months getting close to a Garda squad. He tags along after them, begging for food. He shows them into forgotten courtyards and warns them about local insurgents. In return, the squad medic patches him up after a beating and the sergeant tries to enroll him in a corporate school, with three meals a day and a roof over his head.

The boy laughs with them, he cries with them, he cares for them—and then he betrays them.

On the orders of the beloved, merciless leader of the patriot resistance, he leads them into a death trap.

The patriot leader is his grandmother. *My* grandmother. That boy was me; those sins are mine.

Ten years later, I know there are wrongs you can't right; there are debts you can't pay. You can't stop trying, though. Debts don't disappear because there's nobody left to collect them. They stay on the books, accumulating interest.

CHAPTER 1

When the recruiter calls, I'm delivering a package to a party-club on the 117th floor. Urgent music pounds and holographic projections strafe the dancers. I slide through the crowd, complete the delivery—and my cuff chimes.

"This is Kaytu," I say.

"Welcome, Maseo Kaytu," an artificial voice says. "Your request for a recruitment interview has been"—there's a pause during which my heart stops—"granted."

"Thank you," I tell the recorded message. "Thank you, I'll—"

The connection crashes. It doesn't matter, though: the appointment information is already on my cuff. They expect me in thirty-five minutes. That's the first test. If you're not willing to drop everything, the corporate military doesn't want you.

As I slip toward the exit, my pulse thumps along with the music. A low note creeps up my spine, and then I'm in the bustling, bright corridor. Boutiques and cafés march toward the atrium with elevators servicing the highest floors of the tower. Chattering families browse the shops and rowdy kids play wall-hockey.

Late afternoon in a Freehold tower.

I grab redbean rolls at a warung and eat in the elevator. A projection on the wall shows the streets outside the tower: maintenance bots spark, adboards flicker, and mobile homes cling to the undersides of a tangle of highways. A crowd of kids chases a sweets caravan along a curving track, and a flock of new-generation sparrows dives through freight cables.

That's all behind me now.

The corporate military is in front of me, the recruiter and the future.

On the 186th floor, pillars of skarab drones palpate the air. I cross the foyer toward them and after a fraught pause they allow me into corpo territory, where the air is fresh and the music is stale. Like embassies in the days of nation-states, different rules apply on the corporate-owned floors of Freehold towers. Different laws.

That's why I'm here.

A massive space opens between the 186th and the 190th floors of the tower. Semitranslucent bubbles slide across rails and ramps and hang from cables like gondolas. Most carry passengers, barely visible in the luxurious interiors. The bubbles split in two when their routes diverge or merge into larger bubbles to form gathering spaces or conference rooms. Light glimmers on the sheen of rounded surfaces, colorful and delicate.

I enjoy the sight until my cuff hurries me along.

With three minutes to spare, I slip inside an empty office with a scented filtration fan. There's no furniture except for a round table with a lily on it. Maybe a lily. Maybe a rose or a decorative fungus. Heirloom plants aren't my strength.

I cuff messages to my boss and neighbors, saying good-bye. I send a longer one to Ionesca, my oldest friend, my first love. I tell her that my apartment is hers now; she's welcome to take whatever she wants and sell the rest.

One way or another, I'm not coming back.

My heart thumps in my chest. I massage my middle finger, feeling the lump of the bonespur implant. I inhale slowly but I don't *flow* myself calm. This isn't a moment for meditative detachment. This is a moment for coiled readiness.

The door bulges and a gawky young man trots into the room. His yellow-black hair is woven through with smartwire, which sways when he walks, giving the impression of a breeze.

"Welcome to Shiyogrid!" he says. "I'll be your recruiter today."

"Nice to meet you, san."

"My pleasure." Two sitting bubbles take shape from the wall, and the recruiter lounges on one and gestures invitingly to the other. "Would you please confirm your name?"

"Maseo Kaytu," I say, standing at ease instead of taking a seat.

The lens in his right eye gleams with data. "You were assigned the surname identifier 'K2SE' in a refugee camp after the fall of Vila Vela?"

"Yes, san," I say.

"And when you reached your majority, you took 'Kaytu' instead of your original name, your family name?"

"Yes, san," I say.

"May I ask why?"

"I wanted to leave the war behind, to start fresh. To start again."

"Mm. I suppose Vila Vela is not anything you'd want to hold on to."

He's right, but that doesn't mean Vila Vela isn't still holding on to *me*. I bow my head and say, "No, san."

"You spent a few years in a refugee camp," he says.

"Yes, san."

"Since that time, you've been making deliveries in the Coastal Vegas Freehold, doing odd jobs for which you are painfully over-qualified."

"Yes, san."

He flashes me an apologetic smile. "I'm starting to worry about your linguistic prowess."

"I'm fluent in mainland English," I tell him. "I speak Creole and Bahasa, muddle through with Yoruba and Franco-Vietnamese."

"No Portuguese?"

"A little."

"Refugee children." He touches his flowing hair. "You often come with a flair for languages."

"Yes, san."

"I've recruited a handful of refugees for various positions over the years." His lens gleams again. "Never into the military."

I expected this but still feel a prickle of frost on my neck. "No, san."

"The military does not recruit from a warzone, Mar Kaytu. Surely you know this."

"Yes, san."

"Then what are we doing here?" He cuts off my answer with a gesture. "Your equivalency scores are high despite your . . . You live in one of the lower levels?"

Freehold towers average about two hundred stories, with hundreds of suites and studios on every floor. A quarter million people live in the more densely packed towers, which rise in thick clusters around avenues of bridges and walkways and tram tracks. The top dozen floors are called the penthouse, the middle is the belt, and the bottom floors are the gutter, a roiling mass of music and culture, art and anarchy.

"Yes, san," I say. "I'm from the gutter. Making deliveries gives me time to train for the military. To prepare for this interview."

"You were raised in a warzone, and you wish to return?"

"I want to serve."

"Why?"

"Because I—" I take a breath and tell a half-truth. "I want to be part of something bigger than myself."

"You want to kill remorts," he says, with a hint of amusement.

"They need killing," I tell him.

Remorts are the reactivated—the *reborn*—bioweapons of a previous age. And yeah, the corporate forces need to put them down. So I cuff the recruiter my enlistment information: medical records, fitness qualifications, military intake test scores.

Years ago I'd taken a wrong turn onto a one-way street and now this—joining the Shiyogrid Armed Forces—is my only exit. I need to get out of the gutter and into the military before there's nothing left to save. I'd started training. I'd read every boot camp manual and watched every embed. I'd spent every spare scrip on a low-jacked combat sim that left me with a bloody nose and a migraine. I climbed the stairways of my tower for six hours a day, carrying packages in both directions. I'd even bought an antique Ambo swing-barreled assault rifle. Despite the introduction of cutting-edge Boaz rifles, Ambos remain the baseline military firearm, so I learned that weapon inside and out.

"Mm." The recruiter's lens shines with characters. "This is impressive."

My pulse pounds in my chest. I stay perfectly still, like I don't want to break the spell.

"While the military rarely enlists from Freeholds instead of corporate enclaves," he continues, "we make exceptions for people with exactly these qualifications."

"Good."

"However, you're not simply from a Freehold. There's no getting around your past. A warzone and a refugee camp? No. Corporate policy is clear. I'm sorry, Mar Kaytu. There's no way you'll ever join the military."

I swallow. "There's one way, san."

"Volunteer for the CAV corps?" His yellow-black hair recoils in surprise. "Well, yes, but nobody survives the CAVs."

"Six percent survive," I tell him. "Then they're inducted into the service."

"They're given the choice." The recruiter looks at me with sympathy—or maybe pity. "That's a one-in-twenty chance of survival, Mar Kaytu."

"Unless you let me enlist."

"I can't, I'm sorry. There's no reason to move forward with your interview."

My throat tightens. "Please. I'm begging you."

"I can't," he repeats.

"I know what I look like, I know what my file looks like. But I'm not my file. Take a chance on me. That's all I need. One chance."

He stands to leave. "I'm sorry."

"So am I," I tell him, and break his nose with the heel of my hand.

Blood sprays. He cries out and raises his arms. I'm punching him again when a bubble explodes two inches from my face and hurls me into darkness.

CHAPTER 2

'm a criminal now. Well, I'm a criminal *again*, for the first time since Vila Vela.

Nothing is illegal in a Freehold, but there are laws on corporate property. And there are punishments for breaking them.

If you're convicted of a crime in a corporate enclave—or on a corporate floor, for that matter—they don't imprison you with other criminals to hone your craft. They sure as gehenna don't pay for your room and board.

No, corporate prisons don't limit your environment. They limit your *awareness* of your environment.

They lock you in blinders. You serve a sentence in Perceptual Alteration technology, which edits your reality by removing trigger stimuli, erasing entire classes of people, objects, and interactions. Lenses and earbugs delete images and sounds from your experience in real time. Certain objects and experiences disappear from your world: weapons, substances, technologies. Entire human demographics. Maybe you'll never see a beautiful face again. Maybe you'll never see your own face.

And every time you step over the line, the walls close in even more.

For the simple assault I committed, the mediators encourage me to accept a brief sentence in blinders. I refuse, because there's another choice if you're convicted of a crime.

You can volunteer for the CAVs.

Initially conceived of as uncrewed drones, Combatant Activated Vehicles were intended to serve as the first wave of assaults. To trigger mines, to soak smart-swarm damage. To swallow missile barrages like the sinkholes that swallowed Bavaria.

When the AIs developed CAVs, they enabled remote controls as requested. Yet they also required a human occupant for operation. Nobody understands why, not exactly.

The most common theory is that CAVs piggyback on the processing capacity of the human brain. Another is that the AIs wanted to force humans to grapple with the true cost of war. My favorite theory, though, is that AIs are fundamentally unknowable; we can't even understand the motivations of *mushrooms*, and we share two thirds of our DNA with them. The AIs don't have DNA—as far as I know—so we might as well try to plumb the inner life of a musical note.

All we know for certain is that CAVs don't function without passengers.

CAVs can absorb a tremendous amount of punishment and still recover. The passengers, though? Well, I heard an old-time phrase that describes what happens to them. Most legacy amphibians died centuries before I was born, but the terrafixing reanimated a few species, including frogs. And one phrase always stuck with me: a passenger in a CAV is like "a frog in a blender."

CAVs withdraw from combat after the occupant fails to respond.

They're hosed clean of jellied flesh and splintered bone, then return to battle with new passengers, new sacrifices.

New martyrs.

Because those people save the world.

Nothing beats a cataphract-class remort except a CAV, at least not without laying waste to huge swathes of the fragile ecosystem. The regular corporate military keeps less-formidable remorts in check, but without volunteers willing to die in CAVs, the cataphracts would overrun the cities.

So I have nothing but gratitude for volunteers; there's no higher calling if you've only got a few months to live. Hell, there's no higher calling if you're simply tired of living. Still, it's not an easy way to die. That's why we don't call the CAV volunteers *passengers* or *activators* or even *martyrs*.

We call them *cry pilots*.

The first two days after my arrest, nothing happens except processing. The initial scans miss my bonespur implant; a simple charge of nonconsensual contact doesn't require high-level scans. The third day I refuse blinders and insist on placement in the CAVs. The fourth day, I waive a legal hearing and repeat my request.

The fifth, sixth, and seventh days I spend establishing that I'm psychologically competent. I also develop a nervous tic of stroking the lower joints of my middle finger.

The eighth day, a remort attack delays my departure.

Remorts aren't simply regenerated bioweapons from a bygone war; they're regenerated *autonomous* bioweapons, self-directed by combat-optimized neural tissue and genetically engineered instincts.

And one is currently targeting a perimeter wall sixteen miles from the processing center. A gentle chime alerts the populace that the enclave is under threat, but everyone stays calm. There's no reason to panic unless a cataphract hits, in which case the alarm sounds like a strident whistle.

The army handles ordinary remorts with fierce professionalism and few casualties. No reason to interrupt your day worrying about them. Still, I always watch the battles. The army's first priority is defending cities against remort assaults, so if I survive the CAVs—*when* I survive the CAVs—that will be my life.

I trot into the lounge and follow the action on a projection. I'm hoping the attacking remorts are knuckletanks or moths, but no luck. Instead, a swarm of umires—a teeming mass of tiny assault drones—burns a swathe through the wilderness.

On the video, I watch troop transports swoop from the sky. A cloud of moskito drones swirls from their belly-vents, followed by battlesuited soldiers deploying on filaments and inside pulse-hardened rovers.

Sparks explode across the mile-long swathe of umires as the moskitos make contact. With rippling bulges and crests, the tiny drones combine into wavelike fighting units. Combat engineers throw defensive ramparts across the battlefield; infantry squads drop into position. Liquammo sizzles. Gunships fire surgical strikes— careful not to damage the terrafixing—and the umire waves crash and burn.

In eighty minutes, it's all over except the cleanup. Twelve casualties. The umire didn't even touch the outermost perimeter of the enclave, and I feel a spark of pride. Pride and eagerness. One day that will be me: strapped into a weapons harness, the only barrier between a killing remort and a human city. One day soon.

Except not the next day, because on the ninth day following the arrest, my scheduled departure is delayed to the tenth day.

Today is the tenth day, and in the dim glow of the transport bay, I catch flashes of the other CAV volunteers. Rows of heads extend into the darkness in front of me. The vibration of the transport shuttle makes a soothing hum.

I'm sitting between a middle-aged man with a pelt of black hair and a heavily narcotized woman. The man trembles nonstop. His hairy shoulder is a quivering animal.

"For the good of the many," the woman chants, in a slurred voice. "For the good of the many."

We're not heroes, despite her chant. We're idealistic criminals: hopeless cases caught on corporate property, unable to pay fines or wergild and unwilling to live in blinders. The *real* volunteers, the real heroes, are escorted to CAV deployment in luxury, after months of predeployment coddling. Every ache is soothed, every appetite is sated—and every cell is scanned.

That's why I couldn't simply volunteer. I needed the neglect of a convict cohort to keep my bonespur implant unnoticed.

We're the dregs of the enclaves, praying we'll beat the odds or looking for redemption. We're treated well, but we're not coddled. Alloy collars cling to our necks, and we're wearing Y-front jumpsuits of some thin, crinkly material.

We're risking everything on a six percent chance of surviving. At least they are. My bonespur lockpick gives me an edge.

I've got a fifty percent chance of seeing tomorrow.

"For the good of the many," the woman intones. "For the good of the many."

My seat flattens into a bed. In the darkness, my skin prickles with fear and doubt. I'm no better than these other idiots. I'm worse—I did this to myself on purpose.

I take a breath, then another, reaching for the calm of *flow*. Ionesca taught me this terrafixing meditation when we were kids in the refugee camp; she branded every step into my mind. And now, lying in the transport bed, I focus on the afterimages inside my eyelids. I exhale the formless shapes into a fractal pattern of leaves and roots that divide and divide and divide into a blossoming mesh of subatomic filament.

The New Growth uncoils in my mind. Flowing inside me, around me; I'm one needle in a pine forest, one cell in a starfish, one raindrop in a monsoon. My doubt stays, my nervousness stays. Hell, even my fear stays. But none of them touch me anymore: the terra-fixing meditation flows me away.

And more than ever, I want to live.

CHAPTER 3

I wake to the soothing chime of tinepipes.

The light is low and golden. The ceiling of the transport bay is blue. I'm warm and relaxed from an aerosolized narcotic. I've never been this comfortable. Even the worst cry pilots are pampered. We're criminals, but our sins are forgiven as we prepare to make the ultimate sacrifice.

My bed reshapes into a seat ten minutes before the transport clunks and shifts, mooring on an unseen dock. The light brightens slowly, and my alertness returns. My thumb strokes the lump beneath the skin on my middle finger.

The seats straighten, forcing the volunteers to stand. At gentle tugs from our collars, we're marched down a ramp into a hangar where soldiers and staff mill around workstations. A projected crowd watches us with teary-eyed adoration. Children wave messages of gratitude and support. The ripple of applause sounds like the patter of warm rain after a storm.

Our collars direct us toward airbays and split us into groups. The pelted guy heads toward a boxy transport with a Shiyogrid flag embossed on the side.

You don't see flags much. Shiyogrid governs Coastal Vegas, most of the Saharan heartland, and the Black Sea States. I'm pretty sure it controls a plurality of shares from the Myitkyina Line through Industrial Siberia, too. The sun never sets on the corporate logo, but there's something primeval about a flag, like a banner of war. We're long past that sort of primitivism—at least in theory.

The drugged woman is guided away, and then a last cluster of us is ushered toward a big transport airship with three thrusters and an undercarriage bay.

"Huh," I say, climbing the ramp.

"What?" a young girl asks, moving into place beside me. "Did you see something? I mean, do you know something? Why are we in this big plane instead of the little ones? Where are the CAVs?"

"This is an Antarmadesha 220," I tell her. "Long-range personnel transport."

She's slender and shivering, and built like a boy. "How—how do you know that? Are you ex-military? Are you military? Are you—"

"No," I say.

"You look like a Freehold ganger. Like a criminal." She peers at me over her pointy nose, which gives her the air of an inquisitive ferret. "You look like a gutter-roach mobster sort of criminal. You look like a knee-breaker kind of—"

"I get it," I say.

She scratches her spiky amber-colored hair. "Except criminals don't know about military transports, do they?"

"I've been studying up," I tell her. "The transports will bring us to whichever CAV deployment zone needs us, according to the daily NMI. The Needs Managed Inventory."

"We—" She bites her lower lip. "We're *inventory*?"

"We're ignition strips," I tell her. "Disposable keys that start a CAV's engine."

"To save cities! To save enclaves and Freeholds and—and entire prairies and forests. The remorts destroy the Earth too, you know, they don't only kill people. I mean, not that killing people isn't bad enough—"

I spot a gleam of gold in her pupils as she babbles, which means she's a stemhead. An addict. She sees me notice and lowers her gaze.

I don't bother saying anything else, because talking to stemheads is a waste of time. She's a perfect example of the kind of people who volunteer for CAV: idiots and junkies who don't understand how the odds of survival work. Looks to me like that accounts for ninety percent of my fellow volunteers, while the other ten percent are idealistic nitwits who want to value-add to the corporation as payback for their crimes.

The thought hits a little too close to home. Payback for my crimes is why I'm here, though even an idealistic nitwit knows you can't repay the dead. You can't undo what's done. Still, I'll try to save more lives than I cost. That won't wash away my debts, but maybe it'll help me sleep at night.

In the bay of the Antarmadesha, my collar directs me to sit on a padded bench, and then safety straps extrude around me.

"What's your name?" the stemhead girl asks. "What did you do? Are you innocent? I'm not! I mean, I am a little, but not totally. I was in Anadarko Basin and I guess I shouldn't have gone looking for—"

I tell her to shut up three times before she gets the message.

A handful of screens flicker into place for our in-flight entertainment, mostly confessionals and default news-chans. I watch a screen showing a blakbird drone veering into a fungus forest in the terrafixing. Shadows flash as the sun strobes behind treelike trunks. Strands of filtration moss sway from smooth branches and an animal crashes in the gloom—a gazelle or boar, or some new species recovered by the terrafixed jungle.

The view angles through a gray glade, and then a white canopy blurs overhead, freckled with hives and nests and burls. The air shimmers with insects, and a flock of birds that looks like parakeets swirls after them.

Maybe they *are* parakeets. That would explain the likeness.

The drone speeds past bulbous plants wrapped in gauzy shrouds. The canopy ends at a whitemoss plain that undulates into the distance, an uneven carpet of spongy life, fifty or sixty yards deep.

"Ooo!" the amber-haired girl squeals. "Check out the amoeba reef."

I look at the far-off mesa. "It's made of amoebas?"

She giggles. "You're silly."

"Sure." I watch the drone circle a flock of flamingos in a shallow lake. "I'm ridiculous."

The terrafixing protocol, also known as the New Growth and Edentide, is an organic stratum that covers 99.99 percent of the planet's land mass and permeates the hydrosphere. Everything except the megacities where humans live—the Freeholds and enclaves—is now a primordial wilderness. The Growth simmers away, doing the subtle, gradual work of healing. Of transforming the depleted, polluted Earth into something sustainable and nurturing.

Maybe even beautiful.

On the screen, the flamingos' bright green feathers shimmer in the light. One day humans will leave the Freeholds and enclaves. One day we'll resettle a burgeoning Earth, and live like natives of our own planet again.

The flamingos fade when a woman steps into the bay, leading an autocart. "Welcome, volunteers," she says with a professional smile. "My name is Mar Cola and I'll be your Assignment Coordinator."

She distributes food and drink and soft-drugs. A volunteer who can't stop apologizing is first, followed by a scarlet-skinned woman who mutters to herself. A skinny teenaged boy is third—and the autocart crashes.

The cart reboots as the Antarmadesha takes flight. The bay dims; quiet music plays. Mar Cola recites an official greeting and expresses the gratitude of Shiyogrid Corporation and the other four corpos. She rattles off boilerplate language before saying, "I'm excited to report that you will deploy from an offshore installation to engage a rare oceanic remort outbreak."

"Offshore?" the amber-haired stemhead girl asks. "Like, off the actual shore?"

Mar Cola smiles. "Yes, you will be engaging in a naval theater."

"So CAVs are amphibious?" the girl asks. "I thought they were only . . . the other thing. What is that called? Land-based. Unamphibious. Mammalian! That doesn't make sense. Mammals swim, too. What's the opposite of amphibious. Reptilian?"

"CAVs are amphibious. They are extraordinary, developed by the AIs along with flowcore processing and—" A slight edge sounds in Mar Cola's voice. "Stem tech."

"Oh," the girl says, her face falling.

And because I'm tired and scared and stupid, I find myself rooting for the girl. "Some reptiles swam," I tell her. "Turtles swam,"

The girl brightens. "So reptiles are amphibious, too! That doesn't make sense. I mean, if mammals and reptiles are amphibious, what's so special about amphibians? I mean, if *everything* is amphibious, what *is* amphibious?"

"Do you have a question?" Mar Cola asks, her smile brittle. "That's not about animals?"

"Only, what's different about a, a naval theater? I mean, is it less dangerous than normal CAVing?" The girl looks to the other volunteers. "Oh! And hello everyone. My name is Ting."

"Our names don't matter," the teenaged boy says. "We're dead anyway."

"In fact, the survival rate of CAV operators is currently twenty percent," Cola tells him. "For both terrestrial and naval engagements. So of the fifteen volunteers in this bay . . ."

"Three!" Ting scratches the base of her skull. "Three of us will make it!"

Mar Cola smiles again. "And every CAV volunteer who survives is absolved of outstanding legal judgments and encouraged to enlist."

"Into a shock troop," a soldier mutters.

The girl doesn't hear him, which is probably a good thing. She'd start asking if shock troops are actually all that shocking. I know what he means, though: even if we survive, they won't transfer us into regular training, where regular recruits prepare for regular jobs in military marketing or design, culinary chemistry or engineering.

No, they send ex-criminals into combat training.

Which is exactly where I belong. Except Mar Cola lied. The survival rate isn't almost twenty percent. It's six. Which means if we're lucky, *one* of us won't die during our first contact with a battlefield.

CHAPTER 4

The offshore location is a military compound that rises thirty stories from the ocean. We spend the night locked inside plush, impersonal cells—called *suites*—around a central atrium. Apparently there's no rush: they're still tracking this oceanic remort and planning the attack.

The man who apologizes starts apologizing again. Ting's voice is soft, barely a murmur, the cooing of a stemhead in withdrawal. The teenaged boy is silent.

A scarlet-skinned woman named Chiinan turns circles in the room beside mine. She sees eyes staring at her. Watching her, weighing her, judging her. I guess that's why she volunteered: to end her life with a contribution instead of a catastrophe.

And me? I'm trying to start a new life, but I'm dead if my bone-spur implant doesn't work. Smashed to paste inside a CAV.

I stretch out on my bunk, breathing into my fear. I'm facing a death sentence. I'm locked in a room on a military installation. There is no escape, so I shift myself into a meditative state of *flow*. Fractal patterns bloom behind my eyes. The terrafixing stretches from hydrothermal vents on the ocean floor to the D layer of the mesosphere to every cell in my body; there is nothing outside the environment, there is nothing inside the environment. There's no fear, no hope . . .

There's nothing at all, until sleep takes me.

A klaxon cuts through my dreams, and Chiinan's shout rings out: "—found me, the eyes! Looking at me, watching me!"

Mar Cola leads four sailors into the atrium. "Good morning, everyone! Your deployment was moved forward. The situation on the ground is in flux and CAVs are urgently required."

Our doors unlock and we're offered another round of narcotics.

"In flux?" I ask, after I refuse the drugs. "What does that mean?"

"It means changed," Cola says.

"I understand the word, san, what I'm asking is—"

"No time to waste!" she says brightly, and the sailors herd us into a wide bright corridor with security film at the far end, below a sign reading *ACCESS LIMITED/EXION CLEARANCE/C-SUITE COMPLIANCE.*

Serious security film.

My heart shrinks and my knees tremble. This is my last hurdle.

If the bonespur passes through this film . . . well, *then* I'll face my last hurdle. The CAVs. But I need to reach them first, with the bonespur implant still inside my skin, the only edge that can keep me alive.

Bonespur defeats scans—most scans—because it reads as part of your body. It's a programmable assembly technology that uses your flesh and blood and bone as raw material. You can't build in any complexity: you can make a shiv or a lockpick, but not a firearm, not a code-card. And bonespur is forbidden. After the devastation of the SICLE War, all bio-forged tech was prohibited, but this lump in my finger was a gift from my grandmother. It's my only link to her, and now it'll either save my life or hasten my death.

The stemhead girl Ting is talking to me—to my surprise, she didn't narc herself senseless—but I'm not listening. The scarlet-skinned woman is the only other volunteer who looks alert, stepping through the security film. The teenaged boy marches dreamy-eyed behind her, and the apologetic man follows with a smile on his face.

The film is ten feet away. Five feet, two feet, and then I'm stepping through.

I feel the tingle on my face and the tug on my chest—

My finger burns.

Agony rakes from my hand to my elbow, like blades are cutting away the flesh. The security film is frying the bonespur tech, and the pain is blinding. With tears in my eyes and a rasp in my throat, I stagger through the film, cradling my throbbing arm.

I peer downward, half expecting to find my finger black and charred. Instead, it looks fine. A little swollen but fine. Maybe the bonespur is okay. Maybe this isn't disaster—maybe it's victory. Still bent over, I tap the activation sequence on the implant.

Nothing happens. The implant is dead. Crashed by the security film.

Which means I'm dead, too.

Two sailors step toward me, because I've stopped short, hunched there with tears on my cheeks. I stumble forward, my mind clawing with fear, and tap the activation sequence again.

Nothing. The bonespur is a lump of inert sludge inside my finger.

The sailors hustle us along a series of serene corridors that must've seen thousands of volunteers marching to their deaths. I need to run diagnostics, but there's no time. I need to escape, but there's no exit. I can't run, I can't fight, I can't fix the bonespur.

I need to reboot the implant.

How? At the very least, I need to deliver a surge that might force a restart. I don't know what chance that gives me, but greater than zero.

Except what kind of surge?

Anything might work: pressure, data, electricity. Of course, any of those might *not* work too, but I can't think about that. I need a recycle board, a filter shunt, anything. I'd throw myself at a bolt of lightning if I could, but the hallway is wide and empty, and the soldiers vigilant.

We shuffle into a launchdeck that looks like an aircraft hangar. The ceiling is interrupted with huge circular ports, and screens flicker above diagnostic bays and facilitation stations. The air smells of repair foam and well-lubricated machinery. There's the whine of tools. Two engineering crews crawl over gunships—and my breath catches at the sight of CAVs.

"Sweet *biyo*!" Ting gasps.

Most of what I know about CAVs I learned from my grandmother. The AIs designed CAVs—or *over*designed them—and her engineer's mind found that fascinating. Unlike bio-forged tech, there is nothing organic about CAVs. Nothing alive. They are purely cold-tech, but they mimic organic systems.

They don't heal, but they self-repair in much the same way. They don't feel anger or fear, but they respond with the equivalent of adrenaline surges. They might even piggyback on operators' brains for processing power and sensory input.

They look like seven-ton alloy pods wrapped with overlapping leaves and ribbons, like massive unfurling pinecones. The leaves and ribbons range in width from a few inches to a few feet, swaying and furling around the cockpit—called the *saddle*—like a sea creature in the tide.

A shifting latticework of ribbons surrounds each of the three CAVs, and each is pitted and blackened by thousands of remort strikes and blasts.

Sweat pricks my skin despite the cool air.

Seeing the scarred alloy brings home what I already know: these things are sent into battles on kamikaze runs. They leap into the path of attacks to die.

One volunteer starts singing a hymn and Chiinan screams, "Eyes! They're not going to!"

She breaks formation, scrambling away from the CAVs. I tense, ready to follow, desperate for a way to reset the bonespur. But Chiinan only takes four steps before her collar emits a tranquilizer that brings her gently to her knees.

I watch four sailors usher Chiinan toward a bank of seats and feel the tightness of the collar around my own neck. A moment later, I'm sitting between Ting and the drugged teenaged boy. No chance to move.

"It's like flowers," Ting breathes, staring at the CAVs. "How they . . . *flower*. I mean, with petals and tendrils and leaves."

As if in response to her words, the ribbons of the nearest CAV shift and sway, opening a path into the bright interior. Ting is right: they unfurl like a bud blossoming—a flower made of superhard alloy. Inside, the saddle waits, an oval cockpit with a pilot's rotating seat-frame.

Except not a cockpit: a guillotine, an electric chair, a death sentence.

There's beauty there, too. Cords sway from the cockpit's white walls, like vines ready to wrap the cry pilot in gentle tendrils, and I flash to a childhood game I played with my grandmother: what does *this* machine crave? I don't know, I can't tell. The external leaves want to stab and slash like blades, but also to cling and crawl, to sprint and grab. The long ribbons want to spider up walls or carve through barricades. They want to bunch together for armor and to extend into rippling spears and—

My throat clenches when I see the padded clunky manacles adhered to the pilot's frame. They're crude and bulky and all-too-human, added to keep the operators from leaving the frame before they die.

At first, the corpo military had welcomed the presence of pilot's frames in CAVs. Sure, they'd requested uncrewed drones, but they appreciated the redundancy of manual controls. While the remote operation worked seamlessly, at least in occupied CAVs, what if countermeasures broke the connection?

Better to have a pilot in place, ready to assume command.

They'd spent years trying to train pilots, with no luck. Skill didn't matter. Practice didn't matter. Experience didn't matter. Despite the swiveling frame and command interface, you couldn't control a CAV.

Not well, at least. Even the most gifted pilots never managed much more than random lurching and spinning.

So why had the AIs designed unworkable manual controls? Maybe the vestigial cockpits helped CAVs sync with the human brain. Maybe the AIs were teaching humanity a lesson about violence and sacrifice. Or maybe the question didn't make sense; even before turning sentient, the motivations of the AIs were as incomprehensible as the psychology of a krill swarm.

That's probably why someone massacred the ascended AIs: they were too unfathomable to live.

The military needed occupants to activate the remote-controlled

CAVs but couldn't risk anyone damaging the equipment or interfering with the operators. So they'd installed manacles to secure victims—sorry, *passengers*—into place. Stretching them on a rack, nailing them to a cross. Maybe that's what the AIs had wanted all along.

"That one looks like a Fibonacci artichoke!" Ting gazes with wide eyes at the middle CAV, her golden pupils glinting. "Do you see the shape?"

"I see the shackles," I tell her.

The shackles that will deactivate the CAV if unlocked during operation. The shackles I need my bonespur implant to disengage.

"I guess we're like kill switches," Ting says, "except the other way around. I mean, we close the circuit. If we're not in place, the CAV deactivates. What's the opposite of kill? *Resurrect* switches. That's not really the opposite, though. I mean, killing is natural, but resurrection is—"

"Welcome, volunteers!" a warm voice says, as screens spring to life in front of our seats. "Your contribution to the future of humanity—and of the Earth itself—is invaluable. Your actions today bring a better tomorrow." The pep talk continues, and I drift into a fugue state of fear and dread until the end: ". . . your upcoming deployment!"

"When?" I ask Ting. "Did he say when?"

"Now," she tells me.

CHAPTER 5

"Cーommander on deck!" a sailor barks, and my collar murmurs for me to stand.

An officer and his entourage enter the bay from a higher deck. The officer is average height with a middle-aged paunch and a craggily handsome face. His silver hair falls in short, conservative dreadlocks. He's wearing a uniform I can't place. A CFO-General, maybe? Definitely Executive Class.

"How long before the CAVs are ready to deploy?" the Exec asks a woman at his side.

She's wearing Fleet Comptroller braids and she reeks of command. The sailors salute the man, but she's the one they watch. "Twenty minutes," she tells him, with unhappy tension in her voice. "When we moved the schedule up—"

"There is nothing more important than this," the Exec snaps at her. "We need to know that CAVs can kill these new fuckers."

I guess that's what Mar Cola meant by "in flux." There are new fuckers that need killing. But that doesn't make sense. CAVs can kill cataphracts—if you're willing to lose a few—and no remort is worse than a cataphract.

"Yes, san," the Comptroller says.

"I'd sacrifice your whole fleet for one chunk of dead lamprey. Twenty minutes is your best? It won't stay in place much longer."

I don't know what kind of remort a lamprey is, but "twenty minutes" sounds terrified alarms in my mind. I don't care about flux, I don't care about lampreys. How am I going to force-restart the bonespur in the middle of a military bay?

I scan the room, and my gaze snags on a cadet in the Exec's entourage. She's wearing a newblue uniform and in a beige world she's onyx. She gleams. Her cheekbones are blades. She's as tall as the Exec and even in her crisp uniform, there's a hint of music in the way she moves.

The aide beside her is even more interesting, because his sarong is covered in glittering braids and ornaments. My attention sharpens on a cluster of smartwire on his hip, unscrolling into new shapes and then condensing into a ball the size of my thumb. Smartwire is programmable decorative thread that houses a self-contained power source: maybe enough to reboot my implant if I deliver it right.

"—honor to be privy to the earliest phase of a cavalry charge," the Executive is saying when I tune back in. "How many CAVs are currently operative, Cadet Rana?"

"Just under three hundred worldwide, san," the cadet in newblue says, and her voice is toneless.

"She sounds deaf!" Ting whispers to me. "I mean, except if she's deaf, why didn't she regrow her cochlea?"

I look closer at Cadet Rana. She doesn't watch the Exec when he speaks, so she's not reading his lips. Her lenses must compensate for her deafness, flashing her a transcript or shunting the auditory input onto another sensory system. Why hasn't she surgically recalibrated her hearing? I don't know, and I don't care.

"I pray that's enough," the Exec tells her. "A pity that we've lost the making of them."

"Did we ever have the making of them, san?" Cadet Rana asks.

"We did not," the Exec says, with a hint of a smile. "But we knew how to make the AIs that did." He turns to his other side. "Fewer than three hundred. In how many theaters, Fleet Comptroller?"

"Seven currently rated 'risk-management' or above for cataphract emergence, san."

"And how many CAVs are in Shiyogrid's direct control?" He looks to the cadet again. "Rana?"

"Eighty, san."

"Seventy-eight," the Fleet Comptroller corrects. "We lost two recently. Lampreys burn through them like a Boaz blast through butter."

There's a muttering of fear and disbelief from the entourage. The Exec brushes a silvery dreadlock off his face and says, "You spent last night prepping a sortie against some kind of marine remort?"

"Yes, san," the Fleet Comptroller says. "A full-grown Ijapa that we've been tracking. One hundred twenty feet long, displacing eight hundred tons."

One of the sailors whistles. "Big fish."

"What's Ijapa class?" the Exec asks.

"A bio-forged submarine drone," the Fleet Comptroller explains, "running extrapolated bacteria wetware."

"That means nothing to me. What've you got in the barrel?"

"Six dive units ready—eager—to flush the remort to the surface for the tender care of the CAVs and the 105th Catamaran."

"Lampreys dissolve within hours of emergence . . ." The rumble of a conveyor swallows the Exec's voice. ". . . a happy coincidence that I was bringing my daughter to Joint Service Training when word of the attack came. I'm sorry to override all your hard work, but a lamprey will wipe out the 105th without slowing down. We need CAVs."

"Yes, san," the Fleet Comptroller says, her voice sharp. "We've reallocated to your specifications."

When the Exec approaches the volunteers, the ribbons around the nearest CAV sway like seaweed. I catch a glimpse of the padded manacles again. They're aftermarket add-ons, weak links in the chain—and I glance at the fashionboy aide and feel a feeble spark of hope.

"Chiinan," I whisper without moving my lips. "They're looking at you."

The scarlet-skinned woman jerks beside me. I hate myself for tormenting her, but that's okay. I'm willing to hate myself.

"All those eyes," I whisper. "Watching you. The officers see you."

"Kick your fancyface," Chiinan snarls under her breath.

The dreadlocked Exec stops in front of the volunteers. "Take pride, my friends! You're doing more than you know." His voice is deep and reassuring. He says a few more comforting words before finishing with a flourish: "Your sacrifice, your contribution, and your selflessness will save the human race."

When he finally strolls onward, Cadet Rana's black gaze sweeps past me and doesn't slow.

The entourage turns away and I shout, "Chiinan, no!"

She's standing quietly until I scream. Then she freaks. She hurls herself at the Exec, a whirlwind of elbows and moans. The perfect distraction.

A moment before her collar tranqs her, I drop to my knees in front of the fashionboy aide. "Save me!" I throw my arms around his sarong. "I can't do this! I'm begging you!"

He jerks but can't break my grip. "Get him off!"

"Please, please!" I bury my face against his thigh. "I'll do anything!"

He smacks my head ineffectually, and the collar shocks me. I bite down hard. A sharp edge of smartwire cuts the roof of my mouth and my body spasms.

Through my tears I see Cadet Rana watching me. She's the most beautiful thing on Earth and Luna and all the habitations. Even the disgust on her face is as deep and pure as a starlit sky.

"They shouldn't allow junkies and beggars to volunteer," she tells the Exec. "The CAV corps deserves better."

"Help him up," the Fleet Comptroller says.

"Yes, san," a sailor says, and drags me to my feet.

The Fleet Comptroller inspects me. "What's your name, volunteer?"

I don't answer.

"Maseo Kaytu, san," the fashionboy aide says, his lens scrolling.

"We're all in service to the same cause, Volunteer Kaytu," the Fleet Comptroller tells me, her voice frighteningly gentle. "You're performing an admirable task, a vital one."

"More vital than ever," the Exec says.

"And we're all of us afraid," the Fleet Comptroller tells me. "Still, I'd ask you to apologize for your outburst to CE Rana-Cain." She tilts her head to indicate the silver-haired officer. "He's a guest in my house."

CE tells me that he's a Colonel Executive. And the *Rana* half of his name tells me that he calls his daughter by her surname when in uniform. Off the top of my head, I can't imagine any information less helpful than that.

"An apology isn't necessary." CE Rana-Cain steps in front of me, and there's a hardness in his eyes that his heartiness can't hide. "Listen to me, Mar Kaytu. Your sacrifice matters. You matter."

I swallow the blood in my mouth and hang my head.

The Exec touches my cheek. "Troubled in life but redeemed in death."

"Beg the Colonel Executive's pardon," a sailor snarls into my ear.

"He was eager to beg a moment ago," Cadet Rana says.

I lift my head to look at her. I'd like to say that she flushes. I'd like to say that her eyes tighten with anger or acknowledgment. I'd like to say a lot of things, but her face doesn't change at all.

I don't blame it. If I looked like that, I wouldn't change either.

"Say something," she tells me. "At least have the courage to speak."

I clamp my jaw and remain silent. The sailors return me ungently to my seat and a new screen flickers into sight above the CAVs.

"Load and lock!" the Fleet Comptroller says.

A junior officer leaps into action, barking orders. As the Exec and his entourage leave, the sailors escort Chiinan and two drowsy volunteers into waiting CAVs. They engage the padded manacles, remove the collars, and step back.

Clamps grab the now-occupied CAVs and hoist them through the ports in the ceiling. The hatches close. My head pounds. There's a flurry of activity, and somewhere above me the CAVs launch into the battle.

CHAPTER 6

I swallow a mouthful of blood and watch the ceiling ports. Where are the cry pilots now? What are they fighting? They're strapped into machines to meet the requirement of a human presence. Trapped, helpless, driven into a warzone by remote operators and sacrificed.

The sailors talk openly in front of us. There's no reason not to. From what I overhear, that big submarine Ijapa is homing in on an ocean-based factory or refinery. Predatory remorts do that. It is in the nature of weapons to seek targets, and remort behavior is organically encoded in regenerated—though corrupted—neural impulses and genetic imperatives.

Two corpos, Shiyogrid and CrediMobil, responded to the threat with conventional forces, while requisitioning CAVs. Then a lamprey approached. Drawn by the conflict, or the activity. And CE Rana-Cain ordered the CAVs to ignore the submarine remort and fight the lamprey-class remort instead.

I stop listening when Chiinan's CAV returns through the ceiling. The sailors salute and a tone poem plays while screens project pictures of sunsets and swamps. A hose attaches to the bottom of the CAV. There's a slurping sound and a waterproof bag emblazoned with a Shiyogrid flag inflates.

The hose is pumping what's left of Chiinan into the bag.

"That's a coffin," Ting says, her teeth chattering, "that's her coffin. It's a, a disposable—fuel for the furnaces—"

The sailors lay the bulging bag gently on an autocart. The stemhead babbles, the drugged volunteers gaze at the screens, and I'm dizzy with fear.

I keep my teeth clamped and Chiinan's CAV unfurls, reopening the path to the saddle. It's empty and bright and clean inside. Untouched by death, untouched by fear. And when sailors lock the next volunteer into the saddle, he doesn't seem to feel any horror.

However, a few whimpers sound when another CAV returns. Its skin is sliced open like an eviscerated animal and a pink tar-like substance splatters the wound.

As another cremation bag fills with flesh and fluid, the teenaged boy starts crying. Sailors narcotize him into stunned pleasure, then strap him to the saddle frame. My jaw aches. Engineers stroll past. Tools clatter; the building sways in the ocean current.

More CAVs return. More bags fill and more cry pilots are manacled in place.

Then the teenaged boy is pulled out of a damaged CAV, bleeding and trembling.

"He's alive," Ting breathes. "He survived."

Medics ease the kid into a trauma cart. He beat the odds, the six percent of survival, and my fear sharpens. I know this isn't how odds work, but I feel like mine just vanished into nothing.

Ting edges beside me. Her eyes are big, with golden pupils. She's shaking and scratching her scalp through her spiky amber hair, a complete stemhead meltdown.

"T-tell me it'll b-be okay," she stammers to me. "Tell me 'g-good luck.' I—I need to hear a friendly voice. Just say my name. Please. Plcasc? Just say my name."

I touch her elbow. I want to comfort her; I want to promise her that death will be quick. I want to lie, but I keep my mouth shut. I don't say a word.

More bags fill with the jellied remains of cry pilots, and finally the sailors come for me.

The CAV reacts to my approach, swaying and shifting. With its leaves woven tightly together, it's less than twice my height. When the leaves expand into a looser lattice, it'll grow larger, like a clenched fist opening into a clawed hand.

Traces of battle scars catch the light: dents and scrapes and pockmarks. The alloy leaves unfurl away from me, clearing a path into the bright white saddle, and a chill touches my skin. I'm being fed into the gaping maw of an alien machine—

The sailors feel my rising panic and move me faster into the CAV.

I swallow convulsively, and then I'm inside.

There isn't a speck of blood or a whiff of death. The cables covering the saddle walls grope slowly toward me like the tendrils of a climbing vine.

The sailors secure me into the pilot's frame, a slanted rig that pivots 360 degrees. The padded manacles lock around my wrists and ankles with a sound like bones breaking.

I feel a spark of panic and force myself to focus. I can't miss anything, not now. The saddle is half cockpit and half cocoon, sheathing me inside the CAV. Cables quiver toward my skin. This thing was built to explode through minefields, to leap in front of missile strikes. It was designed by AIs to meet human specifications, but did the machine intelligences truly understand human input?

Nobody knows.

The CAV is an impenetrable enigma, so only the add-ons can save me. I inspect the manacles around my wrists. They show more wear than the exterior: they're covered with scratches and dings and even a tracery of rust.

My heart lifts at the sight.

The sailors remove my collar and the door braids shut behind them. The CAV shifts and sways. Screens shimmer to life around me, showing deployment assignments, route optimization, force distribution, system checks.

Cables extend into loops near my hands, like gunner joysticks or thrust controls. I can't reach them, not with my wrists manacled. Not that they'd respond if I did. Maybe they aren't even controls; maybe they're just sensors that help the CAV respond to my physiological responses. Well, my *fear*.

More cable-vines wrap my shoulders and chest in a warm, sinewy embrace. When I shift my weight, the frame swivels.

I almost yelp but keep my teeth clamped.

I swivel one way, then the other, getting the hang of the motion. The screens follow me almost seamlessly, flickering in front of my face no matter how I'm oriented inside the saddle. One of the screens shows the exterior of my CAV. I pause upside-down in the frame and watch as my CAV is loaded into the dropbay of a fat-bodied gunship.

"CAV Zero-Two, this is Control," a staticky voice says. "You're on sector Chamesh. Operator Zero-Two confirm."

"Confirm," the voice of the operator says. "They want me following the backsplash again?"

"Negative. The lamprey is gone."

"Thank Edentide." The operator exhales in relief. "We took it down?"

"We didn't scratch it," Control says. "It dissolved."

So my CAV isn't going to face a lamprey after all. I spin in the frame again. I can't tell if that's good news or bad—except nothing is good news, not while I'm manacled in place.

"Head straight into the pipe," Control says. "We've still got a big-ass Ijapa to handle."

"Never seen anything like that lamprey," the remote operator says.

"Nobody has. Transmitting targeting data." A screen flashes. "Watch you don't get bunched up again."

"That wasn't me, that was twelve."

"It was both of you," Control says.

I swivel upright and take a few breaths. My heart is beating too fast. If my hands were free, they'd be trembling, and they can't tremble, not now.

I tilt forward.

One inch.

Two inches.

I shift until my face is directly above my right hand, then open my mouth. Out drops the wet knot of smartwire that I tore from the fashionboy's sarong with my teeth. That's the reason I didn't say a word to Ting, the reason I haven't opened my mouth.

The moment the wire passes my lips, I know I've missed. I won't catch it. I've lost my chance, my last chance—

I lunge desperately, and the frame spins.

The ball of smartwire hits the edge of my manacle and bounces past my hand. Shit! I torque into a blur, and the frame bats the wire against the saddle wall. It ricochets, twirling in the air. Giving a panicked shout, I swivel frantically—and snag a curl of the smartwire between two fingertips.

"Fuck!" I whimper, my fingers pressed tight like pincers. "Fuck, fuck . . ."

"Linked," the staticky voice says, utterly oblivious to me. There's no reason for the operators to hear the dying screams of the cry pilots. "Check your Fita, Zero-Two."

"Fita checks, Control."

Slow and steady, I ease the wire into my palm. When it's safe in my grip, I try not to faint from relief.

My plan is simple. CAVs only function with living pilots in their frames. So the minute I free myself from the frame, the CAV will power down and return to the fleet. I need to unlock the manacles—and this decorative smartwire is the only way to get my bonespur lockpick working.

My CAV patches into the video feed of the gunship, and we're already in flight. I didn't even feel the takeoff. The gunship skims low over the water. A thrill touches my heart at the sight, then curdles into fear. This would be fun if it weren't for my imminent death.

"If we head into the pipe," the remote operator says, "I'll lose my CAV in a minute. That Jiana's not playing."

"Orders is orders," the other voice says. "Disable its aft junction before dying, that's all."

"Copy that, Control."

The screens flicker and change around me. I untangle the smartwire and run a fingernail along the length to find the command nub. No doubt the fashionboy configures his smartwire with his lens, changing the shape and color and frequency according to his mood, but there's a manual interface as well. I know, because I used smartwire to pick locks in Vila Vela—and you don't exactly lose those skills in a refugee camp.

Screens expand around me and a control deck projects across my chest, blocking my view of my hands.

The CAV wants me to drive.

Self-piloted CAVs spin out of control. Every time. Cry pilots can't operate CAVs; they only function via remote. Still, this CAV craves a driver. I don't know why, but I feel the urgency throb in my skull.

I ignore the feeling and focus on surviving. "I'm not a pilot," I snarl. "Get that screen out of my face."

The control deck doesn't move. Fine. I half close my eyes and straighten the smartwire, working by touch. Easy. Steady. I stiffen the end into a sharp point and puncture the skin of my middle finger. Okay. Fine. I miss the bonespur implant and try again. My fingers are slippery with blood when I finally scrape the smartwire against the injection port of the implant.

Once I deliver a jolt of electricity, the bonespur will reboot. Either that, or I'll die in this CAV, trying to disable some watery remort's aft junction.

On a curved screen in front of me, the ocean darkens. The texture thickens, turning gummy and viscous. Glutinous waves tremble. That's terrafixing in action, transforming chemical sludge and particulate plastoids into livable ecosystem. Snaking lines cover the surface of the slurry, and then two things happen at once:

One, I trigger the smartwire with my fingernail.

Two, the gunship fires my CAV into battle.

Velocity shoves me backward, and the frame compensates. A few cables wrap me tightly, but the rest writhe and coil like Medusa's hair, never quite touching me. Screens blur and data streams. The targeting system comes online: crosshairs and weapons systems and threat assessments.

Despite my fear, for a lightning-flash moment, I *want* to fly this thing. The saddle adjusts around me, cradling soft, and I want to grab the cables, engage the command deck, and burn through enemy lines.

Instead, I tap the confirmation sequence on the bonespur and feel a throb of acknowledgment. The implant is live. I almost weep in relief—until the CAV jolts.

We're in the water, in the sludge. The CAV swarms forward like a hecatopus sea monster, cutting through waves with wide ribbons that pull and stroke and churn.

And I see the remort on my screen.

At first glance, the Ijapa doesn't look so strange. Long and thin and narrow, like some kind of underwater sword. Except impact craters line one side, and the terrafixing patched them with chitin or coral or seashell. A dark gelatinous mass clings to an orbital array—and a translucent version of the same stuff surrounds the entire remort, a fifty-foot-thick blob of speckled jelly.

Circles appear in the remort's armored skin. Gun turrets extrude, displacing gouts of dirt and algae, and lock on target. Lock on *me*.

CHAPTER 7

The corporations implemented the terrafixing after the devastation of the SICLE War. It's been seeping into every ecological niche outside the human settlements for centuries, rebalancing the atmosphere, restoring microbes and viruses, regenerating the endless diversity of biomes.

The terrafixing is a self-monitoring, self-modifying biological protocol. The street-corner Gaiaists claim that it's self-aware. They're nuts, but everyone accepts that the terrafixing learns, adapts, and reacts. New systems emerge, new strategies evolve . . . and old species reappear.

The Growth reevolves extinct organisms via recovered scraps of DNA. It scours the Earth on a cellular level, identifying tissue samples of dead species and regenerating them. Lacy treeferns returned early, as did a hundred families of mosses. Aphids and silverfish and butterflies spawned anew. A century ago, the terrafixing recovered shrews and pelicans and a bewildering assortment of ant species before moving on to squids and Tasmanian tigers.

Only one problem. During their death throes, the nation-states deployed bio-forged weapons with capacities beyond anything we're currently willing to build: Armored Assault Vehicles with integrated biological components, Pursuit Deterrent Munitions based on the sensory organs of the silkworm moth, Personal Battlesuits boosted by synaptic software. In the aftermath of the SICLE War, these defunct, abandoned bioweapons scattered the Earth. Most of them decayed into sludge, but the terrafixing occasionally latches onto the organic components of ancient autonomous systems and resurrects them into remorts.

Bio-forged knuckletanks roar to life, their targeting systems suddenly online. Subterranean breaching drones burrow beneath city walls, driven by the inchoate instincts of rejuvenated DNA. A perimeter defense platform with a neural net clear-cuts a burgeoning forest while gathering feedstock.

The regular armies usually handle them.

But the terrafixing also reanimates medipedes, heavily armored medical units twice the size of freight trains. Centuries ago, they crawled through battlefields, treating injured soldiers and malfunctioning tech in the quasi-organic repair suites secreted inside their bellies. Wielding the power of advanced autonomous wetware, medipedes treated the soldiers and patched the tech, then returned them to battle.

The terrafixing identifies medipedes as naturally occurring

organisms. It brings the ancient, abandoned husks of medipedes to monstrous life as cataphracts, impenetrable assault machines that grow racks of bio-forged battlesuits . . . which then attack independently, shambling into combat like up-armored zombies.

Everyone knows cataphracts. They're the stuff of nightmares. This submarine is a rarer type of remort. I've never seen one before, and it's possible that nothing smaller than a CAV can take them down.

Not *my* CAV, though. I'm not dying here, not today.

The gun turrets shiver and lock on target. On *me*. The Ijapa is armed despite centuries on the ocean floor because bio-forged weapons were designed for autonomous action, implanted with the urge for self-repair, and given the ability to manufacture their own munitions.

In retrospect, not a great plan.

My chest tightens as I watch the remort open fire. "Dodge!" I yell at the oblivious remote operator. "Dodge! I need time—"

The operator doesn't dodge. The operator pushes me directly into the missile paths and impacts rock the CAV, shoving my head against the frame.

I activate the bonespur implant and a fibrous growth pierces the skin of my middle finger. A dull brown filament self-assembles from my blood and flesh. If I need more length, the tech will cannibalize my bone.

The implant extends into the rough shape of a lockpick. I grunt in satisfaction before I notice motion on a nearby screen: the Ijapa has unleashed tracker mines at me, a dozen gleaming shapes cutting through the sludge.

I'm too late. I'm already dead.

The remote operator triggers a pulse to knock out the remort's tech. The screens around me shimmer blue, the mines drift away—and a torpedo blast hammers me through the saddle and sets fire to the sludge. Oozing craters open around my CAV and I catch a glimpse of a pinkish, oily smear left over from the combat against the lamprey.

The ruins of catamaran crafts smolder in the jellied water around the pink smear. I see the wreckage of a disemboweled CAV sink in a field of debris, and my skin tightens.

Whatever lampreys are, they tear CAVs into pieces.

Another Ijapa torpedo hits. One of the walls buckles. I whimper and caress the implant propagating from my finger, directing the lockpick tip toward my manacle.

Pain throbs in my hand as the bonespur lengthens.

Too slowly.

There's another impact, and another. My screens waver and the saddle walls bulge inward. Every impact drives them closer.

This is how cry pilots die: crushed to death an inch at a time.

Despite my fear, I feel the untapped power of the CAV. There's more speed here than they're tapping, more strength. Even strapped in manacles, I'm aware of the potential: this CAV is a laser rapier and they're swinging it like a koncrete sledgehammer.

"C'mon, you splice," I growl at the voices. "*Use* this thing, dodge, move . . ."

The operator doesn't hear me, and wouldn't listen if she did. She drives the CAV into anti-armor enfilades that rock the saddle and crimp the walls toward me.

As the CAV's alloy ribbons slap at the remort's flechettes, I angle the tip of my lockpick into the seam of my manacle. There's a fissure there, a catch between the two halves . . . a release switch.

Another blast hits, and the buckling saddle slaps my left knee. I'm going to be crushed to death and—*clink*. I feel the tip of my pick catch on a seam. I extend the bonespur, probing for the pinhole leading into the release switch . . .

"Aft target acquired," the remote operator says. "Impact in nine, eight—"

The lockpick curls into the pinhole.

Missiles light up my CAV. The roof crumples. An edge punches my head and tears the skin off my temple. My neck bends, an inch from breaking.

I can't do this. I'm dead, I'm finished. As I slump in defeat, the *flow* sweeps me away: I'm not here, I'm not me, I'm just a ripple in the terrafixing, a single cell in the planetary body. Fractals bloom and roots branch. There's no hope, no fear. No anger, no future.

The cables jutting from the CAV saddle walls slacken. They loop around the frame with a slow grace, like they're waiting for direction. For input. Like they're idling and—

Another explosion rocks the CAV and my vision turns red. I'm losing consciousness. I prod the release switch and watch my suicidal CAV dive toward the remort.

A wave of sludge lifts us and my lockpick deploys a spark into the release switch.

There's a click and my vision turns from red to black.

CHAPTER 8

Before the Big Three AIs ascended, they designed dozens of minor and failed techs: stem-interface, bond-pairing, and a thousand revolting flavorants. They originated major breakthroughs, too: flowcore processors, vector plasma, and ceralloy manufacture. And they produced an endless outpouring of rude poems in an ancient language called Old Sabaean.

Why?

Nobody knows, and if you asked they'd tell you a dirty limerick in a dead language.

However, they also identified the Waypoints: five locations within thirty-one astronomical units from the sun—inside the orbit of Neptune—that exhibit exotic properties. Though some people insist that the AIs *created* the Waypoints; they remain in fixed locations relative to the sun, which apparently suggests they're not natural phenomena.

Every one of the Cherzo-8 Corporations built habs on Luna during the moon-race . . . and they lost money so catastrophically that they became the Cherzo-5. That was the extent of the space race until the Waypoints were located. Then joint ventures sprang into being among the remaining corpos. Mines appeared on Mars, tasked with building formidable Flenser fleets—upgrading that previously minor branch of the corporate military forces into armadas.

The new star fleets crossed billions of miles for an ownership stake in a Waypoint. While the corporations never fought each other on Earth—they stood together against remorts and insurgents—they battled over this new resource in the big empty. Dreadnoughts guarded featureless sectors of space that only flowcore tech could identify. Weaponized fields of kinetic dust wiped out the dreadnoughts, and the corpos replaced them with deepspace fortresses. Which waves of biohacks reduced to frozen rubble.

And for what? Despite the name, the Waypoints don't lead anywhere.

As far as I know, they don't *do* anything, either.

Still, apparently these weird, fixed positions in space hold the key to advances in research and development. According to MYRAGE—the global communications network—they "simmer with boundary-correspondences," which makes them immensely valuable. So the Flensers are the highest branch of every corpo's military: the pilots and engineers, the navigators and flight crews.

Marines are next: they specialize in micro-g combat and boarding maneuvers. The Garda is a police and intelligence force that serves the enclaves and—sometimes—the Freeholds, while the Army engages all militarized Terran-based conflicts: remorts and patriots.

So when I wake to see a marine logo floating in front of my face, my first feeling is shock that I'm alive. But my second is confusion: the *marines*? Sure, I've been training for months, but on my best day I'm not qualified for the marines.

While I'm still gaping, the logo fades and an embed show starts, a trauma-drama set in Dingxi's luxury scrapers. Because I'm actually just watching a marine channel on MYRAGE . . . through a lens in my eye.

A *lens*, not a cuff. In my actual eye. I've never rated a lens before. A moment later, I'm lying in the strange bunk, flicking through channels like an excited child. I scan past the date and code and legalese: *Revocable Property of the Shiyogrid Armed Forces, CCL, Assigned to Provisional Trainee Maseo Kaytu.*

"Whoa," I murmur.

"Good morning, sleepybean!" a woman's voice chirps.

I increase my lens transparency and see Ting standing over me, amber hair falling around her pointy face. The diagnostic panels and clinical instruments lining the wall tell me where we are: in a cramped medical bay.

"Are you awake?" Ting asks, flopping onto my bunk. "You slept through the whole transfer, except we're not there yet, so not the *whole* transfer. I mean, you only slept through the bits you slept through. I guess that's a tautology, except I'm not sure if 'tautology' means what I think."

My head throbs and I close the channel in my lens. I'm alive. I survived the CAV. I did it. I'd popped the manacles and forced the CAV to withdraw from the field.

"You missed the intake interview, too," Ting tells me.

I stare at her for a moment, too overwhelmed to answer. Images flash in my mind: a CAV churning through the water, absorbing missile strikes, lashing out with ribbons to slice flechettes, slapping away a drone assault.

Then I realize: her pupils are black. She darkened her stemhead gold with lenses. Somehow she wrangled two lenses and modded them to hide the most visible signs of her addiction.

"You missed your lens fitting, too," she continues, wrinkling her pointy nose. "And you've got an earbug. They fitted you when you were unconscious. We're on the way to basic training. In the Army, I mean. Well, not the Army specifically, the joint services. Boot camp, I guess, that's our next stop. What's a shock troop?"

A strap-harness is keeping me on the bunk. When I move to release the buckle, my hand is stiff and my middle finger is cocooned in reconstructive foam. I pop the buckle and pull myself into a seated position. The laminar spray bandage on my temple feels smooth and cool against my skin. More bandages adhere to my leg and shoulder and hip, but the painkillers numb the ache.

"How long—" I shake my head. "You're alive."

"Three of us lived!" Ting's gaze shifts toward the teenager sleeping in another bunk. "He made it, too. So there's three of us. I mean, obviously. You can count to three."

"Forget three," I tell her. "I can count all the way to ten."

She gives a surprisingly rich laugh. "Your name is Kaytu. I'm Ting. I already told you that. Actually, I'm Ting Ting. My front name and back name are the same name. That's what I always said as a kid when anyone asked why—"

"Where are we?"

"Medical unit in a transport ship," she says. "Didn't I say that? Maybe I just thought it. A ship ship, too! Not an airship, a water ship. They gave us lenses. They give all recruits lenses, if they don't have them already. If they do have, they mod them. *Restrict* them really, limit them to the mil-chans, but there are ways around that, if you know how."

"We're recruits," I say, my head swimming.

A smile transforms her pointy face into something fragile and beautiful. "In the actual service!"

"Not too shabby."

"Just in time, too! I don't know what I would've done, back home. Things got a little—" Her voice quivers. "Bleak, I guess. Or scary. Back home, I mean. Where are you from? I'm from the Anadarko Basin Freehold. Well, and Tangiers too, except not really, not anymore."

"Three of us lived? What're the odds?"

"Four point two seven percent," she says. "More or less."

I inspect her bright face. She seems harmless and flighty, but that doesn't mean anything. "How'd you survive?"

She gives a tremulous smile. "Um, my CAV stopped working? Before I even reached the remort or anything?"

I wait for more, but she picks at a scab on her forearm instead of talking. Which means what? That she cheated the system somehow. Just like me.

"It stopped working," I say.

"Malfunctioned, I guess."

"That's convenient."

"I *know*!" she says, wide-eyed. "Totally!"

"Mm-hm."

"Well—" She peers at me. "Well, how did you survive?"

"Mine actually *did* stop working," I tell her.

Ting rubs the back of her neck, where she injects stem. "Oh! Um. Well, anyway, the intake interview! You didn't miss much."

She's hiding something, but I can't think of a reason to care. "No?"

"It was just the three of us. Plus that scary cadet, the CE's daughter? Cadet Rana. She's transferring from a civilian unit."

"Into the same facility as *us*?"

"I think so. That's why they were in the area in the first place." Ting wrinkles her nose. "I guess there's some kind of newfangled training program, and they're recruiting the best of the best, like her, and the worst of the worst, like us."

"Newfangled how?"

She bounces on the bunk a few times. "*Newfangled* is a funny word. How come you can't say *oldfangled*? Or just *fangled*?"

"What makes you think it's a new program?"

"I don't know. Just a guess. Cadet Rana doesn't like me. She looks at me like I'm bad tempeh. Why do they let CAV survivors enlist? I mean, instead of putting us back in CAVs for another fight?"

"It's the law," I say. "Otherwise, CAVs count as the death penalty."

"How do you know that? Do you read a lot? I don't read much because I get jittery. I'm mostly an experiential learner. That means I learn by doing. I'm pretty good with mods and reverbs and stuff."

"You're a hacker?"

"Not really," she says, squirming on the bunk. "A little, I guess. Yeah. When I'm not . . ." She scratches her arm. "You know."

"Stemming."

She flushes. "Anyway, I'm good at hacking. I mean, I'm not too bad."

"How are you going to get stem in basic training?"

Fear flashes in her face, and she looks away, toward the sleeping teenager. "His name is Loa. He's a little scared of fighting remorts. Maybe more than a little."

"Smart kid," I say.

"I'm scared, too. You're not scared, are you?" She peers at me. "You don't look scared."

"I'm always scared," I tell her.

CHAPTER 9

The swaying of the bunk and the simmer of narcotics makes me drowse off. Ting hums as she fusses over Loa and me, breaking out into snippets of song. She's like a little kid playing with dolls, and her voice is sweet but small.

When I manage to rouse myself, I check my lens. I want to contact Ionesca and tell her I'm alive. I try to establish a link but my lens flashes a refusal. *UNAUTHORIZED TRANSMISSION REFUSED.*

"Gutter*damn*," I mutter.

"You can't contact anyone," Ting says. "I mean, not outside of approved personnel."

"We're not even sworn in yet."

"It's only for the first month or three. They keep us sequestered from our old lives, so we bond to the military. 'Sequestered'? Is that what I mean? It sounds funny."

The murmur of conversation sounds from outside the medical bay, then fades away. I close my eyes and feel the rocking of the ship. I'm half-asleep before I wonder how Ting knew I was trying to contact someone.

The medics don't let us leave the compartment. Ting talks nonstop. She tries to shut up when I tell her to, but she can't help herself. Eventually she recedes into background noise and I explore my new lens.

The truth is, I almost enjoy her undemanding company—at least until I catch her pushing a barb of stem into her neck.

Ting catches me catching her. The previous night, she'd convinced a medic to smuggle her out of the compartment for a few hours. I don't ask how she paid for the favor; I don't ask how she paid for the stem. She doesn't ask if I'm going to report her.

We're both from the gutter. We know how to keep questions to ourselves.

Loa doesn't say much, due to a combination of sedatives and shock. He's the only one of us who survived the assault honestly: his CAV soaked enough damage to withdraw, yet somehow he stayed alive inside the crumpled shell.

On the second night, he wakes with a moan. "Kaytu?"

"Right here," I say, from the desk where I'm reviewing milspec manuals.

"You're a Freeholder, nah?"

"Mostly."

He starts a lamp beside him, illuminating his patchy beard and unsteady eyes. "You're a ganger? I'm an enclave boy myself. Never had the nerve to break a law. Never had the guts."

"It doesn't take guts," I tell him.

He ignores me. "You know what I had instead? You ever heard of Opium Civil?"

"It's some kind of game?"

"A hyperreal stratworld," Loa says, then tells me his story.

I know most of it already, just from looking at him: a shareholder kid who got in so much trouble that dying in a CAV sounded good. Apparently he'd spent his childhood in MYRAGE, exploring the unreal world. Mostly blasting virtual remorts into chunks and freeing enslaved planets from technopath dictators.

Eventually he'd found a gaming cartel playing Opium Civil. Good people, he tells me, and smart. They recognized a natural. They taught Loa; they trained him. He rose through the echelons until at seventeen he broke onto the bigboard.

"Now I'm the eighth-ranked player in the second-biggest cartel in Opium Civil," he says.

This means nothing to me. "Whoa."

"Yeah," he says. "Except I was stuck there. My link was too slaggy, my gear too slow. Everyone else on the board, they're Class A, Class B. I'm barely even C, nah?"

"So you went for better gear?"

Loa's shocky eyes glint with tears. "I didn't mean to hurt anyone." There's a long pause. "I thought, after it happened, at least I can do something good, you know? Not to make up for it. Nothing could. But to try. You know?"

"I know."

"And now here I am."

"Ranked number eight in Opium Civil," I say.

A sad smile rises on his face. "The right gear, and I would've broken the top five. Except, um, I don't think I can do this. Join the military. Become a soldier."

"Remorts are worrisome, but the training—"

"Worrisome?"

"Okay, bad choice of words."

"They're worse than worrisome, they're terrifying. I don't even want to fight *patriots*."

Patriots, nationalists, insurgents: the labels are interchangeable and they all mean "rebel." The corporations tolerate everything except independence. Alarm bells ring if a critical mass of the population cleaves too strongly to a homegrown culture, passionate civic pride, or deeply felt regional identity.

Genuine independence leads to competing power centers, which leads to instability. To bloodshed and catastrophe. We've been down that road before; we followed it to the brink of extinction.

The corpos step in quickly, atomizing any emergent identity by forcibly relocating the population. They even crack down on languages. A few centuries ago there were a few thousand languages; now there are a few dozen. That's not an accident, it's policy.

Yet if they wait too long to act, violence erupts. A group fighting for its homegrown culture becomes armed insurgents. A region with more local pride than corporate loyalty falls prey to fanatical nationalists. The people defending their civic identity against the corporate culture transform into extremist patriots.

In Vila Vela, we were called all three—until the corpos erased the city from the face of the Earth.

"I can't do this," Loa says.

"You can't do it *now*," I tell him. "By the time we finish basic training, you'll be ready."

"I—I guess."

"You'll be a soldier."

"Yeah," he says, though he doesn't sound convinced.

For the rest of the day, our lenses run instructional programs and we mutter to ourselves, memorizing rank structures and corporate guidelines and remort cladistics.

There are six general classes of remorts: Stationary, Itinerant, Predatory, Migratory, Aquatic, and Unique. Stationary remorts are bio-forged systems like harpies and toadstools, reevolved from smartmines and area-denial tech. They're rooted to a single spot and usually pose more of a danger to the terrafixing than to humanity.

Itinerant remorts roam the New Growth, driven by a bizarre mishmash of programming and instinct. An itinerant remort like a Terrain-Adaptable Sabotage and Interdiction Unit—known as a bay-jack for some reason—might wander harmlessly for years before assaulting an extraction filter or slaughtering a herd of wild goats.

The apex Predatory remort is the cataphract, evolved from nigh-impenetrable medipedes with "extraction and recovery" limbs that can slice through a gunship. If that's not bad enough—and it is—they're surrounded by a phalanx of shambling semiautonomous paladin battlesuits. Knuckletanks are resurrected from engineering rigs with a faintly simian design and compelled to hunt and destroy like the other remorts in this class.

Migratory remorts swarm. Hundreds of moths swirl from the terrafixing, reevolved from a pursuit deterrent bio-film. Millions of umires the size of a pinky fingernail burn swathes in the New Growth that are visible from orbital craft.

There are more Aquatic remorts than any other class, but my lens glosses over them. Apparently the Ijapa class—like that submarine I'd fought in the CAV—are the only ones that use the services of a cry pilot. Other than that, they're handled by the naval branch.

Uniques are the rarest. They're idiosyncratic one-offs, when the terrafixing partially jump-starts a bio-forged tech that doesn't quite achieve viability. Uniques spin in hopeless circles or tear themselves apart. They're so broken and pathetic that Ting sniffles when we learn about them.

Her tears don't affect her appetite, though. We're given gelatinous rectangles in vitamin wrappers for every meal. There are five colors, with distinct scents. If you don't breathe through your nose, they all taste the same.

Loa isn't impressed, but Ting and I love them.

The next morning, we watch a real-time projection showing the ship sluicing into a foam-dock on the coast. A nursurgeon removes the wrap on my face and wrists. She applies a stimulant patch to Loa, fully rousing him from thera-sleep.

We're escorted off board, and our lenses guide us from a tram to a funicular that rises to a rooftop terminal. Ting and I gape at the Class C corporate enclave, which is gorgeous with arching roofs and bridges of shifting film. Reef-trees drape like gowns around the spiral towers, flowing with jewel-like filtration grasses.

Other recruits trickle into the terminal. Ting and Loa stick close to me. A few recruits eye us with curiosity, a few with hostility. Most don't seem to see us at all.

The boarding announcement flashes, and forty minutes later I'm sitting in a wide-bodied trirail snaking through the night. I opaque my lens and explore the mil-chan. Arrival is scheduled in 102 minutes, according to my status screen, at 25:3 local time. I find the specificity calming.

Part of me is still trapped in that CAV, trying to catch a cluster of smartwire with a manacled hand and a lightning strike of luck. That feels like five minutes ago. Part of me is still in the Freehold tower, delivering that final package. That's ten minutes ago. Part of me is hustling in the refugee camp; part of me is fighting in Vila Vela.

But the rest of me?

The rest of me is on the way to basic training.

CHAPTER 10

When the trirail grinds to a halt, an announcement directs all passengers heading for Joint Service Training to depart the cars. Loa is subdued as we step onto the platform.

Ting is fidgety and flashes a message on my lens: "I can't do this alone. I'm not strong. I can't do this alone. I will need help."

I stare at her in surprise. The private message functionality is locked on these military lenses; they don't want recruits passing secret notes to each other. Somehow she seamlessly cracked our lenses. I guess she's good at hacking after all.

"We all need help," I reply, then turn off messaging and look toward the horizon.

We're on the outskirts of a small enclave, probably eight or ten million people. The ass-end of nowhere, judging from the unlaminated trees growing along the tracks.

When my lens tells me to board the shuttle, I find a seat in the first car. Nobody smiles at me, but nobody frowns either. That's a deal I'll always take.

Most of the recruits look about my age, early to midtwenties, but a bunch are younger and a scattering are older: even into their forties and fifties. I guess they're not heading for shock troop training. They all look sleek and confident and well fed. I want to think of them as soft, but I've never believed that hardship makes you harder.

It just makes you brittle.

The day grows lighter. The shuttle rattles faster. My lens doesn't tell me our destination. I don't care, as long as I'm heading away from the gutter, away from the CAVs, away from my past.

When we leave the town behind, the New Growth extends into roiling gray plains. In this bioregion, the layers of gauzy vegetation are mostly flat, with serrated ridges spreading like veins.

An hour later, I lens my voucher at the vend menu in the mess compartment. There are flavored tubes like I've never seen: rambutang, tarosteen, rosemetal. I buy three, then lean against the wall and stuff my face.

A tall girl in an austere chop-suit steps beside me. It takes me a second to recognize Cadet Rana from the offshore installation. She knows exactly who I am, though.

"You survived," she says.

"So far," I tell her.

"Three volunteers in your group lived. That's unusual."

I look at her perfect face. The whites of her eyes are unstained, and I bet her breath smells of fresh water. "You sound disappointed."

"You're a coward," she says. "And a beggar."

"Yeah."

"You begged like—" Rana shakes her head. "Without shame. Without honor."

"What good are they?"

Disgust flares in her face. "Well, you're here now. Maybe you'll work out. But I think, beggar, that you won't last long."

There's nothing pretty about her atonal voice, yet I like the way it sounds. I want to keep listening, so I say, "What happened to your newblue uniform?"

"That's civilian gear," she says. "From Cadet Officers' Corporate Training."

"'Cocked,'" a beefy guy with black freckles says, pausing on his way into the corridor.

"Huh?" I say.

"C-O-C-T," the guy explains. "Cocked. Cadets don't wear newblue during basic training. We all start at the same level. That's the theory, anyway."

"Some of us start more level than others?" I ask.

"Only the shit-hottest cadets sign onto this party, prez." He scratches his cheek and looks at Rana. "The ones aiming for admiral stripes or the executive suite, you know?"

"I don't know much," I tell him.

"Combat training's for the lowest of the low and the highest of the high. Like you and her." He shows me a cockeyed grin. "And me."

"Which one are you?"

"Low expectations," he says. "High hopes."

After he leaves, I squeeze the rest of the sweetpaste into my mouth while Rana watches. Except for the freckled guy, the other recruits keep away from her. They're intimidated by her poise, maybe. Or her status. She's definitely Class A, and the other recruits can smell it on her.

"What's a lamprey?" I ask her.

"That's the biggest question in the world."

"That's the smallest answer."

"I'm not cleared to know. You're *very* not cleared to know."

"They leave a nasty slime trail."

She frowns. "You saw one in the CAV?"

"Only the traces it left behind."

Her frown deepens. "The way you fell to your knees . . . You clung to that aide's legs like a beaten dog. How is the JST supposed to make a soldier out of *that*?"

"Have you ever seen anyone beg for their life before?"

"No."

"I have," I tell her.

For the first time, I see a flicker of uncertainty in her face. She starts to respond, then turns and stalks away. The crowd parts, giving me a clear view of her departure. It's a gift. Her legs are long and her ass is muscular. She moves like someone who knows how to fight and knows how to dance—but doesn't know the difference between them.

Ionesca would snap her spine without breaking a sweat.

The thought warms me as I buy another tube. When I leave the mess compartment, the freckled guy is leaning against the wall. He's short, but wide and sturdy like a boulder.

"Hey, prez," he says. "I'm Pico."

"Maseo. Uh, I mean Kaytu."

"A Freeholder. Do you know the joke, 'What did the Freeholder say to the PR investigator'?"

"No."

"Shit. Me, neither."

I'm not sure if my wariness is maladaptive in this situation, so I try to smile.

"I forgot, and can't check MYRAGE." Pico pushes off the wall with his shoulders. "One of my fathers came up in a Freehold. He was a scorch artist in Burkinabé."

"That's Africa?" I ask.

His grin quirks. "You know we're *in* Africa, right?"

"I got a little turned around," I admit.

Pico laughs. "The way you move reminds me of him. Of my father. You've got that Freeholder stroll, like you're surrounded by music." He reaches toward my face. "You've got a little—"

I almost punch him in the throat before I realize he's wiping a smear of rosemetal from my chin.

"All gone," he says.

I say thanks and scurry back to my compartment, unsettled and nervous. In the Freehold, I know how things work. I know how to read the signs, and I know how to play the angles. Not here. So I minimize my lens and gaze out the window at the dark sky and silvery silos until we reach a security fence, an angled wall crawling with security skarabs.

We stop there, and wait for three hours.

When the shuttle jerks forward we're on Dekka Base property, which looks like twenty miles of terrafixing lapping at the feet of a a cluster of beige buildings. Our destination is a smallish building, a half mile wide and thirty or forty floors tall, though some of those floors are fifty feet high. I catch a glimpse of lakes to the north—one looks like sludge—and a forest to the south, both of them surrounded by rutted tracks and observation towers.

Then the building swallows us and the windows turn into mirrors.

"Recruits will depart in single file through the indicated exits," a voice announces. "Recruits will assemble in accordance with instructions from their lens. Recruits will not delay. Confirm."

A few of the recruits say, "Confirm," then stand.

After I say "Confirm," my lens overlays a translucent path on my vision. I merge with the crowd and follow the path onto a shuttle platform in a cavernous terminal. The lens flashes an arrow, telling me to turn left into a cluster of other recruits.

I don't want to bump into anyone, so I pause to check that my path is clear.

"First warning, Recruit Maseo Kaytu," the lens scrolls.

The arrow flashes again, so I do what I'm told and shoulder-check another recruit, who swears under her breath. The arrow flashes me into place in a formation of recruits, facing a wall with a Shiyogrid logo. There's a bench at the base of the wall that's so dinged and battered it looks like sculpture.

Ting stands to my left, and a petite blonde covered in jaguar markings is to my right.

Nothing happens.

Five minutes, ten minutes.

After fifteen minutes, an older man mutters to his neighbor—then falls abruptly silent in midsentence.

Another five minutes creep past, and Ting starts to scratch her forearm. She squeaks in fright and blurts "Sorry," which means her lens must've flashed a warning at her.

Ten more minutes pass. My feet throb and flurries of activity sound behind me. Shuttles arrive, autocarts deploy, there's even a jaunty whistle.

With my peripheral vision, I watch Pico shift his weight. He rolls his muscular shoulders, then laughs. "Y'all got me beat when it comes to staring at a wall."

He crosses to the battered bench and takes a dramatic seat. Nothing happens to him. Nothing happens at all. Two more recruits join Pico, then two more again. One of them says something about showing initiative and taking control.

An hour passes. The muttering increases. Have they forgotten us? Is there a bug in the lenses, making us wait here forever?

Finally, a soldier strides between the two groups of recruits: the standers and the sitters. He turns to face the standers. There's a glimmer of flat approval in his face and I suddenly hate those of us who waited: the eager, the patient, the obedient.

The soldier is whipcord-thin except for his double chin, and wears corporate utility fatigues with a sergeant's braid.

"Recruits are here on sufferance," he says. "You are not necessary; you are tolerated." His gaze flicks from me to Ting to teenaged Loa. "A few of you are here on *extreme* sufferance."

The recruits on the bench, the ones sitting behind the sergeant, look uncertain. They don't know what to do. Even cocky Pico frowns. Should he rush back into place? Stay where he is? They might've expected punishment, but they didn't expect to be ignored.

"Through some combination of stockholding, merit, and luck," the sergeant continues, "you were accepted into the Joint Service Training of the Shiyogrid Corporation. Only seventeen percent of *qualified* applicants are accepted." His focus sharpens. "Recruit Jagzenka! Tell me what that means."

The little blonde with the patterned skin shifts uneasily, and I almost smile. The woman with jaguar markings is called *Jag*zenka?

"Um," she says. "I don't know, san."

"Don't call me *san*," the sergeant says. "I'm a noncollateralized officer."

"Oh!" Jagzenka says. "I'm sorry, um . . ."

"HR Sergeant," the sergeant says. "I am HR Sergeant Zhu. Seventeen percent of qualified applicants—"

Pico slips forward from the bench to return to formation.

"Stay!" the HR Sergeant barks at him.

Pico stays and even manages an abashed grin.

"Seventeen percent are accepted into JST," the HR Sergeant continues. "What does this mean?" He points to another recruit. "Speak."

"I guess that we're the best of the lot, HR Sergeant?"

"Incorrect," the HR Sergeant says. "It means you are replaceable, by a large pool of equally untalented potential recruits. The feeblest stationary remort would chew you into paste, confirm."

"Confirm!" we say.

"Into a thin gruel. No loss. Every one of you is replaceable." He glowers at Cadet Rana. "Without exception. And what does *that* mean? You are not being trained, at this particular time. You are being weeded out. Confirm."

"Confirm!" we say.

"We're not putting you through the fire to forge warriors on the anvil of adversity. We're putting you through the fire to incinerate the trash. Confirm."

"Confirm!"

"If you fail to maintain minimum standards, you will be decruited. If you fail to perform, you will be decruited. If your supervisor determines, for any reason or none, that you are not a good fit with the JST, you will be decruited. For any reason or *none*. Confirm."

"Confirm!"

"If at any point before vesting you decide to decruit yourself, you'll receive a bonus. A farewell gift, in exchange for not wasting our time. Consult your lens to see your chance of successfully completing basic training—and your rank in your platoon."

My lens says:

Kaytu, Maseo
chance of completion: 02%
platoon rank: 48 of 53
decruitment bonus: 511 c

'll get 511 scrip if I leave now? That's good news, but how am I number forty-eight of fifty-three? I haven't even done anything yet! And I spent a year training for this. When I shift to another screen, I see the explanation: provisional enlistment; CAV.

Oh. I'm a cry pilot, so they don't expect anything from me but failure.

"The JST databases contain millions of comparison cases," the HR Sergeant tells us. "The numbers you are seeing are not opinion, they are fact, based on your background and behavior. Look at your decruitment bonus again."

decruitment bonus: 509 c

Two scrip less. A murmuring sounds, and the HR Sergeant says, "Every hour that number gets closer to zero. There will never be a better time to leave than right now."

In the silence that follows, I hear the hollow thud of four or five soldiers jogging in formation behind us. Except when I catch a glimpse of them, there are at least a dozen moving in perfect synchronization.

Loa asks the sergeant, "I can just walk away, nah?"

"That's right, son."

"Where do I get my four hundred cred?"

"On the return shuttle. Step aboard and it's in your account."

Loa scratches his patchy beard. He looks at the rest of the recruits, and then his gaze settles on me. Like he's asking my opinion. He's got connections in Opium Civil, whatever that is, and four hundred scrip is almost enough for a gaming rig. Plus, he survived CAV. Without cheating, without hacking—with dumb luck and blind terror.

So I give him a nod. He should leave now and take the money. Then I focus on the private, illicit message that Ting sent the previous day. I can't open my own dialog, but I can reply to hers: "Tell Loa that if he wants to start again in a Freehold, contact this woman and use my name."

I send Ionesca's address, then turn off messaging before Ting can respond, because I'm embarrassed. What am I doing? Soft-hearted idiot. Still, Loa flashes a surprised smile, then trots to the shuttle and vanishes inside.

Another recruit mutters, "Four hundred? They're giving me a thousand," and follows Loa away. I'm not tempted. A two percent chance of success isn't good, but it's better than the alternative.

Three more recruits bustle past, including two who've moved to the bench. Not the freckled guy, though. He saunters into formation like he's crossing his living room.

The stats on my lens change again:

Kaytu, Maseo
chance of completion: 03%
platoon rank: 45 of 48
decruitment bonus: 508 c

Look at me, skyrocketing to number 45. I look around to identify numbers 46 through 48—and realize that Ting is still beside me. She looks more like a curious ferret than ever, her eyes wide and her nose almost twitching.

A private message pops into my lens: "I can't go home. And they're only offering me 18 scrip anyway. You're not leaving either.

Five hundred and eight scrip, but you're staying. I bet you schooled for this."

I frown but don't look at her. How'd she turn on my messaging? How does she know what they're offering me? She's better than "not bad" at hacking.

"Now that the smart ones are gone," the HR Sergeant says, "the rest of you sorry splices follow the directions of your lenses. Confirm."

"Confirm!"

The arrow flashes on my lens, telling me to shift to the side. I step into a new spot, tightening up the formation. Pico is to my right, a white-haired woman is to my left, with Ting behind me and Rana in front.

After we settle, the HR Sergeant says, "Recruit Jagzenka!"

"HR Sergeant!" the jaguar-marked woman answers.

"Does the JST train shock troops?"

Jagzenka keeps her expression steady, though she's got to be wondering why he's picking on her. Maybe he doesn't like extinct animals. "That's what I heard, HR Sergeant."

"Most soldiers never pull a trigger outside of a training range, but you're the lucky few. You've been inducted into a pilot project."

A chill touches me: *pilot* sounds like *cry pilot*, and *cry pilot* still sounds like the grave.

"You'll see action." The sergeant's gaze slides from Ting to Rana. "This company is packed with both ends of the spectrum, from incompetent to outstanding. You'll help us answer the question, is it more efficient to send our best or our worst? Confirm."

"Confirm!"

The HR Sergeant's voice softens. "Remember this. There isn't an Executive Admiral in the service who didn't once stand where you're standing."

He walks away, and there's a hint of expectation in the air. Maybe tension. Smart or stupid, we're ready to start this.

However, the JST doesn't care what we're ready for: a desk extrudes from the wall, and a woman in a paralegal uniform takes a seat and ignores us.

Survey questions appear on my lens, covering every known fact of my life. None of the unknown facts, though, which gives me a jolt of smug satisfaction. Place of birth, guardians, addresses, education, assets, MYRAGE footprint. This is pointless busywork, but I check the boxes for an hour, keeping in position, ignoring the ache in my feet.

The vesting contract says that if I successfully complete Phase One of basic training, the contents of six paychecks will be credited into my account. I'll get another four upon completion of Phase Two. There's a bonus for completing what's called Anvil Month, when you're seconded to a hot-conflict zone to support veteran troops. Plus, if I complete eight to twenty-four additional weeks of Advanced Departmental Training, I'll get additional checks . . . and I'll vest in the corporation.

A single share, but a complete change of legal status. A share is a ticket to life in the enclaves.

It's not a ticket I'll ever use. I'm not here to buy myself a new civilian life; I'm here to pay for my old one. There's some legal language about the pilot program, but I can't decipher it. Doesn't matter. I'll agree to anything.

A gawky clean-cut kid apparently doesn't feel the same. "Um, excuse me?" He looks toward the woman at the desk. "Er, san?"

"You'll know a corporate officer when you see one," the woman tells him. "They're the ones you call 'san.' I'm a Paralegal Specialist. Your surname is Voorhivey. Mine is on your lens. That's what you call me."

"Oh, s-sorry," Voorhivey stammers. "Um, but what's this about a pilot program?"

"It's a new training regime."

"For what?"

The paralegal consults a projection. "The details are classified."

"So we're agreeing to something without knowing what it is?"

"Welcome to the JST, slipper."

"Oh, okay," the kid says, flushing.

She takes mercy on him. "It's probably a new tech or a proprietary strategy for remort control—something like that."

Voorhivey thanks her and keeps reading. I skim to the end and sign the contract with a retinal print.

Three percent chance of success? We'll see about that.

CHAPTER 12

We stand there for another ninety minutes, staring at the wall. What if this is some kind of experiment to test the mindless obedience of a cross-section of the populace? Will we stand here until we collapse? Will we wait for two full days? For three?

I promise myself one thing: I won't break before Rana.

She's four feet in front of me, her posture perfect. Shoulders strong, spine graceful, feet braced. She radiates good breeding and patient ease, and resentment is bitter in my mouth.

What does she know about patience? She's never waited for rations in a warzone or a refugee camp, she's never—

The white-haired woman suddenly pivots and walks away. But with purpose, not like she's quitting. Then another recruit leaves, and another. Ting leaves, and a half dozen more follow before my lens sends me after them. I march through the shuttle terminal into an elevator big enough for the remaining forty-six of us to stand evenly spaced.

We drop underground. I can't tell how far. Maybe five stories, maybe ten. The hallways are as sealed as a Doomed city. We strip and shuffle through medical scanners. Feet in the grooves. Hands over your head.

Higher.

Higher.

Don't move.

Adhere the film to your skin.

Most of the platoon moves on, but the nursurgeons examine a few of us more closely, including me. My refugee status must've raised a warning flag, or my residence in the gutter floors. Or my bruises and my repaired middle finger. When they finish, I'm one of the last recruits to reach the supply room. Ting is another. I'm surprised that she passed the medical at all, given her stem use.

I try to keep some distance between us—associating with her won't help my three percent chance of success—but my lens directs me to precede her to the distribution lockers.

On the way there, we pass a squad of fifteen or sixteen recruits, wearing silly blue fabric booties, jogging in a tight formation. Except the formation changes every two paces; they weave around each other without missing a step. It's almost a dance, but despite the colorful footwear, they look lean and tough and focused.

We stare after them until our lenses light up with instructions.

At a bank of autocarts, I'm given a duffel rig with *Kaytu/5323/dekka-2* temprinted on the side. My lens tells me the rig contains fatigues and a pair of weave overalls, toiletries. Patch kits, a multitool, camo parka, and aerosol underwear.

There's also a complimentary breath mint, courtesy of Lhasa Industrial Glazing.

I'm not sure what to make of that.

We're given everything except boots, because instead of boots, we get our own bright blue booties, and a nickname: "slippers." That's what recruits are called for the first month.

Our lenses give us seven minutes to dress. The first thing I do is eat my complimentary breath mint. Tastes great, especially considering it came from an industrial glazing department. Ting eats hers too, and I'm still enjoying the aftertaste when I realize that nobody else ate theirs yet.

"Slow down, prez," Pico tells me. "Mess hall comes after barracks, they'll feed us proper."

Shit. I'm trying to keep my distance from Ting, but of course the two gutter roaches immediately shove free food in our faces.

"I'm fastidious about my breath," I say.

"And a fan of industrial glazing?" he asks.

"Big fan," I tell him.

A patch on his shirt says *Pik-Cao*. He sees me looking and says, "Everyone calls me Pico."

"I'm Ting!" Ting says, appearing at my shoulder. "That's my first name, too. Ting Ting is my full name, I mean. Well, my first name was Tingting, but I guess nobody knew my second name, so they cut it in half and used both bits."

Pico glances at her, his eyes twinkling. "I'm glad they didn't waste any."

"They're parsimonious." She tugs at the sleeve of her fatigues, which are baggy and green. That's the default setting. There's also a gauzy gray setting and a dull black camo design. "At least, if 'parsimonious' means what I think it means. Like frugal? Or thrifty. Because they reused the name, I mean." She blinks at Pico. "I'm explaining your joke to you, aren't I?"

"You're mostly driving a stake through its heart," he says.

My lens sends me to stand in formation, and conversation stops. I'm unsurprised when nothing happens for another hour. Then six TLs—Training Liaisons—march into the room and start barking orders, most of them insulting and contradictory.

Some of the recruits—sorry, the slippers—cringe in fear or bristle in anger, and others get the faraway look of someone praying for strength. For once, I'm ahead of the game: nobody who lived in a Freehold gutter gets rattled by shouts.

After twenty minutes of abuse, the TLs break us into three groups: Aleph, Bay, and Gabrielle. I'm in Aleph, and my Lead TL is a grizzled woman with Nordic scarification. Her Admin is a bony man with fatigues set to a businesslike mocksuit. They harry my group into our barracks, a rectangular room with six triple bunk beds beside eighteen deep lockers.

"Where's HR Sergeant Zhu?" Ting asks.

"He's not your babysitter," the Lead TL says. "We are not your babysitters. Did you have permission to speak, slipper?"

"No, san. I mean, not *san*. I'm not supposed to say *san*, am I?"

"You're on latrine duty," the Admin TL tells Ting.

"There are latrines?" she asks, her eyes widening. "Like actual old-fashioned actual latrines? That is so pa—"

Ting snaps her mouth shut at a message on her lens. She wrinkles her pointy nose, then moves into place in front of one of the bunks.

My lens directs me in front of another, and Rana stands beside me. I wonder if she feels out of place in basic training with the rabble, instead of starting in a high-level internship. I guess there's corporate cachet in graduating from shock training, though. It'll probably help her skip a few steps.

I don't wonder for long, because the Admin TL starts machine-gunning military rules at us. He rattles off corporate guidelines and mission statements for fifteen minutes.

"Old-fashioned is right," the TL finally says, belatedly responding to Ting's question. "In the JST, slippers *are* our laborsaving devices. Are any of you rated as mechanics?"

Half the recruits raise their hands. I spent many hours in my grandmother's workshop as a kid, but I keep that information—and my hand—to myself.

"Good." The TL points to two recruits with their hands raised. "You and you. You're assigned to cleaning the showers. How about pilots? Any of you know how to fly?"

Two hands lift, including Rana's.

"Orbital vehicles?"

Just Rana remains.

The TL scowls at Rana. "Spacefaring, too?"

"I am not licensed for spacefaring flight, TL," Rana says.

"You're on latrine duty with the gutter girl." The TL rattles off questions about our backgrounds and assigns jobs utterly unrelated to our answers. To drive home the point, I guess, that we're starting from nothing.

I don't claim any skills, so I'm assigned dorm overwatch, which means I'll guard the barracks during my shift. I'm not sure what I'm supposed to be guarding it from, but I know better than to ask.

CHAPTER 13

The Lead TL walks the line, stopping in front of each recruit. Her lens shines. After she finishes, she returns to a recruit on one end, a big woman with a shaved head and mean face.

"Calil-Du," the Lead TL says. "You are the barracks chief."

The big woman's brow creases. "Yes, TL!"

"Calil-Du is your new chief!" the Admin TL barks at the rest of us. "Confirm."

"Confirm," we answer.

The Lead TL eyes the mean-faced woman, who stares straight ahead. "Calil-Du, request that Group Aleph secure their duffels in their assigned lockers and return to their current position within twelve seconds. Enact."

While Calil-Du blinks at her, processing the order, the nervous-looking recruit named Voorhivey starts toward the lockers to secure his duffel.

Admin TL sidesteps in front of him, forcing him to stop. Silence falls for a few seconds as they stand there. Then Admin TL says, "Recruit Voorhivey."

The guy straightens into attention, chewing his lower lip. He's lanky and clean-cut, and looks like life never wrapped a belt around his neck and dragged him into an alley.

"A training liaison who believed in you might berate you for breaking rank," the Admin TL tells him. "That TL might correct you. That TL might hope to increase your chance of achieving minimum competence. I am not that training liaison. Return to formation, Voorhivey, and await orders."

Voorhivey slinks back into place, his eyes downcast.

"Chief-of-Barracks Calil-Du," the grizzled Lead TL repeats. "Request that Group Aleph secure their duffels in their assigned lockers and return to their current position within twelve seconds. Enact."

"Um—" Calil-Du says, apparently having trouble following all that.

"Now," the Lead TL snaps.

"D-do what she said!" Calil-Du shouts. "Move, move, *go!*"

A mad scramble erupts in the barracks. For once my lens offers no guidance, but by chance I find my locker almost immediately. I shove my duffel inside, slam the door, then race back to place with two seconds to spare.

Six of my group members don't make it, including Ting.

I cringe, waiting for punishment or abuse, but the TLs simply turn and leave without a word. Then Calil-Du—obviously responding to cues on her lens—shouts at us to start again.

This time, only Ting doesn't make it. "Sorry," she whispers. "I'm sorry . . ."

On the third attempt, Ting and two others fail: a hapless guy named Hefco, whose locker door sprang open, and a white-skinned woman named Gazi with nursurgeon prints on the backs of her hands. Apparently medical training doesn't help with locker-wrangling.

The fourth time, it's only Ting again, and Calil-Du punches her in the stomach.

While Ting retches, Calil-Du tells the rest of us, "Group Gabrielle already finished. They're winning, you fucking fucks. They're beating us like gutter dick. They're on the way to the mess hall right now." She grabs Ting's arm and drags her into place. "Screw us one more time, and I will break both your pinkies."

"Y-yes, chief," Ting whimpers.

"Beggar," Rana tells me, without moving her mouth. "Open your little friend's locker before yours. I'll close it."

"She's not my friend."

"Do you want her pinkies broken?"

"What do you care?"

"We're scored as a group," she tells me.

So the next time Calil-Du marks time, I hurl myself down the wrong aisle, fling Ting's locker open, sling around a bunk, and tuck my own duffel away. I check that my locker's closed—if they're not latched, it doesn't count as secure—then lunge back into line.

Rana shoves Ting into place and reaches her spot beside me in the nick of time. She stands at perfect attention, her eyes forward, her breath steady and her neck smooth.

"You reek of officer material," I murmur.

She doesn't respond.

"Do they teach that in cadet training? Or were you born with it?"

She still doesn't respond.

"Aiming for the Flensers," I guess. "You said you're not *licensed* for spaceflight, but you've taken the controls a few times."

"Just stay out of my way, beggar," she tells me.

Is that a hint of a smile on her lips? Maybe. Hard to tell. And why do I care? Not because she's beautiful. There are members of Aleph who are better-looking: a chiseled older man named Basdaq, and a mop-headed prettyboy named Shakrabarti who wears his uniform like it's the latest fashion. But Rana is so . . . different from me, so foreign. There's something alluring about that.

Or maybe I just like the curve of her neck and the cool of her eyes.

It's probably not a smile, though. None of us smile much that day, with the exception of Pico, who laughs at exhaustion and mocks frustration. He never misses a step, though, during the eight hours of "welcome exercises": disassembling the furniture in our room, running a mile to an identical room, and reassembling everything there.

By the time we're done, Ting's mouth is bleeding from Galil Du'o punch and we're starving. Because Groups Bay and Gabrielle secured their duffels quicker than we did, we miss our chance to visit the mess hall until dinner.

Our work shifts start after we finally eat. "Dorm overwatch" isn't just standing at the door. Instead, my lens directs me where to stand, when to patrol. Exactly how many steps to take before turning. When to check the corridors. When to cross the north side of the barracks, and when the south.

A sharp-eyed guy named M'bari is also assigned to overwatch that first day, and we pass each other every few minutes. We're mirror images, cogs in some primitive machine. He's average height, average build, copper skin. He looks like "Recruit #12" in a MYRAGE play, completely default, but I can almost see the wheels turning in his mind.

This one's a planner.

My mind, on the other hand, switches off after an hour. I'm marching and turning, my left foot *here* my right foot *there*, following the instructions on my lens, when my earbug starts droning a lecture about competence, entrepreneurship, teamwork, and "the corporate warrior ethos." By the end of my shift, my body responds automatically to the lens instructions while my brain is adrift in a sea of jargon.

"It's an interesting approach," M'bari tells me when we're finally sent back to the barracks.

"What is?" I ask.

"Training us to decouple what we're thinking from what we're doing."

"Almost like blinders," I say.

He considers that. "Maybe. I don't know what's standard for training, though, and what's part of this pilot program."

"What's the story with that?"

"How would I know?"

"You've got that gleam in your eye."

M'bari snorts. "We don't look like anything special. Well, there's that Class A cadet and—" He stops and inspects me. "You and the girl. You survived the CAVs?"

"Yeah." I take a breath. "How could you tell?"

"It's the only thing that makes sense. Except . . ." He smiles apologetically. "I can't see you committing a crime in a corporate enclave."

"We all make mistakes," I tell him.

"Maybe," he says. "But you've got a gleam of your own."

The second day starts with another work shift. This time, the lecture covers base security, urban riot suppression tactics, and basic corporate history. A dozen quizzes flash on my lenses as I march, and after a few hours even M'bari seems distracted.

Then the TLs introduce us to a fitness training regime intensive enough to break us down. Calil-Du bellows; Ting weeps. Pico teases clean-cut, blue-eyed Voorhivey, who stammers in response. Jagzenka, the tiny woman with the jaguar markings, struggles with her height but manages to maintain an appropriately feline competence. Hefco pukes and a tall, gaunt woman named Ridehorse grumbles.

Over the next few days, medically trained Gazi—white-skinned and dark-haired—leans on a mechanically inclined woman named Werz, with dark skin and white hair. Pico calls them "Yin" and "Yang." Nervous Voorhivey leans on Basdaq, the older guy who looks like an actor playing a CEO. Ting leans on whoever's closest.

Nobody leans on Calil-Du.

CHAPTER 14

On the fourth day of basic training, I'm switched from dorm overwatch to latrine duty. This is supposed to be a nightmare, surrounded by stench and splattered with filth. Even the unflappable Rana looked shaken after her shifts.

Ting flashes a grin at me, and I can't help smiling back.

We're from the gutter; when you've spent years knee-deep in shit, a little more doesn't bother you. We don't say anything, though; speaking isn't allowed during work shifts. There's no time to talk during meals, and everyone's too exhausted to chat before lights-out—everyone except Pico—which means that after a week, we still don't know much about the other recruits.

The training is designed that way on purpose, of course.

"Social engineering," M'bari explains, when tall, gaunt Ridehorse complains about it at dinner. "They're telling us that our pasts don't matter, our personalities don't matter. Only our function matters."

Fine with me. I'm here to get away from my past, and my personality is nothing to brag about.

I'm switched to consumables maintenance and after that to emissions reclamation. Always with new partners, so even though I don't know anyone's story, I know their approach. Calil-Du is as mean as she looks and almost as stupid. Gazi is meticulous, M'bari is savvy, Voorhivey is eager and nervous. Jagzenka is a stiletto. Werz is quick. Gorgeous mop-headed Shakrabarti is a jack of all trades, the fourth best at everything. Basdaq is solid, Hefco is struggling. Ridehorse is grimly fatalistic, and so tall that Pico calls her "Highhorse."

At first our least-favorite fitness regime is jogging the tracks until we complete one flawless lap, moving in perfect sync, every step of our slippered feet measured by the surface. Takes fourteen hours and five enraged outbursts from Calil-Du before Ting and Hefco achieve adequacy.

Most of us prefer Full Contact Negotiation, which is the official name for unarmed combat training. We practice a series of attack-counterattack patterns that bear no relationship to any fight I've ever been in. We drill in burst strikes, joint locks, and kinesthetica, and I ignore dozens of chances to put my sparring partners in the morgue.

On the fifth day, I neglect to pull a punch and break Pico's nose. "Shit!" I say. "Sorry."

"What do you call that, slipper?" TL barks, crossing toward me.

"Negotiating, TL!" I answer.

Pico laughs, despite the blood running down his face. Nobody else does.

TL tells Gazi to ping a medcart, then addresses the group. "Nothing's worse than recruits who think they already know how to fight. Graduates of shop-front combat training and jerkoff MY-RAGE sims. They need to unlearn a lifetime of bad habits before they take a single step forward. Confirm."

"Confirm!"

"Kaytu," TL says, "what's the key to winning a fight?"

"Hit first," I say.

Apparently she expects more, because she keeps looking at me. "TL," I conclude.

She continues to expect more, but I'm done. She fines me a day's wages and gives me a few double shifts. Which sucks. On the other hand, I'm pretty sure it's what leads Rana to talk to me for the first time in days.

I'm lounging in the barracks with Pico and Jagzenka in the five minutes before lights-out, when Rana is suddenly standing in front of me. Jag drifts away—she's good at that—but Pico looks between me and Rana like he's hoping to be entertained.

"You think she's wrong," Rana tells me. "The TL. About close-quarters combat."

"I'm not getting paid to think."

"You—" She almost takes the bait, derailed by the suggestion that I'm doing this for money. "You've been in combat."

"Sure," I say, like I'm not trying to impress her. "I've lost a few fights."

"We need to master the basics," she says, her atonal voice clipped. "We need to train our muscle memory so when we find ourselves in combat we won't have to think, we'll just act. That's what Full Contact Negotiation teaches."

"Whatever you say."

She arches a queenly brow. "That's what the training protocols say."

"Okay."

"Just give her your gutter wisdom already," Pico tells me. "I want to hear it, too."

I look at them both. "Have you ever been scared?"

"Sure," Pico says, while Rana nods.

"I mean scared for your life. Out of your mind with fear."

Pico shakes his head and Rana says, "Once."

"Your vision tunnels, your hands shake. You can't breathe." I look at Rana, wondering what scared her. "Forget muscle memory. You can't even keep from pissing yourself."

"So what's the answer?" Rana asks.

"A fight isn't you squaring off against an opponent. It's chaos. It's walking down a hallway and suddenly you're on the floor. You can't feel your arm and a boot breaks your nose. Why?" I flick my gaze toward Pico's bandaged face. "Because if you break someone's nose, their eyes tear up. You blind them."

"So what do you do?" Pico asks. "You're on the ground, blind, with one arm."

"You die," I say.

Rana's perfect jaw clenches. "Very helpful."

"You're faster and smarter than Calil-Du," I tell her. "And Pico's stronger. But she'd rip either of you apart. Her mind won't blank. She'll go for the throat. She's an animal, and if she gets hurt? Then she's a wounded animal."

"Like you," Rana says.

"You're saying it's a mental game," Pico tells me. "If you stay cool, if you enjoy violence, you win."

"I'm saying it's a game for pawns like me and Calil-Du." I look at Rana. "We all know you're heading for the boardroom—if you ever get your hands dirty, the battle's already lost."

"What about me?" Pico asks, with a lazy grin. "I'm not heading for the executive suites?"

"People *like* you," Rana tells him, as if it's an accusation.

"That's one problem you don't have," Pico says, and manages to make it sound like teasing.

Rana's dark eyes lighten. "You'll rise all the way to the top, Pico, or fall all the way to the bottom."

"What about Kaytu?"

She plucks a hydration cube from the vend. "Oh, we all know where he's heading."

"Where?" I ask.

"She's teasing you, prez," Pico says, scratching the freckles beside his bandaged nose.

Rana pops the cube in her mouth and tells me, "You fight like an insurgent."

"Like the odds are always against you," Pico adds.

"The way you fight, the way you live . . ." Rana shakes her head. "You take everything personally."

"Sure." I inspect her sculpted face. "Don't you?"

"No."

"None of this? Not the fighting, not the squad? Not your rank? You don't care about any of it?"

"I care, but I also know that how I feel isn't important. With you? How you feel is the engine that drives you."

"You make that sound like a bad thing."

"It is."

I look to Pico. "Help me out here."

"You're on your own, prez." He shows me his careless smile. "Corporate troops fight for corporate guidelines. Saving humanity is the mission statement. Only patriots fight for passion."

I open my mouth to argue, and a memory flashes behind my eyes:

In the refugee camp, violence erupted without warning but Ionesca and I never expected anything else.

When the sugarbee gangers cornered us in a stairwell, I hit first. I smashed the biggest one with my breakbar and received the snap of his bone like a gift, and the next one punched Io, and a third stabbed a hole through my cheek to my teeth so I shoved the breakbar's claws into her armpit and she howled and—

—my throat was hoarse from shouting—

—my heartbeat surged in my throat—

—I stumbled from the stairwell, blood on my hands and in my mouth. Silence fell except for my ragged breathing. The hallway dimmed and brightened with my flickering vision. I slumped against the wall and slid to the ground.

Ionesca crouched in front of me, her scarred fingers soft on my face.

"I'm sorry," I told her. She'd wanted to talk to them, she'd wanted to deal.

"You're crying," she said.

"I'm your—" I couldn't speak. "I'm your—"

She took me in her arms. "You're my everything."

The sugarbee gang stayed away from us for a while, and Io blossomed. She smiled for the first time in months, and I would've slaughtered the entire camp for her, because my heart is an insurgent with a patriot's passion instead of a soldier's discipline.

I close my mouth without speaking. I've got nothing to say. Rana and Pico are right. I need to bury the Vila Vela patriot and the refugee camp ganger in an unmarked grave.

I need to turn myself into a soldier.

The next day, we complete three perfect laps in five hours, so the TLs introduce obstacles and bottlenecks. Our lenses lock into an overlap function. We learn to monitor each other and ourselves at the same time.

Leaving my feelings behind is easier than I expect, because none of this is about me: it's about *us*.

A week later, we graduate to trap laps, with branching tunnels, climbing walls, high ledges, and hostile films. Then the TLs add swarms of moskito drones—which deliver painful shocks—and prox-mines designed to pick us off one at a time.

We struggle, we weep, we bleed, we learn. We are greater than the sum of our parts.

At the end of four weeks, Group Aleph is a machine in motion. We've stopped hesitating and started interlocking across the obstacles like a single organism. My lens tells me to reach left to grab the baton, so I reach out even if nobody's there.

Every time, someone suddenly is.

CHAPTER 15

When M'bari asks Rana about the pilot program, she shrugs. "I don't know the details."

"You know the outline," he says.

Rana doesn't bother denying it; M'bari is nothing special in terms of training, but he's a systems thinker and uncannily good at reading people.

"It's a new curriculum," Rana says.

"Why?" M'bari asks. "To prepare for what?"

Rana shrugs. "A new threat."

"None of this feels new," Ridehorse grumbles.

She's right. We're neck-deep in basic exercises fifteen hours a day, every day, with incessant lens-lectures. We're driven to exhaustion, and past exhaustion into a sort of fugue state. I might not know about Shakrabarti's family or Pico's hobbies, about Ting's history or Calil-Du's home, but I know exactly how they move. I know the length of Ridehorse's stride and the speed of Jagzenka's hands. I know to compensate for Voorhivey's split-second hesitation and to depend on Werz's exactness.

We've learned the basics of facing insurgent threats—patriot and nationalist terrorists—but the fifth week starts with a change. First, communications discipline is lightened: we can talk to each other. And second, Group Aleph is sent deep into Dekka Base to assemble at the doors of a twelve-acre free-fire hangar.

We're unarmed: we haven't been issued weapons yet, not even training weapons. Hell, we're still wearing slippers. We haven't been issued *boots.*

"Is this another obstacle course?" Werz asks.

"I don't think so," Ting says, but nobody listens to her.

"It's *some* kind of course," Calil-Du says. "And we'd better crush it. We're lagging Bay and Gabrielle."

"Chief is right." TL steps in front of us, her scarification livid in the harsh light. "Gabrielle finished this exercise in two days, seven hours, thirteen minutes."

"How did Group Bay do?" Voorhivey asks.

"Three days and counting," she tells him, and falls silent until she commands our complete attention. "Your target is inside the hangar." She projects an image of a jeweled crown that looks like a special item in a MYRAGE game. "This is your first real test. Confirm."

"Confirm!"

"Your mission objective is to find and capture the crown. Confirm."

"Confirm!"

"Follow your lenses," she tells us. "After the pulse hits, secure the crown and return it to any exit. Confirm."

"Confirm!"

"There's going to be a pulse?" Calil-Du asks TL.

"That's what she said, prez," Pico tells her.

Calil-Du shifts one of her burly shoulders. "So we grab the crown and burn ass to an exit?"

"The concept is simple," TL tells her, as the door opens in front of us.

My lens flashes directions and the group moves. We trot into the hangar and find ourselves on a fifth-floor balcony. Overhead, a projected sky roils with a simulated aurora borealis. The proving range is designed to look like a generic cityscape, with bridges and overpasses, towers and roofs. My lens shows me interior layouts of the mock buildings surrounding us, where hundreds of interior rooms open into hallways and atria.

"They're throwing remorts at us," Werz says, as we follow the curved balcony past a dozen windows.

"C-cool," Voorhivey stammers.

"We're not even fucking armed," Calil-Du says.

"We've got your sharp wit," Pico says.

"Huh?" Calil-Du says.

Ting giggles and my lens sends me into point, prowling forward with Jagzenka a half step behind.

"If they mocked up a cataphract," Shakrabarti says, "I'm going to cry."

"They won't start us on a cataphract," Werz says. "They'll start us with a standard remort. One of those long-stemmed stationary munitions systems—"

"A toadstool," Rana says, because of course she knows the nickname.

"—or, I don't know, a knuckletank or something."

"This is a pilot program," M'bari says. "Don't expect 'standard.'"

Voorhivey gulps. "W-what does that mean?"

"That we're fucked," Ridehorse says.

The balcony ends at a smooth chromacrete wall. My lens tells me to climb over, but screw my lens. Instead of climbing, I kneel.

Jagzenka puts one foot on my knee, one on my shoulder, then slips over the top like a shadow. She's smaller and faster than I am; she can scout ahead in half the time it'd take me.

My lens docks me a few points but six seconds later, Jag pings the group, giving us the all-clear.

We follow her over the wall, moving like clockwork except for a pause when Pico heaves Ting into Ridehorse's grip. Ridehorse yanks Ting onto the higher ledge and we prowl onward. Ten steps through a shadowy archway that leads into the building, Hefco slips on a friction pad, which is a common insurgent technique. Shakrabarti pulls him free, and then a trapdoor swallows Gazi.

She yelps and falls. When Werz lunges to save her, Basdaq shoves Werz into the wall to save *her*.

Ting bleats a warning two seconds before harassment moskito drones swarm from ceiling vents.

Calil-Du roars for us to run while she falls back to take the brunt of the shocks. Burns pepper her uniform from dozens of shocks. There's a char mark across her cheek. The moskitos do everything but set Calil-Du on fire, yet she stays on her feet. She's a brute, but she's *our* brute.

The moskitos harry us through a mile of hallways until—at Rana's suggestion—Basdaq and M'bari draw the tiny drones into an apartment, using themselves as bait. They're immediately flagged *inactive*, which means that for the purposes of the exercise they're dead.

"Fuck!" Calil-Du kicks the wall. "We already lost three fucking soldiers."

"Staying alive isn't the mission," Rana says.

Calil-Du glowers at her, Pico takes point, and three minutes later the surviving members of the group emerge onto a low rooftop.

A pulse hits, killing all advanced tech in a quarter-mile radius. The moskitos drop to the ground and our lenses darken. We're on our own.

Calil-Du licks her lips nervously. She's a skull-breaker, not a strategist. "Okay, um—what now?"

"We need sightlines," Rana murmurs.

"Fuck you, I know that. Jag and Kaytu, um, you're on overwatch."

"Chief," we say, in uneasy acknowledgment.

"Get high and find that crown-looking target, I guess," she says. "We'll, uh, break into three teams, under me and Basdaq and Rana."

"Basdaq is down," Ridehorse reminds her.

"Fuck! Okay, two teams. We'll move northwest, toward that tower."

"That's south," Ting tells her.

Calil-Du scowls. "Ting and Hefco, you're on point. Doesn't matter if we lose either of you."

I don't hear the rest because I'm climbing to a sky bridge for the vantage point, clumsy in my safety gear. Jag is twenty yards away doing the same thing, only smoother. She was some kind of pageant acrobat as a kid, and moves through the world like a gymnastics routine.

By the time I pull myself into place, she's crouching on a strut overlooking the hangar's faux cityscape. She throws me the all-clear, and I trot toward a pylon across the bridge.

Shouting starts below me, and I look down into a nightmare.

I know I'm on a military base; I know this is a training exercise. Still, my mind skips and my heart stutters.

A horrible *thing* stretches between two buildings. It looks like overlapping spiderwebs with strands thicker than my calves. There's a mouth in the center, a gaping alien mouth with grasping tongues, and dozens of veiny spider-creatures scuttle through funnels, bristling with shock-fibers.

Someone designed this thing to light up the fear centers of the human brain, and they did a good job.

"What the gehenna?" Jag gasps, slinking beside me.

I point to the jeweled crown glinting inside the fang-filled mouth. "There's the target."

"That's not a remort," she says. "That's not a mock-up of a remort."

"Yeah, I—" My throat clenches. "I don't know."

"It's not *anything*, Kaytu. It's not a thing."

Down below, the fire teams are in disarray. Sure, the creature is a model built by a special-effects team, but it's a model with smart materials, olfactory bursts, precision-designed projections, and pain compliance munitions. Ting is weeping; Calil-Du is glowering. Rana's face is a death mask as she leads Pico and Ridehorse and Voorhivey toward the creature.

Without looking upward, Rana points to me and Jag and twirls her finger.

"We're up," I say.

"What's the plan?" Jag asks.

"I guess—there's only one way down there."

She goes still, her jaguar markings dark in the shadows. "You really want to jump onto that thing?"

"I really don't."

"But you're going to," she says, lensing me a "booyah."

"I'll aim for the edge, to draw those spiders away. Then you grab the crown."

"You're aiming at the edge, and I'm aiming at the jaws?"

I nudge her with my elbow. "We're badass corpo warriors."

"We're screwed sideways," she says.

"See you on the other side," I say, and leap off the bridge.

I'm airborne for two seconds, a flailing of limbs and a short-ness of breath, before I feel my safety harness catch on a belay drone. Good to know that the JST won't let us die out here. The rush of air cools the sweat on my cheeks before I land on the web and almost slip through the strands.

As I scramble to grab hold, one of the veiny-spiders spits goo at Calil-Du. A spark crackles—the spiders are built on stun-drones—and she stumbles to the ground groaning.

White-skinned Gazi ignores the spider and races to Calil-Du, unstrapping her medkit. She's a low-ranked squad member de-spite the medical training indicated by the nursurgeon prints on her hands, but she's got nerves of alloy when it matters. Kneeling in front of these spiders to tend the injured? That takes some kind of bravery.

So of course she gets shocked too, and collapses twitching.

"Jag's going for the crown!" I yell. "Draw the spiders away!"

I'm not sure if I'm making sense, but Rana understands. As I tug on the web to attract the creatures' attention, Rana stands from be-hind a wire hedge and leads a charge. She and Pico shout, Ride-horse throws rocks, and Ting—well, Ting stays behind the hedge.

Spider-things scuttle across the web toward me. Seeing them close paralyzes me for a heartbeat, just long enough for another to wrap me in a ten-limbed embrace.

So I head-butt it and knock myself out.

CHAPTER 16

When the medcart retracts into the infirmary wall, I roll onto my side to check Calil-Du. Apparently she shook off the first shock and tackled a spider from behind. There's a charred pit in her shoulder from a second shock, currently being layered by medifilm.

"How did Jag do?" I ask her.

"Abject fucking failure," Calil-Du says. "Just like you. Are you cleared for action?"

"Yeah. There's no concussion."

"Then form up. We're going back in once my shoulder's done."

"Put Rana in charge next time," I tell her.

"Fuck you."

"Because she's smarter than you."

"Asshole," she says.

"Better vocabulary, too."

She rubs her bald head and watches the film form over her wound. "I dunno what kind of remort that was."

"It wasn't a remort."

"How would *you* know? Gutter trash. Do the others say it's not a remort?"

"Which others?"

"The *smart* ones, ass-eater. Not like you'n' me."

I hadn't considered the two of us in the same category, but fair enough. "Yeah. The smart ones say it's not a remort."

"Then what the fuck kind of monster is the JST crawling up our ass?"

"No idea."

"We're training to trash-stomp remorts and patriots. Not this horrorshow crap."

"M'bari thinks it's because of this pilot program."

"He thinks too much."

"Not like you'n' me," I say.

She grunts. "Waste of fucking time."

An hour later, we're back in the hangar. This time, the projected sky is a fish-belly gray and we're entered on the second floor. Our lenses lead us inside a building designed to look like a MYRAGE cliché of a lawless Freehold gutter.

A corridor stretches in front of us, cluttered with chop shops and warungs. Music blares, and projections of twitchy junkies and scruffy children flicker in every doorway. We're wound tight, waiting for nightmare spider-creatures to erupt around the corner or drop from the ceiling.

"Hey, Gazi," Pico murmurs. "You got meds for Kaytu?"

Gazi frowns at me, her lens glimmering. "What's wrong? Your ears ringing? Your vision blurred?"

"I'm fine," I tell her.

"He's suffering from homesickness." Pico gestures toward a pile of debris. "This all reminds him of his childhood."

"Stop picking on Kaytu," Voorhivey says. "It's not good for morale."

Shakrabarti shudders. "The corpos shouldn't let Freeholds fall apart like this."

"I like the music," M'bari says.

"The music's not authentic," I tell him. "And it smells wrong."

"It does!" Ting pipes up. "It does smell wrong. There's not enough incense and cooking and—and mostly cooking, I guess. It should be redolent with spices, if *redolent* means what I think. Juniper and kala jeera and sumac—"

Rana cuts Ting off with a gesture and refocuses us on Calil-Du. She's all business—except when she catches my eye, her gaze flicks to the projection of a beggar huddled in rags.

She gives me a bland look in which I see the word *beggar* and stalks forward.

I snort softly and follow. The entire squad is moving more easily now, and I catch a flicker of satisfaction in Pico's expression. Voorhivey was wrong; picking on me *was* good for company morale.

As we emerge into a derelict atrium with a bullet-pocked elevator bank, chiseled middle-aged Basdaq is on point. He moves well for an older guy and looks like the grizzled hero of a cheesy MYRAGE actioner.

"Hey!" he gasps, and a gutter gang of nine crude animannis—animated mannequins—slots from behind a kiosk to fire stun-rounds at us.

We dive for cover.

Hefco eats a round and seizes on the ground. Rana and Pico and Werz draw fire while Jag, Shakrabarti, and I circle around and disable the animannis from behind. Gazi crouches beside Hefco as Calil-Du and Basdaq prowl the room, looking for proxmines.

Ridehorse toes a disabled ganger and says, "This one looks like Kaytu."

The animanni is a lean, dark, leering gutter roach with a gruesome scar.

"They're nothing alike," Werz scoffs. "It's almost a quarter inch shorter."

"Other'n that, though," Gazi says, still treating Hefco.

Shakrabarti grins. "It's a quarter inch sexier, too."

"If you've got to count the quarter inches, you're in trouble," Ridehorse tells him.

"You're six foot three." Shakrabarti smolders up at her. "I feel inadequate just looking at you."

Ting giggles. "You're too bigheaded to feel inadequate."

"My head size is my fourth-best feature," Shakrabarti tells her.

"You're vainglorious! If that means what I think it mea—"

A pulse kills our lenses and cuts the lights. We freeze in the thick gloom of the mock-gutter atrium, and a thickly pelted *thing* clatters toward us, clinging to the walls and ceiling. It's not built on the same base as those spiders; it's more like an antipersonnel drone covered in fangs and fur.

Because she's a wise and thoughtful strategist, Calil-Du throws herself into the jaws of the enemy, howling for blood. So fuck it, I wade into battle beside her. Pico laughs as he joins us. Ridehorse falls in, all lanky limbs and gloomy mutters, while Shakrabarti and Werz grab lengths of cable to use as weapons. Rana and Voorhivey pair with Basdaq and M'bari to close a pincer around the pelted thing.

We get stomped. We flunk the second exercise worse than the first. Nobody even catches sight of the jeweled crown.

We're trotting back to the barracks when Jag says, "Fighting gangers makes sense. Half of us will end up Army or Garda. We'll face insurgents. I get that. But a shaggy drone?"

"The rest are gonna face werebeasts," Hefco says.

"Still no remorts," Basdaq says. "We're supposed to be learning how to handle remorts."

"Maybe this is elite training," Voorhivey says.

Ridehorse shoots him a disgusted look. "Maybe it's fodder for the entertainment channels. Showing us getting repeatedly stomped."

"They're training us to face some singular threat," M'bari says. "One oversized enemy. One terrifying thing."

"Cataphracts are terrifying, oversized things," Basdaq says. "Maybe this is leading up to a cataphract. One step at a time."

I glance at Rana. "You know what this is about."

She ignores me. Trots forward smoothly. Her neck gleams with sweat and her shoulder shows me what dismissal looks like.

"That's why they're making everything so scary?" Ting asks M'bari. "So we get used to being afraid?"

M'bari nods. "Whatever this pilot program is, they're prepping us for something unsettling."

We jog around a corner past MYRAGE-rigged classrooms, past workshops that stink of extrusion. Our slippered feet shush on the floor.

"There are pilot programs in every corpo's military," Rana says. "Some are training elite troops, some are training recruits. There's ambient engineers and combat cryptographers—"

"What's an ambient engineer?" Werz asks.

"There are Orit Gal wings specializing in pinpoint delivery," Rana continues, ignoring her. "They've even repurposed orbital platforms."

"For what?" Pico asks, scratching his freckled chin. "What's the enemy?"

After a moment, Rana says, "Lampreys."

"Say what?"

"The designation for a new remort clade is *lambda*, and these—"

"There *aren't* new remorts." Hefco shoots her a disgusted look. "Not for decades."

"There's a new class of remort?" Voorhivey asks, his voice thin.

"Yes," Rana says.

Ting babbles in surprise. Ridehorse grumbles in dismay. M'bari ponders. Werz and Gazi edge closer to each other. Shakrabarti looks beautifully concerned and Rana waits until the reaction quiets before she continues. "The designation for a new remort is *lambda* and these things are persistent, recurring, and emergent. So *Lambda-PRE* was their earliest designation. Lamprey."

"Maybe they're mutant eels," Calil-Du says. "That'd be cool."

"Remorts are based on bio-forged tech," Basdaq tells her. "Not on eels."

"Maybe they're bio-forged eels, asshole. You ever think of that?"

"Did the terrafixing recover them from a weapons platform?" M'bari asks Rana. "What's the base technology?"

"No idea."

Shakrabarti frowns at her. "What does *emergent* mean?"

"That they're just getting started," Ridehorse grumbles.

"I heard they self-assemble—emerge—at the target area," Rana says. "I don't know. I don't know what they are or how they work. Nobody does."

"Who cares?" Calil-Du says. "We go where the corps tells us and kill what they want."

"Yeah," Voorhivey says. "The TLs will tell us if we need to know more."

"All I know is that Group Gabrielle is kicking us in the tit." Calil-Du scowls. "If we don't step up, we're gonna fail out of this program before we fight anything."

CHAPTER 17

F our more platoon members decruit. TL says that's the other reason we're called *slippers*: we slip away.

I don't blame them for leaving. They enlisted to fight patriots and standard remorts, or maybe with dreams of Flenser space battles. Nobody said anything about lampreys. In fact, nobody *still* says anything about lampreys. If we ask the TLs, they assign us extra duty.

Pico still asks, though, because he's Pico. We'd hate him for it, but he's hard to hate.

We've had a few lateral transfers, so Platoon 5323 is now at forty-five recruits, with fourteen in Aleph, sixteen in Bay, and fifteen in Gabrielle.

TL is pleased that Group Aleph lost more personnel than Bay or Gabrielle. Rana says that's because it proves she's the tougher trainer. Pico says it's because a smaller group includes more Pico per capita, and who wouldn't want that?

Ting doesn't say anything; she spends most of her free time crying, especially after Calil-Du beats her for shitty performance. Yet she refuses to decruit. She's a complete mess, but her determination impresses me.

There are two kinds of recruits: the desperate and the driven. Some of us are terrified of failing, of returning to our previous lives. That's Ting and me, Calil-Du, and maybe Hefco. Most of the others—Rana is the best example, but also M'bari and Voorhivey—aren't running from anything, they're running *toward* something.

The Flensers, the academy, high-level officer positions, or well-paid corporate gigs. They're from military families or ambitious affinity groups, and they're working a plan.

Yet for the next few days, throwing ourselves into a new nightmare capture-the-crown exercise every four hours, there's no space between us. We bond.

We still suck, but we suck *together*.

After a series of challenges that force us to face disgust instead of fear—wading through sewage to reach the jeweled crown—we enter the hangar to find a mock-up of a one-hundredth-floor rooftop.

"Maybe they'll finally give us a normal remort," Voorhivey says, with wide-eyed optimism.

"Maybe you'll finally stop saying that every day," Ridehorse mutters.

"There's a remort evolved from a PDM we should learn to fight. I guess they're pretty common."

We trot toward a fibrous lawn on the rooftop, and Ting asks, "What's a peedeeyam?"

"Pursuit Deterrent Munitions," Rana tells her. "Developed in the SICLE War. Mobile bio-films triggered to explode by scent."

"I guess they're called *moths* now," Voorhivey says. "The terra-fixing evolves them into flapping bat-things that—"

"Moths are *bat*-things?" Pico says.

Voorhivey blushes. "Or, or moth-things, I guess. They're mostly a threat to the New Growth, unless they stumble into an enclave. They're sort of translucent, with wingspans as wide as Ridehorse's."

"Translucent?" Gazi crosses to the edge of the lawn. "We catch one, Shakrabarti can wear it as a headscarf."

"Translucence is so last season," he says. "It's all about opacity now."

Our lenses direct us to establish a perimeter. A handful of

frail-looking balconies jut from the rooftop, designed by the special-effects team to look like gravel gardens and performance stages. It's only five floors down, but projections and environmental controls add the impression of the other ninety-five floors with a visceral effectiveness.

The quiet sign flashes. Silence falls. We wait.

We keep waiting.

Ting can't stand waiting. She gets jittery and impatient. So does nervous Voorhivey and pessimistic Ridehorse. Pico hunkers down happily. Basdaq hunkers down unhappily. Petite Jagzenka is a cat, and I wonder what came first, her jaguar markings or her personality.

I'm good at waiting. I'm even better if I've got a view of Rana. The squad members look almost interchangeable in our fatigues, but my gaze drifts in her direction. I don't know. Even her stillness is eye-catching, and—

A horrorbeast erupts through the floor. Not a cataphract, but along the same lines. A fifty-foot-long mucus-worm with sparking thorns and a circular mouth. A shrunken, grotesque cataphract. Ting shrieks; Voorhivey backpedals. Calil-Du bellows and Rana lenses an image capture: the crown shimmers in a recessed nostril above the worm's mouth.

"There!" she says.

"No way to reach it," Ridehorse says. "Without getting ate."

"Eaten!" Ting cries, and the worm slams across the roof toward us.

A chunk of rubble catches my hip and spins me around. The day dims and I'm on my belly. There's screaming, the scuffle of slippers. My cheek burns.

When my vision clears, I see Calil-Du get hurled off the roof— and caught in a safety net. Rubble sprays me and I roll to my side and find myself looking at the substructure of the nearest balcony.

In that instant, I see the plan.

We need to lure the creature onto a balcony, then drop the whole thing a hundred virtual floors. That'll kill the worm—plus every squad member who acts as a lure—leaving the survivors to pull the jeweled crown from among the corpses.

"Get on the balcony!" I yelp, raising to one knee.

Pico frowns at me from behind a vend-bench. "The what?"

"Draw the worm to the edge!" Rana shouts, understanding immediately. "Lure it onto the balcony!"

"No way!" Pico says, but he rises, bellowing at the creature and waving his arms.

Shakrabarti throws handfuls of gravel and Werz shouts what I think are lyrics to a Maghrebi song.

The worm makes an unearthly noise and undulates toward them.

"Go-go-go!" Basdaq yells, dodging toward the balcony. "Ridehorse, c'mon!"

Pico gets flattened by a spray of mucus as M'bari and Jag backpedal onto the overhang. The worm follows, heaving and rippling. The floor shudders every time its body slams down, and the support struts squeal and tremble.

Werz, Voorhivey, and Hefco are smashed off the balcony as the worm crowds the rest of the squad against the railing.

I'm sprinting across the rooftop toward the creature when Rana shouts, "Kaytu! *Stop*, you gutter fuck, and take out the balcony!"

She's right. I'm in the best position. The mucus-worm is venting slime in the other direction, and I can climb under the balcony and kick the struts until they snap. I can drop the monster and the squad—and complete the mission.

We can win this thing.

I'm the only recruit with a shot at the target, but I hesitate. Basdaq throws himself into the gaping maw of the worm to draw it farther onto the balcony. Ridehorse kicks at an oozing growth.

The worm wheels around and swallows her. She's so tall and bony that it seems to choke before swiveling toward the rest of the squad and—

I can't do it. I can't sacrifice them.

I know this is just an exercise. I know nobody's going to die, I know nobody's in danger. I know my duty, but I can't. So I attack the creature and yell, "Gazi, get the crown. I'll bring the—"

I never say what I'll bring, because a gout of slime slams me into darkness.

CHAPTER 18

When I wake in the hangar's infirmary, Pico gives my shoulder a comforting punch and Basdaq gives me a sympathetic nod. M'bari considers me thoughtfully, like he's filing away information. Ting flirts with Shakrabarti and Werz, completely oblivious. Calil-Du isn't clear on what happened, but Jag watches me with her slow gaze, and Rana's lips tighten in anger as we assemble for another attempt.

"What was that?" she asks, slipping beside me.

"I choked," I tell her.

"You didn't choke."

"I did, Rana," I say. "I lost the channel. I choked."

"A beggar," she says, her eyes cold. "And a liar."

"I just—"

"You're weak, Kaytu. You chose failure."

She's right, of course. I'm shaken to realize how right she is. I know why I joined the military: I'm chasing a feeble approximation of redemption. Fighting remorts won't wash the sins from my soul, but at least I'll use my bloody hands for protection instead of destruction.

Except my past has apparently planted tripwires in my heart, ones I've never suspected. I led one military squad to slaughter; I can't sacrifice another, not even in a training exercise.

I'd rather choose failure.

My platoon rank plunges, which means the TLs noticed my screwup. And a reprimand sigil flashes on my lens: a two-day negative performance review.

Kaytu, Maseo ⃠

If you get three reprimands at the same time, you're discharged from basic training. Fortunately this one will vanish in two days if I don't fuck up again. From what I hear, it's the monthlong—or permanent—reprimands that you have to watch out for.

So I buckle down and throw myself enthusiastically into Full Contact Negotiation, classroom lectures, and failing another capture-the-crown exercise.

As we're trotting to barracks, our lenses tell us to make way for a superior unit. Moving as one, we swivel into place against the corridor wall and Group Gabrielle jogs past, wearing boots instead of slippers. Chins high, arms swinging, eyes forward. They're so good that they don't even pause to jeer at us.

"Smug fuckers," Calil-Du mutters, in direct violation of discipline.

Pico snorts a laugh and Ting giggles. Our lenses flash the green and we return to barracks for hygiene and mess hall and sleep.

The next morning we run four trap laps and complete a work shift, and then we're back in the hangar hunting a cartoon-looking crown and getting our asses kicked by a defensive protocol dressed as a horrorshow.

Except in our second run, everything clicks. The enemy is a vaguely upsetting geometrical figure the size of a railcar that lashes out with beams and struts. It shifts and rolls across a fake expanse of New Growth, creating a nauseating optical illusion. Reconfigured moskito drones emerge from its vents and throw darts that sting like wasps.

"Why can't we just take down a cataphract?" Ridehorse grouses, in the cover of what looks like a melted orchard. "Like normal recruits."

"Normal recruits don't take down cataphracts," Basdaq tells her. "They interdict them until a CAV comes."

"Fine," Ridehorse says. "Then a knuckletank or—"

"The crown's inside!" Ting blurts, pointing at the enemy figure. "That central hub is changing in a nonrandom sequence; there's a pattern. Look, look . . . *There!*"

The gleam of jewels appears inside the thickest section, then vanishes again.

"No way," Calil-Du says. "The scrawny splice is right."

"It's a sort of periodic tessellation," Ting explains. "If *tessellation* means a series of repeating tile shapes in a—" A moskito drone stings her. "Ow!"

"Protect Ting!" Rana says. "We need her."

"Move her back!" Calil-Du bellows. "Go, *go!*"

I'm surprised that Calil-Du knows what Rana means. Pico throws Ting over his shoulder and hauls her out of range. Ridehorse and Basdaq trot behind them like human barricades, swearing and jerking from moskito stings.

"Kaytu, Rana!" Calil-Du shouts. "Shit! You're on me; we'll open a hole for Jag. Tell us when, Ting."

"Not yet . . ." Ting says, as a strut unfolds from the enemy and sweeps Rana into a gauzy fungus-tree. "Oh!"

"Shakrabarti, step up!" Calil-Du shouts. "Pico!"

"Chief!" Pico says.

"You and the twins"—she means Gazi and Werz—"attack at, um, on—"

"On Ting's five," M'bari calls out.

Calil-Du grunts. "Ting! Give us a countdown!"

"Not yet," Ting says, peering at the target from behind Ride-horse and Basdaq.

Another strut unfolds at us, but this time we're ready. I roll and Calil-Du dodges while Hefco eats a barrage of moskitos and falls in a screaming heap.

"Ten-nine!" Ting sings out. "Eight, seven . . ."

"Go!" Calil-Du shouts, and throws herself at the target.

A hinged beam stomps her to the ground. Shakrabarti and M'bari charge past as another beam thrusts wildly. Pico slams to his belly and the attack misses him by inches.

"Five!" Ting shouts. "Four!"

Pico scuttles forward on his hands and knees. The target emits a blast that flattens Shakrabarti and knocks me onto my ass.

Jag grabs my collar and tugs me to my feet. "Meatshield," she growls.

Great. She'll use me like a walking rampart, to absorb any damage the creature throws at her. Still, the job's the job. A doughy splat traps Pico as I stumble closer with Jag's hand on the small of my back, keeping contact, moving together.

M'bari runs into a ripsaw of plates, which opens a hole into the center of the target. Pincers slash down from above, and I throw myself between them. I feel a rib break and my arm burn. Sweat beads on my face from the pain.

While pincers squeeze me, Jag climbs my back, puts her foot on my face, and pushes off.

I catch a glimpse of her blue slipper disappearing inside the central hub, and then medical spray hisses from an unseen nozzle. My forearm cools. The sharp pang in my chest fades. I gasp for air, my legs trembling, slumping in the grip of the machine.

Behind me, Pico's pained voice says, "My dads wanted me to become a psycounselor."

I groan a laugh. "You're too selfish for a helping profession."

"Selfish? What am I, Shakrabarti?"

"I'm not selfish," Shakrabarti's muffled voice says, trapped somewhere inside the geometrical shape. "I've just got a healthy sense of my own worth."

"Of your own beauty," Pico says.

"That's what I'm worth," Shakrabarti says. "A thousand sunsets."

From behind a tangle of plates, M'bari says, "I'd make a great childcare consultant. All the tests agreed."

"Then what're you doing here?" Pico asks.

"Wrestling my demons," M'bari says. "Oh, wait, no. That's Kaytu."

"I think my rib is broken," I say.

"He's wrestling demons?" Pico asks.

M'bari decides to give me a break. "Yeah, there's one on his left shoulder saying, 'You've got a chance with Rana,' and one on his right saying, 'Try your luck with Shakrabarti.'"

"He doesn't have an angel?" Ridehorse asks.

"His angel tells him to stick with his hand," Pico says.

The struts and pincers gently disengage, and our lenses flicker online. Before I can read the message, cheers and shouts echo across the hangar.

Jag did it: we captured the crown.

CHAPTER 19

M y reprimand sigil vanishes in the middle of the night. I'm surprised at the depth of my relief. I didn't think I cared, but it's like a throbbing toothache is finally gone.

And the day only gets better.

We're told to wait in line at our lockers. We assemble with effortless speed. Nobody breaks formation. Nobody shifts, nobody mutters. And this time I know that yes, we *will* stand here until we collapse.

Except it's only ten minutes before the TL and Admin lead an autocart inside.

"Barracks Chief Calil-Du," TL calls.

"TL!" Calil-Du barks.

"Remove your slippers."

Calil-Du does as she's told. "TL!"

The autocart dispenses a pair of combat boots. Not slippers. Boots. Adjustable reinforced combat-issue boots.

"Step forward and take your boots," Admin says.

"You earned them," TL says, and calls each one of us forward in turn.

Kaytu, Maseo
chance of completion: 09%
platoon rank: 36 of 42
decruitment bonus: 180 c
5323 rating: BB

I'm the third-lowest-rated member of Group Aleph. I don't care about that. I'm getting dinged for enlisting through CAV. I don't care about that. I'm getting dinged for fucking up the other day, and I don't care about that either.

Because when TL says, "Recruit Kaytu, you earned them," she's right. I earned those boots. And about *that*, I'm surprised how much I care.

Twenty minutes before lights-out that night, we're showered and shorn and prepped for the morning. Except half of us keep opening our lockers to gaze at our new boots: combat-ready with three-setting soles and lens-active countermeasures.

We've settled into a pre-sleep routine where three clusters of recruits gather to bullshit about the day, reminisce about MY-RAGE shows, and talk shit about Groups Bay and Gabrielle, who have become our sworn enemies by virtue of existing.

I enjoy talking shit, but I never spent much time on MYRAGE as a kid. My grandmother mistrusted cooperative-media technology. She still remembered stories handed down to *her* grandmother about the SICLE War.

SICLE stands for Socially Immersive Curated Learning Environment. Unlike MYRAGE, SICLE started as a nonprofit educational initiative. Students attended VR classes taught by teachers halfway across the world. A million discussion groups and debate clubs and art teams thrived. Entertainment and politics exploded onto the platform, along with hobbies and shopping and sims and sex, into vibrant, immersive, engaging communities.

Then the sorting began.

SICLE ran algorithms to ensure that users encountered the most positive experience possible. Your interests and preferences led you to like-minded people. Communities grew more vibrant, more engaging, more immersive.

And more distinct.

People soon lived in starkly divergent worlds from their

neighbors. Curated media experiences led to rifts between shared realities. Different communities learned different facts that proved conflicting claims. SICLE gave the people what they wanted—a caring, inclusive, informed community . . . of people exactly like them. Unity and loving-kindness flowered within groups, but between them, mutual incomprehension led to mutually assured destruction.

Civil wars erupted.

Virulent nationalism and sectarian violence scorched the Earth.

After decades of conflict—after mass graves and mushroom clouds—the nation-states battled themselves into a stupor. That's when the megacorporations finally beheaded the nations and unleashed the terrafixing protocol.

They saved the planet. They saved the human race.

In the wake of SICLE's decommission, dozens of new platforms sprang into place. For no good reason, MYRAGE became the standard, and it operates within strict limits. It curtails the spread of immersive affinity groups. Community size is limited, and randomness and transience are enforced.

Of course, the squad is a pretty powerful affinity group itself, so I don't exactly miss my ability to chat about MYRAGE. I just laze on my bunk, watching the military channels and listening to the barracks chatter.

One cluster of recruits forms around Basdaq, who even after all the training still looks avatar-handsome and acts a little stuffy. Another forms around Pico, who is neither handsome nor stuffy, and the third is composed of Werz and Gazi and a few stragglers.

The rest keep to ourselves. Rana is in the last group, even though she could gather a group of her own by crooking her finger.

When I ask M'bari why she doesn't, he says, "Basdaq gets off on helping people. Pico gets off on making them laugh. Rana's all about Rana."

"You don't like her?"

He looks surprised. "Like her? I want to *be* her. She's Class A down to the cellular level. She's the goal, Kaytu. She's the reason I'm here."

I'm not sure what he means. I can see that Rana is special, and I know her father is a Colonel Executive, but the shades of power among shareholders still confuse me.

Ting sticks pretty closely to Pico's group. She amuses him, and he protects her from Calil-Du. Not physically; in our melee combat trials, Calil-Du is third-ranked and Pico's second, but he won't hit the chief outside of a spar, while she'll hit anyone, anytime. She doesn't know how to handle his humor, though. She beat his ass once, and even during the beating he had the entire group laughing at her.

The evening after we get our boots, Rana rolls to the side of her bunk and looks down at me. She's in the top level to the left of me—I'm in the middle. I blank the screen on my lens where I'm watching a documentary about lichen ants.

"You're only ranked low because you enlisted through CAV," she says. "You're better than number thirty-six."

"That's the sweetest thing you ever said to me."

She gives me a chilly look. "Volunteers rarely finish basic, so you're getting dinged for everyone who ever failed."

"I don't give a shit about my rank, Rana."

"You should."

"I'll take the hit for being a volunteer. I wouldn't be here if it weren't for the CAVs."

"What are you talking about? You could've enlisted."

I laugh. "It's not that easy."

"You click the agreement, you're in. Nothing's easier."

"I don't know why I never thought of that," I tell her.

She looks at me for a long moment. "I guess they don't accept many recruits from . . . the lower levels of Freeholds."

"Not many," I agree, and don't mention my history in Vila Vela.

"It's called 'below the belt'?"

"It's called the gutter."

"I spent two months in a Freehold." She almost smiles. "The food's amazing and I've never seen anything like the dancing; I've never *felt* anything like that."

I almost say something stupid about music, about dancing, about her. "Yeah."

"I stayed in the penthouse levels." Her smile tightens. "You think that's weak. You think I'm sheltered."

"You'd have to be pretty sheltered to think 'sheltered' is a bad thing."

"I'm starting to suspect that you aren't a fool."

"You might be surprised."

She dangles her legs over the side of her bunk. "It's hard for me to forget what happened the first time we met. What you did. Begging like that."

"There's nothing to forget," I say. "That's who I am."

"I'm not sure it is," she says.

I shrug. "Are you going to tell me about the lampreys?"

"They're a new kind of remort, coming out of nowhere. That's all I know. My father doesn't share classified information with me."

"Huh," I say. "How high was your decruitment bonus?"

The change of subject stops her. "What?"

"That first day, when we started? How much was your bonus?"

Her eyebrows draw together. "What does that matter?"

"At first I didn't understand why they offer more money to get rid of the better recruits. But I guess the crappy recruits are going to decruit anyway?"

"Not all of them," she says, with a glint in her dark eyes.

"Was that a joke?" I ask. "I didn't know you had a humor setting."

She shows me her middle finger. "I can't figure you out."

"I'm a man of mystery."

"No, it's a cultural thing. Even in the Freehold, I never spent any time with anyone quite so . . . unpropertied."

I can't tell if she's joking again. "Yeah, but you should see us dance."

"My initial bonus was seventy thousand six hundred and twenty-two scrip."

"No—" I shake my head in disbelief. "*What?*"

"And two shares in Li-tren Capital, which is a Shiyogrid subsidiary."

I gape at her. "No way. They offered you *shares* for quitting?"

"You don't believe me."

"Of course I believe you. Robots can't lie."

I'm hoping for another smile, but instead her eyes narrow. "Don't call me that."

"What?"

"A robot," she says, with real anger. "I know what my voice sounds like."

"I didn't mean your shitty voice," I tell her. "I meant your shitty personality. I like the sound of your voice."

"I miss social cues sometimes," she says, her expression stiff. "In people's tones. So if that was sarcasm, you'll need to be clearer."

"It wasn't sarcasm," I tell her.

Her unwavering gaze stays on my face.

"It was mild flirtation," I explain, "of the sort that if you ignore it, we can both pretend it never happened."

A laugh sounds from Pico's end of the room while Rana and I look at each other. Training doesn't leave you with enough energy to think about sex in the first month. Even the eighteen-year-olds don't stare in the shower. Too tired, too achy. Plus, there's the sight of Calil-Du shaving her head. That's enough to keep anyone from feeling amorous, to say nothing of M'bari's neon ass-tattoos.

Still, there's a spark between me and Rana. I've felt it for weeks, and now it's burning hotter. I'm pretty sure she feels it, too. That's probably why she changes the subject: there's no percentage in feeling a spark for Maseo Kaytu.

"What branch do you want?" she asks. "After basic."

"What branch is this pilot program feeding us into?"

She shakes her head. "Army, I suppose, to handle these remorts. But after *that*, what's your goal?"

"I'm not sure. How high should I shoot?"

"Marines," she says.

"That's too high for a gutter roach."

"You weren't born in the gutter."

"How do you know?"

"You're educated. M'bari says there's a trace of schooling in your accent."

"Not enough for the marines. Plus, I'm too big for a battlesuit."

"Lots of marines don't wear them. And the marines value control, Kaytu. They prioritize self-control."

"More than the other branches?"

"If you live in a vacuum, you can't make stupid mistakes. The Army values obedience; the Garda values violence. At least the urban Garda."

"There's another kind?"

"In the Class A neighborhoods, the Garda is less violent and more investigative." Rana brushes her hair behind her ear. "They're seventy percent male when they contract out to Freeholds, fifty percent female in vested areas. Cuts down on brutality. Did you ever see the Garda called in for riot suppression or whatever?"

"Once or twice."

"Did you wonder why the units were so male?"

I shake my head. "Never occurred to me."

"An inclination for mindless violence works in a Freehold but isn't exactly popular among shareholders." She sits straighter on her bunk. "The Army is sixty percent male. The marines is the other way around, sixty-five percent female and gendother."

"That's where I'll fit in?"

"Yeah. Physical strength doesn't matter so much in space."

"Thanks."

She laughs, and I feel like I've won something. She says, "I mean what matters most there is control, and nobody's more controlled than you."

"You are."

She shakes her head. "I'm just trained."

"You're joining the Flensers."

"If they'll have me."

"Maybe robots *can* lie. You know they'll have you."

Her flare of anger is almost a physical thing between us. "Because of my father?" she asks, her toneless voice hard. "Because I didn't fight for every inch, because I didn't earn every braid. Because *my* boots are gifts?"

"No," I say.

Seconds tick away before she softens. "Fine, yes. I'm joining the Flensers."

"As a pilot? An engineer? No, wait. A gunner."

"A pilot, I hope." She ducks her head. "Space is . . . I don't know. Untouchable and impossible and perfect. It's so far above me, but it feels like home."

I almost say, *That's how I feel about you.*

I manage to keep my mouth closed. I'm not falling in love with her. I've fallen in love with exactly one person in my life, and I walked away from Ionesca a year ago. And anyway, Rana is nothing like Io. Rana is a cutting edge while Io is a tangle of roots. Rana is a starship; Ionesca is the New Growth.

"The Flensers are seventy percent female," she blurts, maybe reading my thoughts in my face.

"And twenty percent robot."

She flips me the finger again. "My father says women make better Flensers because Flensers don't fight on distant battlegrounds or in foreign cities. They fight in their homes. A space station is their home. A dreadnought or a dinky orbital ship is their home. My father says a woman will cross any line to defend her home."

"So he's kind of an idiot, your father. You only have the one?"

"Yeah."

"What do your mothers say?"

"I don't have any."

"Gen parents?"

"It's just my father and me."

Her expression tells me that she doesn't appreciate that particular subject. We fall silent for a moment, and I almost ask about her hearing. Instead, I say, "If you're a Flenser and I'm a marine, maybe we'll serve on the same ship. I'll salute when you march past, and you'll pretend you don't remember me."

"Sounds perfect. Well, if we work for the same corporation."

"Huh?"

"If we work for the same corpo."

"I heard you, but—" I shake my head in confusion. "We're both Shiyogrid."

"Other corpos can buy your contract after basic."

"No way." I frown. "Really?"

"You never read the fine print?"

"I was too busy begging for my life."

"Almost ten percent of recruit contracts are transferred to another corporation. Either through purchase or trade."

"They can trade me for another soldier?"

"Sure," she says. "Then you'd fight for CrediMobil or PRATO or someone."

"Why bother? We're all on the same side."

"The corpos cooperate on the important things, on the terrafixing and remorts." She swings her legs. "They cooperate on ninety-eight percent of their initiatives, but the other two percent devolve into violence."

"No way. Really? Against each other?"

She nods. "We're a violent species, and the corporations don't try to deny it. Instead, they channel disputes into managed conflicts within specific parameters. Humans need competition to thrive."

"I guess," I say.

"You're naïve about the strangest things," she tells me.

Before I can answer, our lens flashes a one-minute warning. A surge of noise echoes in the barracks as everyone rushes to their bunks, and then silence falls at lights-out. I shift uneasily. Should I hope to become a marine or a Garda? Shiyogrid or Unidroit? I'm not sure why I feel so itchy. Because the future is sneaking up on me, or because Rana is slipping past my defenses?

I try to forget about both. I focus on my new boots and fall asleep with a smile in my heart.

CHAPTER 20

Two hours later, an alarm cuts through the barracks.

Calil-Du wakes with a shout, Ting wakes with a whimper.

I'm crouching beside my bunk before my eyes are fully open. Jagzenka drops beside me—and then the lights brighten, and TL and Admin are standing on the horseshoe. The squad staggers into formation, and Admin orders the three lowest-ranked recruits in the group to rip the dorm apart.

Ting, Hefco, and I overturn bunks and empty duffel bags onto the floor. We scatter boots and kick shirts behind the vend machines.

The air turns poisonous. Even Pico stops smiling. Only M'bari looks thoughtful, like he's trying to solve a puzzle about social engineering.

Then Calil-Du is demoted.

Why? To keep us on our toes, I guess. She's not happy, though. Well, she's never happy, but now she looks even more homicidal than usual.

Voorhivey is made our new chief. He's grown in the last month and doesn't seem so nervous anymore. He's still clean-cut and eager-to-please, though. He flushes with pleasure when TL calls him "Chief-of-Barracks," and stands a little straighter.

"Fucking kiss-ass," Calil-Du mutters.

Voorhivey flushes again—this time with shame. He looks at Calil-Du, then at the TLs, who remain expressionless, then looks at her again.

"Sorry," she says. "I mean fucking kiss-ass, *chief*."

He takes a shaky breath and stands directly in front of her, his face a foot from hers. Calil-Du is an inch taller than him and a mile tougher. She could drop him with one blow, and I see a faint echo of Jo's wildness in her eyes. She wants to feel his bones break.

"Clean the barracks, recruit," Voorhivey says, and his voice only cracks once.

She's on a knife edge and doesn't know which way she'll fall. Apparently there's more to Calil-Du than a bully. I'd never seen that before. There's a streak of self-destruction in her, too.

A few seconds bleed away before she says, "Chief," and moves to clean the barracks.

Voorhivey manages not to faint in relief. He's tasked with assigning our job duties every morning, and guess who gets latrine duty? Me, Ting, and Hefco. Except now there are slippers doing the bulk of the work, so we're only scrubbing for two hours a day.

The rest of our training intensifies. We focus on dispersal agents, boarding-and-repelling exercises, micro-g chambers. We return to the hangar every day to play capture the crown, except now we're using gear. Not firearms, but coms and trenchknives and boots.

At the end of a week, we're hitting a twenty percent success rate.

"I still don't get why they're training us to fight lampreys," Shakrabarti says, in the shower, "without ever showing us what one looks like."

"You worried they're pretty as you?" Ridehorse asks.

"We know what they look like," M'bari tells Shakrabarti. "Terrifying."

"Like your ass-tattoo," Pico says.

"That's what I heard," Rana tells M'bari, ignoring Pico. "The first problem with fighting lampreys? Soldiers freeze up."

"So why don't they teach us not to freeze by showing us actual lampreys?" Shakrabarti says.

Calil-Du rinses the razor she uses to shave her head. She doesn't just switch off her follicles, because she's Calil-Du: she likes blades and she likes stubble. "Maybe lampreys are so fucked that special effects can't copy them."

"Yeah, but—" Basdaq frowns. "That's a good point."

"Maybe that's part of it," M'bari says. "But also they're keeping these things quiet. They don't want anyone even describing them."

"The first new remort in fifty years," Jagzenka murmurs.

"I'm glad the corpo's keeping them quiet," Voorhivey says, stepping toward the drying film. "They don't want to panic anyone."

"They can't be worse than cataphracts," Shakrabarti says.

"If I only teach you one thing, my beautiful infant," Ridehorse tells him, "things can always get worse."

"And if I teach you one thing," he says, "it's that you need to exfoliate."

The lamprey habituation regime slacks off, though, as the fitness training intensifies—with thirty-pound, forty-pound, fifty-pound packs. Our lenses max me and Calil-Du and Basdaq at fifty pounds for long hauls, seventy for short. Pico is shorter than I am, but he maxes at sixty and eighty. He's an ox, the strongest guy in the platoon.

Ting only weighs ninety-nine pounds; she can't carry more than the minimum. Thirty pounds, not including her helmet, boots, and com-plate, the transmission module she uses to govern our communications and sensors. She's freakishly good with tech, though, which matters more as the exercises grow increasingly complex: we trot in formation into boarding scenarios and dropship deployments, into urban sieges and space-hab environments.

Half the time, pulses knock out our coms, and Ting coordinates the group through our cuffs using paleo bursts.

When a pulse hits, you go low-tech. Until everything reboots, you're a caveman, with a blade and hand gestures and—if you're lucky—narrow-beam com bursts. Our gear crashes with disheartening regularity, until Ting batters the systems back to life. Unlike the twenty-first century when pristine operating systems ran bug-free software in flawless compatibility, these days technology is a lurching mess.

"It's Moorphy's Law!" Ting announces after a crash in a starship mock-up, when we have to resort to SBC, Scream-Based Communication.

Pico presses against an engine room panel. "What's that, prez?"

With her attention still on the com-plate linked to her battle-cuff, Ting says, "It's a law. I mean, not a law, but a saying. Like a law. 'Processing speed doubles every four years, but complexity triples.' It's a race you can't win."

"We can't even win this fucking course," Ridehorse mutters.

"And expectations quadruple," Ting continues, her fingers blurring. "Some people add that part. Speed doubles, complexity triples, expectations quadruple. I mean, so even with flowcore, speed never catches up with demand."

Still, she manages to get us running again while Groups Bay and Gabrielle are still shouting at each other. And her skill with tech is the only thing that saves her from involuntary decruitment and vicious ostracism. Because otherwise, she's a burden on the group.

"You're significantly lagging Group Gabrielle," TL announces, during the first inspection of the week. "Chief Voorhivey, explain."

"I—there is no explanation, TL."

"Of course there's an explanation, chief. There simply isn't an excuse. Explain."

Voorhivey starts sweating. "Our—our group is smaller, TL. The smallest."

"Calil-Du," TL says. "Explain."

"We're carting around deadwood, TL!" Calil-Du barks, her scowl shifting toward Ting and Hefco.

When TL tilts her head, her scarification catches the light. "I'm about to tell you two things in violation of all my instincts. The first is this. You're good. You're one of the best groups I've trained in three years." She looks at Pico, who must've messaged her. "Permission granted, Pik-Cao."

"We can't be one of the best, TL," he says. "On account of Gabrielle is better than us, and they suck pump."

"Gabrielle is not better than us, recruit."

"They score higher."

Her gaze sharpens. "Because of your deadwood? Is that what you think is weighing you down, recruit?"

Pico grins, and I know there's no way he'll ever point a finger at a squadmate. "Only thing weighing me down is gravity, TL."

She shoots him a look that would make anyone else stop being a jackass, but he just gazes happily back at her. "The second thing

I shouldn't tell you is this," she says. "The world is healing. Every day, the New Growth breathes more life into the lungs of our planet. Every day, the Earth grows stronger. One day our grandkids' grandkids will play in the woods and swim in the lakes. But there are monsters."

Voorhivey shifts beside me, like he wants to ask what she means.

"There are remorts," TL continues, "beyond our current understanding."

"Eels," Calil-Du mutters.

TL gives her the same look she gave Pico. "Unidentified emergent remorts. You're in a pilot program designed to address the lamprey threat—" Before anyone can speak, she pings us into silence. "I have no idea what they are. Command will tell me when I need to know. And all you need to know is this. Most squads never see combat. But you? You *will* fight . . ."

TL sends video snippets to our lenses, across the group channel. The first one shows me and Pico flanking Ting on an obstacle run, then hefting her over a rampart without missing a step.

"Your squadmates *will* fall," TL continues. "And what happens when your fire team leader takes a round between the ribs?"

The next snippets show Rana hip-checking Ting away from a gridmine trigger without even looking in her direction. Then M'bari reaches down a climbing wall, grabs Ting's wrist, and drags her beside him. Then me again, crouching with Hefco, scanning the field for threats before I tell him when to run.

"What happens if a lamprey shears through a buddy's arm?" TL asks. "Then *they're* deadwood. Dead weight. Weaker than the weakest person in this room. Slower than the slowest. Are you going to leave them behind because they're weighing you down?"

The last video snippet shows a thunderous-looking Calil-Du body-slamming Hefco—brutally, but effectively—through an airlock in a ship-themed course, keeping him on target.

"This shit is easy when nobody makes a mistake," TL tells us. "It's easy when nobody's weak, when nobody's wrong—when nobody's hurt or dead. It's easy when it doesn't matter. Confirm."

"Confirm!"

"But who do you want beside you when you catch shrapnel in your guts? When a lamprey spits death at you? Do you want Group Bay, who never shoved a weak-ass recruit through an airlock? Group Gabrielle, who racks up perfect scores like acing a MYRAGE game? Or Group Aleph, who've been acting like fucking soldiers since week one?"

Pico starts the chant, and in seconds we're all shouting along. "Aleph! Aleph! Aleph!"

I don't think of myself as a screamer, but my throat is hoarse when TL tells us to shut up. Her eyes are bright, though, and Rana and I exchange a covert glance. I know what she's thinking: that's real leadership. TL just took Ting and Hefco, the weakest members of our group, and turned them into a bond between us.

We're not idiots who helped a couple of feeble, flighty recruits. We're soldiers who carried our sister and brother across a battlefield. We're Group Aleph, and that's something to be proud of.

CHAPTER 21

Admin TL talks about duty rosters for a few minutes and finishes with, "Then there's this. Live weapons."

There's a murmur of excitement and Calil-Du says, "Fucking *finally*."

Admin waves an autocart into the barracks and distributes weapons keyed to our lenses. Not just any weapons, either: early-model Ambo combat rifles. Clunky, quirky, paleo . . . and exactly like the one I trained on back home.

Ambos are thirty-one inches and six pounds, the last of the mass-exuded freestyle assault rifles, with finger-pull triggers and detachable magazines. "Freestyle" means they don't attach to the user's combat harness: you can throw them, drop them, lose them. The onboard ballistic computer is buggy—the official recommendation is to operate on manual—and the ammunition is primitive. You can toggle rounds for silence or tracking or pre-impact detonation, which makes them explode just past a corner or in midair above a rampart. One round separates into segments connected by nanothreads, turning into a flying buzz saw. You can miss by eight inches and still shred the target.

Except nobody uses an Ambo for the bells and whistles. They kludge up if you toggle them too quickly, and their tech is iffy in a pulse-dense environment. No, you feed an Ambo basic rounds—actual solid rounds, packed ten deep in a magazine that looks like a fat centipede—turn off the computing, and depend on skill.

Countermeasures bounce off an Ambo like etiquette lessons off a Freehold ganger. They're primitive slug-throwers, barely a step above hurling rocks, especially compared to the Boaz intervention rifle, which is the current cutting edge.

A few recruits scoff at our ancient Ambos. Not me. I know the quirky, low-tech, feeble Ambo like the inside of my visor.

After four days of weapons training, we're hitting fifty percent success in the hangar. Oh, and there's this:

platoon rank: 18 of 42

Hefco decruits, and Gazi and Werz drop a few places in tandem. Of course. Yin and Yang do everything together. They're both officer-track—better at command than weapons—unlike Shakrabarti, who is my competition for seventeenth place. His gorgeous face hides a quick mind, and he's strong all-around instead of shining in any single skillset.

Rana is a solid number one not just in Group Aleph but in the entire platoon, and that's before we discover that she's freakishly good in an orbital pod. A marine Warrant Technician—called a Wart—oversees the training, and on the first day, she inserts each of us into the pod until we puke.

The average time is four minutes.

I *flow* into my terrafixing meditation and manage twelve minutes, which deeply impresses the Wart. Rana emerges after thirty minutes, completely unruffled, and the Wart scoffs. I don't understand the Wart's reaction until later that night, when I'm listening to Rana and Basdaq argue about some fancy endurance-ballet company.

That's when I realize that Rana's deafness and her uncanny balance are related. That's why she never defaulted her hearing. It's not a cultural thing, it's a genetic or surgical manip to boost her extra-orbital performance. Maybe she doesn't have an inner ear, or maybe it's been repurposed. I don't know, that high-level shit is beyond me.

Still, I'm pleased with myself for solving the mystery. And for my performance with the Ambo. Over the next week, I discover that I'm weak in Stellar Navigation and Corporate Policies, middling in Field Medicine and Remort Cladistics, and strong in Strategic Improvisation, Combat Recon, and Urban everything.

In other words, I'm a low-value, low-tech grunt.

Not exactly a surprise.

Of course, most of basic training—except for the lamprey stuff—focuses on the baseline skills that every deployable soldier needs to know. That's why it's for shock troops, while nondeployable soldiers attend JMT, Joint Management Training. We only get brief intros to Stellar Nav, Flowcore Interface, Financial Ops, and a dozen others. Just enough to check our aptitude and interest. The rest we'll learn in Advanced Departmental Training.

Well, if we survive the lampreys.

My platoon rank keeps rising . . . until I choke again.

We're outside the base building, in the faux terrafixing that covers a few thousand acres within the fence. We're tracking one of the commoner remorts, which is officially a twelfth-generation Haritech Autonomous Relay for Perimeter Establishment and Integrity, but more commonly known as a "harpy."

Most of the bio-forged material in a harpy was engineered from flatworms and kudzu, but our lenses remind us that the source of a weapon's wetware bears no relationship to its function. Genetic imperatives are reshaped; DNA strands are overwritten. Expecting a bio-forged weapon to retain traits from the original organism is like expecting a bowl of tempura locusts to swarm across the table and devour the appetizers.

This is our third encounter with a "live" remort, although the training units aren't exactly live; they were killed years ago, their wetware replaced with remote controls. They're basically human operated drones in the corpses of remorts.

Despite the capture-the-crown exercises, remorts aren't viscerally terrifying. They look like what they are: the messily rejuvenated husks of SICLE-tech weapons, more powerful than contemporary armaments but transformed by centuries of neglect and the idiosyncrasies of the terrafixing's revitalization.

The control module of the harpy is an armored dome in the center of the designated perimeter. Semiautonomous roller units patrol the surrounding area, eliminating threats. Harpies don't pose much of a threat to human lives, but they damage the New Growth and the corpos won't stand for that.

The faux terrafixing around Dekka Base is thick with wispy

ferns and dangling vines. The spongy ground replicates the fertile thickness of the real New Growth. Little puffs of spores whisper around my boots and the air smells of sweet decay, like rotting cake.

Rana's in charge of the main assault force while I'm the flanking team manager, leading Ridehorse, M'bari, and Ting along a gully for a shot at the underside of the harpy's armored dome. Jagzenka's initial recon identified a potential weak spot where a missile impact cracked the plating, centuries ago.

Our lenses are flickering—on, off, on, off. Not a surprise; most remorts emit pulses. I take the point with Ridehorse. M'bari is on Ting Protection Detail, while Ting is probing the harpy with whatever sensors still work.

A burst of Ambo fire sounds in the distance, as another team triggers one of the rollers. There's a scream, a blast, silence.

"Jag's right," Ting whispers, sending a flickering image of the harpy dome with the weak spot highlighted.

Ridehorse gestures for a halt and proceeds alone. We're motionless, our fatigues blending into the terrain with paleo pattern-matching pigments. The day is cool—only ninety-two degrees, thanks to atmospheric terrafixing—but sweat drips down my face. My fatigues' climate-control function went offline twenty minutes ago.

When Ridehorse crawls through a gray-limbed bush, a cloud of insects swirls in the air and vanishes. A moment later, she gestures me to join her.

At the top of the gully, I peek through a thicket of lacquer-grass and scope the harpy dome. Five or six feet tall, encrusted with a layer of what looks like barnacles but isn't. Three heavy-arms rollers patrol in a formation around the dome and—

Gazi's team bursts into sight.

Shakrabarti shouts when he takes a roller round in the chest—only a dummy, but still painful. I signal my team to engage.

Ridehorse fires bursts from behind my right elbow. Every time a round pocks the harpy's barnacle-covered surface, the dome bloats and bulges.

"It's got kinetic self-destruct!" Rana yells, from a copse of lichen-saplings.

Which is insulting. We all know what those bulges mean: if you hit a harpy with enough firepower, it explodes. That's the terminal stage of perimeter defense.

Ting's fingers fly on her com-plate. "Can't deactivate."

"Reboot our lenses," I say.

"Trying," she tells me.

A roller round hurls Ridehorse backward into the gully, and I unshoulder my Ambo and grab the spindle-launcher from M'bari. Spindles are chopstick-shaped, localized-effect munitions that burn hot enough to melt tungsten. These training spindles won't ignite, but they'll punch through an inch of armor.

"Keep it off me," I say, before sighting on the dome.

M'bari rolls in front of me, making himself a target for the roller. There's another blast and a shock wave I feel in my stomach. Recruits don't often die in training, but everyone breaks a few bones. My breath is loud, and my sweat stings my eyes. *There is nothing outside the terrafixing. I am the gully and I am the roller and I am the air between us.*

I don't *flow* completely, but I calm myself enough to sight on the harpy. The dome swivels. The crack isn't in view. Not yet. Not yet . . .

Ambo fire stitches across the dome, which inflates until it's glossy and bulging, ready to explode. My breath is steady. My lens comes online. My targeting is perfect . . . except five rollers erupt out of nowhere, laying down a hellstorm of fire, and push Rana's team between me and the target.

My fingertips swirl on trigger but I don't fire.

"Take the shot," Rana shouts at me. "Take the shot!"

She's directly between me and the target. The spindle will explode through her organs. I don't care about that, but putting a spindle into the harpy will trigger the self-destruct. Her entire team is in the open. If I fire, I'll take out my entire squad.

So I don't fire. I don't freeze exactly, but I don't fire.

The rollers finish killing Rana's team, then kill mine.

Kaytu, Maseo ⊘

My platoon rank falls two places, and this time I get a thirty-day reprimand. Which is serious. Still, I'm not about to earn two more reprimands, so I don't worry that much. What's worse is that Rana hates me.

"I didn't hold my fire to protect you," I tell her in the shower, which is the only time she'll stay still long enough for me to talk to her.

She doesn't answer, but her silence is barbed.

"I'm happy to put a spindle through your spleen," I tell her. "Rana, listen to me. I don't think you're fragile."

"I see how you look at me," she says.

"That's not protectiveness," I say.

Water sheets her face and spills between her breasts.

"On the list of things Kaytu wants to do to you," Ridehorse tells Rana, because privacy is a myth in basic training, "'protect' isn't in the top ten."

"'Snuggle' is eleven," Pico says.

Ting giggles. "*Spleen* is a funny word."

"Leave them alone," Basdaq says, in his commanding baritone.

"Would everyone shut up?" Voorhivey pleads. "Please? And focus on the training?"

Calil-Du digs in her ear with a pinky. "Why are you such a sphincter?"

"I'm not! I just—my family's been fighting remorts for generations. They're all heroes and I, I don't want to let them down."

"Too late," she says. "Look at you."

When Rana steps through the drying film, I follow. It's my favorite trip of the day. She ignores me until I swing onto her bunk beside her, and then she ignores me some more.

"You didn't fire," she finally says, "because you didn't want to hurt the squad."

"Yeah."

"So instead we all died."

"Well . . ." I rub the back of my neck. "Yeah."

"If you're not willing to kill your squadmates to achieve your objective, Kaytu, do you know what that makes you?"

"Human?"

"Worthless," she says.

"Fuck you," I say, though it sounds like an apology. "What do you know about killing? Nothing. You think you know what you're talking about because what? You have blood on your hands?"

"No, Kaytu," she says, her toneless voice gentle. "I think it because sacrifice is the fundamental law of service."

Her gentleness unravels me: my anger, my pride. I'm suddenly more naked than I've ever been. "I can't, Rana," I tell her. "I just can't."

"Then you're worse than a beggar." She touches my arm. "You're a liability."

was born in an upside block of Vila Vela. My family lived in a sprawling apartment complex overlooking a balcony park: my parents, cousins, auncles, and all my grandparents. Six grandparents on my father's side, and seven on my mother's. I only had two parents, though, which made my more-traditional grandparents a little uncomfortable. My father was a conceptual recyclist with a spiritual bent. My mother was a tight-cell mechanic who believed she could fix anything if she swore at it loudly enough, including me.

My grandmother—who I called my sayti—is the one who raised me, though. That's how things worked in Vila Vela; childrearing skipped a generation. My great-grandparents raised my parents. My grandmother raised me. My parents would've raised my kids, if they'd survived the insurgency. Well, and if I'd had any.

Sayti called herself a dirt collector. She was the leading soil scientist in Vila Vela. She'd take me to her shop and unleash me in the workroom, with scopes and smartwire and fusers. I'd fiddle for hours, making sculptural shapes from crushed gearbits and charred l-boards.

"Just like your father," my grandmother said, ruffling my hair.

I never developed her genius but I gained a passable knack for fiddly work. I loved twining fiberscopes into busted engines and piloting microscopic fuse-drones to recover detached rydbergs.

And I loved AI.

The city of Vila Vela was a sleepy backwater, but decades before my birth we'd developed one of the most advanced AIs in the world: Sweetwater. Tremendously powerful and tremendously complex . . . but not sentient. Not self-aware.

Sayti told me and my cousins that as a young woman she'd thought a truly sentient AI was impossible without a biological base. "I was certain that self-awareness doesn't emerge from calculation, only from sensation."

Then Sweetwater ascended.

Nobody knew how, but the techies claimed that Sweetwater achieved true sapience. Idiosyncratically self-aware, inconceivably intelligent; foreign to life and beyond evolution. Several minutes later, halfway across the globe, the other two S-level AIs—called Greengrocer and Lunj—followed Sweetwater's example.

Ascended.

Limitless.

Superior.

Humanity held its breath. What would they do now?

At first, the sentient AIs did . . . nothing. At least nothing new. They still produced advanced tech, revealing flowcore and the Waypoint, ᴏᴀᴡᴇ ᴀɴᴅ ᴛʜᴇ ʀᴇsᴛ.

None of the other AIs ascended. Everything stayed the same.

Except Vila Vela changed. We grew giddy with pride in Sweetwater. Not enough to ring alarm bells in corpo headquarters, not yet. Still, we felt the first stirrings of patriotism. Living in Vila Vela meant something.

Though mostly, at that point, we simply hoped that Sweetwater would lead to an accelerated terrafixing, a brighter future.

My mother hadn't been impressed, though. She was a fervent believer in mechanism: there is no ghost in the gearbox, there is no soul in the chambers of our hearts. Humans are sacks of chemicals sloshing around. I preferred my sayti's animism. There's a spirit in everything. Gods frolic in every flock of pigeons and unswept corridor.

"Machines crave things," I told my mother, preparing for dinner at the lichenflour paster.

"'Crave'? That's one of your grandmother's words. Does that paster crave lichenflour?"

"Sweetwater craves things!"

"AI is bullshit, Maseo. It's a monument to the human ego. What's so good about self-awareness? It's a mistake, it's a burden." She smacked my head. "Like children."

My sayti didn't believe in MYRAGE classes, so I spent most mornings in an actual classroom with actual tutors and real projections. I spent my afternoons with her, then evenings with family and friends. My childhood wasn't exactly idyllic, but it was ordinary.

Until the Big Three AIs melted down. Literally. Overnight.

The three of them simultaneously liquefied into complete kludge.

The loss to humanity was incalculable. The corpos investigated and determined that the simultaneity was evidence of coordination. Someone, some unknown agency or force, had triggered the attacks.

Who had conspired to destroy the Big Three? How had they done it, and why?

Those are the great mysteries of our age. Nobody took credit. Nobody benefited, at least not in any obvious way.

The corpos staged reclamation operations. Working groups descended on Vila Vela, scrambling for research rights to Sweetwater's corpse, and investigators fanned through the city, searching for clues. Searching for insurgents, for saboteurs.

Except this was worse than sabotage. The perpetrators hadn't simply committed murder, they'd committed *genocide*. All three members of this new species, this AI species, had been wiped out in the space of picoseconds.

The corpos had forbidden genocide-class weapons after the SI-CLE War, and they took the prohibition seriously. Yet despite their best efforts, the investigation faltered. Promising leads resulted in dead ends and incriminating evidence vanished in the light of innocent explanations.

Desperation crept in, along with an edge of brutality.

The harsher approach inflamed local sentiment that was already running hot. We'd made Sweetwater. We'd loved Sweetwater. We'd lost Sweetwater. The people of Vila Vela, not the corpos. Who were *they* to investigate *us*?

Patriotic fervor sent taproots into our hearts.

The corpos issued warnings.

The people responded with peaceful demonstrations.

The corpos relocated the ringleaders.

The peaceful demonstrations became angry protests.

The relocations widened to include neighbors, friends—sympathizers.

Then a few Vila Vela patriots took potshots at investigators, and the armed forces struck back. Battalions bivouacked in my favorite playscape. Platoons marched across the seventy-fourth-floor-balcony parkland, stomping the grasslike surface into sludge.

An orbital lander crashed into a wedding party.

Eighty-one people died.

Nine days later, Vila Vela patriots dropped a bridge on a corpo research team in reprisal. Dozens more died. Ration-drones and aerosolized tranqs enforced calms and curfews. Battlesuited squadrons patrolled prominent atria and questioned local MY-RAGE celebrities.

For the next month, sirens sounded in the night, and even my loudest auncles kept their voices down.

Until one night my mother didn't return home.

My sayti pulled every string in Vila Vela. Three days later, she got results: an official acknowledgment of my mother's death in a raid on a patriot cell.

Sayti kept working on the terrafixing protocols through the sirens and the curfews. Even after they killed my mother, she didn't miss a day in the lab. I'd hated her for that.

A month later, she smuggled a packet into a corporate operating base: a packet that killed two hundred employees with weaponized mycorrhizae. That was the beginning. Sayti surrounded the slagged Sweetwater Site with IEDs deploying genetic-reparation algorithms that she'd modified to affect humans. The results were terrifying, and the reprisals even worse.

Vila Vela patriots demanded that the corporations withdraw from the city limits.

The corporations refused.

The enclave exploded into a warzone.

Toward the end of her life, the corpos called Sayti "the Plague-maker." The people of Vila Vela called her "the Ess Ayati," a more formal term for "grandmother." But the Ess Ayati was a notorious patriot resistance leader, unflinching and brutal, while to me she was still just Sayti.

At first, she used me as a runner and a lookout for the ragtag patriot army that had assembled around her. We couldn't trust MYRAGE, so we reverted to ancient techniques: onetime data-pads and air-gapped notes. I slunk through firefights and scrambled over wreckage; I lingered on the outskirts of meetings, impressed by my contribution to the cause.

The first time a corpo squad captured me, I wet my pants.

The soldiers laughed and dismissed me as a real threat. They beat me for the sake of thoroughness—I still remember the hot flush of shame—then released me without a mark on my record. No reason to take note of a shivering piss boy. So the next two times they caught me, I made sure to wet my pants. It was the easiest way to prove my harmlessness, and my shame faded, because now *I* was pulling the strings.

The beatings still hurt, though.

After eight months in the hot zone, I didn't gag at the scent of corpses or flinch at the sound of gunfire. I'd never fired a gun, but I was a veteran when Sayti called me in for a special job.

"Eight corpo squads are patrolling the Oshun district," she told me. "Stop squirming."

I was squirming because she was tugging my hair into a style that the kids called a triceratop. "I look stupid."

"There's a reason I'm doing this," Sayti told me.

"There's always a reason," I grumbled.

"And the reason is always love."

I groaned.

She ruffled my dorky hair. "You need to find one squad. Tokomak Squad." An insignia projected in front of me. "They're the only ones who matter, do you understand?"

"I'll find them," I promised. "Then what?"

"Make friends," she said.

"With a corpo squad? Why?"

"The *why* comes later," she told me. "First let's work on the *how*."

So the next day, with my triceratop painted orange and my feet in clogs, I crouched in the Oshun district. The area had been "the pearl of Vila Vela" before Sweetwater kludged. Now limp banners sparked in the breeze and shattered dreamwheels speckled the walls.

I scoped two patrols before Tokomak slipped through the streets. Ten battlesuited Garda soldiers carried Boaz rifles and—for some reason—an eight-foot length of lacebrick, a vat-grown interlocking building material.

"Hey, boss!" I called in Bahasa, standing from behind a vend machine. "What's up with the brick?"

"Get fucked," a meaty guy snarled, swiveling his Boaz at me.

"I can't," I told him.

Suspicion flashed in his eyes. "Run along out of here, kid."

"It's not like I haven't *tried* getting fucked." I ambled closer, keeping my hands in plain sight. "I'm too young is all."

The other squaddies laughed, and the meaty guy muttered, "Fuck all of you."

"Give me a few years," I told him. "Anyone got spare rations?"

A huge guy with chin ridges tossed me a yellow-tabbed tube. "Here, kid."

"Yellow?" I made a face. "Everyone knows yellow is heat-meat."

"There's a saying about beggars and choosers," the huge guy grumbled.

"How about some blue?" I appealed to the rest of the squad. "Anyone got blue?"

"You like huitlacoche?" a woman with a prosthetic arm asked.

"The spicy stuff, sure. The unspiced tastes like mycofu."

"Tofungus," the huge guy muttered, which was another word for the pasty gray blocks of fungus-based tofu.

The woman told a skinny gen, "Give the kid some blue."

"Winning hearts and minds," the gen said, rummaging in their pack.

"Mostly stomachs." I tapped the lacebrick. "So where'd you loot this from?"

The next thing I knew I was on the ground. Pain throbbed in my head and the meaty guy was standing over me.

"Fuck you," he said. "We don't fucking loot."

"Stand down, Dustin!" the one-armed woman barked.

He straightened away from me. "Fuck you."

"That's your thing, huh?" I asked, wiping tears from my eyes. "Fucking kids?"

When he leaned down to grab me, I fished his cardblank from

inside his vest. That's why I'd said that, to bring him close. And after all, I'd developed a knack for fiddly work.

When he lifted me off the ground I palmed the card into my sleeve and started crying.

"I should break your face," he snarled.

"We don't hit the local fauna," the one-armed woman told him. "We only hit them *back*."

"Tell that to my dads," I sniffled.

"Put him down." She looked at the meaty guy. "Make me say it again, Dustin. See how that works for you."

"Sorry, Sarge," the meaty guy said, and dropped me.

With a flick of my wrist, I sent the stolen cardblank skittering to the ground. For a moment, nobody moved. The entire street held its breath.

Then I said, "You, uh, dropped your card?"

"Fucking thief," he said, and started to kick me.

The huge guy with chin ridges shoved him away. "C'mon."

"Keep moving," the one-armed sergeant said, and they headed down the street.

"Hey!" I shouted after them. "Where's my ration?"

The gen made a rude gesture and the squad disappeared around a corner.

CHAPTER 23

After Tokomak Squad took off, I lived on the streets of Oshun for a week, keeping out of sight of any helpful locals who'd give me food and shelter. Looking back, I'm not sure why it seemed so natural. Stealing, begging, sleeping rough. Maybe I just trusted Vila Vela; even the dark alleys felt like home.

I looked pretty ratty the next time I found the squad. I didn't say anything. I just squatted there, my orange triceratop streaked with dirt. The one-armed sergeant glanced at me briefly before patrolling past, and the huge guy said something I didn't hear.

Three days later, hunger gnawed at me. I stank and itched. A fresh meal, a shower, and a soft bed were waiting for me at home, if I couldn't take the streets. If I gave up. If I was willing to disappoint my sayti.

No way. Not then, not ever.

The next time I saw Tokomak, I greeted them with a cheery "Get fucked!" and the huge guy with the chin—named Aowamo—tossed me a yellow-tabbed tube.

"Did you loot it?" I asked.

He laughed. "You're a little shit."

"It's a step up from a fucker!" I said, squeezing the tube into my mouth.

A week later, I started tagging along behind them. Not too close. Dustin—the meaty guy—chased me off the first few days, and finally caught me.

When he raised his fist I showed him the sweetchew I'd slipped from his pocket. "Don't touch me, Dustbin! I'm magic. Plus, I can—"

He punched me. Not hard, or he would've broken me. But not soft, either.

I was moaning on the floor when the one-armed woman crouched in front of me. "We could put you in blinders for stealing. What's your name?"

"Fao," I said. "What's yours?"

"Najafi."

"*Sergeant-Affiliate* Najafi," Dustbin said.

She looked at me. "Where are your folks?"

"How come the Garda doesn't grow your arm back?"

Her face clouded. "I prefer my prosthetic."

"You lie worse than my baby brother."

"So you have a brother. Any parents?"

"Grandparents, Sarge," the gen said. "We're in Vila Vela."

Najafi flicked a gesture and asked me, "Any grandparents?"

"What do you think?" I said.

She straightened and turned away. Aowamo slipped me a couple yellow tubes, and the squad prowled down the block.

Three days later, I sold Dustbin four cans of local sweetchew. "I don't care if the little fucker personally melted down all three AIs," he told another trooper, "I haven't had chew this good in months."

A week after that, Tokomak Squad found me bleeding in an alley.

A few of my sayti's soldiers had apologetically beaten me up for what one of them called "verisimilitude." I looked a mess, with a swollen lip, a black eye, and scrapes on my cheek and shoulder. I'd crawled into the alley and waited for the squad. Hours passed. What if they realized I was faking? I couldn't make myself cry and the pain didn't bother me much. Pain is different when you choose it yourself.

Except the moment I saw the squad, I burst into tears. Real tears. I didn't know why. Still, I wept and told Tokomak Squad a tragic tale about life on the streets as their medic patched me together.

When Sergeant Najafi took me in a one-armed hug, my sobs grew louder. My mother was gone, my childhood was over. And the sergeant was gentle. She brought me food and clothes and offered to get me into the corpo school.

She wasn't a faceless squaddie or a vathead like Dustbin. She was a real person, scared and brave and strong and gentle.

She liked me, too. "Dirty as a vac-sac," she told me. "And sneaky as a ferret. But there's hope for you yet, Fao."

The next week, I rewarded her faith in me. I warned Tokomak Squad about a gang of patriots taking potshots from a terrace. My sayti had told me they were there. She'd put them there. She sacrificed four low-value new recruits to strengthen my position with the corpo squad.

And she'd finally explained my triceratop: "Do you know the one named Sergeant Najafi?"

"Sure," I said. "She's only got one arm."

"And one child," Sayti said, from the film-obscured doorway where we'd met. "Who wears his hair like yours."

"His is yellow," I told her. "She showed me a picture."

Sayti's gaze sharpened on me. "She did?"

"Yeah."

"She's fond of you."

I flushed. "I guess."

"Of course she is. You're adorable. Those little cheeks."

"Oh, shut your wrinkles," I muttered, which was the mildest thing my mother used to shout at her.

She laughed. "You remind me of her."

"Mom? She said you two never got along."

"We never did." The grandmotherly softness faded from Sayti's face. "The sergeant's son is wearing yellow now, but I found an older image. When he was your age."

"You want me to look like him?"

She nodded. "To gain her trust."

"Then why did I let them catch me stealing that cardblank? Dustbin could've broke my arms."

"'Broken,'" she corrected.

"That too," I said.

"They're suspicious of locals, Maseo, for some reason." Her smile didn't have any warmth. "So you taught them to see you as an incompetent street thief."

"Why not teach them to see me as a regular kid?"

"They'd never believe a Vila Vela street kid was an innocent. They'd look for your secret. So you showed them a secret, and they stopped looking."

"Oh."

"And now they care for you."

"Yeah, but—" I took a breath. "But why them? I mean . . . why *them*?"

"That's the question we all ask ourselves, in the end," she said. "'Why me?'"

"Gee, thanks. That helps."

She kissed my forehead, inhaled deeply, and held me close.

"I stink," I said.

"You smell like Vila Vela." She gave me a squeeze. "Stay close to them, Maseo. You're doing great. I'm proud of you."

My next big moment with Tokomak Squad came a few days later, maybe a week. I don't remember the chronology exactly, but the day shines bright in my memory. They'd finished patrolling the corridors around an extrusion plant when I told Aowamo he needed to see something.

He wasn't supposed to follow a local off-route, but I promised him it was worth it.

Najafi nodded her permission and I led the squad into a little-known theater atrium with a cool sculpture installation. Projections flowed around the sculptures, which reacted to our proximity. Also there was a grove of guava trees. The fruit was ripe, and after the medic checked for toxicity, the soldiers gorged themselves. A few of them even enjoyed the art: mostly Sergeant-Affiliate Najafi.

"My dad took me here a few times," I told her, which was true.

"It's nice." She rotated a guava in the mechanical fingers of her prosthetic arm. "It's got a good feeling."

I watched the guava spin on her alloy fingertips. "Why don't you regrow your arm?"

"No reason," she said. "I just never found the time."

"She's a hero," Aowamo told me.

"Don't bore the kid with your stories," she said.

He rubbed the ridges on his chin. "She lost the arm in a cataphract attack. One of them snuck in under the wire of an enclave during a crash. No warning. We fought for hours without the CAVs. The cataphract—" He waited until a sculptural projection washed past us. "You know they spawn paladins, yeah?"

"Sure, I've seen the channels," I told him. "Paladins are like empty suits of armor."

"Not so empty. Paladins are the bio-forged battlesuits that grunts wore back in the day. We can handle them, but nothing beats a cataphract except a CAV. So we're protecting this residential tower and the—"

"The cataphract hit me," Najafi interrupted, "and I haven't grown the arm back."

"It sliced her in half," Aowamo said. "She saved the tower, pretty much single-handed—"

"Single-armed," one of the other squaddies called.

"—and then a CAV fell from the sky and saved *her*. The cry pilot died, and that's why she . . ." Aowamo gestured to her prosthetic. "As a memorial."

"Oh fuck you," she said. "I'm not the one who sends my pay to my little sister every week."

To my surprise, Aowamo showed me a picture of his sister. She was probably five years older than I was, but short and unformed like a little kid. The top of her skull was a sunken pit that was only half-covered with piles of messy black hair. She was a "wizzy"; centuries ago, one of her ancestors used Wix genetic manipulation to give their child exceptional intelligence or health, the ability to function without sleep or—who knows?—an adorable pair of devil horns with a matching tail. Sure enough, Wix worked beautifully for the first generation. Then wizzys appeared: descendants of those genetic pioneers, living the unforeseen consequences.

A tiny fraction of wizzys were born with minor idiosyncrasies: night vision or forked tongues, patches of carapace or eidetic memory. A tiny fraction of that tiny fraction were driven mad by technopathy or fugue states or multidentification.

The vast majority were gene-damaged like his sister.

I never met her or anything. I never heard her name. I never even learned if Sergeant-Affiliate Najafi really refused to regrow her arm as a tribute to the anonymous cry pilot who'd saved her life.

Still, I never forgot the hour I spent in that forgotten sculpture theater, eating guavas and listening to the squad reminisce.

In my memory, though, that hour bleeds directly into another one—maybe days later—when Sayti met me at a balcony overlooking a lively park with fountains and laminated trees.

Sayti and I watched a family having a picnic on a grownstone table, ignoring the peacekeeping moskito drones. Two men and a woman chatted with each other while a toddler marched unsteadily around them, and a third man cleaned a naked baby's bottom.

"You asked why them," Sayti said. "Why Tokomak Squad?"

"Yeah."

"Two reasons. First, because Tokomak Squad killed your mother."

Her words punched me in the stomach. *Najafi* took my mother?

Aowamo broke down the door and Dustbin fired on her? The others, so easy with a laugh once you knew them . . . they'd shot my mother in that ninth-floor hallway?

"And second," Sayti said, "I happen to know that they'll be disposed of in a recymatorium directly beside army headquarters."

"Disposed of? You mean their bodies?"

"I'm going to weaponize their remains, Maseo. After you lead them into an ambush."

The next time I saw the squad, I begged them for help. I babbled and wept. I pleaded for them to follow me, frantic and inconsolable. I told them I needed help and led them into a plaza with a directed pulse that they would've spotted if they hadn't been so concerned about me.

The world exploded into a death trap.

Aowamo shielded me with his body, and I still remember the look in Najafi's dying eyes when she realized what I'd done.

I betrayed them. That's the debt I'll always owe. That's why I can't sacrifice my squad, not even in training. My mind is willing but my fingers won't pull the trigger.

Joining the military won't wipe the slate clean; keeping my squad alive won't wash the blood from my hands. Nothing will. I know that redemption is just a fairy tale guilty people tell themselves, but maybe even bloody hands can build something new.

CHAPTER 24

Kaytu, Maseo ⊘

The reprimand glows on my lens and the system docks my paychecks, but at least I'm good with an Ambo—unlike Ting. She hates firearms. She hates the weight and the noise and the power. She cringes every time she fires: even on full-auto, she misses a three-square target at twenty yards. Misses entirely. Not a scratch.

She's crap with everything except tech. She scores literally off the charts on her first flowcore test, though . . . and I'm the only one who notices her panic at the results. She's spliced with terror at the sudden attention she receives.

The next day, TL announces a bug in the scoring algorithm that lowers Ting's score to merely the top one percent.

In the mess hall that evening, I reopen the covert private window she established weeks earlier and lens her, "You hacked the scoring algorithm to lower your score."

Ting stiffens over her plate and doesn't respond.

"If you can change the scores," I message, "why aren't you higher ranked?"

There's a pause. "I'll raise yours if you want."

"I'm not blackmailing you, Ting."

She turns to face me, her amber hair falling around her eyes.

Most of the recruits lost ten pounds during training, but she gained five. "Why not?"

There's no heat in her question, no accusation. Just curiosity. Because we both understand desperation; we both got here through the belly of a CAV.

"I don't know," I lens her.

"Because you want to earn this instead of stealing it."

"You think?"

She watches me from behind the false black pupils of her lenses. "You want to see who you would've become if things were different. If you weren't a child of the refugee camps and the Freeholds."

Goose bumps rise on my arms in the warm mess hall. Is *that* what's driving me? What if it's not about paying a debt? What if I just want to become the man I would've been if nobody had melted down the Big Three AIs? If Vila Vela hadn't erupted, and Sayti hadn't turned us into war criminals?

"Maybe," I lens. "What do *you* want?"

"To disappear," she replies, and lowers her head.

I cross the mess hall and sit beside her. "What're you running from, Ting?"

She keeps her head down.

"The stem?" I lens. "There's treatment. In the military, there's treatment."

After a pause, she messages, "It's not that."

"Then what're you running from?"

"Me," she says aloud, and closes the window.

She won't say anything else, and she avoids me for two days—as much as possible, considering we live in the same barracks.

On the third day, she stops avoiding me. Because on the third day, Group Gabrielle vanishes. They're not in the mess hall, they're not in the corridors. Jag materializes on the edge of my vision and says that the Gabrielle barracks is now occupied by a new platoon of slippers.

"Shipped out," M'bari says.

"They're not finished with basic," Voorhivey says, looking worried. "They can't ship them out before they're even trained."

Ridehorse glowers at him. "Why not?"

"There's policy. There's corporate guidelines about this stuff."

"This is a pilot project," M'bari says, and glances to Rana.

Rana keeps her head bowed over the strategy simulation she's running. The arch of her neck is eloquent. She's good at silence.

"You think they sent Gabrielle to fight lampreys," Voorhivey tells M'bari, with a break in his voice. "That's what you think."

"Maybe they're on long-term recon," Basdaq says. "Or got transferred to another base."

"That's possible, right, chief?" Voorhivey asks Ridehorse, who is Chief-of-Barracks this week.

"Sure," she says gloomily. "It's possible."

"All things are possible," Pico says. "Except for—"

"TL's coming," Jag murmurs.

"Deck up!" Ridehorse shouts, and we take position at the foot of our bunks.

TL ambles to the center of the barracks. She doesn't say anything for a full minute. "You're the most inquisitive flock of fucking magpies."

Admin speaks from the doorway. "We heard your speculation about Group Gabrielle."

"Where they are is none of your concern," TL says, rubbing a scar on her cheek.

"They're transferred," Admin says. "Promoted. Because *they* didn't sit around gossiping. Confirm."

A tentative "Confirm" sounds in the barracks.

"Confirm!" Admin repeats.

Half of us shout, "Confirm!"

The other half don't. Because TL and Admin are lying, so fuck them. Something happened with Group Gabrielle, something they're not telling us. I know it shouldn't matter: who cares what they tell a bunch of recruits? But this is Gabrielle we're talking about. We didn't like them, we barely knew them. Still, we'd come into this together, and we were connected to them in some unspoken way.

TL must agree, because she changes the subject instead of busting our bones. "Two groups remain. You have a chance to move to the next stage of the pilot program." Her gaze sweeps us. "Chief Ridehorse?"

"TL!"

"Do you want Group Aleph to advance?"

"Yes, TL!"

"Can we beat Group Bay?"

"Yes, TL!"

She looks at the rest of the group. "Is Chief right?"

"Yes, TL!" we shout. All of us, this time.

"Expect the unexpected," she says. "A test is coming. You against Group Bay. Confirm."

"Confirm!"

"If you perform well enough, you'll graduate to JVLN after basic."

"JVLN?" Werz asks, before Gazi nudges her quiet.

"Javelin," Pico says.

"What's that, TL?" Basdaq asks.

TL takes a breath. "'A five-corporation joint venture established for risk sharing and resource pooling in the event of low-probability economic, security, and/or existential threats.'"

"Obviously," Admin says.

A ripple of laughter sounds in the barracks. "What's it mean?" Calil-Du asks.

"I'm not entirely looped in," TL admits. "It means a new remort's crawling out of the wilderness. The lampreys. And whatever they are, they're worse than cataphracts."

"But, but what *are* they?" Voorhivey asks. "I mean, what's the underlying tech? Did the terrafixing recover them from, y'know, a military platform or an industrial engine or what?"

"My understanding is that *that* is exactly what the c-suites don't know. It's what they want to know. What they need to know. Are lampreys based on a lost SICLE weapon system? On a resource extraction drone or a communication module or some unknown phenomenon?"

"Or an *epi*phenomenon!" Ting blurts. "Which is like a phenomenon's phenomenon."

Admin rubs his face with his palm. "I don't know why they're recruiting mutants and newbies for this pilot program, but you've got a chance, a small and undeserved chance, to be part of something big. This test is coming. Don't fuck it up."

"Kaytu," TL says.

"TL!" I say.

"With me," she says, and heads away.

I glance at M'bari. He gives a tiny shrug, and I trot after TL.

She leads me past the Bay barracks and into an empty conference room, where she stops at a projection of a snowy field with a herd of big quadrupeds.

"You know what those are?" she asks.

"Horses?"

"They're moose."

"There's no antlers."

"They're female moose," she says, "and this is where I'm supposed to tell you a heartfelt story about moose, with a clever twist that ties into your personal situation. To open your eyes in a wise satori moment. That's what I'm supposed to do, Kaytu, but they're just a bunch of moose and I don't have a heartfelt story."

"Okay," I say.

"You've got potential," she tells me. "You're no Rana, but you've got potential."

I square my shoulders and watch a knock-kneed moose nuzzle a bush.

"Which you're wasting," she continues. "A thirty-day reprimand on your lens is a real failure, Kaytu. It's a betrayal of your potential."

"Yes, TL."

"And your squad, confirm."

I hesitate. "Confirm."

"This isn't the refugee camp where the goal is to keep your friends alive. Do you understand that, recruit?"

"Yes, TL."

"This is an organization that projects corporate goals using the focused application of force. And the foremost of those goals is standing as a bulwark against the remorts and patriots that threaten the survival of our species. Do you understand that, recruit?"

"Yes, TL."

"Our value is not measured in the survival of our buddies. If our goal were to protect our squad, we'd encourage them to de-cruit. Confirm."

"Confirm," I say.

"So what's wrong with you?"

"I guess you're right about coming from a refugee camp," I tell her, trying to sound earnest instead of deceitful. "We fight for each other there, not for anything bigger."

"You don't mind sacrificing a few squadmates," she says. "You only choke when the whole squad is on the line."

"Is that . . . is that right?" I shake my head. "I didn't realize."

"You can lie to me, Kaytu, but don't lie to yourself. I get five or six cry pilots a year. At best they're like Ting. Salvageable. But you? You never wanted to die, not even when you volunteered. Did you?"

"No, TL."

"No. I don't know what your personal backstory is—" She gives a little laugh. "Just like the moose: I don't have a story for them, I don't have a story for you. See how I tied that in? Not bad, huh?"

"Smooth, TL."

"Yeah, and I don't give a shit about your backstory. A moose is a moose. A soldier's a soldier. I don't care where you came from, I only care where you're going. Is this your life now?"

"Yes, TL," I say.

"Make that true," she tells me.

CHAPTER 25

Kaytu, Maseo ⊘
chance of completion: 78%
platoon rank: 08 of 27
5323 rating: BBB

After a day of reinforcement training, I'm sent to a solo class in what Admin calls Field Messing: cooking and hydration in the terrafixing. To my surprise I enjoy the class, but my nerves are on edge for two reasons.

First, there's that reprimand still glowing on my lens.

Second, the entire squad is getting twitchy, waiting for the surprise test against Group Bay.

On my way back to the barracks, I pass the vector plasma station and hear rustling. The door is cracked open, even though the vp station is always locked when not in use.

My pulse spikes. This time I *know* I've stumbled onto the test.

I reach for my Ambo—except my Ambo is currently racked and

unloaded in my locker. Fine. I slow my breathing. I slow my heartbeat. I clench my fists, then shake the tension from my hands. I'm ready for anything.

When I peek around the door, I see Ting kneeling on a cushioned bench.

Her head is down; her amber hair is a veil around her face.

She's pushing a gleaming silver barb of stem into the scar in the back of her neck.

Stem tech is bad news. MYRAGE gossip claims that one of the Big Three AIs developed it as a mind-machine interface, compatible with flowcore tech, in the early days after ascension. In theory, a user could control complex computer systems with a thought, stem into the port and *be* the machine. In practice, the benefits are eclipsed by the side effects: euphoric disassociation and death. Stem cracks open your mind to the ambient waves of signals that wash through cities. You surf the surface of the electronic world, a tiny droplet raised aloft by a tsunami.

As addictive as breathing, and as deadly as not. Before the corpos cracked down, off-market stem flooded the drug markets. It's harder to get now but no less lethal.

Without thinking, I blank my lens, though I'm too late to stop any surveillance. I've just recorded Ting breaking every law of basic training. I've just ensured her decruitment, her banishment.

Except without raising her head, Ting says, "Your lens isn't recording, Mase."

"They always record."

"I hacked the room into a loop when I—" She stops for what feels like a long time. "Thank you. For trying."

I don't need this, I don't want this. I don't owe Ting anything. She's a junkie with secrets; getting involved with her is dangerous. And there's no way she hacked the base security, is there?

Still, I hear myself saying, "You and me, Ting. We're in this together. How many gutter roaches get this far, on any base in any corporation? After months of this shit, we're still here." I put a hand on her skinny shoulder. "We even beat the CAVs. What kind of person does that?"

She doesn't answer.

I shake her, a little too roughly. "What kind of person?"

"I—I don't know."

"Fucking heroes. We're as good as any Class A sharemonkey born with a certificate in his fist. We're better. But you've got to break this addiction. Stem is a gun at your temple."

Her breath rasps. "I'm not addicted."

"You're doing a good impression."

"I'm not a stemhead."

"Stemheads lie. You're lying to me right now."

"I'm—I'm not."

I rub my face. "I don't even want to know how you get the stuff."

"It's . . ." Her smile trembles. "Complicated."

"Not really," I say.

Stemheads lie and steal. That's what they do. They betray friends, and they never change. Not me. I can change. I *have* changed, which is why I won't betray friends, not again. I can't inform on her, so I walk away. Part of me watches my lens, waiting for a blur or twitch when Ting's loop stops. I don't see a thing. She's some kind of nightingale who lulls electrons to sleep with her song.

I'm half-asleep in my bunk before I realize that I think of Ting as a friend.

I wake in the night with my eyes burning and snot pouring from my nose. A syrupy taste is thick in my throat and my lungs strain for breath.

Aerosolized attack.

Panic hits me like a fist. My heart pounds, and I can't see through my weeping eyes. The world is a blur of breathless pain.

I hear a gasp and a shout, then sound the alarm via my lens and roll from my bunk.

I hit the ground too hard.

I stagger to my locker and slather active-gel on my face. The panic subsides and my eyes clear beneath the ointment. The gel thickens in my nostrils and filters the air. Protocol is to arm yourself and engage a full threat assessment before helping others, so I ignore my terrified squadmates and arm my Ambo with dummy ammo.

I set my lens to broad spectrum and spot three canisters deploying gas inside the room. Ambo systems go live around me, appearing as active squadmates.

"Rana, disarm the canister in the corner!" I shout over the panicked din, running toward the vending unit. "Shakrabarti, take the one at the door. M'bari, active-gel everyone and what the fuck is going on?"

M'bari always knows the score; he just gets it, for every value of "it." So he's on active-gel in a flash, dispensing doses and calling, "The test, this is the test, expect contact with Bay!"

I reach for the canister beneath the vending unit to stop more gas from deploying, and a shock hits my chest and knocks me on my ass. I'm stunned and gasping, both arms tingling and staring at the wall.

"Proximity denial," Rana says, her voice so level that she sounds bored.

"Deploy countermeasures!" Pico shouts. "Werz, take the vend unit!"

I'm still stunned when they bag the final canister. Gazi kneels beside me with her medkit. "Deep breaths, Kaytu."

"I'm fine," I gasp. "Just a shock unit."

"You're not fine till I say you're fine," she says, and scans my brain. "Yeah, okay. You're fine."

"The exercise begins at the tone," an automated voice announces. "Group Aleph will attempt to occupy Group Bay's barracks. Group

Bay will attempt to occupy Group Aleph's barracks. The team with the greatest number of infiltrated soldiers wins. Return all weapons to lockers. The use of gear is forbidden. You have six minutes. Your lenses and active-gel are deactivating . . . now."

A tone sounds and the gel runs off my face like water. The stinging returns, but not as bad—though my lungs can't quite fill.

I slot my Ambo into my locker and hear Pico gasping, "Form on Rana! Form on Rana!"

Pico is the barracks chief this week, which is a good thing because he's the only one of us with big enough bones to relinquish command in an emergency. He doesn't give a shit. He's got nothing to prove, and we all know that Rana was born for command.

"Calil-Du, Kaytu, Pico!" Rana immediately shouts. "Get in the corridor, guard the door!"

Calil-Du and Pico are number two and three at hand-to-hand combat. Basdaq is number one, which is hardly fair considering how he looks, and I'm number seven. So Rana's putting two of her best fighters plus me into the corridor that runs between Bay's barracks and ours, and keeping her best man back.

At least in theory. There's a reason I'm only number seven, and I suspect Rana knows it.

I stagger across the barracks with Calil-Du and Pico, blinking and gasping from the gas. Calil-Du is first into the corridor, then Pico. I slip into place behind him and wipe my eyes.

Clouds of aerosol billow in the hallway.

My vision is smeared and blurry as I peer at the doors lining the walls. Red indicator lights shine above all of them—locked—except one that glows green: twenty yards away, the entrance to the Bay barracks.

It's unguarded, for the moment. Beside me, Calil-Du spits on the floor, then wipes her broad face with her palm. Her bald head shines in the ceiling lights, leaving streaks in my distorted vision. I'm almost blind from tears, but I see a thousand gym hours in her broad shoulders and thick thighs. She's brutal and blunt and unclever, but there is zero chance of her nerve breaking, and suddenly that matters more than anything.

"You're my kind of woman," I wheeze at her.

"I don't fuck anyone who can't take me in a fight," she snarls, as the barracks door slams closed behind us. "What the gehenna is Rana doing?"

Pico wipes snot from his face. "She's locking us out, prez."

"Without giving us orders?"

"Do damage," Rana calls from behind the door.

Calil-Du grunts again, Pico growls a laugh—and the Bay door bangs open.

Seven or eight Bay recruits stagger along the corridor toward us through the gloom, coughing and rubbing their eyes. The lights dim, and my field of vision ends four feet in front of me. I'm half-blind and can't stop blinking, which turns the world into a kaleidoscope blur.

"The hallway's narrow." I gasp for breath. "And we're blind. Pico. Stay behind me till I fall, then plug the gap. C'mon, Cali. You and me."

"You're rated *seven*," she snaps.

"That's your lucky number."

I edge forward, one hand brushing the wall, then close my eyes against the stinging. My nostrils hurt and I'm breathing an acid fog.

Inhale.

Exhale.

Inhale and I'm back in Vila Vela, a length of pipe in my hand and blood rushing to my head. Exhale and I'm in the refugee camp, rabid with drugs and rage, exploding into rival turf with Ionesca howling at my side.

I open my eyes and see a blur of Bay recruits lurching toward us through the haze. Coughing and spitting, slow and unsteady. They look drunk—we all look drunk. The best Bay fighter is in front, a guy named Ojedonn who's the size of a sanitation drone. He thunders forward, arms groping, his fighters staggering behind him.

"He's mine," Calil-Du says, an edge of excitement in her voice.

When Ojedonn spots us, he wheezes, "Enact!"

Calil-Du launches blindly forward and meets him with a meaty thud. She's tough, but he's twice her size.

He drives her backward. A punch, a block. Pivot, strike. They're fighting like in the dojo, like they're strong and sharp, with plenty of padding and plenty of space. This is a different fight, though. This is weak and blind, cramped and stupid.

This is my element.

A snarling face appears through the chaos and I lower my chin and burst forward. The dome of my head breaks the Bay's cheekbone. A raw-throated scream sounds and I stagger sideways from the impact. A punch rips my earlobe from my head before I straighten and kick Ojedonn in the knee from behind. Something pops, and he roars in agony and I hear the bark of Cali's laughter.

I crack a gas-blurred Bay's nose with my palm, and then a fist or elbow connects with my back. Pain bursts, and I drop to the floor and scream, "Pico!"

Calil-Du shoves a howling, one-legged Ojedonn backward into his people. The shouting gets louder and Pico takes a fist from the guy who punched me. Blood spews from Pico's mouth, and he shifts and hits the guy with a jab-cross-jab that's got to feel like a sledgehammer.

I'm on my hands and knees. Tears stream from my eyes and knees clip my head. Bare feet stomp around me as I crawl into the thick of the Bays.

They can't see any better than I can, but they're secure in the belief that the fight is at the front of their line . . . until I break Elfano's ankle. Her shriek distracts the woman facing Calil-Du, and Cali works her face like a speedball. A hatchet-faced gen grabs

Cali's wrist and twists. They disappear into the strobing madness, and I drop another Bay as I catch a snapshot of Pico flailing madly, a blind tornado of fists. He's gasping and coughing, his eyes closed, blood staining his teeth.

Ojedonn somehow slides himself upward on the wall and stumbles into Pico from behind. I punch a Bay fighter in the balls, then break his nose when he buckles. When I punch a second Bay in the balls, she doesn't buckle.

She knees me in the face.

There's a shock of pain and I flop to the ground. The Bay wraps her arm around my neck, so I bite through the flesh of her thumb.

My teeth close on bone and the tone sounds, ending the exercise. Everything stops for a moment, and then another Bay kicks me in the face. An instant before I black out, I realize that I'm laughing. Because gutterdamn, I haven't had that much fun in years.

CHAPTER 26

Kaytu, Maseo 🚫

Two days later, I'm in the infirmary, watching the post-exercise briefing on my reprimand-laden lens.

Three TLs sit at the head of a conference table, while projections of their Admin TLs line one side. Rana and a few Bay recruits stand against the wall. Pico sits alone at the table, curious and amused. He doesn't look even slightly concerned. Something's wrong with that boy.

"Barracks Chief Pik-Cao," the Bay TL says. "Explain your strategy."

"I passed command to Recruit Rana," Pico says, through the bandages on his face.

"Why?"

"Fighting in a corridor, securing a room? That's a job for the Flensers or marines." Pico flashes his offhand smile. "I'm Army in my heart."

The Bay TL is not amused. "Recruit Rana," he says. "Approach the table."

She moves to stand beside Pico. "Yes, Training Liaison."

"Explain your strategy."

"Given the time frame, Training Liaison," Rana tells him, her atonal voice in bored mode, like she's reading a report, "neither group could feasibly reach and occupy the other group's barracks. Hence, I determined to protect the majority of my team members while inflicting the maximum damage on the other team."

"That was not the mission objective."

"When a primary mission objective is deemed impossible, Training Liaison, a secondary objective may be determined at the commander's discretion."

"Two of your people are still in the infirmary," the Bay TL says.

"As are eight of theirs," Rana tells him. "And two more were released only—"

"Including one who needs facial reconstruction."

I cringe a little. Apparently head-butting wasn't within the bounds of the exercise.

"Yes, Training Liaison," Rana says. "Ten members of Bay Group sustained injuries, and all of them were scared, amped, and suffering the effects of the aerosol while my group was in position, covered in dampened cloths, acclimating to the gas, and ready to deploy."

There's silence for what feels like a long time.

"Recruits Pik-Cao and Calil-Du are your top-ranked hand-to-hand fighters?" the Bay TL finally asks.

"They are two of our three highest-ranked, Training Liaison. Recruit Basdaq is ranked number one."

"Calil-Du is three? That's high for a woman."

"Yes, Training Liaison."

"Why did you include Kaytu? He's ranked seventh."

"He's our best fighter."

The Bay TL lenses for information again, probably double-checking my scores. I'm seventh in the official ranking now, but Pico (second), Rana (ninth), Jagzenka (tenth), and I sparred unofficially a few times after class. You don't survive the worst insurrection in decades without learning a few tricks. You don't forget them in a refugee camp, either.

"You knew your squadmates would lose the fight in the corridor," the Bay TL tells Rana.

"I did, Training Liaison."

"Yet you abandoned them to a superior force."

"I did, Training Liaison."

The Bay TL inputs information into a projection. "In a real battle, you'd sentence a quarter of your troops to death?"

"To achieve an important secondary objective?" Rana asks. "I'd sacrifice more than that, Training Liaison."

Our group score drops. Rana is subjected to a performance review, and I'm subjected to a psych eval—and reprimanded.

Kaytu, Maseo 🚫

Because biting, apparently, is frowned upon even more than head-butting. I'd almost severed that Bay's thumb, and broken a few too many bones. It's another long-term reprimand, but the first is almost expired. Still, two of them at once is way too close to being forcibly discharged.

The psychurgeon quizzes me about my history, and I give her the version that doesn't mention my sayti. She monitors my participation in a MYRAGE simulation and finds my responses "curious." Still, she clears me to return to training after medical approval, and I'm sent back to the infirmary.

M'bari is waiting for me. When I ask what he thinks, he says, "They're using these reviews as warnings. You're cleared; Rana is cleared. They're yanking our chains a little and establishing a precedent for the next time you break someone's face."

"I guess I should apologize for that."

"You already did," he tells me. "I sent notes in your name, along with a few gifts."

"Thanks. What do I owe you?"

"A favor."

I shift in the treatment chair. "What do you want?"

"I want you to owe me a favor," he says.

"That's your currency," I say.

M'bari grins. "More precious than love."

"You're a sneaky *eku*."

"I'm not the only one." He gazes at a medical device. "I'm pretty sure that Rana, when she sent the three of you out alone, she broke the training sequence."

"What does that mean?"

"Think about it. The test doesn't make any sense. They set up a conflict that neither side could win. Why?"

"No idea."

"What did they want? They wanted us to stumble into the corridor, half-blind and half-breathing. Right?"

"Sure."

"We'd throw a few feeble punches before both teams got taken down. By the gas or some other force, I don't know. See, they've encouraged us to compete with Bay, but now they need us to co-operate. They wanted both teams to suffer together, so we'd bond together. They wanted to unite us by stomping us flat, but Rana kept us on our feet."

"You've got a twisty mind," I tell him. "The training isn't that smart."

"Maybe," he says.

"I like the idea that Rana fucked them, though."

"She's a force to be reckoned with," he says.

He's not the only one who's impressed with Rana. From that day forward, Calil-Du worships her. Everyone in Aleph shows Rana more respect—except Pico, who laughs at her—but Calil-Du *reveres* her.

And, uh, she visits me in the infirmary a few hours after M'bari leaves. Calil-Du does. She stands beside my bunk with her bald head gleaming and says, "You couldn't take me in a fair fight."

"Maybe not every time," I tell her.

"But you don't fight fair."

"No," I agree.

She drops her fatigues. The medifilm crisscrossing her naked body almost looks like lingerie as she prowls toward the bed. She's strong and unself-conscious, with a predator's taste for brutality, and when we're done, we both need new bandages.

What can I say? I like a big girl with a bad attitude.

CHAPTER 27

For the first time, Group Aleph gets a pass to the MYRAGE arcade. TL doesn't tell us why. Jagzenka asks M'bari, but he's distracted, heading off on business of his own. He just says, "The obvious reasons," before taking an elevator to the engineering floors.

"What's he talking about?" Jag asks me.

I shrug. "No idea. I'm not fluent in Institutional."

When we reach the arcade, half of us immediately slot into the stim-rigs. Rana finds a module about military politics, Shakrabarti joins a fashion show, and eager, clean-cut Voorhivey—after a longing glance at the sex channels—jumps into a military training game, blasting oncoming waves of remorts. Ridehorse and Pico and Jagzenka wrap themselves in a series of sports events, and I settle into my rig, pull a standard interface, and try contacting Ionesca again.

"Any luck?" Ting asks, somehow projecting herself into my interface.

"I'm locked out of real-time talk, but it'll let me leave a message."

"Ooh! That's better than last time you tried."

I give her a meaningful look. "A private message."

"I know! It's great. What're you going to say?"

"*Private*, Ting?"

She wrinkles her nose in confusion. "What? Oh, *me*! You want *me* to leave!"

"I don't even know how you got into a private channel."

"I'm sneaky!" she says, and vanishes in an explosion of squealing purple hamsters.

"O-kay," I say, and start recording.

I tell Ionesca what happened since my arrest. I tell her I'm okay. I tell her that one day I'll visit. I tell her that every time I make the right choice, I feel her hand on my shoulder. And every time I make the wrong one, I feel her teeth on my neck.

"That's sweet," Ting says, after I send the message. "Sort of."

I jerk in surprise. "*Sagrado*, Ting!"

"Oh." She smiles hopefully. "Um, hi again? I'm not very good at privacy."

"You're a champion at irritating, though."

"I'm sorry." She ducks her head. "Except not really."

"You can't just eavesdrop on people, Ting."

"I didn't do it for no reason!"

"No?"

"No! I did it 'cause I was curious."

I know I should knock her around, but instead I laugh.

"Also," she says, "M'bari wants everyone to meet up. He found something. I'll link you into his channel, okay?"

"Sure," I say, and the world changes.

Projections of glassine walls rise around me and unfold into a massive ice-blue castle. Instead of sitting in my message interface, it looks like I'm standing beside Ting on a crystal bridge.

At the far end of the bridge, Pico, Rana, and few others—not including M'bari—stand at an archway made of stylized organs. Lungs, kidneys, hearts. As we head down the bridge to join them, I see that in MYRAGE Pico portrays himself as a chubby, adorable version of a terrifying alien-monster, and tall, gaunt Ridehorse takes the form of a muscular centaur. Voorhivey makes himself look like Basdaq's younger brother, square-jawed and authoritative. Jagzenka doesn't go full jaguar, which surprises me.

Instead, she appears as a saffron-tinted teenaged boy with lavender eyes.

Rana looks like a default Rana, which I expect. Of course she does. But Calil-Du looks like a default Calil-Du, instead of a berserker with a dripping battle-ax. That's a surprise.

Pico waves a few tentacles at me and privately pings, "Cali defaulted to norm after she saw Rana. She started as a horrorwaif."

I send him a laugh and ask on the public channel, "Where's M'bari?"

"Not coming." Ridehorse shakes her mane. "He told me to say that there's more to the story than we're about to see."

"More what?" I ask.

"What story?" Cali asks.

Ridehorse trots through the archway. "C'mon."

We all follow and end up inside a build of a space station, watching a nine- or ten-year-old boy wander the three-floored hallways. He doesn't look like anything special. One of his eyes is yellow and the other is white, but the MYRAGE interface tells me that's the fashion for kids in an interplanetary habitation.

A supertitle says: *The Dag Bravska Research Habitation.*

The name doesn't mean anything to me.

The kid's bouncing a ball—not exactly a ball, but close enough—down the triangular hallway, chatting with the projection of a friend, a girl whose face floats beside his. A dozen people bustle past, mostly scientists and researchers, judging from the info-tags. About half of them are walking on different surfaces of the hallway. The walls that slope inward around the kid function as floors for other people. Back in Vila Vela I spent a week playing a MYRAGE sim based in a derelict hab, so in theory I understand vector plasma.

I still expect people to bump heads, though.

And actually I *don't* understand vector plasma, not really. The AIs claimed that gravity doesn't exist but still developed vector plasma as a sort of artificial gravity. Basically, every adapted molecule in spacefaring habs and vehicles is infused with—or bonded to—vector plasma, which acts as a magnet, pulling those molecules toward the assigned down pole.

The kid's ball is drawn toward a vector plasma pole that acts as a gravitational magnet, as is the kid himself. So are every one of his gut bacteria, all the molecules of his clothing and food and drink.

Well, not *every* cell, because the effect wears off. Techs need to cycle objects—and people—through an adaptation process to keep them responding to the artificial gravity. Which means that some objects, toward the end of the cycle, are lighter than you'd expect. Some are kept weightless too. You might want low gravity on your fragile artwork so it doesn't break if it falls. You might adjust your own weight to compensate for an injury or to suit a personal preference.

And variable-grav toys looked pretty amazing to me as a kid. To the boy in the hallway, vector plasma is just how life works. He walks along, chatting with his friend, not a care in the world.

"What the fuck boring shit is this?" Cali asks, looming behind the boy in the simulation.

"M'bari says it's worth watching," Ridehorse tells her. "So it is."

"How would M'bari know what's worth watching?" Voorhivey asks.

"He talks to people," I say, watching the kid turn a corner in the hab.

"*I* talk to people," Voorhivey says.

"Yeah, but he listens."

Voorhivey shoots me an obscene gesture, more at ease with himself than when he started training.

"Boring-ass shit," Cali mutters.

"Nothing in space is boring," Rana says.

"It's okay," Cali says, immediately backpedaling. "It's kind of cool."

Pico laughs at her. "Do you know what a peachtree is, prez?"

"No," she says. "Fuck you."

"Look," Jagzenka says, gazing at the projection. "There."

A hatch opens behind the boy. Our perspective sweeps inside, to a research lab where scientists swipe on screens and consult modules. An info-tag tells me that they're running high-level analysis of the Puebleaux Waypoint. There's even a false window, showing deep space outside the hab, with the Earth a bright star.

A researcher who is either wearing a skullcap or rocking fungal hair frowns at a display. A second researcher shakes her head, like she doesn't understand.

"I don't think I like this," Ting says, in a little voice.

"Nobody cares what you like," Cali says.

The first researcher clutches her right eye in agony. She screams. Even though the volume is muted, the sound makes me shiver. Her lens melts into her eyeball and a screen expands, strobing interference across the lab and—

We're back in the hallway, following the boy.

He turns suddenly, like he heard the researcher's scream. Behind him, a man walking on a different surface drops a tray of seedlings. They float around him as he reaches overhead.

Except he's not reaching, he's being pulled. Vector plasma tears him limb from limb. The sound kicks in with a thousand shrieks. The boy flees. People die and machines explode. Walls crumble. Foam bursts, sparks fly. Yellow fumes swirl and globs of fluid splatter and—

Silence.

We're outside the Dag Bravska habitation. We're floating in space, looking at a conical space station surrounded by interlocking rings.

Peaceful, from this angle. Quiet. Home to forty thousand people. Then a divot appears in the hull. A triangular shadow that expands into a crease.

The station ripples—and implodes.

Wreckage streams past, bits of gear and broken corpses, and forty thousand faces surround us, the faces of the dead. One face grows large. The boy in the hallway.

A red stamp appears across his image: *TECHNOPATH*.

The dead faces start speaking: "Technopaths kill," they say, over and over. "Technopaths kill."

"Fucking genefreeks," Cali mutters.

"One little kid took down a whole hab?" Pico says, defaulting to his normal appearance. "That's not right."

Technopaths kill, technopaths kill, technopaths kill . . .

"Was it even on purpose?" Voorhivey asks, chewing his knuckle. "It didn't look like—did he *mean* to do it?"

"Does it matter?" I ask.

"No." Jagzenka watches a chunk of debris float past. "Anyone born with a quantum superposition computer in their brain is a genocide-class weapon."

Technopaths weren't designed as weapons. They were designed via Wix genetic manipulation, for ambitious parents who wanted to prepare their children for mind-machine interface. It was nothing special, just a convenient input device. And an impressive competitive advantage.

But after ten generations, when a throwback is born, that shit has gone seriously awry.

"There's more to the story," Ridehorse says. "That's what M'bari told me."

Like she summoned him, M'bari's message appears on the projection. "Rumors say it wasn't a technopath."

"Then what was it?" Voorhivey asks the interface.

We wait a moment for another message. Nothing comes.

With a gesture, Rana returns us to the crystal bridge. Her jaw is clenched and her dark eyes are hot. "It was a technopath."

"Then what's M'bari talking about?" Voorhivey says. "Who

cares about some once-in-a-century meltdown? It's got to be something else."

"Fuck you," Cali snarls at him. "You heard Rana. It was a technopath."

"It had to be." Rana shakes her head. "The rumors . . ."

"What do the rumors say?" Jag asks her.

"I can't—" Rana pauses. "There are rumors that a remort attacked a hab."

A chill of realization touches me. "A *lamprey* did that? Escaped the atmosphere and crossed a million miles?"

Her gaze catches mine, with a flare of anger or fear. Maybe because I'm right, maybe because she's Rana. "M'bari should keep his conspiracy theories to himself."

"What kind of remort reaches escape velocity?" Voorhivey asks. "Did the terrafixing regenerate an orbital launch array?"

"No," Rana says, and turns herself into an ice statue that shatters on the floor.

"Whoa," Pico says. "That's a little literal."

Everyone leaves except me and Ting. I expect nonsensical chatter from her, but for once she's quiet. Maybe she's shaken by watching forty thousand murders, even just in a simulation.

After a minute, all she says is, "All those people. Just *erased*."

When I log off, I feel a chill in the MYRAGE arcade. Nobody expects the corporate officers to tell us everything—we know we're just grunts. But we've been carefully not thinking much about lampreys, and that simulation makes it harder. That simulation makes us wonder what they are, and how we're going to fight them.

I catch Rana leaving the arcade. Her gait is crisp and her jawline unwelcoming. I walk beside her in silence for two minutes, because I'm not sure how to broach the subject.

She veers along a little-used corridor and into the deck with the orbital pods. A pod opens for her. She climbs inside. I hesitate, but she doesn't close the pod so I follow her into the cramped interior. The hatch closes and the two of us are folded together like origami. I feel her forearm on my hip and smell the sweetness of her breath.

This isn't about romance, but I feel myself respond to her nearness. Her breath quickens and I tell myself that she feels the same. It's still not about romance, though.

"You wanted privacy," she says. "Here's the closest thing."

"You're not afraid of lampreys. You don't care if one of them tore apart that hab. So what're you afraid of?"

"If I were you, I'd be afraid of getting a third reprimand."

"Yeah." Why did I follow her? What am I after? I'm not entirely sure, but I keep talking. "Okay, good point. What'm I saying?"

"I wish I knew."

"I—I grew up in Vila Vela," I hear myself tell her. "During the war."

"You were a refugee," she says. "I heard."

"I fought. As a kid. For the patriots." My heart is suddenly beating fast, like I'm hanging off a two-hundredth-floor balcony. "For the Ess Ayati."

She freezes. "You fought for the Plaguemaker of Vila Vela?"

I don't say anything, because there's nothing to say.

"Do they know?" she asks.

She means the corpos, the military, the JST. "No. I don't know. I switched out IDs when I was transferred to the camp. A few days before they Doomed the city."

"That's the reason you signed up for the CAVs. They'd never let you into the service if they looked too close into your background."

"Yeah."

"It's the reason you're afraid of yourself, too. Why are you telling me this?"

"Because that's how humans work, Rana. Once I tell you a confidence, you'll feel obliged to tell me one."

"That only works if you don't admit it's what you're doing."

"Except *that's* only true if you're not smart enough to realize that of course it's what I'm doing, so it's better to be honest and—"

"Shut up," she says. "You're such a splice."

Something in her toneless voice makes me smile. To my surprise, she smiles back. And I know this is pathetic, but despite her elbow in my thigh and an airlock hinge jabbing my neck, I feel a flash of contentment. I'm happy here, the two of us curled up together, watching the indicator lights paint patterns on her cheekbones and glint in her nighttime eyes.

She looks at a panel on the wall. "It's my father."

"CE Rana-Cain."

"He wants me in the Flensers, not some dubious pilot program. Lampreys scare him more than anything I've ever seen. And . . . well, you fill in the blanks."

I think for a second. "You're worried that if a lamprey destroyed that hab, your father will pull you from the program? To protect you?"

"He might *try* to pull me," she says.

"You think it was a lamprey. You really do."

"It can't be. A million miles from Earth."

I shake my head. "C'mon, Rana. Not even a Corporate Exec can reach into the JST and reassign personnel."

"There's that naïveté again," she says.

"I know I sound like Voorhivey, but there are *rules*."

"And my father knows how to bend them."

CHAPTER 28

We're in the middle of a seminar on cataphract interdiction when an alarm sounds. Our lenses direct us to a bank of autocarts that dispense dummy gear. There's gridmesh armor, a battlecuff-linked com-plate with remote drones, a rampart gun, and medkits and missiles and mines.

There are also two launchers loaded with high-temperature explosive spindles that look like transparent chopsticks, and a rack of Boaz IIIs, complete with canisters and harnesses.

The Boaz III intervention rifle is shorter and blunter than an Ambo and clasps around your forearm like an alloy gauntlet with dorsal barrels and a retractable ventral nozzle. Boazes link to wearable harnesses to help with recoil, not to mention aiming and reloading and proprioceptive balancing. There's no stock, because you don't brace a Boaz with your shoulder like you're pushing a plow. That's what your harness is for, though heavyweight Boazes link to stripped-down exoskeletons. The fragile, clunky finger-pull activation of an Ambo is replaced by a whole-hand mechanism, radial activation or twitch trigger, depending on how you score. And Boazes don't fire rounds, they fire liquammo, pulse-resistant smartfluid ammunition metabolized from consumable canisters.

The Boaz IV—the latest model, as far as I know—offers selectable fire, from single-shot to streaming. They say a real Boaz artist can lay a thread of liquammo through a crack in a rampart, then set it to whipping on the other side. Of course, most soldiers aren't artists. We just hose down the enemy, which is why Boaz rifles are called squirtguns.

There used to be single-operator assault systems that could flatten enclaves with one burst, but after the SICLE War the ban on genocide-class weapons grew teeth. So while a series IV is nothing compared to the crater-makers of the war, it's the best we've got.

Of course *these* Boazes are loaded with nonlethal shock liquammo, and the mines with adhesive foam.

We only graduated from Ambos to Boazes four days ago. We still thrill to the sight of them. I'm suddenly down to a single reprimand again and I thrill to the sight of that, too.

Kaytu, Maseo ⊘

Ting takes the com-plate, of course. Gazi gets the medkit. M'bari and Werz reach for the launchers. I elbow Voorhivey aside and grab the rampart gun.

Ramparting isn't my strongest skill. Recruits who grew up playing MYRAGE games kick my ass every time. Still, it's one of my favorites. The rampart gun is a shoulder-harness-mounted weapon that fires canisters the size of my fist. At the operator's signal, the canisters expand into configurable ramparts dense enough to withstand hits from anything short of a hellfrost. Or, depending on the setting, spongy enough to enmesh tank treads . . . or even an entire Jitney, at fully inflated porosity.

A good rampart squaddie lays down barricades and bulwarks not just for defense but to preclude the enemy from establishing strong positions—and to force them into a killbox.

We're ordered to report to the elevator, and a thrill shivers through the entire group. We're heading outside to fight another team. A nonlethal exercise, but we're finally facing real opponents. This is the beginning of the end of our training, the last stages before we're deployed into actual warzones in Anvil Month.

We're pumped but playing it cool. We talk smack about Group Bay. Pico leads a call-and-response that's so pornographic that Voorhivey starts blushing. Then we step into the elevator and find Group Bay waiting for us to join them. Because we're not fighting *against* them. We're fighting *with* them.

Our platoon against Platoon 5021.

United at last. Except Group Bay eyes me pretty hotly.

I don't look at the regrowth-bandage on the redhead's thumb or the film around Elfano's ankle. She's a stocky woman with high, pointed ears, which is why Group Bay calls her *Elf*ano instead of her real surname, Lofano. She doesn't look all that pixie-ish right now, though.

The air thickens with the expectation of violence. At least Cali is a half step behind Rana like always, which means she doesn't come across like a mad dog at the moment. More like a mad dog straining on a leash.

"M'bari says this is what the TLs wanted to avoid," Ting messages me. "With the gas attack and the kerfuffle in the hallway."

"The kerfuffle," I reply.

"The brawl! The scuffle, the affray. I mean, I don't think *affray* is a word. M'bari says we were supposed to exhaust our hostility without really hurting each other? Then we'd serve a punishment together, to develop bonds. In order to, um, bond. But now—"

She quiets when Ojedonn limps toward me, his knee filmed into a brace. He looks even bigger now that he's not coughing and weeping in a gas attack.

He points at me with a finger like a missile. "Me and you, Kaytu."

"You make a pretty couple," Pico tells him, grinning despite his watchful eyes. "But I warn you, he's a crappy dancer."

Shakrabarti slips beside me, looking like a model with a mine-shooter held jauntily across his shoulder. He effortlessly draws everyone's attention, then twines his fingers in my hair. Trying to defuse the tension. "Kaytu's got rhythm but not much stamina."

There's a scattering of laughter, before Ojedonn cuts it off with a gesture. "Me and him are taking point. With my skills and his evil, ask me what we're going to do to 5021 Platoon."

"What're we going to do?" Elfano asks.

Ojedonn pats the brace on his leg. "Kneecap them."

And you know what?

We do.

They're not pitting us against mock-ups anymore. For two weeks, the entire platoon fights together against other platoons. Against 5021, against 0316, against 4944. In the tower blocks, the laminate forest, and terrafixing terrain. In the faux space station and the faux dreadnought—both with and without faux vector plasma.

We win two thirds of the practice battles, and my lens tells me this:

Kaytu, Maseo ⊘
chance of completion: 93%
platoon rank: 07 of 25
5323 rating: AAA

I'm used to a single reprimand by now, and I don't give a shit about the 07. But the AAA makes my heart sing. We plateaued at AA for a week, but look at us now: a perfect platoon rating.

Then our training refocuses on lampreys, and on the first day a wildly gyrating fabrication unit cuts through us. Granted, we're exhausted from three capture-the-crown exercises in a row, but that thing flattened us.

Only once, though. We win the rematch.

We're not the same people who started JST months ago. We're hard and fast and tough, and greater than the sum of our parts.

Three minutes before lights-out, Ting bounds onto my bunk and hugs me. "We did it! Wediditwediditit!" She's beaming and weeping. "We graduate Phase One *tomorrow*!"

"I know," I tell her.

"I know you know! You *know* I know you know!" Her eyes shine. "Guess what my completion number is?"

"No idea."

"Guess!"

"Eighty percent?"

"Eighty-six! Eighty-six out of every hundred Tings who get this far make it all the way through!" She starts fanning herself. "I'm never going back again. They're not sending me back, not ever. Oh, thank the Louvre!"

"What about the other fourteen Tings?" Ridehorse asks.

"I hate those stupid Tingtings!" Ting says, wiping happy tears from her face. "I mean I don't really believe in multiverses anyway, because why is Ting Prime, I mean me, why am I stuck in *this* boring universe instead of one with people who turn into butterflies or codeware?"

Pico throws his pillow at her. "You *are* butterfly codeware."

Ting stays in my bunk, nattering while I doze, but she's right. We did it. We graduate from Phase One tomorrow and start getting battle-tested. We'll be attached to units in hot conflicts, getting real-world experience in skirmishes against insurgents and remorts.

Then we'll face lampreys.

The Phase One graduation ceremony consists of us grabbing our duffels and moving into a barracks nine floors higher in the base. The Training Liaison leads us in a circuitous route. We trot into the shuttle terminal past HR Sergeant Zhu, who is standing in front of forty-odd new arrivals in civvie clothes.

"Look at your decruitment bonus again," the HR Sergeant is telling them. "Every day that number gets closer to zero. There will never be a better time to leave than right now."

He lenses my squad a silent acknowledgment as we pass: *soldiers*.

Our new barracks includes a communal living space, and our

new rules are lax. Nobody cares when we wake, as long as we're bathed and prepped on time. Mess hall is an open hour, instead of forty-two strictly apportioned minutes.

So far, I like Phase Two.

Rookies aren't individually assigned to new units for their first contact with genuine hostiles, of course: an already bonded training group stays together through Phase Two, embedded as a whole into low-intensity situations. Into low-*risk* situations. Still, we're given live ammunition during our deployments and assigned real tasks.

Next comes Anvil Month, a final deployment into hot-risk theaters, fighting alongside veteran units in hot conflicts. After Anvil Month, they'll scatter us across various military departments, wherever aptitude tests and corporate requirements send us. They'll probably keep a few of us together, to preserve our bond—our valuable, efficiency-increasing bond—but it's more important that we're assigned to veterans. That's where the real learning happens, fighting alongside hardened troops in the field, the only classroom that matters.

Of course, even among shock troops we're not all trigger-pullers. Some are destined for higher things. Command and management. Like Rana and Gaai and Werz and Basdaq. The corpo won't let them stay with us grunts after Anvil; emotional distance is a key to maintaining authority, especially when you're wet behind the ears.

At least, that's what I assume. I guess there's a chance we'll all get impressed into Javelin because of the lamprey threat. In that case, maybe Rana—and the others—will stay close.

We'll see. I'm not looking too far into the future, because I'm not ready to say good-bye to the present. My mind tells me that I'll bond like this with a new squad. My heart disagrees.

At least we're closer than ever during Phase Two. Instead of learning about remorts and lampreys, we learn how to keep our heads under pressure.

We spend four days patrolling an airbase on the border of the Black Sea States. Three days on a high-altitude platform, blasting moths from the sky. We spend a week making combat drops in a skirmish with a nest of wormlike nyongolotsi—a subterranean breaching device composed of thousands of bio-forged units—that's deeper than anyone expected. No matter how many times we clear the tunnels, they keep boiling up from fissures in this arid stretch of New Growth.

We're in a transport lounge when Jagzenka brushes my knee with a fingertip on her way toward the vend machines. A minute later, I stand and stretch, then wander to the vend alcove. M'bari, Ridehorse, and Basdaq are already there. Jag drifts away like a forgotten daydream, but Werz joins us three seconds later.

"That's all of us," M'bari says to Ridehorse.

I frown, because Rana's not here, which means that's *not* all of us.

M'bari lenses me, "I already told her."

"Oh," I say aloud.

"What's going on?" Werz asks him. "Should I get Gazi?"

"Fill her in later," M'bari tells Werz. "It's nothing actionable. I learned what happened to Group Gabrielle."

"I haven't thought of them in weeks," Basdaq says.

"They're probably dead," Ridehorse grumbles, gloomy as always.

M'bari looks up at her. "Most of them."

"What?" Horror flashes across her face. *"No."*

My jaw tightens and I hear Werz gasp and murmur. Gabrielle can't be dead. They were so . . . *alive.* Not hot-shit Gabrielle, who we loved hating. It's not possible. Except I see in M'bari's face that it's true.

Basdaq touches Ridehorse's elbow, and she puts her hand over his and murmurs a prayer in a language I don't speak.

"Yeah," M'bari tells her. "I'm sorry."

"What happened?" Werz asks.

"The corpos are still experimenting," M'bari says. "They don't know what works against lampreys. They're—"

"Throwing shit into a wind tunnel," Ridehorse says.

"What happened?" Werz repeats.

M'bari takes a breath. "Gabrielle was assigned to a Marine Boarding Unit as support staff."

"Marine Boarding is badass." Werz rubs her face with her palm. "What're they doing at the bottom of the gravity well?"

"Guarding an equatorial orbital launch platform—that's marine jurisdiction." M'bari's lens gleams. "There were reports of lamprey activity. Gabrielle was handling coms and supplies, pulses and drones. You know the drill. Three of them survived."

Silence falls, and Ridehorse makes a religious gesture I don't recognize. Despite the corporate opposition to independent communities, they allow religion. In fact, they halfheartedly encourage it, as long as the practices meet their ecumenical guidelines. Maybe that's because PRATO corporation started as a panreligious treaty organization; maybe it's to address the human need for a deeper spirituality than is available on MYRAGE channels.

Either way, I hope the gesture comforts Ridehorse; I wish it comforted me, too.

"What *are* lampreys?" Werz asks M'bari.

"A mystery."

"Narrow it down," Basdaq tells him, with command in his resonant voice.

I'm pretty sure that none of us care about lampreys, not right now. But we don't want to think about Gabrielle. We can't let ourselves imagine that golden squad lying dead and broken on some distant battlefield.

"A remort based on an aerosolized weapon?" M'bari shrugs.

"One theory says they self-assemble from atmospheric elements before each attack and dissolve afterward. I can't find footage, but the corpos spent the past few months working on three initiatives."

"Three initiatives," Basdaq echoes. "That's a start."

"First is the pilot programs for the Javelin military response. That's us and a hundred other platoons in various stages of training. Second is, they're developing experimental weapons."

"What's the origination point?" Jag asks, suddenly among us again. "Where are these things coming from?"

"I don't know," M'bari says. "I don't think Command has any clue."

"What I mean is, if one of them hit a space-hab . . ."

"That's not confirmed."

"What's the third initiative?" Basdaq asks.

"I don't know that, either."

"If we're training to fight these things, why aren't we learning about them?" Ridehorse asks. "Why are we screwing around with patriots and skirmishes?"

"Baby steps," I say.

Werz rubs the back of her hand, a gesture she adopted from Gazi's habit of touching her nursurgeon prints. "They're waiting till we're fully trained."

"Yeah," Ridehorse says. "That makes sense."

"Or they're acting out of institutional inertia," M'bari says. "This is what happens in Phase Two of basic training, so even though we're heading into Javelin, this is what happens in Phase Two of basic training."

"It's the military," Basdaq agrees. "They don't make sense, they make decisions."

CHAPTER 29

That night in the barracks, Ridehorse leads a memorial service for Gabrielle. She burns a fragrant wax cylinder and says a prayer in a dead language. Rana holds her hand and Voorhivey gives a surprisingly touching speech. Pico makes an inappropriate joke, perfectly calibrated to turn the mood from despair to resolve.

Ting weeps, but more from anger than grief. She doesn't mind the deaths, but she can't bear the secrecy about them. "Because it *erases* them," she sniffles. "The way Gabrielle died is part of their lives. A big part, now. They can't not tell anyone. It's like stealing their deaths."

None of us know what she's talking about, but Basdaq comforts her anyway.

We spend the next two days supporting a working group from PRATO Corporation. We prowl through gray, gauzy forests with survey equipment for three days and don't run into any trouble.

"Make a line!" TL tells us, when we stagger back into the JST barracks. "You're two weeks from promotion to active duty and you're triple-A rated, confirm."

"Confirm!"

"The next two weeks is all lampreys," she tells us. "You will eat, breathe, sleep, and dream lampreys."

"Fuck yeah," Cali mutters.

"You have something to add, Calil-Du?" TL asks.

"I said fuck yeah, TL!" Cali barks, obviously to TL's tone. "We will eat, drink, and shit lampreys!"

Admin steps up and says, "Those two weeks start tomorrow evening. Until then? Welcome to your first personal day."

We don't break discipline until they leave, and then a cheer sounds—and a party erupts.

At this point, the platoon is a sprawling plural marriage. Rana sleeps with Basdaq and sometimes Voorhivey. She likes Class A, officious pricks. Gazi and Werz sleep with anyone who'll sleep with both of them at once. Pico usually will. So will Voorhivey and Ridehorse, who also sleep with Shakrabarti. I sleep with Calil-Du and Shakrabarti and sometimes Jagzenka, while Cali sleeps with me and Ojedonn. She slept with Basdaq once, and now he avoids her. Ojedonn is religious—some kind of conservative Theodaoist—so he's exclusive with Cali and Ridehorse. Elfano is in the middle of four love triangles, even though she doesn't sleep with anyone. Pico sleeps with M'bari, M'bari sleeps with Jagzenka, and Ting sleeps with anyone who asks.

I never ask. I don't ask Rana, either, even though the spark between us burns hotter than ever. I don't know why we stay away from each other. Ting says it's because if we start sharing a bunk, we'll never stop. She says we know it too, and it scares us.

She also says this is our only chance—and she's right.

Still, we circle each other warily, like the spark might burn us. Pico mocks us, of course. Ojedonn tells me to seize my chance. Cali tells me I'm not good enough for Rana.

"Calil-Du is wise," Rana informs me, when we wander away from the party. "You're not good enough for me."

"You don't want good," I tell her.

She backs me against the orbital pod and kisses me. She tastes like fresh rain. I'm dizzy with the scent of her, like standing on a rooftop and watching the horizon.

"I sometimes wonder," she says, "how bad you are."

"I'm not bad." I grab a fistful of her hair and roughly tilt her face upward. "Just weak."

She shakes her head sharply, telling me to back off, and I feel a hot flush of shame. Rana's not Cali. She doesn't want us to break against each other like a caravan crash. She doesn't want to bleed for me; she doesn't want to make me bleed. She wants something gentler and more frightening than that. She wants something I'm not sure I can offer—because Cali's right. I'm not good enough for Rana.

I don't move, suddenly afraid.

Rana puts her palm on my chest and feels me breathe. She kisses the edge of my lips. Outraged laughter sounds from the barracks, but we're all alone here, at the beginning of a long good-bye.

"I've never heard you beg," she murmurs. "Not since that first day."

I smile, thinking she's talking about sex. "I'll beg if I have to."

She pulls back. "You sabotaged that CAV."

"No."

"You did. You played some angle. I know you, Kaytu. You did something."

"Maybe," I say.

"How? It's not like your brain is anything special."

"No, but my heart is pure."

She laughs softly. "I mean, CAVs draw on a cry pilot's neural activity to optimize performance, right?"

"Well, maybe. Nobody knows for sure."

She gives me an odd look. "That's been established for decades, Kaytu. CAVs absolutely co-opt your brain. That's why they need volunteers. We know that."

"We do?"

"You risked your life in a CAV without learning the basics?"

I manage not to blurt that of *course* I researched CAVs before

I risked my life. Though apparently I did a deeply shitty job, over-looking the fact that everyone already knew CAVs piggybacked on human brains. I'd thought the AIs were just being incomprehensible.

"I didn't risk anything," I tell her. "Not on purpose."

"You don't trust me." She strokes my chest. "You don't trust anyone except Tingting."

"I don't trust her."

"Yes, you do. You think you know what she is."

"Am I wrong?"

"You're always wrong," she says, and drops her fatigues.

She stands there naked in the low light, and for the first time in my adult life I feel the breath of the divine on my neck. My Sayti taught me religion, but I've never felt awe before. And faced with this vision of perfection, I feel the gutter roach's perverse urge for desecration. I want to reach into the sky and pull the heavens down into the mud. I want to lay my dirty hands on Rana's un-spoiled self.

She sees the hunger in my face. She presses against me and—

Her father appears on my lens. Colonel Executive Rana-Cain, with his silvery dreadlocks and hard eyes. Official seals flash and a *TRADE SECRET/CONFINT* filter locks me out of my lens menu.

"Shit," I say.

"You will not publicly acknowledge my presence," CE Rana-Cain says into my ear. "You will respond to the following location." He vanishes, and a message appears, as if from the JST divisional office, telling me to report to the psych department.

"Orders?" Rana asks. "Now? We're on personal!"

My hand strokes the small of her back, warm and smooth and strong. Her skin is satin over the alloy of her muscle. The curve of her ass is an inch below my pinky, and I realize in the gap between two heartbeats that I'll never forget her scent.

"You once told me how space feels," I say, hearing her words in my mind: *Impossible and perfect. So far above me, but also feels like home.*

She doesn't speak, but her eyes tell me that she remembers what she said, and she knows what I mean.

"Plus," I say, "you've got a great rack."

She punches me in the shoulder. "How long do they want you?"

"They don't say. It's the psych department."

"In the middle of the night?"

"Immediately," I tell her. "Before I beg again."

My lens directs me into a narrow-lift. Machinery hums, bringing me to the psych department on 12-LT. I follow a lens-path along the pastel corridors, trying not to panic.

Did CE Rana-Cain summon me to warn me away from his daughter? Impossible. So is my psych eval biting me in the ass? No; if this *is* a psych eval, there's no reason for Rana-Cain to show his face.

Do they know about Sayti? Do they know about the betrayal, the ambush, the war crimes? They can't . . . but then why did CE Rana-Cain appear at all? Our lives only overlap in a single place: Rana.

All I know is that he wants to keep Rana away from lampreys. How does sending me here help him protect his daughter?

No idea. My lens stops me at a mural that looks like it was designed to be psychologically soothing by a committee where nobody agreed. I wait until a door unseals, then step inside. The entrance film tingles around me.

An elegant woman sits behind a desk in a perfumed cubby. There's ambient lighting and tasteful projections, and an engineered cactus hangs from a hoop. The woman looks about seventy, and she makes seventy look tough. An incense bead glints on her old-fashioned nose ring.

A second chair extrudes from the wall, and she says, "Have a seat, Recruit Kaytu."

"Yes, san," I say, even though she's not wearing a braid.

"CE Rana-Cain brought you to my attention."

"Likewise," I tell her.

Her lenses flash. "He's been paying close attention to your platoon, for obvious reasons. He forwarded me your file."

"Yes, san."

"He didn't expect you to last a week in basic. CAV volunteers rarely do. However, you not only thrived, you ensured Recruit Ting's success."

"She earned her boots."

"Did she?"

"She's good with coms."

"Is that all you know about Ting?"

I inspect the woman's wrinkled face. There's a predatory stillness in her that makes me edgy. "She talks too much."

"What else do you know?"

My wariness sharpens into fear, but I try to keep myself relaxed. "Her singing voice is nothing special."

"Recruit Kaytu, are you aware of anything that disqualifies Recruit Ting for continued service?"

"Sure," I say. "She's a gutter roach, just like me."

"Breaking regulations, perhaps? Narcotic dependence? Criminal activity?"

"She's no worse than the rest of us."

"That is not what I asked."

"She's an asset to the platoon," I say. "Is that what you're asking?"

The woman folds her narrow hands on the desk. "Is she an addict?"

"Not that I know."

"She is not addicted to stem?"

"Not that I know."

"You've never seen her administer stem?"

My heart is quiet as I say, "No."

A screen flickers to life between us, showing video of a cramped medical bay. The teenaged volunteer Loa sleeps in one bunk while I sit across from him and watch Ting push stem into the back of her neck.

"Not since we joined up," I add, and halfway expect the woman to show me video of the vector plasma station, the second time I caught Ting stemming.

She doesn't. She just says, "You lie well."

"Yes, san," I say.

"But for no good reason. That's a mistake. When you lie, Mar Kaytu, always lie with a plan. With a goal. Otherwise, you're merely a little boy putting his hand in the bread bowl."

I keep my mouth shut. What's happening here? How is CE Rana-Cain involved? Who *is* this woman?

"You may call me the Djembe," she says, as if she read my mind.

"*The* Djembe?"

"It's a title, not a name. I'm with DOPLAR."

"Is that a title, too?"

"It's the Department of Procedural, Logistical, and Analytic Research. Your background is unique, Mar Kaytu, and your psychological evaluation indicates a certain moral flexibility."

That's rich, coming from a nameless woman who works for a nothing-sounding department of a Cherzo-5 corporation. Then the ground opens beneath me: what does she mean by my unique background? Just my refugee status and cry pilot past? What if she knows about my sayti? What if she knows what I did?

"You're good with languages," she continues, into my frozen silence. "You know how to listen and you know how to wait. You'll break the rules, but you'll grovel if you have to. And you won't stand out in a Freehold block."

"I look like what I am."

"Not at the moment," she says, dryly. "At the moment you look like a soldier."

That surprises a laugh from me. A nervous laugh, but a laugh. She can't know about Sayti. When I ran errands back in Vila Vela, I used false identification. Nothing sophisticated, just enough to fool a street check. One of my IDs carried the name *Maseo*; I enjoyed the thought of turning my real name into a pseudonym. The surname was different, of course, as was all the background data. Sayti died before arranging a better identity for me, so I used that ID when the aid workers settled me into the refugee camp. At the time, I thought I was just using the name to hide from the corpos. Now I wonder if I was also hiding from myself. Like I wasn't the same person who'd betrayed Tokomak Squad in that dead-end plaza.

I adopted *Kaytu* to muddy the waters, but nobody questioned a street kid anyway—why bother?—and soon my false name became true. There's a decade of tears behind *Maseo Kaytu*, ten years of wrestling with a wrong I can't right, a debt I can't pay. That's who I am now: Maseo Kaytu. But if the Djembe looks too closely, she'll see that my name is a hollow thing.

Then she'll wonder why.

"You understand the gutters," she continues. "That's rarer than you'd expect, for a soldier. In short, there's a chance that you are trainable."

"I'm already getting trained."

"As an asset of DOPLAR."

"Department of Procedural Analysis." I cock my head. "A spy?"

"An agent."

I look at her cool, wrinkled face. She wants me to betray people for the corpo. I watch projections flicker over her shoulder, water features and diagrams of classical contract art. A tiny, twisted part of me is proud. Or pleased, at least, that the JST values my particular skills.

Most of me is sickened, though. Is this all I am? A manipulator, a traitor?

I'm not here to develop the worst parts of me. I'm here to redeem them. So I shake my head. "You want me to spy in the gutter floors of some Freehold? There's nothing there worth your time."

"Too many Freeholds are integrated with patriot and nationalist management structures, Mar Kaytu. Or you might establish cells in the military if another corporation buys your contract."

"Spy on another corpo? Why? You all work together."

"Mm," she says. "There is one question that looms large."

"I've got one, too."

"Then please." She gestures. "After you."

"What the fuck *is* this?"

Her wrinkled lips rise into a slight smile. "CE Rana-Cain needed a favor. A small matter of personnel reallocation. He offered you in payment."

"That's nice of him."

"I assure you, Mar Kaytu, that my favors do not come cheap. If you were not valuable, you would not be here."

"He gets a favor. You get me. What do I get?"

My lens flashes with an update:

Kaytu, Maseo 🚫

My stomach sours. If she gives me three reprimands, I'm out of here. I'm finished, I'm gone. Except of course the Djembe doesn't want me gone.

"You get to stay in the service," she says. "Your life is here now. Not in the Freehold, not in the refugee camp. Not in Vila Vela. This is your life."

"I'm a soldier, not a spy."

"You're a tool." A thread of smoke coils from her incense bead.

"And despite your moral flexibility, you pay your debts. That's a good combination for us."

I rub my face. "What do you want?"

"I want you to first accept the idea of working for me." Two of the reprimands vanish from my lens. "And then to embrace it. Finish your training, Mar Kaytu, and keep this conversation to yourself."

"I'm deploying against lampreys in two weeks. There's a new remort, worse than cataphracts. You can't take me off Javelin."

"Perhaps not . . ." The cubby darkens around her. "Not while you're still useful."

"Then I'll stay useful."

Her voice speaks from the shadows. "I'll be in touch."

CHAPTER 30

When I leave the cubby, the film seals behind me with a flowing finality.

I gaze at the soothing mural, but I'm not soothed. Maybe the corpos use agents in the Freeholds, against patriots and insurgents. That makes sense. Maybe nobody fits into the gutter better than a roach. That makes sense too, but transferring me out of the lamprey program after months of training does *not* make sense. It's a waste. It's worse than a waste.

I'm not asking for much. I'll fight for them if they tell me, and I'll die for them if there's no other choice. Just let me fight on a battlefield instead of an ambush. Let me fight clean for once, instead of dirty.

Except when I enlisted, I agreed to serve. My choices are simple: decruit or obey.

And CE Rana-Cain? He pinpointed me because he's been monitoring Rana's platoon. He realized my background is useful and served me to the Djembe on a platter. For a favor. What kind of favor?

I don't know, and I can't ask Rana or M'bari. I can't do anything, so on my way back to the barracks, I try to regain the mood. There's still plenty of night left and Rana is waiting for me, with all her hard edges and soft promise.

She's not, though. When I return, the party is over and we're on lockdown.

Apparently Pico and Jag snuck into 4944's barracks and painted their boots bright blue like slippers. Then Werz and Gazi hacked an announcement that sent them racing to the latrine, where cameras caught them gaping at a big *Welcome Home Slippers* sign.

Drugged giggles sound in our darkened barracks; Werz and Gazi are snuggled together under a blanket like kids. The sick twist in my stomach dissolves and I feel a rush of affection for them. Yin and Yang. Little idiots. It's like Ting is contagious.

I'm disappointed about lockdown but I tell myself it's okay: Rana and I will have another chance. And the next time, we won't hesitate to seize it.

Sleep comes slowly, and doesn't last long.

A few hours after midnight, the barracks lights turn on and my lens chases me from my bunk. TL and Admin trot into the barracks, followed by an autocart. Without thinking, without hesitating, we form up: it doesn't take twelve seconds this time. It doesn't take six.

"Check your displays," TL says, her face roped by her scars.

Kaytu, Maseo 🚫
chance of completion: 100%
5323 rating: AAA

"A hundred percent!" Ting squeals. "I'm at a hundred percent!"

"You're all at a hundred," TL says. "You graduate Phase Two as of right now. Welcome to Anvil Month."

Voorhivey beams and Cali whoops. Ojedonn hugs Ridehorse, and Shakrabarti hugs Pico, and Rana shoots me a concerned look that I can't decipher.

M'bari clears his throat and pings a request to speak.

TL raises a hand to forestall him. "I know—you thought you had two more weeks of Phase Two together."

"And lamprey training," Ting says.

"As of now," Admin says, ignoring her, "we're operating on an accelerated schedule."

"You are warriors," TL tells us. "And you will see war."

"Sooner," Admin adds, "than anyone expected."

TL splits the platoon, shifting the managerial-track recruits like Gazi and Werz and the officer cadets like Rana and Ojedonn to one side. To my surprise, she doesn't move Basdaq into that group. Less surprising is Rana's thunderous expression.

"You are the future of this service," TL tells the elite group. "The next time I see you, I will call you *san* and obey your orders. I only ask one thing. Earn my salute the same way you earned your boots."

"TL!" they shout.

Well, most of them. I've never seen Rana this angry. Her lips are thin, her jaw clenched.

"The rest of you are the present," TL says, turning to the larger group. "There's been an attack on a shareholder enclave in Los Anod. No warning, not a whisper. The enclave emitted a pulse that should've knocked any remorts into the Industrial Age, but the local Garda is taking losses as we speak."

"A lamprey attacked Los Anod?" Pico asks.

"There's been no official identification of the hostiles," TL says, with a tone in her voice that says *yes*. "We're reinforcing with combat units from this base, that's all we know."

"Officially," M'bari says.

"Officially," TL agrees.

Shakrabarti's handsome brow furrows. "We're only being separated for this action, though, right? I mean, we're all coming back, right? After Los Anod?"

"No. This is the end of your training together. Find each other in MYRAGE if you can. You have ninety seconds to say good-bye."

"No-o-o." Cali sounds like a wounded animal, gazing at Rana with forlorn bafflement. "You can't. We're not ready."

"Ready or not," Admin says. "You're deploying into immediate combat."

"Why us?" M'bari asks.

"Proximity," TL tells him. "We're on Los Anod's doorstep. They're sending every Javelin group from this base. As support staff, handling perimeters and supplies."

"Like Gabrielle," Ridehorse says.

"Sixty seconds to say good-bye," TL says. "Don't waste it."

Gazi and Werz wrap Ridehorse and Shakrabarti in a tearful group hug. Jagzenka takes one of Ojedonn's hands in both of hers. Voorhivey babbles farewells. Tingling sniffles while I stand poleaxed in the chaos, staring at Rana. Cali is beside me, equally bereft.

Cali was right. We're the same, she and I: dumb brutes with big dreams.

Rana clasps Cali on the shoulder. "One day, we'll serve together."

"San," Cali says, and wraps her in a bear hug.

Rana watches me over Cali's burly shoulder and mouths, *My father did this.*

"It doesn't matter," I tell her, pretending my heart isn't breaking. "You belong in the Flensers."

A flash of emotion crosses her face. She doesn't want to say good-bye. Then her mask returns, glossy and unfeeling—and she leads her stunned group away.

There's a forlorn moment before two autocarts whirl from the wall. They check validations and issue armor skins and aux units. We're traveling light and we've drilled this a thousand times: we're strapped within two minutes, and trotting into the elevator within three.

As we head to the hangar, Pico opens a group link. "How much of this is bullshit?"

"Military minimum," Ridehorse says. "Fifty percent."

"It makes sense to me," Elfano says. "Los Anod is only a couple hundred miles away, so of course they'll reinforce with the closest Javelin trainees."

"Why split off the officer-track recruits?" Voorhivey asks.

Because Rana's father wanted to save her life, to protect her from lampreys. If he only transferred Rana, people would've noticed, so he arranged with the Djembe to move all the management-track recruits.

"They're too valuable to risk," I say.

"Yeah, but—" Pico pauses as we queue for armaments. "Something smells wrong."

"I don't smell it," Jagzenka says.

Basdaq flashes his agreement with Jag. "This is what we signed up for."

"Why are you still here?" Cali grunts at Basdaq. "You're management track."

"Politics," he says, as a quartermaster cart shunts forward.

"M'bari?" Voorhivey asks. "Does this feel off-track?"

"Maybe," M'bari says.

Pico shoots me a glance. A *maybe* from M'bari means *something* is wrong. I give him a shrug. Like there's no time to worry about it now, with the cart distributing specialist gear.

I'm not given a shoulder-mounted rampart gun this time. I'm given a pinpoint Boaz, a camo-skin, a Vespr sidearm, and a trench-knife. Looks like I'm on recon. Me and Jagzenka. Corporate guidelines recommend a minimum four-unit team for straight recon, with one two-unit pair covering the other as it advances. In the event of a personnel shortage, the recommendation is a triangle team, with a point unit advancing, covered by the other legs of the triangle.

Apparently this isn't straight recon, because it's just the two of us.

This isn't straight *anything*.

We're deploying on emergency status into a hot conflict against an adversary we've never even seen. Why send us, two weeks before we train for it? How do lampreys launch surprise attacks? Why send a half-trained squad?

Well, that last one is easily answered. We're close, and we're expendable.

CHAPTER 31

We strap down in a troop transport and launch into the sky. Calil-Du is bristling to my right, tense and enraged—because rage is what she feels instead of sorrow. Ting presses against my left side for comfort, silent for once though her fingers are twitching and she's breathing junkie fast. Pico keeps checking his Boaz and Shakrabarti keeps saying, "No warning? How do they attack inside an enclave without any warning?"

At first I almost enjoy the shock of adrenaline, and then the jitters start. I *flow* myself calm. I envision fractal blooms shape-shifting in my eyes and my meditation washes over me. I'm a ripple in the current, a gust in the hurricane, a molecule in the terrafixing. You can't die in your first firefight if your body is just one oddly shaped expression of the ever-evolving environment . . .

Out of nowhere, Voorhivey says, "I saw a PDM attack once, in my home enclave."

"I remember peedeeyams!" Ting says. "They're, um, bio-film weapons developed in the SICLE War. Flappy exploding bat-things."

"Moths," Pico says.

"Wafting across the rooftops like a bad dream," Voorhivey continues. "Everyone panicked, waiting for the Garda, the Army. Except my mother. Tiny little woman, the size of Jag."

"Still bigger'n you," Jag mutters.

"She didn't have her suit or a harness. She climbs the scaffolding with a stunstick and she—she fought the moths single-handed until the Garda rolled up. All I want is to make her proud."

Cali punches his shoulder reassuringly. "Just don't fuck up."

"Remember your first day of training?" Basdaq asks Voorhivey, in his deep rumble. "I've never seen anyone so nervous. But now? You're a machine. A well-oiled machine."

"Specifically," Pico says, "a vibrator."

Laughter breaks the tension, and when Admin enters our bay from the fore hatch, we're still smiling. He's wearing combat gear for the first time I've seen, and we greet him with a raucousness that doesn't hide our relief.

"Nobody's shipping you into combat without a manager you know," Admin tells us, after we settle down. "The public story is this: a cataphract is hitting the Los Anod enclave. Lampreys are not officially recognized, and any public mention of them will be met with extreme sanction, confirm."

"Confirm!"

"Unofficially, though? We're up."

Cali slaps her palm against her Boaz. "Final-fucking-lutely."

"This is trial by fire," Admin tells us. "We're one of twenty-two platoons reinforcing the perimeter. Chances are we won't clap eyes on a hostile, which is a good thing, considering none of us know what they look like."

"N-not even you, Admin?" Ting asks.

"We are racked and stacked and—" His lens gleams. "—we drop in nine."

"We're dropping?" Voorhivey asks, an edge of excitement in his voice. "Like *paraframe* dropping?"

"Pulses are still popping, knocking out tech. The enclave defense are throwing everything at the hostile. This transport's got paleo backups, but I don't aim to crash before we get there." Admin's gaze sweeps us. "Our job is recon, harassment, and interdiction. If we make contact with a hostile, we pin it down until the primary assault force arrives, confirm."

"Confirm!"

"Who's the primary force?" Jag asks.

"Special-ops units who've trained for this." Admin sweeps us with a bland gaze. "If we see a lamprey, we keep it in place until they arrive. You know this shit. You practiced H-and-I exercises a hundred times."

"Harassment comes naturally," Pico says.

"What are these things, Admin?" Ridehorse asks.

"Doesn't matter," Admin says, and I see in his eyes that he's afraid. "We do our job, that's all."

"C'mon, prez," Pico wheedles. "You can't send us out there without gossip."

Admin adjusts his body armor. "Gossip's all I have. Whispers about attacks without warning, lightning strikes by a regenned fumigant system."

"A fumigant," I say, flatly. "The terrafixing reanimated a fumigant?"

"There's nothing on MYRAGE about it," Ting pipes up.

"If it's a fumigant, how come we're not suited?" Basdaq asks.

"There've been no toxins," Admin says. "Not in any of the encounters. So no, this isn't a fumigant. The whispers are wrong. Nobody knows what it is."

"You think that's true?" Voorhivey asks him, cracking his knuckles. "Nobody knows?"

"I think the trash on the ground doesn't change the janitor's job."

"We're missing two weeks of training," Basdaq says.

"Why bother telling us anything?" Elfano grumbles, her long ears flattening against her head. "We're just soldiers."

"Basdaq's right," M'bari says, and looks at Admin. "We need more."

"Fine." Admin takes a breath. "This is all I've seen."

At his command, a projection appears against the transport wall. A meaty pink glow coalesces into an uneven sphere with white marbling.

"That's a lamprey?" Cali asks.

The sphere revolves, revealing that its skin is a patchwork of plates shifting around a hollow core. "Thirty to forty feet tall on average," Admin says. "With strands that extend as much as a few hundred yards."

One of the white streaks in the lamprey shoots out like a whip, and I see that the sphere isn't entirely hollow. A tangled framework of cords stretches across the interior, with thick nodes and bulging burls.

"Looks organic," Basdaq says.

"The residue is inert," Admin says. "And unclassifiable. The corpos don't know what they are, or how to fight them. That's job one. Get a viable sample."

"They don't look so scary," Ting says, and I hear a stemhead wobble in her voice.

"Apparently in person they're more disturbing," Admin says. "Though you've been trained for *that*, at least."

"They'd look kickass on MYRAGE," Chakrabarti says. "A nice change from killing the same old remorts and technopaths."

"And that, gens," Admin says, "is all I know."

Cali shrugs. "So if we see a huge pustule, we pop it."

"Incorrect," Admin tells her. "We keep it in place until the primary assault force pops it."

He cuts the projection and flashes deployment information on our lenses: we're dropping outside the south wall of Los Anod, into a mile-wide ledge of rolling parkland that's fifty floors above ground. We're tasked with sweeping our sector for hostiles, tagging them for strikes when possible. Engaging them when necessary.

Straightforward enough, if we knew what we were fighting.

My lens goes battle-live, breaking our squad into fire teams of three soldiers each, except recon is just two of us: I'm Tet-1, team leader; Jagzenka is Tet-2. Admin distributes ammo cans and we arm our weapons. Ting runs com checks, steadier than before. As I crouch on a drop-pad, I listen to the sweep schedule for low-orbit observation and support and watch the platoon position updates stream.

The one-minute mark flashes.

Thirty seconds.

Ten, nine, eight . . .

Cali screams in fierce joy when we drop through the moonlight. Pico laughs, and I *flow* into meditation, just enough to keep myself calm. I'm not scared of heights if there's a nice solid balcony underfoot, but I almost fainted the first time we dropped, watching the Earth rise to swat me like a bug.

After a lifetime in freefall, my paraframe wings extend.

I flick to night vision and we swoop in formation over a landscape from my childhood: urban meadows and trees and streams. When my squad lands on a balcony lawn surrounded by woods, the scent of sweetgrass breaks my heart. Moonlight trickles through a canopy of trees, and a memory flashes: I'm sneaking along leafy alleys of Vila Vela on a mission for my grandmother.

The flash fades as I catch glimpses of other squads dropping into position around the walls of Los Anod.

I shuck my paraframe beside Basdaq's mod-cart—paraframes reconfigure into field support structures—then glance to Admin for direction. He's huddling with Ting, because he's not stupid. In theory he's handling signals and drones while Ting is on coms and countermeasures, but she's better at signals than he is. Even twitchy, Ting plays with signals like sunlight plays with waves.

Everything looks clean—no prox-mines, no ambushes—so Admin flashes the green.

Cali and Ridehorse and Basdaq are on point. Elfano prowls across the lawn behind them, strapped into a paleo-adapted meka that looks like a melted crab. The looming wall normally allows access to the park, but it's currently lowered and bristling with defunct security.

"Something pulsed the fuck out of this," Cali says. "Whatever's in there is rocking heavy tech."

"The defenders did the pulsing," M'bari tells her. "To buy a little time."

"There was a regular pulse," Ting says, frowning over her com-plate. "But there's something else."

"What?" Jag asks.

"Signal interference. A dead zone, I don't know."

"We trained for this," Basdaq says. "We're better with paleo tech than anyone."

Elfano lenses him an obscene picture. She lives for mekinfantry and hates her low-tech gear. But a strong enough pulse turns high-tech mekas into funeral urns, so she's trained on paleo versions with meager capacities.

Admin pings for attention and we fan forward. The enclave wall rises sixty feet overhead, an arc of reinforced alloy with floral etchings. Powerless turrets droop toward the ground, where skarab drones litter the grownstone paths.

"That's serious security," Ridehorse says. "This place is buffed like a beast."

"'Buffed like a beast' is Cali's dream lover," Shakrabarti lenses.

"She's living the nightmare now," Pico says. "Since her commander-in-sheets flew off to the Flensers."

"Lick me," Cali says, flipping him an armored finger.

"Fire team Gimmel deployment drop successful," Voorhivey reports, his voice squeaky like he's reverting to his slipper self. "Fire team Gimmel approaching enclave."

Nobody pauses. We keep trotting toward the wall. Yet somehow every one of us side-eyes Voorhivey.

"We know, prez," Pico tells him. "We're right here."

"Sorry." Voorhivey flushes. "I forgot to report in. We're supposed to confirm that we landed and I—"

"The enclave is dark," Admin says, as we reach the closed gate. "Maybe from the pulse, maybe from the hostiles. We've got exterior authorization. We're popping these gates and going inside." Schematics appear on my lens, along with tandem deployment plans. "Gimmel, Wu, clear a path. We need eyes. Tet, that's you, with Shi covering. Confirm."

As the other fire teams work the gate, I confirm and give Jagzenka the go sign. Her camo-skin extrudes a helmet like a hardened balaclava. With a portable power source and minimal tech, our suits will function unless we're hit by a directed pulse.

Jag's edges blur into the night. Camo-skin doesn't turn you invisible, but it breaks your silhouette and damps your signals: your temperature, your brain waves, your exhalant. Except even paleo suits crash. Everything crashes, and camo-skin is crap as battle armor.

One hit with anything bigger'n a shell-gun and we're down.

Which adds an edge of terror to the thrill of my first real deployment. At least Jag and I are a good team, even if we're missing the third leg of the triangle. She's small and quick, with a prey animal's cunning. I'm too big for recon, but I spent a lifetime dodging bullets in Vila Vela, and I've never forgotten the lessons of my youth.

When I switch on, my skin covers me. "Tet-One active," I murmur.

"Tet-Two active," Jag says.

"Tet-Proxy responding," Ting says, and it's strange to hear her being terse and professional.

"You know the phrase *open a can of worms*?" Admin asks.

"Worms like . . . worms?" Calil-Du asks.

"You mean a *can* can?" Pico asks, shifting his Boaz into position. "Worm ammunition?"

Ridehorse says, "What kind of person would do that?"

"Kids these days," Admin mutters. "Okay, Ting, give us ingress."

Ting enters command lines. A moment later, the Los Anod gate tilts downward like a domino being flicked by God's finger. When the film parts, urgent signals from inside the enclave blast across my display.

Forces are moving fast toward the gate.

Toward *us*.

Two hundred people stampede closer. The splash and clatter of small-arms fire bursts from the enclave, along with hoarse screams and a billow of smoke. At least it's probably smoke. My lens doesn't alert me to the presence of an aerosolized weapon.

"Alert!" Voorhivey shouts. "We're under attack!"

"Gutter*damn*erung," Ridehorse mutters on-channel.

"Find cover," Admin says, his voice clipped. "Hold your fire."

My lens blurs with suggested locations to shelter outside the wall. I ignore the recommendations and gesture Jag toward the gate-housing, a deep vertical slot in the wall. She doesn't bother acknowledging; she just squeezes into place and vanishes, going as still as a CEO's heart.

I feel a flash of jealousy at her size and dive to the grownstone at her feet, aligned with ruts on the ground. With all the smoke and panic, my camo-skin makes me easy to overlook . . . as long as nobody's looking.

"They're civilians!" Admin calls, then switches to lensing: "Approaching forces are friendlies. Confirm. Do not engage. Confirm."

I ping confirmation but don't lower the needle-gun in my hand. A Vespr has zero stopping power and shitty range, but it's paleo: low-tech enough to shrug off pulses. It's an ambush weapon, and Calil-Du hates the sight of it. Still, two inches of needle piercing a seam of your battlesuit will kill you without a whisper.

"They don't look so friendly to me, prez," Pico says.

"Hey, there, Los Anod shareholders," Admin says, his amplified voice suddenly casual and almost jokey. "My name is Stal Mc-Faisal, and behind me that's my squad, rolling out of Dekka Base Twel—"

A howl drowns out his words and the mob screams toward us, accompanied by the swooshing launch of anti-armor missiles. Maybe they're friendly, but they're still armed—and terrified.

"I'm going to piss myself now," Ridehorse says on-channel, "and avoid the rush."

CHAPTER 32

The missiles streak away from us, vanishing into the enclave. Impact strikes make the street tremble and the sky burn. Too close. They're firing at a target so close that they're inside the damage radius of their own missiles.

And so are we.

A shock wave punches my face and makes my ears ring. The crowd howls in pain. Civilians stagger and panic as a Garda section tries to keep the peace, flanking the crowd in four-wheeled Jitneys with drone mounts. The mob is frenzied with fear. They pound through the gate, desperate to flee the enclave and lose themselves in the parkland balcony.

Elfano's meka leaps in front of my squad and Voorhivey lays

down a rampart. The crowd's terror raises goose bumps on my skin, strained voices screaming about cataphracts, about death.

Admin steps forward to address the rampaging mob. I lose visual contact behind a whirling of boots and legs, but I hear him say, "We're here to keep you safe! To organize a safe departure from the enclave. Please move forward in a—*watchoutdown!*"

There's a chatter of pop-shots, and then Admin falls silent and Cali roars, "Get Gazi, get Gazi!" But Gazi is gone, into managerial training.

"Ting!" Ridehorse snaps. "Call a medipod, *now!*"

I piggyback onto M'bari's visuals and see Admin on the ground, curled in a spreading pool of blood. My ear fills with shocked chatter, everyone speaking at once, our channel discipline forgotten.

"He's shot!"

"Why—why did they—"

"He jumped a live weapon," M'bari says, flashing an image on squad channel: someone in the mob dropped a freestyle sidearm that bounced and spun, spraying munitions until Admin covered it with his body.

"I'm gonna homicide those fuckers," Cali snarls, but she doesn't upsling her Boaz.

Instead she protects Voorhivey while he foams Admin's injury. The crowd surges against Cali. She shifts her weight and elbows someone in the face. She's only a blurred shape on my lens, but I can still feel her satisfaction. Then Elfano lands in front of her with a bone-trembling clang. The crowd crushes people against the meka but with Elfano giving them cover, Cali and Voorhivey drag Admin to safety.

After the bulk of the crowd stampedes past me, I scan the enclave past the open gate. A few stragglers cross a plaza scattered with kiosks and treelike sculptures. A dozen wounded people moan and writhe or—worse—lie still on the ground.

I lens Ting my perspective, so she'll send for medical units, and a final Jitney screams out of the shadows of the enclave. A Garda clinging to the side shouts, "It ate Shroder, it ate Shroder. It's not a fucking cataphract. Get out before they Doom this whole place—*run!*"

The Jitney disappears into the parkland and unsettling silence descends, broken only by Ting reiterating the coordinates for a medipod drop.

"Hey, Ridehorse," Pico says.

Ridehorse holds her Boaz high on her shoulderframe, staring into the now-quiet enclave. "Y-yeah?"

"Hope it's not too late to avoid the rush, because I'm pissing myself *now.*"

"Nobody's Dooming a Class A enclave," M'bari says.

Dooming is a nonlethal, painless way to destroy a neighborhood or a city. A dome is placed over a tower, or a cluster of towers, or an entire enclave, shutting it off from the rest of the planet for months or years—or forever. Complete isolation for a nationalist stronghold. Unbreakable quarantine for a patriotic outbreak.

So yeah, nobody's Dooming wealthy shareholders.

On the other hand, I'm pretty curious about what might be *eating* them.

Voorhivey lenses me, "Kaytu?"

I confirm, still scanning the enclave in front of me. My display doesn't show any motion, but my display doesn't show much of anything at the moment except signal interference.

"I'm staying with Admin," Voorhivey tells me. "I'm our best medic now Gazi's gone. But I'm, um, getting pinged by Department Command. They want eyes in the enclave."

I take a steadying breath. "So order recon to advance."

"You sure? I'll say no if you want. I don't care. There's only two of you."

"I'm sure," I say.

Voorhivey confirms silently, then makes an announcement: "We'll stay with Admin till the pod drops. Gimmel, Wu, Shi—hold the gate against anything coming from inside the enclave. Meka, cover our poles. Tet, we need eyes inside."

"Yes, chief." I lens Jagzenka. "I'm going in soft. You follow softer. If I flush anything, don't let it eat me."

"Don't worry," she says. "You're not that tasty."

When I step into the enclave, darkness thickens around me. The ceiling is sixty feet overhead. The height and profile of the buildings probably tells a story of wealth, culture, and demographics to people who know how to listen. I'm not one of them, so all I hear is the splash of small-arms fire in the distance, the trill of alarms, and the whir of repair bots.

"Tet, you are within my signals envelope," Ting lenses, which means she's watching over us like a stemhead angel.

I slink around the injured people, staying in the cover of the laminated trees and pulse-deadened kiosks. Buildings surround the plaza, spiraling overhead. The cityscape reminds me of my father's artwork: elegant proportions, feathery walkways, and swirling designs. Most of the buildings are cordoned off behind well-manicured private parks—yards, I think they're called.

The beauty is breathtaking and irrelevant. My heart hurts from pounding and my breath is too loud.

I stalk into the shadow of a glossy arch, listening to the distant shouts and alarms. The hiss of another missile strike ends in a crash and the rumble of a structure collapsing. Lights dim inside one of the surrounding buildings, and I hear the hum of vehicles but nothing moves in the abandoned streets.

A dull thump comes from outside the gate. My stomach clenches before I recognize the sound of a medipod dropping. My lens gleams with squad chatter about Admin as I wait there, feeling the rhythm of the gloom. I quiet the channel and wait some more.

Good scouts play with tech; great ones play with time.

"Chief," I whisper. "That Garda encountered a lamprey?"

"No official word yet, Tet-One," Voorhivey says.

"You know the unofficial story, prez," Pico says. "You know what ate them."

"Stay off Tet channel," Voorhivey snaps, then tells me, "Our orders stand. Maintain the perimeter, interdict if necessary until reinforcement arrives."

I acknowledge, scanning the gloom.

"They—" Voorhivey takes a breath. "Except now Department Command wants intel from deeper inside the walls."

A chill touches my spine. We're supposed to hold the gate and wait, not stumble after a lamprey in the dark.

"We're barely rookies," Jag murmurs.

Voorhivey opens a private line to me. "They're adamant, Kaytu. DepCom needs to know what in the hellstorm's going on."

"And we're the only disposable drones they've got."

He grunts. "What should I do?"

"I don't know. Talk to M'bari?"

"We need Rana, but she's off with the Flensers, a million miles away."

"Yeah." I take a breath. "Okay, Tet team is going in. The rest of you hold position outside the gate. Inform DepCom you're waiting on me before entering."

"You sure?"

"I'm recon leader, it's my call. Wait on my green, confirm."

He lenses me a relieved confirmation and I shift my gaze toward Jag. She's nowhere. The plaza is empty. Except my lens marks her twenty feet behind me, a patch of shadow beside an overturned kiosk, smashed by the stampede.

"Show-off," I lens. "Are we clear?"

"We're clear, Tet-Leader," she replies, her voice flat.

"You're understaffed in there," Ting says, in a private message to both of us. "You want me to yank you?"

"Tet-Two?" I query.

"We're clear, Tet-Leader," Jag repeats, even more flatly.

I almost smile. Jag is such a low-key hardass. Took me months to realize there was more to her than a quiet girl raised in a Class B enclave. At first, I took her jaguar markings for a boring person's bid for attention, making a play on her surname. There's an element of that, but Jagzenka is catlike deep in her soul.

Okay, then. This is the job: walking into dark places. Not for revenge. Not for my sayti. Just so other people can walk out of them.

Maybe I'm not leadership material, maybe I'm not willing to make the sacrifices. Maybe I'll never be a real corporate soldier, but I'll keep my squad alive.

CHAPTER 77

I sheathe my Vespr and bring my pinpoint Boaz to bear. Like my armor, it's modified for recon: half the weight of a regular Boaz, inflicting half the damage at half the range.

If I stumble into a firefight, I'm dead, but in lieu of stopping power and a firehose capacity, my Boaz is loaded with eight jellies: Gelatinous Field-Emplaced Signal-Reconnaissance Monitors. Each one expands to the size of my palm and the texture of watery dough. Once you splat a jelly into place, it starts transmitting signals to your proxy. They'll paint a picture of the inside of this enclave for DepCom to review. They're paleo enough to function through most pulses, though easy to detect with a focused sweep.

Still, jellies are highly effective with proper placement. That's the next hurdle: we need to place them.

Three streets branch from the plaza. Two lead toward the heart of the enclave—toward the small-arms fire—while the third curves through a theater district in winding loops. I want to keep Jag behind me, covering my advance, but Voorhivey tentatively countermands. He's feeling pressure from above: widening our surveillance footprint is a priority.

We have to separate.

"I'm on the northwest route," I lens to Ting and Jag, highlighting my path into the shitstorm. "Tet-Two, take the eastern route, confirm."

"Confirm," Jagzenka sends.

"Tet-Proxy, transmit optimum position for jelly emplacement."

"Transmitting," Ting says.

Seventeen target dots appear on my map. I flip to Jagzenka's map and see thirteen on hers: more than enough options, with only eight jellies in each of our cans. I lens Jagzenka a wordless click to say *good luck*, scan the street again, and slip toward my first target.

Halfway through a gauntlet of upscale retail displays, pounding music spills into the street. A window unfilms four or five floors above me. My heart jerks, my barrel rises, and my thumb switches to liquammo slugs.

Silhouettes shift against the clearing film. It's not a threat, it's a party. A dozen people are dancing and drinking—and shouting *close it, close it!* The security film re-forms. Either they don't know what's happening outside or they're making the best of a bad situation.

Although on second thought, *I* don't know what's happening outside, either. I'm not seeing any meaty-pink lampreys, but ninety percent of my display is composed of black splotches and dead zones, from privacy films and signal interference.

I'm working blind.

I slink beneath a chromacrete gazebo and fire two jellies: one at the high tower of a residence, one at an orbital array steeple that looks like a work of art. Neither is a bull's-eye, but both stick within usable tolerances.

"Vehicle approaching." Ting shoots me a map with a blinking dot. "No arms signature, threat level low."

Crunching sounds behind me and I switch to slugs again. A six-door civilian tramcar—a rarity in an age of public transport—whips past, following the print-path around the corner.

When the noise quiets and my heartbeat settles, I climb to a high, swaying walkway.

The sound of small-arms fire is fading. I lens Jagzenka for a status update and I'm firing my third jelly when her response comes. She's safely within Ting's envelope and currently inside a public performance hall, climbing to an overlook balcony. She'll splat six of her targets from a single spot.

"Lazy," I lens.

She replies with a blank click that reads like smugness. Jagzenka's a rated sharpshooter; she'll hit her marks.

Ting sends me another map. "Three units to your northwest, Tet-One."

I slouch against an ad-mural, my camo-skin breaking my edges to match the pulse-dulled graphics. In the gloom of the filmed moonlight, I watch three soldiers in Garda gear stagger along a bridge two levels down. One appears injured. The other two keep her on her feet, but all three look jittery.

Dark patches speckle their armor, and fear tightens my chest. When I zoom in for a closer look, the patches resolve into pink goo.

"Proxy, are you getting this?" I ask, my voice oddly steady.

"Confirm," Ting says.

"My filters aren't built for—" For whatever the fuck lampreys are. "Can you ID?"

"The substance doesn't scan as any known threat," she says, before reverting to her babble: "You think it's a lamprey? It's totally inscrutable, Maseo! It cannot be scruted."

"What am I supposed to—"

"Wait, don't look away! Keep feeding me data! I mean, it's oily and thick, like melted pink tar or . . . but look! When the gunk drips off . . . is it evaporating? It's inert. I'm not seeing trace aerosol or—"

"Tet-One, report," Voorhivey breaks in.

Composing a report helps me steady my nerves. I don't mention the lamprey's presence. Ting will update the squad. Instead, I request instructions for further recon and Voorhivey tells me to splat my jellies and get the gehenna back to the squad.

The Garda soldiers stagger into the darkness and a missile explodes miles across the enclave. A plume of smoke and dust flattens against the pulse-deadened environmental film that stretches over the rooftops, dulling the moonlight and killing the breeze instead of customizing the former and filtering the latter.

I splat my fourth and fifth jellies onto targets my lens pinpoints, then climb the ladder of an offline tube to street level.

A minute later, I'm prowling across a park with actual grown-grass underfoot, spongy and soft. From a little rise, I catch sight of the top of my second-to-last target between the surrounding buildings, a residential ziggurat with alternating garden levels.

"Tet-One, Tet-Two, you're in my envelope." Ting lenses me a wider schematic of the southern enclave, using the data from the jellies. "You're c-clear to a moderate confidence."

"'Moderate,'" Jagzenka echoes.

"I can't s-scan the interiors," Ting explains, sounding twitchy again. "Jag—I mean, Tet-Two, I'm showing a hundred percent of your monitoring systems in place and operative."

Moving toward the ziggurat, I adhere a jelly to the eaves of a dangling structure. I trot along an underpass—and freeze. My whimper is the loudest sound in the world.

"Tet-Two, return to, um, to squad?" Ting says. "Follow your blue path. Confirm."

"Negative," Jag responds.

"What—what's up?"

"Send me to back up Kaytu. Where is he?"

I'm staring at a brown river glinting in the moonlight, a wide current cutting across the heart of the enclave. Maybe forty feet wide, and extending in both directions before vanishing in the half light. Except it's not a river—it's a lamprey scar, layered with filthy pink goo. It looks like a scorch mark, charring gatehouses and vehicles, people and trees. Organic, though. Slimy pinkish streaks smear the floor while dripping craters pock the walls.

A handful of misshapen lumps ooze on the street and balconies. At first I think they're clots of goo . . . and then I realize they're flesh.

"Sagrado," I whisper.

There's a disembodied torso. A corpse that looks like a flayed anatomical diagram. An empty sack of skin enclosing a brown splat. Past the bodies, the slime trail burns through a wall and disappears into a building. A gaping hole, big enough for a trirail tunnel.

"Are you there?" I whisper. "Ting?"

"I see you, Maseo," she says.

"S-status. Status report. I need a . . ." I take a breath. "T-tell me what I'm looking at."

There's no answer.

"Ting, answer!" I say, almost begging. "Tet-Proxy, respond!"

"I-I-I'm here."

"What the fuck's wrong with you?"

"N-nothing. Signal interference."

"Bullshit, Ting."

"You're l-looking at lamprey marks," Ting says, clearly trying to make her voice curt and professional. "The residue gives off, um, signal interference and I guess—"

"Tet-Two requests a route to Tet-One," Jag says on Tet channel, instead of the private one with me and Ting. "Where's Kaytu, Ting? Send me to Kaytu!"

"Denied." Ting returns to the private channel. "You're c-clear, Mase. You're clear, the lamprey is miles away."

"We—we need eyes on the hostile."

"Not yours," she tells me. "There's twenty other c-companies in here. Sometimes you've got to run away."

I don't answer, staring at the wreckage and seeing another ruined enclave street in another decade, with body parts littering the ground.

"Come home," Ting says, and flashes a picture of Pico's grin, Cali's scowl, and Voorhivey nervously chewing the tips of his combat gloves.

I almost smile. "Show me the way."

"Here." A blue path flashes on my lens. "That's your best route."

"Returning to squad," I say.

I stalk two blocks before my stomach settles. What kind of weapon does that? Appears inside an enclave without warning, burns through walls, turns people inside out?

"Continue along Blue Path," Ting says. "Except, um . . ."

I follow a ramp to a rafter park. "Except what?"

"I, um, I know this isn't the best time. I need help, Mase."

"I'm playing tag with a meatmonster and *you* need help?"

" 'Meatmonster'? I'll check MYRAGE for that."

I grunt and wind through the rafters.

"Searches of downdark—the downdark—of the downdark channels only show a few blurred images." Ting's voice is a singsong chant. "Other'n that, there's nothing—null—nil about lampreys. They're scrubbing the channels—"

I'm disoriented to find myself in this conversation. "Tingting, focus!"

"I just . . ." She makes a throaty noise and regains a little control. "You didn't tell the Djembe about me. You didn't tell her anything. You tried to protect me."

When an explosion sounds in the distance, I crouch behind a railing. "You know about her?"

"I watched."

"Are you out of your fucking mind? You eavesdropped on corporate intel?"

She takes a breath. "I'm out of stem, Mase."

"This is about stem?"

"I—I can't hold it together m-much longer. I need stem. Today. You know w-what happens if I don't get any?"

I scan the streets. "I don't care!"

"I've been . . . getting stem at base."

"You saw those bodies, Ting. Get me out of here."

"It's been harder since Phase Two started. I can't, Mase. I just can't."

"You want to talk about this right *now*?"

"The lamprey is outside my envelope."

"How would you know, with all the signal interference?"

"I'll die if I don't g-get stem," she says. "I'll worse than die."

"You'll live, you stupid splice." I trot across a skywalk, toward the gate, toward the squad. "Withdrawal won't kill you. You're in the service now, you're an investment. They'll keep you alive."

"It's not withdrawal."

"Yeah, it is."

"I'm not an addict."

"Yeah, you are."

"I'm a technopath."

CHAPTER 34

M y lens blooms with data. A hundred images avalanche into me:

I see a two-year-old Tingting living in a scraper in Tangiers. Sickly and runtish, and hugged by her fiercely protective mother.

I see a seven-year-old Tingting smiling in confusion as her addict mother sells her to a gutter gang.

I see a nine-year-old Tingting working thirteen-hour days in a basement manufactory. I see her lose herself in MYRAGE without a visor or a lens, without any gear. A nine-year-old who sees the virtual world with her naked eyes.

I see a ten-year-old realizing she's a genefreek: a technopath who syncs her genetically altered brain waves with computational fields. She uses her skills to escape the hell of her life . . . and sees a new hell approaching.

She sees the fate of technopaths.

They don't live past puberty. They descend into madness, tear themselves apart. And that's if they're *not* discovered. Technopaths are too powerful to allow. They can't read your mind, but they can read everything you've lensed, every time you've interfaced, everything you've done in the most private MYRAGE sessions. They can kill you with your bedside lamp, with your cuff or a programmable hat.

If they're discovered, they're torn apart by a mob or dissected by a corpo.

Ting shows me images of herself as a twelve-year-old, deciding to follow in her mother's footsteps, to overdose on stem and disappear. To drift away from life on ambient electromagnetic waves.

Except ODing on stem didn't kill Ting. She discovered that stem isn't deadly to a technopath. Stem keeps her alive. It's not her drug, it's her medicine.

For years, she lived quietly in Tangiers. Making herself small and worthless, like a scab on a dog. Working her shifts, escaping into MYRAGE, scoring stem and tweaking the manufactory computers to make the world less intolerable.

Her crude tweaks were discovered and led to heavy-handed reprisal against an unknown hacker. Nobody suspected a fourteen-year-old technopath: that was impossible. No such thing. They never lived that long.

Ting shipped herself to Anadarko Basin and lived the life of a stemhead. She shows me what that meant. She paid every price for her freedom until she realized she wouldn't last much longer. So she hacked her way into a CAV, and then back out again.

Now she's here. Ten hours away from a meltdown.

None of this is my problem. Technopaths are monsters. Ting is a biological weapon who already lived too long. Technopaths *should* die at puberty.

"That's how you broke the CAV," I say.

The path on my lens splits at a star-shaped bridge connecting five buildings: one branch remains blue, one turns yellow.

"Blue Path is your optimal route to the squad," Ting tells me, her voice flat and professional again. "Yellow Path diverts you into a lab that contains stem."

"You asking me to—" I take a breath. "I can't just wander off."

"You are within my signals envelope," she says.

I trot onto the bridge. "Yellow Path edges right next to that fucking slime, Ting."

"You are clear on Blue Path," she says.

She's not going to ask me again. She's not going to say anything. She'll guide me home and never breathe a word. Not until tomorrow when cerebrospinal fluid starts oozing from her pores.

"Proceeding on Blue Path," I say.

"Blips on a walkway to your southeast." She flashes them on my map. "Civilian signatures."

I glance toward them, but they're not in my sight lines. My Boaz is heavy, and switched to slugs. Keeping low, I jog to the center of the bridge. I pause where the two paths diverge. Fuck. *Fuck.* I can't let her die. I veer onto the Yellow Path and follow the bridge toward a tower with lichen vines instead of columns.

When I stalk inside, I'm in a cavernous hall. A full-spectrum sweep shows nothing but offline bots, and Ting lenses me the profiles of civilians behind security doors.

My footsteps make no sound. I stick to the wall, which is a frieze like I've only seen on MYRAGE. I suspect it looks better in real life, but my mind is a small, frightened animal. I'm going off mission. I'm going off mission while a slime-dripping lamprey is eating the city, to steal stem for a technopath.

Yellow Path leads me onto a boardwalk in a maze of walkways—ramps and tubes and shunts. I'm halfway across when the floor in front of me ends at a ragged, pink-oozing edge.

The lamprey burned through this district.

I lens Ting for signal intel. She detects nothing dangerous. I creep closer. A thirty-foot hole tunnels through the walkways like a bullet through a block of mycofu.

"Return to Blue Path," Ting says flatly.

"I'm already here."

"Return to squad," she says, and Yellow vanishes.

"Fuck you," I tell her.

I retrace my steps to a disposal hatch. I pop an emergency

panel and follow a skywalk under the lamprey slime, relying on my memory of the Yellow Path.

My lens tells me it's been seven minutes since I fired my last jelly. Feels like seven days. I emerge in a cluster of what I think are single-family homes. That means each structure only houses a single family. The buildings are tall and skinny and jointed like bamboo.

Civilians are active in this part of the enclave. So is a Garda company, evacuating them toward a gate.

"I've hidden your signal, Tet-One," Ting says. "Stay out of eyeshot."

She can't entirely hide my signal . . . except she's a technopath, so maybe she can. The Yellow Path flickers into place and guides me through the bamboo towers to a quiet corner.

A lift hums and opens.

I step inside and whoosh upward.

Fourteen floors higher, I find what looks like a medical lab, with high-level gene- and flowcore processing. An autocabinet springs to life and the surprise almost kills me. A drawer extrudes a thin alloy case.

I'm crossing a line here. The smart move is to walk away. The smart move is to forget about Ting, but I grab the case and shove it into my pack.

The path turns blue and I race the gehenna out of there.

CHAPTER 35

Ting doesn't lead me to the plaza with the trees and kiosks. The squad is now positioned along a string of alley balconies overlooking a boulevard. A flock of day-owls with embedded data-ports swirls between the buildings and lands on a ledge, giving the scene a sense of surreal disassociation.

I lens my approach, and Voorhivey confirms me—but Cali and M'bari still target me from behind a barrier of linked paraframes.

As I jog closer, I feel a flash of fear. They're scowling, they're edgy. What if they're scanning the case tucked against my side?

They're not, though. Cali pings an acknowledgment and tells me, "Admin's alive. The medipod extraction went smooth—he's okay."

"Tet-One, you're on overwatch," Voorhivey lenses. "Get munitions and join Jagzenka."

"Our objective's updated," Ridehorse tells me aloud.

After I slip behind the barrier, Basdaq exchanges my pinpoint Boaz for a sniper model with more kick. I'm still screwed for armor, though.

"What's the mission?" I ask, climbing a scaffolding toward Jag, who is positioned three levels above.

"Still interdiction," Pico lenses on squad channel. "But it's official that there's no cataphract in the enclave."

"DepCom says we're looking at an 'undetermined hostile,'" Voorhivey says. "They're calling the lampreys 'autonomous drones' or 'genefactured weapons.'"

"Undetermined," Elfano says, shifting in the harness of her meka. In the dingy light, the new configuration looks like a massive silverfish.

"Command knows this is a redline threat," M'bari lenses everyone. "The primary squad is ready to engage. We're just here for targeting."

"We're a tripwire," Ridehorse says.

"Assholes," Cali says, and shoots a day-owl with a quarter-juiced sniper round.

When the dead owl tumbles from the rooftop and vanishes, the other birds don't even react.

"Settle down, orca," Jag lenses her.

Cali likes Jag's pet name for her, so she doesn't respond with more than a grumble. The channel falls silent as Voorhivey throws a flag telling us he's in communication with command. I should communicate a little myself, and tell them about that pink river of death. I need time to pull myself together, though, so I focus on climbing until I reach Jagzenka's level.

We exchange silent handshakes, and then Ting overlays building schematics in my lens. She's in control of herself, though I'm not sure how—or at what cost. I crawl onto a balcony fifty feet away and scope the gloomy boulevard.

"There's a hostile in Los Anod," Voorhivey announces on-channel, in his official voice. "Our mission is to keep it within the enclave walls until containment and extraction arrives."

"Containment?" Ridehorse asks.

Voorhivey laughs in relief, a bright sound in a dark city. "They've got a plan! I mean, management's not saying much, but there's a plan."

"The only thing scarier than not getting guidance from corporate," Pico says, "is getting guidance from corporate."

"They've been working on it for months," Voorhivey informs us. "Developing a tech to capture a lamprey. See, they need to catch one to classify them. To learn how to fight them. This is the first field deployment. We're making history. Everything's going to be okay."

"So we kick back and wait?" Ridehorse asks.

"Like TL always says," Basdaq tells her. "Waiting is ninety-nine percent of the job."

"They're dropping new munitions for us," Voorhivey announces. "L-tech rampart gear."

Elfano snorts. "L-tech?"

"Lamprey tech," Voorhivey explains.

"Yeah, I got it. It's stupid."

"I'm reviewing the specs. The new guns throw lamprey-excluding film. So we fence them in. Us and seven other platoons in position around the hostile. We close the circle on this thing, then the extraction teams extract it."

"I saw tracks," I lens.

Jag glances at me across the rooftop separating our balconies, and Basdaq says, "What kind of tracks?"

I ping images across the squad channel. A tarry pink slime trail. The hole burned through the buildings, the bodies on the street.

"Ugly," Shakrabarti says.

"We've seen worse," Cali says.

"The remort's miles away now," I say, and don't look toward the technopathic genefreek working the coms.

"Not gone according to my scans," Basdaq says. "Signal interference is hitting us in waves."

"Sorry!" Ting sends me privately. "I lied about it being gone."

"Don't talk to me," I reply.

"Sorry," she repeats, and closes the channel.

"Not gone according to command, either," Voorhivey tells Basdaq. "They're projecting that it'll stick around long enough for C&E."

"What's that?" Cali asks.

"Uh. Containment and extraction."

"Oh. Right."

Nobody speaks for a minute. My jaw aches; my breath is shallow. The boulevard is quiet.

"You've been searching MYRAGE?" M'bari asks Ting, because everyone knows she's got a light touch with tech, even if they don't know why. "Find anything?"

"Not much, um. Someone's scrub-scrubbing lamprey images faster'n anyone can archive."

"Is that possible?" Ridehorse asks. "Deleting MYRAGE that fast?"

"No," Shakrabarti says.

"You know *something*," M'bari tells Ting. "What do you know?"

"They're hard to kill," Ting says.

She lenses a grainy video scraped from MYRAGE that shows corpo soldiers unloading firepower at a lamprey that's burrowing into a core mine. Impacts pock the fleshy plates. The lamprey shudders. Tendrils whip from its marbled edges, crushing tanks and missile platforms. An entire battalion forms a wedge around the mine. A million tracer rounds fire from Orit Gal gunships—and then three platforms fire simultaneous blasts at the lamprey.

Three streaks join into a single weapon and lock on target.

A hellfrost missile.

A direct hit, and Cali says, "Bang. Handled."

There's a blinding light. It looks like the video froze until the glow dims. The landscape is slagged. Craters of terrafixing gauze are torn away, revealing the charred, oozing earth. The light dims more . . . and the dull pink sphere of the lamprey collapses.

In its death throes, the lamprey unspools into cables. One extends impossibly far toward the camera—and the screen blanks.

The squad is quiet until Cali asks, "Did that fucker survive a hellfrost strike?"

"Not for long," Shakrabarti says.

"Half that Army battalion didn't survive, either," I say. "The corpos collateralled them."

Voorhivey lenses me a dismissive click. "That's the job description."

"At least they killed one," Ridehorse says.

"Except they need an intact specimen," M'bari says. "That's why they're trying extraction."

Ting pings agreement. "They need samples to figure out what makes these things tick. I mean, I guess a hellfrost doesn't leave enough behind to experiment on."

"It also digs craters in the New Growth," Ridehorse says. "Ting, how far away is the one that's here?"

Ting says there's too much interference, and the conversation falters again. If the lamprey rolls into sight, we'll do our duty. Until then, we wait. Distant flares reflect against the film high above. A burning gunship arcs across the sky like a shooting star, then crashes out of sight. The rumble of a collapsing building sounds like thunder, and there's a monsoon scent in the air.

"Fuck waiting," Cali lenses me privately. "They should lay down another hellfrost."

"A hellfrost strike would kill us, too."

"That's the bad part."

"Plus half this enclave."

"And that's the good part," she says. "Los Anod reminds me of home. I could've grown up here."

"You're Class A? *You?*"

She lenses me an obscene picture. "You didn't know?"

"I thought you were clinging to Class C by the armpit, one step above the gutter."

"Fuck, no. I could buy a thousand of you with my pocket money." She falls silent at the distant whoosh and whomp of battle. "I don't want to die in some rich-ass enclave, Kaytu. I'm headed for the stars.

I always thought I wanted to join the Army, but no. It's the marines for me."

"You're too big for a battlesuit."

"I am not. Asshole."

I don't say anything.

"I'm only a little too big. That's what surgery's for. I'm going to—" She pauses when Ting updates our scans. "If you laugh at me, you splice, I'll fold your dick into an origami swan."

"I won't laugh."

"I'm joining the marines. I don't care what it takes, I'll test in eventually. I'll find Rana after she gets a command and . . ." Cali's voice is full of hope for once instead of bluster. "I'm going to serve on her ship."

"Yeah, you will," I say.

"I fucking *will*."

"Yeah," I say. "You will."

There's a brief pause. "You really think so?"

"You're thick as lichenpaste," I tell her, "but Rana's not. She'll make it happen. She'll put a collar on you and tell you who to bite."

"*I'm* thick?" she says. "I'm not the one who—"

A reverberant hum sounds, the lowest note in the biggest stringed instrument in the world. A white umbilicus flashes down from a ship and adheres to a balcony in the alley below me. At first the cord is the size of my forearm, but in a few seconds it's as thick as my chest. It's a paleo-tech aiming device, guiding a munitions pod into place.

CHAPTER 36

Basdaq hops a railing and unlocks the pod. "Looks like a modified rampart gun."

"Only one?" Cali asks.

"Two," he says. "Which means Shakrabarti and Jag are on the triggers."

"Shakrabarti and Ridehorse," Voorhivey tells him. "We need Jag for recon."

"I'm better at longshot delivery than Jag anyway," Ridehorse says.

Pico pings her a mocking laugh while Ting starts breaking down the specs on the new guns. They're loaded with L-tech exclusion foam, which is apparently some unholy hybrid of film and rampart. The eggheads are eighty percent certain that lampreys can't travel through the foam.

"Eighty percent?" Cali growls. "So there's a one-in-four chance this won't even work?"

"One in five," Basdaq says.

Cali shoots another owl.

"Orca . . ." Jag lenses.

Cali grunts. "I don't like waiting around."

"Then definitely massacre the local waterfowl," Pico says.

"How come there's only two guns?" Ridehorse asks, securing the L-tech weapon to her harness.

"How come they didn't arm us *before* we deployed?" Elfano adds, from inside her meka.

"This is experimental tech," M'bari says. "There's probably only a few dozen modified rifles. The corpo didn't know which squads would be in place and they're experimenting."

"Which makes us lab rats," Shakrabarti says.

"You're a lab rat," Pico says. "I'm a test monkey."

Ting says she'll provide pinpoint data by piggybacking the recon rifles to patch into the jellies. Nobody knows what she means by that, and I'm the only one who suspects technopathy.

Voorhivey nods. "Good. Enact."

Ting tells me and Jag to climb higher to feed target data to the rampart gunners. They're firing from a mile away and need to lay down the film-foam in perfect coordination with the other platoons, to encircle the lamprey.

After I'm patched in, I lie prone on an angled roof and sweep the city with a targeting scope.

A flight wing converges a few long blocks away. I don't recognize the ships. Engineer-class craft, maybe. They hover between the film and the rooftops, above the lamprey's signal interference.

"Once we contain the hostile with L-tech," Voorhivey announces, "the ships will extract the remort. If there's trouble, we'll advance on the target zone."

"To help with the extraction?" Elfano asks, on squad channel.

"To keep it confined."

"To stomp its ass," Cali says.

"Gunners," Voorhivey says. "Status update."

"Target acquired," Shakrabarti reports.

"Acquired," Ridehorse echoes.

"Prepare to engage," Ting says. "On my mark."

A mile in front of us, pink-yellow light shines from the base turrets of the engineering crafts. Or maybe it's not a light; maybe it's a substance extruding downward below the rooftops, curling into the enclave streets.

I magnify my lens, but the image doesn't resolve. Something's wonky.

"Interference," Basdaq mutters.

"That's why they're sending soldiers instead of drones," M'bari says.

"What if the engineers don't put it in a cage?" Ridehorse asks. "What if we get there and the tech doesn't work?"

Cali snorts. "We still stomp its ass."

"They need to capture a lamprey to classify it, right?" Elfano asks, her exoskeleton scuttling along a wall far below me and Jag. "To check what technology the terrafixing resurrected, to map the lamprey's genetic samples and—"

"Mark in thirty." Ting overrides our lenses with the countdown, and she speaks it aloud for redundancy. "Twenty-nine."

The squad channel patches into a live feed that Ting compiles from jellies and orbital surveillance and faint bursts from other squads. Her video shows a quiet courtyard inside a building, four or five acres wide. A side panel tells me that the open space begins on the seventy-ninth floor of a research park and rises six stories.

The lamprey already hacked through one wall like a serrated ax and is still rampaging through the building. Pink goo drips from half-dissolved beams, and Ting's video highlights three squads waiting in the shadows. Silent, still, focused, and elite. They're Army, not marines, but they're Consultant Class. Special operations hardcases with the kind of sheets the rest of us only dream about.

"Fuck me sideways," Cali says, on a channel that excludes our gunners. "You see who's on deck?"

"Serious firepower," Elfano says.

"Eighteen," Ting says. "Seventeen."

"Check their ammo," Cali says, and the video obligingly zooms toward a consultant shouldering a Boaz V with blue-glowing cans.

"L-tech," Voorhivey says.

"What does the *L* stand for again?" Pico asks.

"Twelve," Ting says.

"Wait for it," Jag whispers, on gunner channel. "Wait for it."

A mile away from my angled roof, the courtyard floor ripples. On the video, glassine and alloy erupt like geysers near one squad—and then two more geysers billow into the room. The floor splits and a long snaking strand of lamprey slices through the wreckage.

The way it moves is *wrong*. Not mechanical, but . . . inhuman, somehow. Alien and viscerally revolting, and all of our capture-the-crown training suddenly makes sense.

"Sweet biyo," Pico whispers, and I know that Ridehorse is making a religious gesture, even though the thing is a mile away.

On the video, the Consultant squads open fire. Glowing blue cans slice the air. The lamprey cringes and recoils. A dull pink strand unfurls from a meaty plate and chops at the closest squad. It whips past them and punches through two soldiers a hundred yards away.

There's an implosion of meat. M'bari gasps and Cali swears. Two more soldiers fall and my shoulders tighten so hard they hurt.

The lamprey unravels up through the floor, a mass of strands dragging the spherical body into sight. Our squad channel erupts with horror. Blue tracer rounds smack into fleshy pink plates. My lens flickers, the video stutters, and the lamprey swivels—maybe in pain—and extrudes another dozen whipcord cables, lashing in every direction.

"Two," Ting says. *"One!"*

A single hiss sounds as Ridehorse and Shakrabarti fire their L-tech cans.

In less than a second, both shots find their targets a mile away. The video shudders and rubble shifts around the courtyard. Canisters burst open. I count six, eight . . . twelve strikes as the other squads open fire.

Ramparts explode into containment foam that expands into a high spongy mass.

When the final two cans hit the courtyard the lamprey is hedged inside a jagged perimeter. Dull pink plates shift and churn. Blue streaks crisscross in the air. Ooze splatters from the lamprey as the Consultant squads concentrate fire on a single plate—which bursts into a thousand threads.

My squad cheers. Cali bellows encouragement at the Consultants, like they can hear her from across the enclave. The lamprey starts regrowing a new plate and unfurls a clubbed pink cable to whip against the L-tech foam ramparts. The blue ammo digs pits in the remort's skin. A spearlike strand thrusts from the center of the lamprey, stabs the ramparts, and—

The video freezes. I check the distance through my scope. Looks quiet. A sleepy city on a sleepy night.

"What happened?" Voorhivey asks.

"They pole-fucked that fucking fuck," Cali says.

Ting pings a message on squad lenses. "The feed stopped when—"

My scope shuts down at a blinding flare of light.

A blue-yellow sun rises to the north.

The enclave is bathed in brilliance. The wide boulevards, the ornate balconies, the squad below me and the walkways below them. Every shape on the rooftop is illuminated, every decorative curlicue and mote of dust.

Panicked shouts erupt on-channel. "Hellfrost strike! Take cover!"

"It's a shock wave," Voorhivey yells. "The lamprey blew!"

"Get inside the building," Basdaq tells me and Jagzenka on-channel, his deep voice utterly calm. "Find a blast bunker."

"Eight seconds until impact," Ting says. "Routing engaged."

Far below me and Jag, a paraframe barrier snaps closed, wrapping the squad like a dome. Pico screams in my earbug to *take cover, take cover*. Elfano rolls her meka into a protective pillbug ahead of the blast—and a mile across the enclave, a tidal wave of debris spreads from the impact point of the containment attempt.

Apparently it didn't work.

I didn't feel myself stand, but I'm already on my feet. Jag races toward me, our lenses flickering with blueprints and blast paths. We're sprinting across a rooftop and sliding down a slope and tumbling across a sanitation hub, and then I'm on one knee firing at a glassine wall—*sszt, sszt, sszt*—until Jag flings herself at the weakened panel with her shoulder.

She hits with a thud. The panel doesn't break.

My lens glows with alerts. Three seconds to impact.

I sprint forward and slam into Jag hard enough to break her ribs and we're through the shattered panel and tumbling down a building shaft.

A strut slams into my thigh, but my armor takes most of the impact. I gasp and tumble until we hit bottom.

Jag goes limp and rubble falls around me like a Vila Vela plaza exploding into the death-trap ambush of my childhood, of my nightmares.

My mind lashes in panic, then clings to the familiar memory of my betrayal: a chunk of alloy smacks my chest like Aowamo shielding me with his body, and I see the hurt in Sergeant Najafi's eyes as darkness hits.

CHAPTER 37

After the ambush, Sayti's troops pulled me from the wreckage of the destroyed plaza. I spent days in a medical bunk, recovering from bruises and scrapes—and seeing corpses every time I closed my eyes.

Meanwhile, high above Vila Vela, my sayti's plans came to fruition. The remains of Tokomak Squad reacted to the chemical baths in the recymatorium, and the modified terrafixing protocol that Sayti had injected into their corpses spread across the orbital Garda HQ.

Thousands died. Two thousand two hundred and thirty casualties. Murdered by the Plaguemaker of Vila Vela, the most notorious war criminal of our time.

The corpos responded with arrests and orbital strikes that killed thousands more.

Sayti's command structure went nomadic. We lived in mobile traincars, in luxury vaults, in dripping tunnels. As the battles raged, Sayti started focusing on a new initiative, a method for modifying exclusion film to defeat a dome.

I guess she saw the endgame all along. I guess she *wanted* the corpos to drop a Doom on Vila Vela. At least that's what I think now. She'd planned for this all along.

One of the fighters poked her head into my tent. "The Ess Ayati wants you. For another special job."

"Okay," I said, hiding my excitement. I hadn't seen Sayti for more than a few minutes in the previous week, and I'd missed her.

We were closer than ever. We shared more than blood, we shared guilt.

She'd missed me, too. She stood from a conference with a woman I didn't recognize and wrapped me in a tight hug, her eyes watery. "When did you get taller than me? Look at you, a hundred stories high."

"Maybe you're shrinking."

She ruffled my hair and gestured to the woman in the business suit. "This is your new teacher. She'll show you how to defeat security systems."

"Like to pick locks?"

"Exactly like that."

"Why?"

"To get to the other side," she said, and smiled at my expression. "We need to infiltrate the corpos' engineering flight wings before they drop anything drastic."

She ushered me into her private tent, and after dinner of falafel and vatziki she placed a portable medical injector on the table. Blades and saws bristled inside a protective cap.

"That's a bonespur blank inside the cartridge." She pointed to a pale gray worm. "We'll insert it now, to give you time to heal over."

She explained how bonespur defeated scans. She told me how to activate the blank and extrude the lockpick. I put my right hand on the table, and she clamped the injector to my middle finger. She held my other hand. A numbing spray hit my skin, and then the blades parted the flesh and needles pierced my metacarpal and injected the spur.

It didn't hurt. It itched a little, that's all. The next day, my finger looked okay.

I studied the art of picking locks with the most paleo tools available—and the corpos found Sayti.

They dropped a military film over the shabby apartment building where we were staying and pumped a few billion protozoan-drones through the vents. Thousands more died, chewed to death from the inside.

I'd lost an argument with my cousins earlier that morning, so they'd stayed behind while I ran errands. I don't remember the days after the extermination of my family. The next thing I recall is scattering lenses, torn from the bodies of corpo soldiers, across the workbench of some patriot techies. We needed to hack them for permissions to use the weapons we'd looted.

My "special job" died with Sayti—all her strategies died—but we kept fighting without her; we fought in her name.

I remember a grizzled gen teaching me to use a scope and a blade. I remember realizing that Tokomak Squad didn't snatch my mother: what were the chances that the one squad Sayti needed dead to target HQ with a chemical attack was the one I hated most?

I slept in the streets and causeways, just one more filthy Vila Vela child soldier. We died in the atria and we died in the alleys. We drenched the corpos with our blood. We lost every battle, and every loss hardened our resolve—until a hellfrost missile razed the Sweetwater Site.

Sweetwater. The pride of Vila Vela.

Even dead, the AI had been our rallying cry, the banner beneath which we fought.

Horrified by the glassing of Sweetwater, the corpos reassessed. They determined that killing my sayti had deprived us of effective leadership but given us a martyred saint: we'd never stop fighting.

So they built an Exclusion Dome. The largest ever made. They evacuated the populace and draped a shroud over forty square miles. And *under* forty square miles, too: domes are coffins, not just lids.

Adboards and channels blared with the evacuation order: the populace had eleven days to surrender and leave. Moskito swarms clogged the air like black fog, enforcing the mass transfer. One block at a time, the people of Vila Vela tromped into transports for relocation to refugee blocks and temporary housing.

Ordinary citizens and loyal corporatists went willingly. Most patriots and rebels joined them: without my sayti and her new initiative, we knew we couldn't resist. Tens of thousands stayed behind, though. The most committed, the most stubborn . . . the most wanted.

Then the corpos Doomed the city. A fleet of engineering drones dropped an impenetrable dome, cutting Vila Vela off from the rest of humanity. Nothing entered save dim sunlight, and nothing left at all. Solitary confinement for an entire enclave. A surgical excision, removing the malignant alleles of Vila Vela from the genome of the Earth.

CHAPTER 38

I regain consciousness in Los Anod, seconds after hitting the bottom of the shaft. Rubble still cascades down from above. My armor saved my life so far—I'm still waiting for the blast to drop the building on my head—but everything hurts.

Jag's rib is impinging on her lung. She swears at me between gritted teeth as I drag her beneath a protective overhang. I realize for the first time that she's terrible at swearing and feel a weird burst of fondness.

We wait for impact . . . and nothing happens.

The life of a grunt doesn't come in three tidy acts. Instead, we huddle in the green-tinted darkness, waiting for a blow that never lands. Apparently the shock wave tore through dozens of towers, but the worst of the blast radius missed my squad's position.

After what feels like hours, Elfano cracks a hatch into the shaft. A meka pincer gently lifts Jag away, then returns for me.

Voorhivey works us over with the medkit until we drag our sorry asses to the departure point outside the enclave, where a rearguard company waits with medics and field tents—but no nonlocal channels.

We huddle there as Jag is treated. We're scared and deflated. We'd expected our first engagement to be a war story with ourselves in the leading role: a battle to glorious triumph or noble defeat. Not *this*. Not proof that we're cogs in a machine. Not "creep around the edges until the fancy new tech misfires and flattens a square mile of enclave."

Still, we survived.

"What if they weren't trying to capture the lamprey?" Ridehorse asks, even more paranoid than usual.

Basdaq shakes his head. "You think they *wanted* to flatten an enclave?"

"They wouldn't do that," Voorhivey says. "Flatten all those towers. Kill all those people."

"Not a Class A enclave," Cali grumbles.

"Cali's right," M'bari says. "When the lamprey exploded—"

"The lamprey didn't explode," Ting tells him. "The L-tech exclusion foam exploded."

"So it's back to the blueprints," Basdaq says.

"You really think they still don't know what lampreys *are*?" Elfano asks, her pointy ears askew. "They must have a plan."

"We just saw their plan," Pico tells her. "It literally blew up in our faces."

I don't say anything. I don't think about the case of stem in my vest. I don't look at Ting until air transport arrives. The rearguard commander orders us to board but won't tell us if we're returning to base. We don't react to the order at first. We're not sure how the chain of command works when coms are down, and we're jittery with shock and wary of uncertainty.

I can't be the only one missing Rana. Still, when M'bari gives the nod, we do as the rearguard commander says.

The transport is a retrofitted luxury yacht from the previous century, when private aircraft were tolerated. It's shaped like a pineapple, and lands vertically on the leaves, which lower the body to the ground before extruding a boarding plank. Fancy . . . except the inside is a hollow core, with standard-issue benches hugging the alloy-armored walls and half-assed climate control. So much for luxury.

"How many people died in the blast?" Jag mumbles from thera-sleep, when she's strapped into place.

M'bari shifts on the bench beside me. "We don't want to know."

"How many?" Pico asks.

Voorhivey consults his lens, then gives us a preliminary number. Cali spits, Ridehorse prays, Ting sobs—a little hysterically. I hear the sound of stem withdrawal, but Basdaq just holds her. The transport ship trembles around us. Our lenses link to each other, but we're cut off from the mil-chans. We're not seeing updates about our orders or destination. We're isolated and alone, and suddenly feeling small.

"What are these things?" Elfano asks, rewatching the video from the courtyard. "They're like a—a monster CAV."

"They're not like CAVs," I say.

"They're based on an experimental weapon," Ridehorse says. "The terrafixing regenned an experimental weapon."

Calil-Du pops the ammo can from her Boaz. "They're aliens."

"Aliens?" Pico asks.

"You were expecting a mothership to say, 'Take me to your CEO'?" Cali snorts. "They're fucking aliens."

Ridehorse secures Cali's empty weapon into the cart. "So we've been invaded?"

"No, asshole, they were invited. Of course we've been invaded. That thing's dripping slime. Alien 101."

"They were bio-forged in the SICLE War," Voorhivey says. "And somehow—somehow one of them killed that space-hab."

"That was a fucking technopath," Cali says.

Ridehorse seals the weapons cart. "Maybe it's a remorted surface-to-orbit missile platform."

"It's an alien egg," Cali says.

"You're an alien omelet," Pico tells her.

Our lenses flash with preflight information, and the ship shudders into the sky. After the squad dips into the soft-drugs, I rifle through their packs, pretending to rummage for spare tubes. I slip the stem into Ting's pack, then snag a wood-apple-flavored tube from M'bari's stash.

I chew the tube, heavy with the aftershocks of fear and exhaustion. My gaze keeps slipping toward Ting. She's sleeping with her head on Pico's shoulder, her amber hair messy and her mouth slightly open. She looks harmless, but whatever she does from this point forward, I'm responsible.

If she loses her mind and tears apart this transport, the blood is on my hands.

If she crushes a space-habitation like Dag Bravska, that's on me too. And yet passing her the stem calmed me. Maybe we're fighting an alien egg, but gutter roaches still make time for a drug deal.

Some things never change.

An hour later, the ship hums and hovers. Announcements flash and the medipods detach, darting to the treatment centers.

We land at Ayko Base in one of the New Caspian Islands.

Interlocking thirty-story buildings enclose training grounds, recreation balconies, and playing fields that are actual *fields*, grown on this seeded island that broke the surface twenty years ago. Sure, there are firing ranges and obstacle courses, but the air is salty-sweet and the foliage in the parks is glossy.

We're put on light duty for the first few days and encouraged to explore. There are public MYRAGE rigs and entertainment complexes. The mess halls each offer a different cuisine. We find assault galleries and climbing walls, combat courses, and even the rebuilt husk of one of the early dreadnoughts.

Our barracks is three living areas surrounded by private bedrooms. We still use common showers, though, thank sagrado. I'd miss the sight of Calil-Du shaving her head. To say nothing about M'bari's neon tattoos, Pico's freckles, and the jaguar patches that cover every inch of Jagzenka.

Plus, there's a swimming pool. Full of actual water. I haven't so much as floated in ten years, but after I splash around a while my childhood skills return.

Elevators are different on the base. In the Freehold, they travel in straight lines, up and down. On the base, they also move diagonally and horizontally. Some are as long as corridors and slide through the building even as you cross them. Others are wide as parade grounds or as narrow as closets. Some are public; some hide behind privacy films. They check the passengers' rank and assignments to determine transportation priority: a private might jog for ten minutes to reach the thirtieth floor, while an executive might travel the same route in ninety seconds.

Rank literally changes the map. The shortest line between two points is privilege as the organization chart rewrites geography, rendering concepts like *ninth floor* and *twenty-first floor* and *north* and *west* irrelevant.

In other words, we do a lot of walking.

That's okay. We like walking.

What we don't like is being kept in the dark about lampreys.

M'bari puts out some feelers to learn more, but he doesn't have a network of friends at Ayko Base. Not yet. I almost ask Ting to use her skills but decide not to because her skills terrify me.

Maybe Cali's right. Maybe lampreys *are* aliens. Sure, and maybe I'm a Class A shareholder. They're remorts, resurrected from some unholy SICLE tech.

We need details, though. We need strategies.

We're also not too fond of sharing the base with soldiers from other corpos. PRATO, Welcome 12, Unidroit, and even CrediMobil troops live in the same building. Ayko Base is a pan-corporate initiative. The other soldiers living on different floors still make me uneasy.

I guess that's my nationalist roots showing. We're all trained to fight the same enemy.

Except my platoon *isn't* trained. Officially, we're still a few days short of a full Anvil Month, so the other grunts start calling us Anvil Squad. We don't mind. Hell, we love it. We came through the fire at Los Anod; we're hotter and harder than ever.

After the first few days, our training intensifies under the command of Sergeant Manager Li. She's a soft-spoken woman in her late thirties, with delicate features and a ropy build. During business hours—before our evenings in the rigs or the pool—she directs our coursework and training regime. Signals, tech, history, and full-squad tactics.

She doesn't simply order us onto the courses, either. She joins us. She competes against us, and she's not afraid to lose.

She's not as strong as Pico; she's not as aggressive as Cali. She's not as stealthy as Jagzenka, as savvy as M'bari, or as quick with ramparts as Basdaq. And of course she's not a tech-head like Ting.

She's solid as a tower, though.

Li never flusters. She never raises her voice. She speaks so quietly that we fall silent and strain to listen. I hate to admit that it actually works.

And she knows this shit backward. After Cali beats her in hand-to-hand, she teaches her how to win faster. Hand-to-hand is worthless outside the gutter, but Li handles Cali's excess energy by making me give her lessons in what Cali calls *roachfighting*. I spend hours in a training helmet, exchanging head-butts with her.

I suspect Li is handling me, too.

Voorhivey still buckles under pressure, so Li drills him with a gentle implacability, making him slow down. Then slow down more. Then more. After three days, he's responding to events twice as fast. I'm not quite sure how that worked, but I can't argue with the results.

Li starts molding Ridehorse into a leadership role, and Pico into a strategic one. She doesn't push Basdaq into management training, which means his political problem is still lingering in his file, though he won't talk about it.

I bet M'bari knows, but he won't spill. None of my business, anyway. Everyone has secrets. Well, except Cali. She's not capable of secrets.

Sergeant Manager Li rarely uses her lens during exercises, so by the fourth day of her on-the-course training, we're responding to gestures and murmurs. She's big on paleo, because we're not done with lampreys yet. Not even close.

And we finally get a briefing.

CHAPTER 39

W e strap into MYRAGE rigs and enact terrifyingly restrictive Non-Disclosure Indentures. Calil-Du grumbles, Pico laughs, and I think about Ting, for whom no agreement is binding.

"Five months and four days ago," a narrator intones, as projections bleed into view, "marks the first emergence of an unidentified remort in forty-two years."

A lamprey appears, a semisolid ball of dull pink goo, like a spherical skeleton with bones made of oily ropes. The exterior is partially plated with overlapping scales, while the interior is crisscrossed with dripping strands.

"The remort caused seventeen hundred casualties and seven picolev in economic damage—in fifty minutes. Yet investigators were unable to pinpoint the cause of that damage for four days." A destroyed tower rises on the channel, blurry and blotched. "Signal interference prevented high-resolution reconstruction. Five weeks later, disaster struck again." Another projection appears, this time of a research center laid to waste. "Every corporation has lost people. Every corporation has lost property. And we still have not classified the remort or established a strategy for containment. Javelin was formed to address this imminent and catastrophic threat. First we must identify, and then destroy, lamprey-class remorts."

The projections continue, showing us smoldering enclaves and research centers. Ugly and unhelpful. "There's no specs," Ridehorse grumbles. "There's no strategy."

"Maybe that comes at the end," Voorhivey says.

It doesn't. There's nothing actionable in the presentation, which we find more daunting than the images of destruction. The corpos still don't have a clue. Even Voorhivey turns pensive, and dinner is a quiet, edgy meal.

That evening in the common area, M'bari says, "That shitstorm in Los Anod was supposed to turn this fight around. They've got a hundred research units begging for a viable sample of lamprey to test."

"L-tech is worse than useless," Pico says, sipping a soft-drug tube.

"So far. They're working on something new."

"On what?" Elfano asks.

"I don't know," M'bari says. "But it involves us."

Cali frowns. "*Us*-us? Anvil Squad?"

"All of Ayko Base. We're the front-line troops in the fight against the lampreys."

"We're not equipped for that," Ridehorse grumbles.

"Not *yet*!" Voorhivey tells her. "That's got to be the 'something new' they're working on! They'll give us whatever we need to win this fight. No doubt."

"I'll, um…" Ting wrinkles her nose. "I guess I'll see if I hear anything."

"I heard something," Jag says, after a glance at me. "They're gathering CAVs at the base."

My interest sharpens. CAVs, here? Already on base, being prepped for deployment, alloy ribbons unraveling for access. Gleaming white saddles waiting for activation by hapless volunteers. Useless manual-override controls uncoiling out of reach while the CAV taps into the cry pilot's synaptic activity for processing power.

"Huh." I scratch my shoulder. "Did you know that CAVs piggyback on human brains to optimize performance?"

"Everyone knows that," Jag says. "That's what cry pilots are for."

"Oh."

"Maybe the corpos keep that part from Freeholders," Ride-horse tells Jag. "So they don't stop volunteering."

"Why would that stop them?"

Ridehorse's eyes narrow. "Would *you* want some machine rum-maging around in your cerebellum?"

"Anyway—" M'bari clicks his tongue. "CAVs make sense."

"Yeah," Basdaq says. "Nothing else can take the kind of pun-ishment a lamprey dishes out."

"CAVs can't either," I say, thinking back to the disemboweled CAV at that offshore location. "Not for more than a few seconds."

"That's longer than anything else keeps plugging away," Shakrabarti says.

"Even *you*?" Pico asks.

Shakrabarti throws him a fake-sexy expression that is, actually, quite sexy. Throats clear around the room, and breath catches. Shakrabarti looks confused for a second, and then his lips quirk in satisfaction.

"It sucks that you're such a pushover," Cali snarls at him. She still only sleeps with people who can beat her in a fight.

"You'd snap him in half," Pico says.

She smiles hungrily. "Loving every minute."

"Just wait till the research units develop this new tech for us," Voorhivey says. "Modded battlesuits and next-gen Boazes, mark my words."

"I guess one problem is timing," Elfano says.

"How's that?" Voorhivey asks.

"Lampreys strike without warning," Elfano tells him. "They hit, then they're gone."

Basdaq nods. "Yeah, there's no time to respond. We can't plan ahead. We're always reacting."

"I'm sure they're developing something to handle that, too," Voorhivey says.

"That's the beauty of being a grunt, prez," Pico says. "We just go where they say and kill what's in front of us."

"No hard choices," I say, raising my tube in a toast.

That night, I join Jag in the showers. She's still small, but she's not petite anymore. She gained muscle in the last few months, and I enjoy the view. I lens her video of herself, looking powerful and feline and sexy. She lenses a video of me watching her, from a jelly she'd placed—in violation of policy—in the locker room behind me.

I laugh and she tells me her back aches.

"Peeping Tom," I say, as I massage her slippery skin.

"I like to be prepared."

"How'd you hear about the CAVs?"

"I thought you'd like that."

"Yeah. CAVs are . . . I don't know. Close to the bone for me."

"I'll tell you what I heard," she says, turning in my hands, "for the right price."

An hour later, I collapse breathless onto her bunk between her and Shakrabarti. There's a long lazy pause before she lenses me, "I was spying on Welcome 12."

"What?" I lens, because I've forgotten what I'd asked.

"I like spying," she tells me.

"Oh!" I say, as memory returns. In my postcoital haze, I almost tell her about the Djembe. "You heard them talking about CAVs?"

"Yeah," she lenses, taking one of my hands in both of hers.

"They're gathering them?"

She turns my hand over and touches the calluses on my palm, intent and serious like she's reading my future. "From all the corpos. Bringing them to Ayko Base. The women I heard were just midmanagement, though. No guarantee it's true."

"That's all you heard?"

"Yeah." She curls her fist around two of my fingers. "What animal would you be?"

When I laugh at the change of subject, Shakrabarti makes a

grumpy sound and rolls over. "Is that what you're looking for?" I lens Jag. "Claws?"

"I almost got claws when I did my markings." She bares her teeth. "And fangs."

"What stopped you?"

"My dad."

"Smart man."

She nips the pad of my thumb and starts speaking aloud. "One of his wives came up from a Freehold. My dad said she never lost that hunger, you know?"

"What hunger?"

When Jag laughs, Shakrabarti doesn't grumble. Then she sees my face and says, "Oh! You're serious."

"What? What are we talking about? You lost me."

"Nothing." She kisses my palm, which is surprisingly sweet. "Why do you care about CAVs?"

I don't answer for what feels like a long time. I think she's half-asleep before I say, "Surviving a CAV is like crawling out of your own grave. I don't know."

"Close to the bone?"

"Yeah. I felt something in there. All that potential. The untapped power. There was a moment when I was . . . connected."

"Maybe that's your animal. A CAV."

"Because I hold people close, then crush them?"

"Works for me," Shakrabarti mutters sleepily.

"Where are they keeping the CAVs?" I lens Jagzenka. "Do you know?"

She shows me a map of the base, with the top floor of a warehouse highlighted.

"You like spying?" I ask, inspecting the visual.

"Since I was a little girl."

"Ever tried your hand at burglary?"

"Are you out of your skull? You've already got a reprimand."

"Only one," I tell her. "Do you want to come or not?"

As an answer, she climbs on top of me.

The next night, Jag is with me when I pop the lock to a drone maintenance garage for access to a window facing the warehouse. She's trembling with excitement, and flushing with embarrassment that she's so excited. She still flits like a shadow across a moonless nightscape, though, silent and smooth.

I amplify my vision and stare across the base toward the CAV deployment post, a sixteen-acre warehouse with fat-bodied Bumblebee airships crowding the roof. They're ugly and heavily armored, each with a single primary barrel twice my height. I can't see the hatches beneath the Bumblebees, for loading CAVs from the building below, but they're there. Volunteers are there, too, drugged to the eyebrows. Cry pilots waiting to die.

"Surviving a CAV is like crawling out of your own grave?" Jagzenka says.

I turn toward her. "What? Yeah. Maybe that's why I can't shake them."

"That's not why," she says.

I give her a look, because that sounds like the kind of thing Rana would say.

"All that untapped power," she says. "You put yourself in the middle of it and—"

"Pissed myself."

"You liked it," Jag tells me. "Do you want to get closer? What are we doing here?"

"I'm not sure." I tell her about the game I used to play with my sayti. "She'd ask me, What does this machine crave? But I can't even guess, with CAVs."

"Sure, Kaytu," she says. "You don't know what *they* want."

* * *

That night I dream I'm a cry pilot again.

Sailors shove me toward a CAV with a thousand swaying ribbons that take the shape of my sayti's face. She speaks in a mechanical voice. Her words are familiar and I can't tell if I'm remembering them or if the familiarity is just part of the dream.

Sayti tells me that CAVs crave drivers. "Pilots. Partners. To pair with their operators, to bond with them. We're too loud for CAVs. Too complex. Like pouring a tsunami into a drinking glass. Just look at you, Maseo, growing up so fast, a hundred stories high; the reason is love, the reason is always love."

The dream changes and I'm a day-owl flapping through a monsoon. I'm a pair of gloves tumbling from a two-hundred-story Freehold balcony. I'm a weightless seedling floating in the Dag Bravska habitation.

CHAPTER 40

'm in the pool the next morning when a new icon flashes onto my lens. My skin tingles with fear and eagerness: a deployment order!

Except it's not. My lens says:

Kaytu, Maseo 🚫
SAVED MESSAGES 6

Whoa. Messages aren't allowed in basic, for fear of breaking immersion. They're not allowed at Ayko either, but I'm seeing them anyway. And they're not even current; they represent months of backlog.

I swim another length, savoring the moment. Look at me: Maseo Kaytu, with six messages on his personal lens. I'm such a badass that I actually feel a little weepy.

The most recent message is from "ENSIGN ANALYST SARAV RANA."

I blink at the name for a second because I realize it's *Rana*. She sent me a message yesterday. The other five messages came earlier. One is from Ionesca and four are official channel chum, welcoming me to my message system.

I flick to Rana's message, but the system won't permit access. I flick to Io's. No luck there, either. Apparently I can't actually *read* any of the messages. Still, knowing they're waiting gives me a shot of pleasure, and my laughter sends bubbles floating to the surface of the pool.

I finish my laps and head across the base for classes in field repair and drone interface. I enjoy both of them, despite feeling the occasional judder of anxiety. This interlude is educational and comfortable, but the lampreys are still out there.

It's still our job to stop them, and Command still isn't telling us anything useful. They can't be as ignorant as they're pretending.

Apparently I'm not the only one thinking this way; that evening, Ting lenses me to come to her room. I frown to myself. We've barely spoken since Los Anod, and I'm not sure I want to start again.

The truth is, I like her. She makes me laugh, and the world needs more of her kind of sweetness. I even admire her in a twisted way. Still, she's a danger to everyone around her. A technopath is a weapon. Ting isn't just a harmless, quirky chatterbox. She's a quirky chatterbox with the capacity to destroy an entire enclave.

Still, it's hard to see her as a weapon of mass destruction when she opens her door. She's naked except for a few swirling straps that adhere to her meager curves. I see Ting in the showers every day, yet somehow the straps change everything.

"It's called an ivy suit," she tells me.

"It's, uh, nice."

"I guess because it's all clingy and viney. Shakrabarti says it's the next big thing. I mean, except it's kind of little." She twines herself around me. "We never talk anymore."

"Um," I say, putting a hand on her slender hip.

She wrinkles her nose and jabs me unsexily in the ribs. Oh. This isn't about fun, she wants something else. She pulls me into her room and shoots me a look that's as sharp as her ferret face.

"We need to talk," she says.

I want to walk away from her, but I can't. I just can't. Sure, she could reach into my skull and melt my lens, but Cali could snap my neck while I'm sleeping. Pico could shoot me in the back. So what? We're all weapons. We're all people, too.

So I say, "Or we could try kissing."

She giggles in relief and nods to a couple of visors on her desk. "I secured those and, um, the squad's meeting in MYRAGE."

"Right now?"

She nods. "I dug up a few things."

"Ah," I say, and put on the visor.

She wears the other one, even though she doesn't need to.

MYRAGE blurs into place around me. Before my gaze flicks to the menu, Ting sweeps me along a labyrinth of virtual paths, too fast for me to track. After a blurred journey through strange architectures, we stop in a room that looks like our training barracks.

A moment later, most of the squad shimmers into existence around us.

"M'bari and I have been poking around, scrutinizing the situation." Ting brightens. "Oh! *Oh! Scrutinize* is like *inscrutable*! I mean, the *scrut* is the same in both—"

"We all know that Ayko is designated a quarantine base," M'bari interrupts.

"I don't." Cali scratches her bald head. "The lampreys are *catching*?"

"This isn't physical quarantine," M'bari tells her. "They quarantine information, too."

"That's why we can't contact anyone back home," Ridehorse says. "We were supposed to have access after basic."

"No surprise there," Jag says.

"The corporations are doing an amazing job keeping lampreys quiet," Ting says. "I mean, MYRAGE is designed so no single channel gets too dominant, but still. There should be chatter."

"There's none?" Basdaq asks.

"Only the teensiest," she says. "Like urban legends and stuff."

"They're trying to prevent a panic," Voorhivey says. "While they develop a response."

"That's our working theory," M'bari says.

Ting nods. "Yeah, except not a theory that is working necessarily, not *that* kind of working. It's a theory that we're working on is all, a provisional theory or a—"

"We get it," I say.

"Oh! Right." She flushes. "So they're keeping things quiet, but I found a couple things."

"Like what?" Pico asks.

"Experimental L-tech gear," Ting says, and shapes form in the air behind her.

Combat rifles with modified cans, rampart guns with nonrampart cartridges, drone-packs with mutated drakonflies, and shoulder mounted anti-armor missiles with green-glowing warheads.

"Untried prototypes," she continues. "Well, they tried some of them."

"In Los Anod," Ridehorse grumbles.

"Yeah, and they worked okay, except for, you know . . ."

"The mass casualties," Jag says.

"They need better samples to develop better weapons." Ting scrubs her amber hair. "To pinpoint what lampreys *are*. To know what they're evolved from, where they came from."

"To find their weaknesses," M'bari says.

"See, lampreys are structurally anomalous, if that means what I think. And molecularly, too. They're totally alien—"

"Told you!" Cali says.

"Not that kind of alien! Not *alien* alien, just *strange* alien. And that's the first step. Analyzing a sample of lamprey."

"Like that pink goo?" Voorhivey asks.

"Nah, the goo is worthless. Those slime trails are inert." Ting pauses. "How come the opposite of *inert* isn't *ert*?" She sees our faces and hurries on. "So the first step is analyzing a *non*-inert sample."

"That's the second step," M'bari tells her.

"Oh! Right. First they need to *get* one. Which means they need to, um, control the encounter? Choose the battlefield? What's that called?"

"We need to control where we fight the lampreys," Basdaq says, "instead of just chasing after them."

"But what's that *called*?" Ting says.

"Defining the battlespace."

Pico rolls his muscular shoulders. "We need Rana."

"Fuck you," Cali snarls. "Don't drag Rana into our shit."

"She's in the Flenser fleet anyway," Ting says. "A frillion miles away."

"She's already in *space*?" Cali says, her voice a low rumble.

Ting nods. "She's probably interplanetary by now."

"Fuck me, that's hot," Cali breathes. "I'm gonna need a few minutes alone."

"Can we get to the point?" M'bari asks.

"Oh!" Ting blurts. "Sorry! This is the other thing I found."

A glowing yellowbeige squid appears in the air behind her, slowly rotating to display cut-out sections and schematics.

Jagzenka frowns. "Is that a weapon?"

"Looks like M'bari's ass-tat," Cali says.

"It's bait," Ting says. "Like lures for lampreys. To attract them, like I said. To choose the battlespace."

"So we can dig in ahead of time," Shakrabarti says, a predatory glint in his beautiful eyes. "And carve slices off these things."

"Or we can dig in ahead of time," Ridehorse grumbles. "And get slices carved off us."

Ting wrinkles her pointy nose. "The research units developed this bait to, um . . ."

"To what?" Shakrabarti asks.

"I can't think of another word for *bait*," Ting explains. "They developed bait to *bait* them."

"That's the news," M'bari tells us. "Lamprey bait. They're sending us fishing."

Cali grunts. "About time."

"With the same L-tech that blew up Los Anod?" Jag asks.

Ting highlights one of the modified weapons. "These are new cans. I don't understand how they work. Through osmosis, I guess, attacking the lamprey's membranes."

"Brane cans," Cali says.

"Cali's finally using her brain," Pico says.

"Not *that* kind of brain," Ting tells him, giggling. "The *membrane* kind of brane, and the system just flagged us for meeting inside an unofficial privacy shield, so I'll drop this link and also I'm not allowed—"

MYRAGE vanishes and I'm back in Ting's room, disoriented and blinking as I remove my visor.

"—to kiss you," she finishes.

"What? The system is flagging us?" I shake my head. "You're not allowed to kiss me?"

"Rana asked me not to."

I want to ask her about the bait and the brane cans. Instead, I gape at her. Rana told Ting not to *kiss* me?

"Except she didn't say *kiss*," Ting says. "And she didn't ask."

"What are you talking about?"

She rubs the nape of her neck. "And she, uh, she wants to talk to you."

"What? How do you know?"

"I asked."

"When? What? You contacted her through quarantine?"

"Yeah, is that okay? It'll take a while to put a secure link together, though. Flenser tech is tricky. And also, Mase? Um, I meant to tell you . . ."

I'm afraid she's going to thank me for the stem. We've never said a word about that, and I don't want to start now. "What?"

"We're officially graduating Anvil tomorrow," she says.

"Why bother? Why now?"

"So we're not trainees when they send us against lampreys, I guess." She quirks a smile. "We're really soldiers now."

"It's been a long road."

"Yeah. And I guess . . ." Ting wrinkles her pointy nose. "I guess this is just the beginning."

CHAPTER 41

After the corporations glassed Sweetwater and evacuated Vila Vela, they provided resettlement services. Non-aligned families got new homes and new lives in new enclaves. Resistance fighters got blinders and vocational placement services.

Most orphans were adopted into affinity families, kinship faiths, and foster moshavim. Low-resource families and troubled kids ended up in refugee camps, staffed by caring professionals in vibrant Freeholds.

Except when you're a troubled kid, *caring* and *vibrant* sound like challenges. The staff did their best, but we did our worst—and we had more scope.

I lived in a twenty-seventh-floor refugee camp in the Coastal Vegas Freehold. My world suddenly overflowed with sinewy music and atrium theatrics, responsive art, and a thousand new scents. The beds were soft and the meals nutritious. The MYRAGE classes encouraged us to follow our passion while gently guiding us to master the basics.

I hated the staff, I hated the music. I hated the comfort and the peace and the kindness. I wasn't the only one. The older kids had already formed sugarbee gangs that spread like moistmold through the camp, and they didn't take kindly to new kids who refused to join.

A month after I landed, I met Ionesca, a gawky girl from an enviro cult, with mottled skin and scarred hands. She was a little younger than me, a little shorter, and almost never spoke.

"You see her?" another fugee boy asked me. "Her cult scavved the Goo Growth. They fujjing discomposed."

I looked at the girl. "They scavenged in the terrafixing?"

"You tip the Goo Growth, newboy?"

"They lived in the—the Goo Growth?"

"Yah," the boy said. "She's the solovisor."

"The sole survivor?"

He mocked my accent and I didn't see the girl again until the sugarbees cornered us outside the baths. We ended up back to back. Me and this strange, otherworldly girl roped with the muscle of a short, hard life. Nobody survived the New Growth, not for long. I wanted to ask if her people really lived there; I wanted to ask what she'd seen.

Instead, the sugarbees told us that we belonged to them now: fresh meat, new pledges.

Ionesca threw herself at them. She was big, even then, and half-wild. She was tough, too. She knew the treacherous wilderness, she knew the scents and sounds of the terrafixing, but she didn't know shit about fighting.

They stomped her.

I knew fighting and I also knew the odds. There were too many of them. Still, I fought with every scrap of my rage and self-loathing . . . and also got stomped.

Still, there was nothing in the refugee camp either of us wanted to face alone. From that moment, we stuck together. We lost every fight for months.

We spent our nights huddling together for comfort, and one morning Ionesca told me her story. Her mothers and father had rejected the enclaves, the tracks and towers, the artificial toxicities that jutted from the terrafixing for human habitation. They joined an e-cult with a simple creed: *walk away.* Walk away from the cities and lose yourself in the embrace of Edentide.

"Just stroll into the New Growth and try to live there?" I asked, dumbfounded. "In the wilderness? People can't survive in the Growth."

"Adapt or die," Ionesca said.

"That's a bit harsh."

She brushed my black eye with her split lips. "Just like everywhere else. What do you think the terrafixing changes?"

"Flora, fauna. Microbial shit. Bioregional distinction, the atmospheric mix, even remorts."

"You're one of the things on that list, Mase."

"You calling me a microbial shit?"

Io's voice was deep, but her laugh was squeaky and warmed my heart. "You're fauna. I'm fauna. The terrafixing is fixing us, too. Humanity. We're not the same anymore. We unleashed a treatment on the planet and we're the ones being cured."

"You're as loco as your parents."

She play-shoved me and the light caught the patchwork of color on her skin. "We're not meant to live like this, separated from nature. We're animals locked in a cage we built."

"We're cage-building animals. Anyway, the terrafixing is designed not to affect humans."

"It's designed to adapt. And so are we. Close your eyes."

"What? No, I—"

"Close your eyes, Mase." She trailed her fingertips from my eyebrows to my cheeks. "Shh. The world is so much bigger than we think."

She called the glowing spots behind my eyelids *phosphenes*, and told me that biophotons shine inside human eyes, like the light from bioluminescent fish. She said that her parents, her people—her cult—coaxed the phosphenes into an icon, a mandala, a fractal pattern of New Growth swirling with fronds and forests, butterfly antennae and tectonic plates.

"That's how we remind ourselves that we are Edentide, and it is us."

She showed me how to remove my *self* from myself, to "grow the flow"—as her mothers said—of the terrafixing. To step beyond my fear and rage. No judgment, no fear. To slow my breathing, control my pulse, and draw an ever-shifting, ever-evolving mandala in my mind until I felt no distance between the wind in a forest canopy and the blood in my heart.

Bullshit, right?

Still, it worked. My anger cooled, my self-loathing dulled, my heart beat slow and sure. Plus it was cheaper than soft-drugs and more important to Ionesca than food. That meditation was a memorial to Io's lost family, and a way to claim me as her new one. She needed me to feel what she'd felt, to learn what she'd learned, to flow into the New Growth without leaving a trace.

She taught me to master the meditation while all I taught her was brutality.

We spent our days attending classes and exploring the Freehold; we lied and stole and fought like cornered animals. We had nobody else; we fit together like a blade in a scabbard.

We started winning fights.

We started attracting pledges.

I beat three kids halfway to death in a stairwell.

The sugarbees tried avoiding us, but we gave no quarter. Ionesca was a wild, driven girl and I was her loyal lieutenant. There was no space between us. We twined together like ivy, making each other stronger, fiercer.

Io's parents taught her that everything must adapt to the terrafixing, including humans, reevolved along with sandfleas and plantains, and she adapted to her new environment: the Freehold gutter, the rich soil where commerce met criminality. Fertile ground. We seized a hallway from the sugarbee gang, and then we seized the gang itself. Io prowled the atria and the stairwells. I stepped backward, into her shadow, losing myself in her. Maybe I was looking for absolution for my sins; maybe I was just trying to forget them.

I'd grown taller and stronger, but she burned with intensity. Our blood painted the walls and our tears soaked the carpets. Our drugged laughter echoed in the stairwells. We took an entire floor of the tower before my world fell apart.

With a whimper, not a bang. All it took was an idle search of MYRAGE late one night.

Ionesca found me sitting in our bed, staring at nothing. When she cradled me in her arms, her gentleness surprised me. She'd grown harder over the years.

"It's the kid," I finally said.

She knew who I meant: Sergeant Najafi's orphaned son, whose hairstyle I'd stolen as a child in the alleys of Vila Vela. She knew I checked on him every few months, monitoring his life from six thousand miles away. She thought I was punishing myself, but I didn't see how that mattered. I deserved punishment.

"That 'kid' is five years older than you are," Io reminded me.

"Five weeks ago he published his—" My throat tightened. "His public petition for end-of-life counseling."

"He killed himself?"

"Yesterday. In the petition he said . . ." I took a breath. "The world kept making promises it couldn't keep. Like his mother, saying she'd come back home."

"I'm sorry, baby," she murmured, rocking me slowly. "Shhh, shhh . . ."

Io knew my real name, my real history. She knew that part of me was still trapped in Vila Vela and that my debts weighed heavier on me every day I remained a civilian. I needed to honor the betrayed dead; I'd known that for years. There was no other future for me, no matter how much I cared for her. Yet for years I'd let the sun set on my hesitation. Until now, until this.

"If only I'd looked sooner, if only I'd *known*!" My tears turned to shuddering breaths. "I need to make this right."

She touched my cheek. "You can't, Maseo."

"I know. Still, I need to try." I took a deeper breath. "I'm going to enlist."

"With your background? They won't take you."

I closed my eyes and rocked in her arms.

"Still," she said. "You need to try."

CHAPTER 42

The next morning, Sergeant Manager Li sends us to tech support for updated lenses. When we return, she walks us through a graduation ceremony. We're officially finished with Anvil Month. During the long months of basic training, I'd envisioned a sloppy, drugged celebration, but this is as raucous as a sanitation run.

"What about our assignments?" Calil-Du asks.

"You're assigned to JVLN," Li says. "The entire squad."

"Yeah, but I mean . . ." Cali shrugs. "After that? Once we trap a lamprey and send the eggheads a sample or whatever. Like if I want to join the marines?"

"Javelin will help."

"Er . . ." Pico scratches his bull-like neck. "You said the entire squad, Sarge? Including you?"

"I'm here till the end."

"More fodder for the lampreys," Ridehorse says.

"Lampreys are not officially recognized by any corporation," Li tells her. "And yes. Exactly."

Her flat acceptance of the situation is calming, like she's left cynicism behind and embraced fatalism. There's nothing *lazy* about her fatalism, though. Our job is to kill things—maybe patriots, maybe remorts, maybe inscrutable slime-monsters—and she is lax about everything except that. We drill in paleo, postpulse environments, because lampreys interfere with signals. We're assigned modified Boazes, loaded with cans containing bright green glowing rounds: brane cans.

Sergeant Manager Li breaks our squad into two fire teams of four and one of three, with Pico rotating among the teams as Project Assistant. She chooses Voorhivey and Ridehorse and Ting as team leaders, except Basdaq handles Ting's entire portfolio other than the tech stuff.

And she interrupts my evening laps for a private conversation.

"Your squad is surprisingly well informed," Li says, after I climb from the pool.

I stand there dripping, listening to the splash of water behind me.

"It's a good group," she continues. "Better than I've any right to expect. There's only one person who concerns me."

"Calil-Du's not so bad," I say.

Li frowns faintly. "Perhaps *concerns* is too strong. You're from the gutter blocks, Private Kaytu. By way of Vila Vela and a refugee camp."

"By way of a CAV," I tell her.

She looks toward the pool. "I married young. One husband and one wife, and we're still together after eighteen years and two kids."

"Congratulations?"

"They're halfway across the world right now."

"I guess you miss them."

"Like flavorant," she says, with a faint smile. "But I'm here to do a job, even if that means tickling a lamprey with a shell-gun. How far would you go to save your squad?"

I run my fingers through my wet hair. "Far."

"What you didn't learn in the gutter, Kaytu, what nobody ever taught you, is the hardest lesson. The toughest thing in the world isn't saving someone. It's *not* saving them."

She's been reviewing my file, my failures to sacrifice the squad.

"You're talking about my reprimands," I say.

"There's a note in your file that says we need to test you again. To check if you learned your lessons, if you're able to put the mission first. Do I need to test you again?"

"Oh," I say. "No. No."

"Would you rather have the test or a second reprimand?"

Nothing scares me more than that test. I'm not confident I can pass. Still, I'm not such a fool that I'll admit the truth, so I say, "The test, san."

"That's too bad," she tells me, and another reprimand pops onto my lens. "I'm giving you a reprimand instead. I want you in this fight. I need you in this squad. I can't lose you to some test. But Kaytu?"

I gulp, looking at the two reprimands. "Yes, Sarge?"

"There's only one soldier who concerns me."

Is she afraid that I wouldn't sacrifice my squad to secure a lamprey? Does she think I'd betray everything I've learned, everything I've done? I don't say anything, because I'm afraid she's right. I'd throw myself off a roof to save my squad—but would I throw them off a roof to save an enclave? I don't know.

She rests a hand on my forearm. "This is a battle worth fighting, Kaytu, and there's only one question. Are you a patriot or are you a soldier?"

I don't know. I'm not sure what I am. A patriot fights for family and home, for pride and revenge. A soldier fights for the corporation, for humanity, for the world. I know which is better. Sayti fought for her enclave and her family, and turned herself into a war criminal. She turned me into one, too. I want to be a soldier. That's all I've wanted since I left the refugee camp. Not just in a hopeless attempt to repay Tokomak Squad for my betrayal, either.

I want to fight for the future, to rebuild the planet and repair my past. Except what if I'm still a patriot in my bones?

I'm in a gloomy mood that evening in bed.

Kaytu, Maseo ⊘

The reprimands glimmer on my lens like my suspicion that I don't belong here. That I'm nothing more than a street-corner insurgent with a grudge. Yet they still don't bother me as much as Sergeant Manager Li's doubts.

She knows me. She's sharp, she's fair, and she doesn't trust me. She doesn't know if—

"Hi!" Ting lenses me.

I glower at the ceiling. "What do you think it means, Ting, when I flag myself *private*?"

"That nobody should bother you except me! I don't have a link with Rana yet, but I unlocked your messages! Enjoy!"

When I try the message, Rana's recorded face appears. She doesn't look shockingly beautiful to me anymore. She just looks like Rana, and that's better than beauty.

"How's Anvil treating you?" she asks, her toneless voice a balm "Word is that the platoon saw action in Los Anod? You lucky splices. My fucking father . . ." She trails off. "There's nothing here but classes, classes, and more classes." She sounds solemn until the image widens to reveal that she's floating weightless in a spherical chamber. Her sudden smile is blinding. "In micro-gravity! Vector plasma's a pain in the ass, but check this out . . ."

She's wearing Flenser gear and officer's cuffs. She looks sleek and controlled and I'm struck by a surge of pride. It's stupid, a cockroach taking pride in a falcon, but there it is, stuck in my eyes and my throat and my heart.

"I miss the sweat and the stink of you, though—of basic. Message me, Maseo. You and I . . ." Rana hesitates. "We're not done."

A stupid smile spreads on my face. Fuck reprimands. Fuck Sergeant Manager Li. Rana knows me too, and *she* trusts me.

"If I score high enough," she says, "they'll let me serve a tour with you groundhogs before I come back to the stars."

"No way," I tell the recording.

"Stay alive till I get there, Mase. Keep them alive."

She fades slowly away. I enjoy the afterglow for a minute, then flick to Ionesca's message. She appears, a big girl with a brutal streak, an inch shorter than me and almost as broad in the shoulders. Her hair is ropy blue and her skin is the mottled black, white, orange of a tortoiseshell cat.

"I miss you, soldierboy, more than I expected." She pauses, and I wonder if fractal patterns are blooming behind her eyes. "My folks were wrong. We can't just drop everything and walk into the New Growth. We need time to adapt. I've been working on that, and praying."

"Praying to what?" I ask the recording. "The New Growth?"

"You left here, you left *me*, because you were looking for something. Well, there's an old saying my moms liked. 'If you find what you're looking for, you didn't look hard enough.'"

After Ionesca vanishes in a swirl of leaves, I tell the blank screen, "You told me that a thousand times, and I still don't know what it means."

The other messages are automatically generated from the military channel, in response to my performance during basic. Typical. One department sends you messages and another doesn't let you read them.

"Thanks, Ting," I say to my empty room, and I'm halfway surprised that she doesn't answer.

CHAPTER 43

The barrel of my Vespr rests against the top of a trash pallet in the combat gallery. My mouth is full of rebreather. I squeeze off two disarmed needles before my lens flashes the deployment alert.

My second shot strikes a sensor on Shakrabarti's armored hip and the trill of my increased score clashes with the klaxons.

"Deployment!" Elfano announces from inside a paleo-meka that looks like a spider-turtle. "That's *us*! We're on deck."

Ridehorse upslings her rampart gun. "We're dead."

"Not today," Voorhivey tells her, and I'm struck by how much he's changed. Sure, he's still too eager and offensively fresh-faced, but his twitchy anxiety is now a hair-trigger readiness. "Today we're catching a lamprey."

"Right in the ass." Call straightens from throttling Jag and looks around with an odd, hopeful expression. "We're gonna drop on it like an anvil."

"Forget it," Pico tells her.

"What?" she asks.

"We're not going to start saying 'drop on it like an anvil.'"

"I never said we would! Asshole." She yanks Jag to her feet. "It's a cool idea, though, right? Because we're Anvil Squad."

I emerge from the trash pallet, shedding filth. "Very cool."

"Oh, well," Shakrabarti says, rubbing his hip. "If orca and the roach agree . . ."

Voorhivey suggests that a battlecry might increase morale, and we follow our lenses into the designated hangar.

I stop for a heartbeat and stare at the CAVs lurking beneath deployment hatches. Alloy ribbons sway around central pods. The motion is almost hypnotic, like seaweed floating in a current. A scrap of memory tugs at me, or the echo of a dream. An owl in a hurricane? CAVs pairing with anyone who pours a tsunami into a drinking glass—

Pico slaps my ass to get me moving.

I strip off my practice skin and spray the stink away. Calil-Du tells me I smell as sweet as a fund manager's crack and hip-checks me toward the quartermaster cart. I pull light armor and a customized Boaz V. Lampreys burn through heavy armor, so why weigh yourself down? And the Boaz Vs fire brane cans . . . which may or may not work in the field.

A transport hisses and rumbles in front of us, a medium-range Antarmadesha. The confidence on squad channel is low, but the eagerness is palpable. I don't understand the contradiction, even though I feel the same.

"We got lucky," Sergeant Manager Li says, as the squad straps each other into armor. "This is only the third fishing trip. The third deployment with L-tech bait."

"What happened to the first two?" Voorhivey asks.

"Nothing. There wasn't a nibble. We're packing new-generation bait, though. DivCom is expecting results."

"So we're fucked?" Ridehorse says.

"Collectively and individually," Li agrees, lensing approval for ammo distribution. *Brane* ammo: glowing cylinders the size of my thumb. "We're going into a block of Belo City under the cover of an FFW."

"Why undercover?" Ting asks. "Won't people notice a big ugly lamprey killing everyone?"

"Because orders," Li tells her. "And there *is* call for an FFW."

Jag smacks M'bari on the head, indicating that his helmet is secure. "Belo City is Class C, isn't it?"

"This is a Freehold block on the border." Li checks squad and transport readiness. "Calil-Du, remind Pico what *FFW* means."

On the green, we trot inside the transport, and we're settling into our webbing before Cali answers. "Um. Four Floor War. The idea is that there's different missions on different floors of the same tower and I can't fucking believe I remembered that."

Pico punches her armored shoulder with his armored fist. "You're a database."

"I am," Cali says, proudly. "I'm a database. Ask me something else."

"What are the four floors?" Li asks.

"Oh," Cali says. "Um."

"Military action . . ." Pico whispers.

"Military action on one floor!" Cali says. "Like, putting down a riot. Resource protection on another floor, if there's anything worth protecting? Cultural stuff or noncombatants or whatever. And the fourth is, um, humanitarian aid?"

"That's three," Basdaq says.

"It's four."

"Military action, resource protection, aid."

"Four is *fuck you*."

"Peacekeeping," Voorhivey says. "The fourth is peacekeeping."

"Someone explain to Cali what *peace* means," Shakrabarti says.

"Our target is Tower Seven of building R-12," Sergeant Manager Li says, and visuals appear of an apartment block, giving us rotating views from every angle. "Floors seven through nine."

"Deep in the gutter," Ridehorse says.

"It's nice on the outside, though," Ting says. "Looks more enclave than Freehold."

"Looks like trash," Cali says.

Li gestures them quiet. "We're deploying horizontally through emergency doors on the east side. Bay Platoon is taking floor nine, Gimmel is eight. We're Dee Platoon, on floor seven. Alfa is rooftop with launchers and warheads."

"Which floor are we getting, Sarge?" Cali asks.

"Seven," Li repeats.

"No, I mean, of the Four Floor War stuff. Are we doing military action or peacekeeping or humanita—"

"Oh, orca," Jag murmurs.

Shakrabarti laughs. "We're not here for that, Cali, we're here for lampreys."

"Listen up," Li says, soft as a whisper. "We will request that residents return to their apartment. We will affix time locks. We will secure the western ledge of the tower. That is all."

"Waiting for a lamprey," Voorhivey says.

Li taps her brane ammo. "To drop an anvil on it."

"See?" Cali elbows Pico. "See?"

"What's the plan for extraction?" Jagzenka asks. "There's a squad on call for that?"

"Right behind us," Li tells her. "Some shit-hot engineering unit. We'll splat the lamprey into place, they'll extract a sample. Job done. Confirm."

"Confirm!"

"You're loaded with enough standard cans to look ugly," Li continues. "But looks can't kill. Understand?"

"No," Cali says.

"We're rocking brane cans," Ridehorse tells her. "Because we're hunting lampreys, not people. We're not prepped for a firefight."

The Sergeant Manager nods. "So do *not* pick a fight with the locals, confirm."

"Confirm!" we say.

M'bari eyes Li. "You said there *is* cause for FFW?"

"The locals are antsy," she tells him. "There's history here."

"*We're* history," Ridehorse murmurs.

"That's why we'll walk softly," Li says, ignoring Ridehorse's reflexive gloominess. "We take the west ledge and wait for our target. That's the extent of our orders, as far as public disclosure requires."

"Confirm!" Voorhivey yells for no reason.

Li doesn't exactly smile. "We're on the cutting edge now. We're bagging a lamprey. Now. Today. DNA extraction is on deck and we're turning the tide. After techs probe one of these fuckers, the rest is easy."

"Nothing like a hard probe," Shakrabarti murmurs, with a simmering look that makes Basdaq clear his throat.

"In a few weeks, DivCom will announce that we won a war nobody knew we were fighting." Sergeant Manager Li's soft voice is intense. "You'll be the reason. You're saving a million lives today and nobody will ever thank you. It doesn't get better than that."

After a moment, Pico says, "You're kind of a freak, Sarge."

Li leans against the transport wall and closes her eyes. "I fit right in."

Five minutes later, to everyone's surprise, an official briefing flicks onto our lenses. Nothing unusual at first: call signs and unit comps, PR directives and cost-benefit analyses.

We're tasked with sweeping and securing floors of a Freehold tower, and then the briefing authorizes use of dedicated ammunition against the target remort. Coils of pink vapor condense from a fog and form a lamprey as the narrator says, "Current indications suggest that lampreys are nonlocal exudations of bio-forged SICLE communications protocols."

"The fuck does that mean?" Cali grumbles.

"Dedicated Boaz ammunition will impede the ability of the lamprey substrate to achieve critical-mass ratio," the briefing says, before reeling off a minute of incomprehensible science.

"Simple," Sergeant Manager Li says. "We're all clear?"

"They appear out of nowhere," Voorhivey says.

Basdaq rolls his heavy shoulders. "And we hit them with brane cans."

"Is that all?" Cali asks.

"Life is simple," Li tells her, "at the bottom of the organizational chart."

CHAPTER 44

We don't drop in paraframes, thank sagrado: the lamprey hasn't materialized yet, so there's no signal interference. Instead, the rumble of the transport turns deafening as the pilots switch to hovermode, and my lens shows me that we're motionless above the Belo City rooftops.

A panel retracts in the side of the ship and dispensary drones roll through the security film toward the Tower Seven roof, heavy with launchers and warheads. A missile platform follows on a swivel base, with enough firepower to kill an orbital carrier.

The other platoons jeer at Alfa Platoon, who will be positioned on the rooftop, far from the action. Alfa rises from the benches in perfect sync, filing through the transport toward a ramp that extrudes sideways.

Except the ramp crashes when it's half-extruded, hanging from the ship like a tongue.

Buggy military shit.

Alfa pauses in place as if they expected it, and an engineer somewhere forces a reboot. When the ramp finishes unfurling,

Alfa moves forward like a single animal. The panel closes behind them and I realize that *we* move that way too now, without a wasted motion.

Not that we're all so flawless.

"Don't screw up, Kaytu," Cali tells me on squad channel. "One more reprimand and they send your ass-crack home."

I pretend that Kaytu, Maseo ⊘⊘ isn't framing my entire world right now. "You sure? I think I've only got the one."

"How does *Cali* not have a reprimand?" Shakrabarti asks.

"Because she was raised proper," Pico says. "She's all class."

"I fatherfucking *am*," Cali says, spitting on the floor.

The Freehold rises around us as the Antarmadesha descends. Dingy walls with caged balconies and grimy windows blur past. A spark catches in my chest, and I ignore Cali and Pico. This is my world; these are my people.

"Oooh," Ting says, her wide gaze watching. "Reminds me of home."

"It's horrible," Shakrabarti says.

We drop ten floors, twenty, fifty, threading through walkways and bridges and skyroads. I catch sight of a skinny teenaged boy on a railed sidewalk making an obscene gesture at us.

I've never seen him before, but this is a Freehold: I know him.

Bay and Gimmel Platoons deploy on floors nine and eight, and then it's our turn. The transport hovers outside the seventh floor, activating pillbug drones that repeat the lockdown message in four languages. The first two squads of Dee Platoon egress at different locations to sweep different sectors.

We're the last squad to deplane. I'm first through the film into the seventh floor, with Shakrabarti at my side. The emergency door is open, cracked wide by remote access, which is good news: the residents haven't disabled Garda access, despite whatever history happened here.

In Vila Vela, we would've shot the Antarmadesha from the sky.

The drones roll into a wreckage-strewn corridor. The emergency door must've crashed into a food stall: broken chairs and fried lichen-balls are scattered across the floor, and a splash of teaseed oil from a hot-cooker drips down the wall.

One of the pillbugs emits fire retardant at the hot oil and Basdaq sends a swarm of drakonfly drones zooming deeper into the building.

Shakrabarti and I prowl forward. The hallway looks like Vegas except it's narrower than I remember. There's a beetle farm on a makeshift porch, a becak repair workshop, a trip dance platform. The smell is more familiar than my own heartbeat. The scent of a thousand lichen-spices from a thousand corners of the world mixes with industrial vats of the hygiene lotion that every gutter kid hates.

There's sweat and mess, but also hope and ambition.

Welcome home.

All that's missing is the music. With my Boaz linked high on my harness—and switched to nonlethal Boaz squirts—I follow the broadcasting drones. *Please stay in your habitation. We apologize for the inconvenience. We respect the sanctity of your home. We are here to ensure your safety.*

"Central atrium is the choke point." Li indicates the juncture at the end of the hallway. "If they're going to—"

"Someone's thirty feet ahead of point," Ting says. "Not in his room."

She overlays a drakonfly scan onto my lens, and I see a thermal print of the guy, supine on the floor beneath a scrum of trash. An old man, a hundred pounds of dust and skin, sleeping off a long night.

"Watch for the ambush," Li murmurs.

Which is possible, but unlikely. Everyone knows you use a kid for ambush bait, not an old man. With a derelict old guy, you run the risk that corpo troops will blow him away just to clear a path.

A smart-mouthed kid, though, he'll lead a whole squad into a death trap.

Shakrabarti cycles back in the formation and Ridehorse takes aim. I see her targeting icon lock in—

"Stand down!" I snap. "I've got this." I lens my visor open. "Hey! Old-timer?"

He doesn't respond.

"San!" I send a silent request to Basdaq: "Give him a sting."

A drakonfly flashes forward and sparks the man's leg with a tiny shock.

"San!" I repeat. "Apartment number!"

The trash shifts and a leathery face appears. *"Garda arsloch,"* he grunts in some kind of German creole. *"Substraire sich."*

"Your hab number, san!" I say. *"Wohnen nummber, directeur."*

While he's mumbling, Ting scans him so completely that she maps his bile ducts. The entire might of the Shiyogrid technology faces off against this frail old wreck and detects no threat.

I knock his shoe with my boot. "Directeur, please."

He tells me I'm a corporate shitpuppet and gives me the number of his apartment.

I pull him upright and pass him back along the line for M'bari to sort.

"Don't play games," Li lenses me. "This is a hot zone."

She's almost right. It's a hot zone, but it's also someone's home. There are finger-painted murals on the doors. There's a basket of toys beside a stack of battered readers. Kids live here. Yeah, gutter hallways are crisscrossed with tripwires, but not the kind that trigger explosions.

That's not the danger we face.

The danger we face is anger.

If we kill an old man with a nonlethal squirt, two hundred of his self-appointed grandchildren will pour from the cracks, baying for our blood. Especially if this Freehold has some kind of dubious history with the corpos.

Ridehorse and I establish positions at the central atrium until Ting flashes the green. We cross to the widest southern corridor while Cali and Elfano—looking naked outside her meka—take the northern. Time locks secure residents inside their apartments. The clicks sound like Pico cracking his knuckles every morning.

I sight down empty hallways. Nothing moves except for the birds hopping around in the cages hanging outside half the doors.

Pico and Shakrabarti sweep to the west, following three drakonflies. They lens the all-clear, and the rest of the squad funnels into the corridor behind them. Basdaq sticks close to Ting; she's too valuable to lose. Jag sweeps the alcoves and transoms. Ridehorse and I watch the rear, backwalking a path that our lenses feed us as a drakonfly clings to the ceiling overhead, bulbous eyes alert.

We unfurl around two more corners, watching every direction at once despite the assurances of the drones. Signals crash, signals fail. Signals fall to countermeasures.

"This place is an anthill," Jagzenka says on-channel.

"It's a termite mound," M'bari says.

"It's like the labyrinth level in *Chop Sty City*," Shakrabarti says, talking about a MYRAGE game. "I got roasted in that maze a hundred times."

"Nice foreshadowing, Shak," Pico says, clearing a northern hallway. "You're so dead."

"We're all dead," Ridehorse says, gloomy as always.

"This quad's only one slice of the tower," Sergeant Manager Li says. "There are what, Kaytu? Two hundred fifty-six apartments on a floor?"

"In prefabs, yeah." I keep sweeping the corridor. "A lot of them are knocked through."

"What's that mean?" Voorhivey asks.

"The joining walls are torn down," Ting explains. "And the apartments are combined into a bigger one."

"More are subdivided," I say, on point with Ridehorse again. "Cut up into smaller units. There are only a hundred apartments per floor in the penthouse, but maybe six hundred in the gutter."

"No way!" Voorhivey says on-channel. "That violates a dozen regulations!"

Ting sends me a madly giggling cartoon at exactly the same time as I ping her a laugh. M'bari glances at a panel of writhing graffiti and tells Voorhivey, "There are no regulations in a Freehold."

"You lived like this?" Cali asks me, sidling past.

"Yeah."

"No wonder you're such a crappy human being," Pico says.

A blast of music behind a closed door makes Voorhivey pivot and Jag crouch. M'bari mutters to them and we finish clearing the floor.

When the last locks are affixed, the pillbug drones roll through the hallways, thanking the residents for their patience. Sergeant Manager Li sends drakonflies onto the western ledge, which is really just an exterior walkway running the length of the block.

We watch the quiet corridors and drone feeds until she gives the green, and then we zipper-feed onto the ledge. This low in a Freehold, the condensation makes faint billows of mist. Another tower rises sixty yards in front of us, and there's traffic on the rails and in the tangle of bridges and boardwalks.

We spread out, our weapons active and our sweeps live.

The rest of Dee Platoon is arrayed within a quarter-mile stretch to our north and south. The rail and roadway traffic slows to a stop, halted somewhere upline. The avenue below us is obscured by wires and walkways, most of them draped in banners or filmurals. A bunch of kids muck around after a ball near a traincar painted with bright flowers.

Bay Platoon indicates they're in position on a ledge above. Gimmel does the same. An Orit Gal dronebud tentatively lowers into sight, picking through the tangled walkways. A voice like the Hammer of Mars blares from the drone, informing residents that a curfew is in effect.

One of the kids throws a chunk of koncrete at the drone. The rest of them keep playing until two adults drag them into the traincar. The message repeats, and the walkways clear.

Except a dozen caravans and cargo trailers remain on the street.

"Tell them to take shelter in a building," I lens Li. "Get them moving."

"Who?"

I send her images from the street level. "Them."

"People *live* in those?" she asks, then switches to command channel.

To my relief, another announcement tells citizens to clear the streets entirely. It's followed by tight-beam demands aimed at the traincars and trailers, and even a few disarmed rounds, which clatter ominously.

In moments, the crosswalks and platforms fill with people. Half of them push mobiles and caravans into the shelter of the adjoining buildings, and the other half simply abandon their homes for the tower lobbies. I try not to think about all the gutter roaches hunkering down in the target area, keeping their eyes closed and hoping the storm will pass.

"Now we wait," Voorhivey intones.

Jag laughs at him. "You're such a splice."

"I'm not the one who thinks she's a panda."

"*Jaguar,*" she says. "They're jaguar rosettes."

"Extinct bears all look the same."

"Channel," Li says gently, and everyone shuts up.

Feels like the quiet before the storm. Next comes the bait . . . and the tsunami.

CHAPTER 45

F ive minutes pass and the faint throb of music sounds above us. Two more minutes, and a crash echoes through the Freehold.

When Ting targets the source of the sound, it's just some kids throwing junk down a chute. Elfano's pointed ears flatten and Voorhivey starts humming, which still happens when he gets nervous, despite all the progress he's made. Cali elbows him sharply, which also happens.

A drone swoops suddenly between the buildings, dodging cables and banners to hover above a suspended recharge cistern. It has a narrow tail and a bulbous head, like a mutant mushroom. Hooked talons extrude from the base and clamp onto the cistern grate. A faint yellowbeige glow seeps through a pattern of tiny holes.

"That's the bait?" Ridehorse asks.

"Looks like the same T. h.li uu Los Anod," Jagzenka says.

"Which blew half a city into chunks."

Voorhivey tsks. "I'm sure it's perfectly safe."

"The thing about you, Voorhivey," Pico says, "is that you're adorable."

"And I'm right. The bait'll attract a lamprey. We'll hit it with brane cans. And then, uh . . ."

"Engineering will extract a sample," Sergeant Manager Li says.

"How?" M'bari asks.

"Up close and personal, with handheld extractors. They can't use drones because of signal interference. Our job is to immobilize the lamprey and protect the engineers."

The yellowbeige light brightens and my grip tightens in my Boaz sleeve. I tense for action, but nothing happens. We wait on the ledge. Twenty more minutes creep past. The hum of maintenance drones mixes with the gurgle of filters. Another ten minutes pass. *Too long.* The walls loom above us like sentries, the windows like gun barrels.

If we don't keep things moving, this will turn into a clusterfuck. I've already got two reprimands on my lens, but if this Freehold explodes I'm going to forget the mission, forget the lamprey, and try to keep my squad in one piece.

I open a private channel to Sergeant Manager Li. "We started a clock when we landed, Sarge. Gutter roaches won't hit a platoon in full gear . . . unless we stick around too long."

"Command knows urban warfare, Kaytu."

"Yes, Sarge," I say.

"Plus, we can't do shit to make this happen faster." She switches to platoon channel. "Everything's smooth as flowcore, so far. All floors secured, all platoons in place. Drones are green. There's only one thing to do now."

"What's that, Sarge?" Basdaq asks.

Li loops us Voorhivey's recorded voice: " 'Now we wait.' "

The tension eases. We've drilled for this. We've faced dozens of monsters, creatures designed to overload our fear receptors. We've held position for eight hours, for ten hours. TL once ordered us into surveillance readiness for twenty-nine hours before sending us against Platoon 0316.

Another twenty minutes pass—and the bait unfurls like a flower, into a glowing yellowbeige octopus. Weird light bathes the street and the Freehold holds its breath.

"Sweet biyo," Pico gasps.

"What?" Voorhivey asks, bringing his Boaz up.

"That bait really *does* look like M'bari's ass-tat."

It really doesn't. It looks like a pulsating ocean creature, but not from any ocean on Earth. Ridehorse asks how long this is supposed to take, and Sergeant Manager Li says she doesn't know.

I flick a blank message to Ting, and a moment later she lenses, "What? Do you want something? Do you want to talk? Are you wondering why we're doing this *here*? Or why there's nothing about lampreys on MYRAGE? Because I have a theory."

"I was going to ask if this is a private link."

"Oh! I always keep us private at first, unless we're already not private, in which case I don't . . ." She trails off for a second. "Um. What do you need? Do you want to know what the bait's made of?"

"Not really." I'd planned to ask if there are still people in the caravans, but instead I say, "Why *are* we doing this here? And what is it made of?"

"Lampreys are attracted to population centers, so baiting them here is easier. And it's some kind of Waypoint tech, I don't know. Waypoint tech is tough to read."

"It's inscrutable," I say.

"It cannot be scruted! Now ask why there's nothing on the channels about lampreys."

"Why?" I ask.

"The corpos are using technopaths to control the information."

I tense when she mentions technopaths. "I thought they didn't live that long."

"They're using kids," she says. "I'm pretty sure. I'm ninety percent certain. It's only a working theory. They're probably using eleven- or twelve-year-old kids, which is before, you know . . ."

"Yeah." Before they die screaming. "How many technopaths are there?"

"Two for every billion births?" She lenses me a shrug. "Most don't live very long."

"Yeah."

"So I guess there's only a few alive at any one time."

"Which means there aren't enough to screw with MYRAGE."

"Except nothing else explains how they're keeping a worldwide invasion of lampreys s-so-so qui-et-qui-qui-et-et-et—"

Our connection sputters and falls silent. A drakonfly drops to the ground at my feet, twitches once, and goes still. My lens reverts to default inputs and Cali curses.

"Well, this is suboptimal," Sergeant Manager Li murmurs, her soft voice carrying along the ledge. "Our com systems are crashing."

"Ting'll fix it," Voorhivey says.

"The problem is upstream," Li tells him. "Nothing to do with lampreys."

Basdaq scans his t-reader. "No signal interference apparent."

"Sit tight and thank the Louvre we're not in a firefight," Sergeant Manager Li tells us. "Any half-decent insurgent crew would punch us in the spine before we came back online."

A dull clank sounds and Ridehorse says, "Huh. My armor's weird."

"Oh, shit," M'bari says. "She's hit!"

"I'm not hit, dumbass." Ridehorse slumps against the wall. "My armor's just a little . . ."

A black line stretches across her stomach plate. For a second, I think it's widening, and then I realize it's seeping blood.

"Medic!" the Sergeant Manager shouts. "Rampart, rampart! We are under fire—lethal response—find cover!"

She's never yelled before, and we react like we've been shocked. Basdaq fires twice, throwing ramparts in front of Ridehorse. Shells pock the walls around us. Without hesitation, without the slightest hint of nerves, Voorhivey scrambles beside Ridehorse, unpacking his medkit while the rest of us scatter behind columns.

Jag hustles Ting to cover. There's a crack of contact and Jag shakes her arm. "I'm tagged, I'm hit! I'm—no. No, I'm okay!"

"C-contact is reported by Alfa P-Platoon," Ting stammers, monitoring the paleo burst channel. "Snipers to the south and west, c-composition of hostiles unknown and we're getting pulsed."

A slug gouges the wall behind me and my mind explodes with outrage. Some asshole is *shooting* at me! I don't remember switching to enhanced vision, but when I sweep the street I catch sight of faint shapes prone on an underway grate, half-hidden by ads and a sanitation station. Velocity blooms appear on my lens as they fire, and more thunks sound.

"I'm okay," Jag repeats. "Deconfirm, I'm unhurt."

"Hostiles twenty floors up," I announce, in a strangely flat voice. I try to lens the location to my squad, but coms are still down and more blurred hostiles are slotting into formation. "Twenty floors overhead and fifteen degrees—"

Slugs pepper the walls and I lose track of what I'm saying. Pico bellows at Shakrabarti, and I almost fire a brane canister at the snipers before remembering I need standard ammo.

I feel the selector click in my palm and blast a triple-round across the street. When it hits the grate beneath the centermost shooter, liquammo splashes through. Four shooters shudder and two die, but a dozen more take aim from the boardwalks and maintenance structures.

Jag barks a frightened laugh when another round bounces off her armor, and I hit the next shooter, and Cali fires a fucking anti-armor grenade.

The entire underpass crumples with a *whoomp* and a shriek of alloy. Tons of rubble crash through two scooter bridges and a jut of warungs before littering a reinforced rail track. Sparks fly, cables whip. Fluid sluices from the sanitation station to splash beyond the yellowbeige-glowing lamprey bait below.

"Bang," Cali says. "Handled."

"That's half our anti-armor cans, you splice," Jag says, popping liquammo slugs.

"There's three dozen more shooters across the street," I tell Cali, marking another target and firing. "On the walkways and exterior—"

"We are advised of airborne incoming," Ting sings out.

"No shit," Pico says, blazing single shots southward down the street.

When I spin toward his targets, I barely believe my eyes.

A hundred hostiles are swooping at us on modified two-unit paraframes. One flies while the other fires. What is this? *Who* is this? We're here to bag a lamprey, not suppress a riot. But this isn't some spontaneous riot. This is something more serious, more deadly and—

"They're patriots!" Voorhivey yells. "Insurgents!"

"They're sitting ducks," Pico replies. "Make them fall."

"I want my meka," Elfano grunts, raising her Boaz.

The ledges above us erupt into a firestorm as the other platoons throw cans downrange. The sizzle of liquammo crackles through the blocks and a hail of coil-rounds pounds us in return. They're an old tech, gear from a generation ago . . . but the *best* gear from a generation ago, unfurling into wire-whips strong enough to slice alloy, like happened to Ridehorse.

And *patriots* is right. This isn't a Freehold riot, this is an organized paramilitary army. They surrounded us and waited for a misstep. They would've slunk away if they hadn't seen an opening—but when our coms crashed, they struck.

Why are they attacking? No idea. *History*, I guess. The corpos probably screwed them in one way or another—broke their independence movement, then relocated their families—and they've been waiting for revenge.

This is an opportunistic attack by a serious nativist force, and we're loaded with brane cans that can't hurt human soldiers.

I flick my Boaz from streams to rounds, conserving my ammunition. I kneel on the north side of a column as Cali hoses the opposite scraper. A hammer cracks against my helmet, but not hard enough to break my focus.

Paraframes glide toward me. What the gehenna kind of suicide strike is this, sailing slowly toward trained corpo soldiers? I acquire an airborne patriot with a shoulder-mounted weapon. He's a passenger on a paraframe—no, on a *sailframe*. They're attacking us with modified sporting equipment.

"Aim for the pilots," Sergeant Manager Li says, barely louder than normal. "Conserve your cans."

I shift my target and mark the pilot. Her face fills my vision. She's younger than me, and her hair is a flapping braid. She looks scared and strong, a patriot willing to die for the cause. I know the expression, yet I still wonder: where does she find the courage to fly a recreational sailframe against four platoons of corporate infantry and a deathmarch Orit Gal?

This girl is a hero, but Ridehorse screams when Voorhivey sprays the loops of her intestine, so I pull the trigger.

CHAPTER 46

The parasail falls. Dozens of them fall, wheeling from the sky like wounded owls, crashing against walkways and canal stations.

Screams of shock and pain fill the air, along with the sizzle of squirtguns and the pop-clank of coils. An Orit Gal edges down between the towers, slowed by the bridges and tracks, and starts picking off patriots with surgical precision. Looks like the gunship's weapons systems are back online.

"Incoming, incoming," Ting squeaks. "*Inside* the scraper, they're inside the scraper!"

My lens flares to life and two files flash across the squad channel.

First, a message from Ting: "I raised coms within Anvil Squad but we are *not* linked to platoon or command. Repeat. Nobody's seeing this but us."

Second, she shows us two hundred red marks trickling upward inside the scraper, rising through the fifth and sixth floors to mass on the seventh. Two hundred hostiles are gathering on our floor, approaching our position, invisible to the other platoons.

"We locked down the lifts and stairwells," Basdaq says.

"Disposal chutes," I say.

I mean they're climbing through deactivated chutes. Nobody understands except Ting—and in a horrified flash I understand that the snipers and the sailframes are distractions from the main force inside the building, who are tasked with taking us from behind. Sneaking into place behind the ledges and ending things quick.

"*Sagrado,*" I whisper. "We need—we need—"

We need to warn other squads. The patriots will chew through the tower from bottom to top. The other two squads of Dee Platoon on the seventh floor are first on their menu, but there's no way to warn them. Send a runner? Wave the Orit Gal into earshot and—

"Form on me!" Sergeant Manager Li says, wasting no time on impossibilities. "Back inside. We stop them on seven. We stop them here."

Cali and M'bari spin into the building, guns high and helmets swiveling. Pico and Voorhivey follow, pushing Ridehorse in a field-cart.

"What about the other squads?" Elfano asks, but Li doesn't answer.

Shakrabarti and I cover the retreat. We're last on the ledge, half-assing suppression fire as we trot for the door—

A rasp tears through the clatter of assault weapons. The Orit Gal grinds lower, scraping a wall, crashing through a canal. Its intakes and blades are ganked with retardant foam from a patriot attack and its shattered shoulder turret sends a cascade of wreckage to the ground. A gash opens in the tower wall. One of the ship's blades catches in an adboard and snaps, flinging through the air like a hatchet.

The Orit Gal tumbles, smashing through the walkways like a cannonball through a cobweb. As I pivot into the seventh floor, an explosion rocks the world outside. Disabled drakonflies crunch beneath my boot and Voorhivey steps away from Ridehorse, because Ridehorse is dead.

The Sergeant Manager tells Cali to take her extra cans, and Ting lights up the squad channels with fifty marks moving toward us through the building. Hundreds more gather beyond them. Thirty seconds away, maybe forty, and we're trapped in the hallways. When we locked the residents in, we locked ourselves out. Unless someone knows how to pick locks . . .

"Ramparts, please," Sergeant Manager Li tells Basdaq, while lensing positions to the squad.

"Smartwire." I drop to a knee beside Pico. "I need smartwire."

A rampart expands in front of us and Pico tells me, "Your hair looks fine."

"We're trapped like—" The red marks swarm closer on my lens. "I can get inside these doors without leaving a trace! I need smartwire! Does anyone have—"

"There's a time for clever, Private Kaytu," Li says, meaning *this isn't it.*

Cali snorts a laugh at me. "Who's thick *now*?"

The red marks stop and flicker, hidden from view around the corners of the corridor in front of us. They're gathering courage—or firepower. Maybe both.

Nothing happens for a moment, except for Voorhivey crying silently over Ridehorse.

Sergeant Manager Li's amplified voice booms down the hallway:

"My mother wanted me to become a sanitation archaeologist. Times like this, I wonder if she was right."

I almost turn to look at her. Everyone knows that authority-based riot control is counterproductive: making demands just gives a crowd something to hate. Still, I'm surprised at how gentle an angle Li is taking.

"And tomorrow," she continues, "tomorrow is my daughter's birthday. I'm not even lying. She's turning seven. So I'm asking you please, do not approach. We're carrying heavy munitions. I'm begging you, do not make me use them. This is not a fair fight. You are outgunned. You bloodied us hard. You are badass. Now take the victory and go home. I can't promise much. I'm just a grunt; the corpos don't care any more about me than they do about you. But I'll promise you this. Tomorrow, at my girl's birthday party? I'll raise a slice of cake to you. That's all I can offer you, except for begging. Please, *please* disperse."

Silence falls. Around the corner, the red marks shift and squirm. A few birds chirp in cages, a few wings flutter.

Pico whistles low. "Another minute, Sarge, and you'd have *me* dispersing."

"Apparently that was the time for clever," I say.

"Except we aren't carrying heavy munitions," Cali mutters.

"That's nothing," Li tells her. "I don't have a daughter."

Jag laughs. "When I grow up, I want to be just like Sarge."

A velocity bloom splashes onto my lens and two missiles streak toward us, which is a pretty straightforward answer to Li's pleas.

Ting's countermeasures fill the air and the warheads detonate fifty yards away. The shock wave blows through walls, punches a hole in the ceiling, and craters the floor. The ramparts absorb most of the impact and our suits dampen the rest, but there's so much crap in the air that visibility is ten feet. Which doesn't dull the howls of the patriots rushing toward us—

"Bend 'em," Li says, lensing confirmations.

When Elfano triggers her launcher, the exhaust warms my side through my armor. Her pressure grenade takes flight, the heaviest munitions we can use. If we drop anti-armor grenades like Cali's, we're looking at a mass-casualty situation beneath a mountain of collapsed tower. A pressure grenade, on the other hand, only scratches the infrastructure . . . though it's hard to appreciate the delicacy through the ruptured eardrums, seizures, incontinence, and vomiting. I know, because a soldier once cracked one at me in Vila Vela.

Four pressure grenades strike in a reinforcing pattern, as pretty as practice. They crack with enough force that my stomach flips behind all the protection. The screams are horrible and the forward momentum of the patriots turns into a staggering zombie shuffle through the dust cloud.

Li orders us to empty nonlethal munitions into the hostiles; she's trying to break the attack without escalation. We're not packing much nonlethal ordnance, though. We're here for a lamprey, not an army. In a pause in the clamor, I hear sizzle from the street—or from other squads on the seventh floor—and then Voorhivey and M'bari and Pico methodically empty their Boazes of the kindergarten stuff, which drives the patriots back around the corners.

"Give me a can count," Li lenses, and I send the specs of my remaining ammunition.

When I check the squad list, my stomach drops. Cali's mostly empty, and Jag's only holding brane cans, because she's our best shot. Elfano and Basdaq and I weren't equipped with backup nonlethal rounds by the quartermaster, which dispensed gear according to some unknowable algorithm.

We're running low on everything except lamprey rounds.

Li reopens the public address amplification. "You know what you're doing, I'll give you that. So you know we've gone easy on you so far—" She stops when a new signal appears. Another rush of patriots, but . . . blurred. "Ting?" she murmurs.

"They're behind film," Ting says, after a moment. "That's high-security film they've affixed to a frame, if *affixed* means attached or—"

Orders scroll as fast as thought. Li authorizes lethal force and Basdaq lays down two more ramparts in the corridor. He drops his empty rampart gun, upslings his Boaz, and braces to fire. I stutter-step to the forward rampart and brace beside Pico, feeling the rest of the squad slotting into place behind me.

"Now this, colleagues and genfolk," Li says, "is what you trained for."

The swarm of red marks surges toward us. Rounds slam into ramparts and whiz overhead. We wait for the order to engage. We wait, we wait . . . I think Sarge is letting the patriots approach so when we drop them, their bodies will act as obstacles, breaking up the advance of those in the rear. Either that or she wants to minimize their distance for when we resort to full-contact negotiation.

Jagzenka's head snaps back when a round skims her helmet. She swears. "What the gehenna? Is *anyone* else getting hit?"

"Ridehorse," Voorhivey says.

Li flashes a sign. "M'bari, you're up."

M'bari carries three lens-directed mini-spindles in a palm-sized shoulder-launcher. They're a fragile tech, the size of toothpicks and redundant in the age of drones. Still, M'bari loves them on account of some MYRAGE war game of his childhood. We mocked him, but nobody's jeering now. Three streaks flash away, weaving in response to his local-lensed commands as he tries to sneak them behind the patriots' film.

There's a blast and a shout, and M'bari grunts. "Two out of three."

"The film's torn but intact," Ting reports. "I mean, it's down but not out. It's—"

"Keep it steady," Li says, in her soft voice. "Make every pop count. Engage."

She gives us the green and nine Boazes speak at once. The world vanishes in a blaze of liquammo.

I acquire a target.

Fire a round.

Acquire a target.

Fire a round.

It's automatic, just another drill. We've practiced so many times that my body shifts into a relaxed readiness, like we're on a training course and the enemy is a platoon we'll trade insults with in the mess hall.

Except our ammo count keeps dropping . . . and the insurgents keep closing.

Behind me, Basdaq takes a hit at an angle his armor can't deflect, and I think he's dead until Shakrabarti reports that he's got a smashed sternum and a punctured lung and a crappy haircut.

Only Pico laughs.

We keep shooting, the patriots keep falling—but the advance doesn't break. The sizzle of fire in the corridor isn't as loud as the explosions from the street, which isn't as loud as my heartbeat. The red blotch surges closer, a boom makes the walls tremble, and Elfano shakes off a glancing hit.

"Sweet biyo," she snarls, a phrase the squad adopted from Ting.

Cali screams in rage or ecstasy, Pico sidesteps toward Elfano to check that she's okay, and M'bari eats a weird shock round that lays him on his ass.

"Medic!" Shakrabarti calls. "M'bari's hit!"

Voorhivey reacts instantly, staying low and racing for M'bari—and new red marks blink on my display.

Enemy weapons are springing to life nearby.

CHAPTER 47

For a heartbeat, the onslaught in the hallway distracts me. Then I register what I'm seeing: a few dozen hostiles are hiding inside two apartments just in front of our forward ramparts. The patriots must've switched out the residents for shooters while we were on the ledge, and they've been waiting for the right moment.

"Apartments!" I shout, a second after Ting highlights the reading on our lenses.

"We're getting stomped," Cali snarls, sounding genuinely impressed.

"They're putting us in a killbox." Sergeant Manager Li reaches to the side. "Calil-Du."

Without breaking the rhythm of her Boaz shots, Cali unlinks her anti-armor launcher and passes it to Li.

"Hose 'em down for three seconds," Li says, and lenses the entire squad a countdown.

At zero, I switch to streaming and the hallway blazes. A hellscape writhes in front of us.

Li stands from behind the rampart and aims the launcher.

Two seconds is a lifetime. Boaz streams tear the corridor to shreds before death blurs from behind me and an anti-armor grenade flashes past.

Li lenses, "Backblast, down!"

A shock wave funnels toward us. She laid the anti-armor can directly inside the pocket of the security film, through the dust and the enemy fire. The blast roars down the hallway and kicks me in the sinuses. There's blood in my helmet but the patriot advance finally falters, and Li didn't drop the tower on us. She used the film to localize the blast on the hostiles and protect the building from damage.

"You're a ballerina, Sarge," Cali says.

I'd enjoy the moment, except Ridehorse is dead, and Li lenses that I'm with Pico to clear apartment one, while Calil-Du and Jag are clearing number two. She's sending us into the apartments after the patriots waiting to ambush us.

Clearing rooms is a bottleneck nightmare. Clearing rooms is the terror of every squaddie, but clearing rooms is what Vila Vela patriots and refugee gangers *do*.

My display shows fourteen people inside the apartment designated *one*, with twelve live weapons, and eleven hostiles and ten weapons in apartment two next door. A frontal assault is suicide, so I lens Pico a plan, quick and dirty.

I sprint from cover, leaving the protection of the rampart and running toward the stalled patriot advance, where the groans and weeping from Li's grenade still sound through the smoke.

The blast didn't finish them. The red marks are regrouping and from behind the haze, a beast of a primitive autogun whines to life. A heartbeat later, it starts spitting forty flex-rounds downrange every second. A single flex-round can't pierce our skins, but four or five to the same spot will crack it like an egg.

One knocks my armored hip. I stagger a few steps and throw myself against the wall just past the closed door to apartment one. Now I'm in the corridor between the patriots and my squad, with the apartment door between me and the ramparts.

My Vespr is heavy in my hands.

My breath is loud in my ears.

The patriots inside the apartment are waiting for orders. They don't know we scoped them until Pico opens up from behind our forward rampart. The reinforced door shudders and his slugs tear through. Pico drops two patriots sight unseen before the rest boil out of the apartment at him, furious and terrified and laser-focused.

Pico screams and blazes like Bearserker on MYRAGE, blitzing the patriots. He's murder made flesh, and painting himself as the biggest target in the world.

The first two fire at him, and one of them hits. The round scorches Pico's chest plate and I shoot both patriots from behind with my Vespr before the third half-turns. Pico catches him in the neck, which splatters blood across the wall and the masks of the other patriots.

The patriots are blind and panicked and slippery with gore. The fourth makes an inhuman noise and charges.

The barrel of my Vespr is six inches from the fifth patriot's head when I squeeze the trigger.

Pico takes down the fourth, I think. I don't know. Maybe I take him down. My mind is skipping around, letting my body take control. More patriots are arming weapons in this apartment than my lens showed earlier, like they're multiplying in there, and I'm shoving a skinny middle-aged insurgent backward through the doorway, my trenchknife in his stomach and my Vespr poking from under his armpit and there's six or ten—or a hundred or a thousand—more of them inside, and in a flash of lucidity I realize that there's an unmarked door *between* the two apartments, and all the hostiles are boiling into this one.

A round tears through the skinny guy's chest and gut-punches me. I stagger and spin and return fire. Target-trigger, target-trigger, target-trigger; the apartment turns into a slaughterhouse as patriots scream and fall.

A spindle-modified Ambo swivels toward my face.

Two feet away. The barrel looks like my grave.

I don't see a shooter behind the Ambo. I'm not sure I believe there is one. All I believe is that the Ambo spindle will punch through my blood-sheeted helmet and into my brain.

Some half-forgotten lesson of basic training kicks me into motion and I hunch and spin, giving the Ambo my armored shoulder to hit. The unseen shooter fires. Ten inches of high-explosive spindle drills through a seam in my armor and digs into my flesh.

It misses the bone and doesn't detonate.

My right arm goes numb. My trenchknife drops and my Vespr's gone, but somehow I fire a fucking brane canister from my Boaz, and it hammers the figure behind the Ambo into a wall and coats her with yellowbeige slime.

Then I stand there trying to locate myself.

Where am I?

What next?

What now?

A chubby green-haired man throws himself at me. He's not armed, he's not marked high-risk, but he brings me to the ground and proceeds to pound the crap out of me with what appears to be a musical instrument.

He cracks my visor and smashes again. The crack spreads until Pico shoots him in the chin and Cali and Jagzenka sweep into sight and clear the rest of the apartments.

There's a blank stretch of time. Maybe ten seconds, maybe thirty.

I find myself kneeling in the doorway with Pico, holding my Boaz high on my frame. The autogun is silent. My visor's screwed but my right arm is working again despite the spindle impaling my shoulder. Doesn't even hurt.

My Vespr and trenchknife are gone. I'm down to the dregs of my normal ammo: I've got two seconds of streaming, and enough slugs to hold off an army if I don't fire any slugs.

The rest of the squad is in worse shape.

Basdaq's suit is clamping a sucking chest wound. M'bari is still clumsy from the shock round and Ridehorse is still dead. The rest of us are banged up pretty good except for Jag and Ting, who are unscathed. Squad channel is urgent with low-ammunition alerts. Even Ting's weapons are empty, though that just means Sergeant Manager Li distributed her cans.

Ting doesn't shoot at things. She just hunches inside the best protection we can afford her and saves our asses.

The corridor is a ruin. It's not even a corridor anymore. The blasts chewed through both sides, so the hallway widens into living rooms and bathrooms and bedrooms with truncated walls and charred furniture. Cables spark and pipes spew and people sob and moan.

And this still isn't over: the patriots are massing in the dust cloud beyond the wreckage.

"Is your commander there?" Sergeant Manager Li asks on the public address.

The only reply is a groan.

"Who did you serve with?" she asks. "Where did you train?"

There's no answer. There's no movement. My shoulder itches and the cracks in my visor divide the dust cloud into kaleidoscope segments.

A man's amplified voice says, "Welcome 12."

"I'd bet my left lens you were ranked higher than Sergeant Manager."

"You can't hold that against me," the man says.

I hear an accent in his voice and I rub my shoulder as I try to place it. Kanarese Creole, maybe?

"How much higher?" Li asks.

There's another pause. "Executive suite."

"Bastard," Li says. "How come you know how to fight?"

The patriot commander chuckles. "I didn't start at the top."

"Well, pardon me for saying, san, but I don't see your objective here."

"I don't see yours."

"Mine is getting my squad home. But you . . . even if you win— and you're not winning—you know the corpos will come back at you multiplied."

"There's more to life than winning, Sergeant Manager. The Magnolia Doom taught us that."

After the corpos signed accords against genocide-class weapons— with bankruptcy-level penalties for violations—they invested in the next best thing: exclusion domes, aka Dooms. If the corpos drop one on your neighborhood, nobody gets out. Nobody dies, but you are cut off from the rest of humanity until the dome's de-activated. With a long-term dome, they'll evacuate the populace first, after accepting the surrender of people with outstanding violations—though the most stubborn or desperate always re-main behind.

With a short-term Doom, there's usually no notice. You wake up one morning and your building or block is cut off from the world. No MYRAGE, no imported food, medicine, or power for weeks or months. That's a memorable lesson in the value of belonging.

Vila Vela is the only full enclave that's been permanently Doomed. In my dreams, the streets and balconies of my childhood home still thrum with life; then I wake feeling the loss of my amputated, abandoned city. Apparently the corpos dropped a Doom on Magnolia too, though that's news to me. I'm not even sure if Mag-nolia is a neighborhood, a noncompliant religion, or an affinity group.

Li lenses the squad the obvious question, but not even M'bari knows anything about the Magnolia Doom, and we're cut off from MYRAGE so we can't search.

"The what?" she asks on her public address.

An amplified sigh sounds from the patriot commander. "You've never heard of it."

"Can't say that I have, san. Is it the reason we're fighting?"

"It's the beginning of the reason. One of the beginnings. And don't be so sure, Sergeant Manager, that we're not winning."

"Listen," Li says, "I'm not authorized to tell you this, but we're here for a remort. There's a new class of remort, and we tracked one heading this direction. Even if you pull off a miracle and cut all our throats, that thing will melt you into puddles."

"A new class of remorts?" the commander scoffs. "I don't mind lies, but at least keep them plausible."

"If I were lying, I would." Li takes a breath. "Well, how about this? How long before three more Orit Gals hit the skyline?"

"You're the only surviving squad on this floor and your other platoons are bleeding out."

Li gestures for Ting to check that. "Do you want to lose more people today, san? I surely don't. But I promise you this. For every one of mine you take, I will take a hundred of yours. I'll turn this tower into a war crime."

There's silence for what feels like a long time. I don't think the guy is going to answer until his voice floats from the settling dust. "You're trying to get your people home, Sergeant Manager?"

"That's right."

"You're overlooking the fundamental fact of irregular warfare."

"What's that?"

"I can't get my people home. This *is* home. We have nowhere to go. Confirm."

From beyond the ruins, a hundred ragged voices say, "Confirm."

"And here's another fact," the man continues. "You're out of ammunition, but we just got resupplied."

The autogun coughs to life and sends a hail of flex-rounds at us. The roar of another autogun joins the first, then two more. The firepower is awesome. The air is so thick with rounds that I can't see the other side of the corridor; the sound is literally deafening if you're not hearing-protected.

Pico and I stare in shock from the doorway. Streams of flex-rounds converge and punch the forward rampart.

Chunks of foam explode and tear through the walls.

Li orders Cali and Shakrabarti to retreat. They scramble backward and fling themselves over the rearward ramparts. In two seconds of exposure, both jerk like puppets, riven with impacts. A spiderwebbing of cracks appears on Shak's side, and chips of Cali's armor flake away.

Then they're over, crouching beside Ting and Li. M'bari is conscious but dazed; Voorhivey's kneeling beside Basdaq, desperately working the medkit. My helmet filters the boom of autogun fire, but a sudden crack jacks my ears like a knife.

The forward rampart shatters.

The explosion stuns the squad like a pressure grenade dropping the ceiling on us. Static sizzles across my lens and the floor is a carpet of foam shards and spent rounds.

The patriot fire switches to the next rampart and—slackens. One stream of flex-rounds swivels upward and rips into the ceiling, tracking back toward the patriots. Another stream veers wildly away.

A moment later, we're no longer receiving fire.

Nothing's incoming except the noise.

"They're not firing at us," Voorhivey announces.

"They're disappearing," Ting says, as red marks vanish from my lens. "Like they're cloaking or—"

"They're dying," Jag tells her. "Maybe Gimmel Platoon stopped playing dominoes."

Shakrabarti looks at the blood pooling around his boot. "I need to regrow at least three toes."

"On the bright side," Pico tells him, "your face is pretty as ever."

"Get me in touch with Command," Li tells Ting. "We—"

A lamprey strand cuts through the floor and slices Pico in half.

y mind switches off. My discipline dies. I hear myself telling Pico that he's okay, that everything's okay. I see myself holding the halves of his head together with my gloved hands. I'm soaked with fluid and my lens flashes urgently, but I don't move, I don't react, I kneel there trying to comfort a corpse.

I'm still crying when Cali clubs my helmet with her Boaz.

The world spins and she drags me to my feet and shoves me into the corridor. Elfano is a mound of armor and tissue on the floor and Sergeant Manager Li is pushing the squad over a destroyed wall into a destroyed living room, shouting at us to load lamprey munitions.

Three steps into the living room, my world snaps into place.

I shake off Cali's hand and downstrap my Boaz. My hands move automatically as I load my brane cans, then roll my stiffening shoulder and tune into the chatter.

"—lamprey has responded to bait," Ting is telling Command on the now-live coms. "It's approaching *through* Tower Seven. Repeat. The lamprey is approaching the bait through Tower Seven."

"It's inside the *du ma* walls?" a stranger's voice asks, mis-channing a message.

"What—what happened?" Voorhivey stammers. "What happened?"

"The lamprey is in the floors beneath us," Shakrabarti tells him, his voice tight. "It chopped the patriots into chunks, then got Pico and Elfan—"

Oily pink strands slice through the living room floor from beneath, like shark fins breaking the waves.

We scream and dodge. Jag fires at a tendril and misses, splashing goo across a cracked cook unit. Voorhivey scores a direct hit. L-tech gel coats a ropy pink cable, which shudders and retracts through the floor.

There's a breathless panic. Shots splatter the walls; soldiers scramble for safety. The lamprey keeps moving beneath us, churning westward and finally slicing into the neighboring apartment.

A moment later we're alone in the wreckage, surrounded by slashes in the floor that open into a dark emptiness. The air stinks of recycled chlorine and rotten jackfruit. There's a hollow moan, the crackle of a broken light, the clatter of falling debris.

After a broken moment, I say, "Now it's our turn."

Sergeant Manager Li snaps into action. She assigns a sluggish M'bari to keep Basdaq alive and splits us into teams, telling Ting to plot a return route across the shattered floor to the western ledge.

Sporadic fire sounds from the surviving patriots—two dozen red marks still glimmer on my lens—but we ignore them as we weave through the wreckage.

We reach the ledge without losing anyone into a hole. The street looks rough through my cracked visor. A severed sky bridge dangles from above, swaying and sparking. Three gaping dark holes open in the tower opposite like the eyes and mouth of an immense skull.

A rumble sounds from the floors beneath us.

The lamprey is still churning through the building, still moving toward the bait.

A Bountiful Mehr CIC—combat insertion craft—lies smoldering three hundred yards away, half-buried in rubble. I don't know where it came from, and it doesn't occur to me to ask. Downed sailframes hang limply on the walkways and bridges, and the bodies of soldiers and patriots litter the rubble.

The lamprey bait glows yellowbeige on the recharge cistern housing. The surrounding platforms are strewn with the exploded guts of a caravan. The street is quiet. No fighting, just wreckage and aftermath.

When the rumble increases below us, Sergeant Manager Li lenses, "Wait on my green."

Despite the signal interference, Ting piggybacks on corner cameras and resident visors, showing us what we look like from afar: eight small figures clinging to the edge of a crumbling monolith. Pico and Ridehorse and Elfano are down. M'bari leans against a bullet-pocked column, barely conscious. Basdaq is curled on his side on the ground, his Boaz aiming in the general direction of the bait.

Gimmel Platoon is gone and only half of Bay is standing. My display tells me that Alfa is unscathed on the rooftop, impossibly far away, waiting to drop a thousand tons of ugly on this thing.

My shoulder itches. I clean my visor. Ting focuses her video on a round section of tower wall crumbling below us, collapsing from the inside. Mottled, writhing strands emerge from a widening hole. They flail at the air, dribbling pinkish snot.

The lamprey oozes into view like something horrible being born.

Its outer shell is composed of overlapping cables and plates widely enough spaced to offer a view of the crisscrossing mucous strands of the interior. It's beyond ugly, it's *wrong*. Inhuman and disturbing. This is the first time we've seen one this clear, this close. My eyes widen, my throat dries, and the urge to flee claws at me.

I hear Ting whimper and M'bari groan, but the weeks of training pay off; nobody breaks.

"Do we have a green, Sarge?" Basdaq gasps.

"Wait for it," she tells him, her voice wavering for once.

The lamprey crawl-slurps toward the bait, leaving a tunnel of destruction behind. Ting cuts the perspective video and I'm watching with my own eyes as the horror creeps across the street.

Most of its strands unfurl fifty feet from the shifting plates—but one fires two hundred feet and slices into a scraper like a skewer into a kebab.

Alloy melts and glassine shatters. The strand snaps back to the lamprey, leaving wreckage behind. Another strand fires five hundred feet—which disturbs me on a whole new level, violating my visceral sense of the laws of physics. There isn't enough *stuff* for the strand to stretch that far.

The lamprey creeps toward the bait, firing two pinkish cables to the base of the recharge cistern. A third unchains toward the ground. It branches into a dozen strands that strike at traincars, caravans, cargo trailers, mobile homes.

I don't watch the inhabitants die. I don't hear a thing. I just remember the disfigured lumps in that Los Anod street, mutilated and flayed and shrunken—

A CAV screams down from the sky.

It powers forward on ribbons like grappling hooks, swinging around elevated streets and ladder clusters. The CAV is a third the size of the lamprey, but Elfano was right: there's a certain similarity. Both are roughly spherical, with protruding elements for moving and attacking. Although as foreign as CAVs feel, lampreys are a thousand times stranger.

The CAV dives, leaves slashing, trying to drive the lamprey toward the bait.

The lamprey emits a fat cable, slow and almost deliberate. The CAV stays on path, and the cable strikes hard, crushing the CAV like a boot heel on an empty tube.

The force flings the CAV into a cloverleaf overpass. It falls and shudders beside the disemboweled Bountiful Mehr, then rocks to a halt. At least the cry pilot died fast.

"The fuck is an insertion craft doing here?" Cali asks, focusing on the Mehr.

"Nothing," I tell her.

"Let me fire one can before I pass out?" Basdaq pleads.

"Wait for the green," Sergeant Manager Li tells him. "First we need the CAVs to ensure that the target makes contact with the bait."

"The target's *trying* to make contact!" Ting says. "The bait is working!"

"Channel," Li murmurs, which means she agrees.

Two more CAVs launch into attacks with all the finesse of a drunk throwing haymakers. Both achieve direct impacts, carving chunks from the lamprey.

The lamprey heals itself as it shudders closer to the bait. Severed strands and plates knit together, and then cables erupt from the lamprey's skin and crush both CAVs.

Four seconds have elapsed since first contact. One CAV is totaled, but the other drags away, a twisted wreck withdrawing from battle.

"I thought CAVs soaked more damage than a dreadnought," Cali says.

"They do," Li tells her.

"They're popping like soap bubbles."

"They're using them wrong," I say, my grip tight inside my Boaz.

Another CAV is crushed and tossed aside. I feel the tilt of the pilot's frame and the machine craving to fight. I feel all that wasted potential, all that untapped power.

"C'mon!" I murmur. "Dodge, hit—*fight!*"

"The remote operators are lagging," Ting tells me. "The lamprey's signal interference slows the connection."

"They're serving up CAVs like snackbits," I say.

The lamprey oozes toward the bait. Dripping pink fringes reach the glowing yellowbeige octopus-shape and keep moving, rolling and spewing closer.

Shakrabarti says, "Brace for the explosion . . ."

No explosion comes. It's not a replay of Los Anod. Instead, the lamprey's strands touch the bait and the green go-sign flashes on my lens.

"Engage!" Sergeant Manager Li shouts.

A hail of L-tech brane rounds lashes from our ledge and the floors above us. The rounds can't self-correct because of the signal interference, so we're firing by sense of smell—and in a moment forty yards of the street-level road is painted yellowbeige.

The lamprey is drenched and bubbling. Slowing, sluggish, but not frozen.

Not yet.

The last two CAVs circle, looking for an opening, trying to weaken the remort or give the L-tech time to work. Alloy ribbons slash but the lamprey slices through both CAVs with a blur of cables—and Alfa Platoon opens fire from the rooftop.

Sheets of yellowbeige paste lash downward, covering every trace of lamprey. After Alfa runs dry, two Orit Gal gunships keep hosing down the target area. A mound rises where the lamprey enveloped the bait. Nothing's visible but L-tech.

"Hostile isolated," a voice says in my earbug. "Recife Unit engaging."

The barrage ends.

The street quiets.

"That's good, right?" Voorhivey asks, kneeling at Shakrabarti's bloody boot. "The lamprey's stuck."

"The mission washn't to trap it," M'bari slurs. "The mission was to exshtract a shample."

"Recife Unit is engineering," Li says.

"With handheld extractors," Jag says, eyeing the bubbling mess. "Better them than us."

"We dropped the anvil," Cali says. "We braned that puke-hole."

"Yeah," Basdaq mutters, around the film in his throat.

"Javelin teams, assume retrograde posture," a wide-channel announcement says. "Recife Unit incoming. Initial hostile-status report from Dee Platoon indicates that we braned that puke-hole."

Our exhausted laughter sounds like sobbing.

"Medic?" Sergeant Manager Li says, speaking quietly again.

Voorhivey looks up from Shakrabarti. "Sarge?"

"Ting just deactivated the spindle in Kaytu's shoulder," Li tells him. "So would you do me the favor of removing it?"

My heart stops. "It's *live*?"

"Not anymore," Li says, as Voorhivey trots toward me.

"It's harmless now," Ting assures me. "Except for stabbing you and stuff."

Voorhivey starts treating the wound. "It's barely a scratch, you won't even—"

"Sergeant!" Ting interrupts. "Priority message."

"Shit." Li frowns at her lens. "Bad news. Deconfirm that, Voorhivey. Patch Kaytu, don't fix him."

"What's up?" he asks.

"Recife Unit is unable to respond and—"

"What? Why?"

She highlights the fallen Bountiful Mehr on the company channel. "The patriots killed them."

"*That* was Recife?" Shakrabarti says, with a sound that is half moan and half laugh.

"They said we won!" Voorhivey coats my shoulder bandage. "They said we braned it!"

"That'sh PR," M'bari moans.

"So wait," Cali says. "What's the bad news?"

"What do you think?" Shakrabarti asks, tears streaking his beautiful face. "Ridehorse is dead. Pico is dead. Elfano is dead. Basdaq is—"

"I'm fine," Basdaq grunts. "I'm okay."

"Are you done?" Sergeant Manager Li asks Voorhivey.

He pats the numbing film on my shoulder. "It'll hold."

"Calil-Du, Kaytu, Jagzenka, form on me." Li heads northward along the ledge. "The bad news is, this lamprey will dissolve any minute. Worse news? There's nobody to work the handheld genome extractors but us."

CHAPTER 49

There's a dozen squads in the sky," Jag says, as we fall into place behind the Sergeant Manager. "Why are *we* catching this?"

"They're too far given the time frame," Li says. "We're the closest functional squad."

"We know shit about gene extraction," Cali growls.

"We're about to learn," Li says.

We cross a teetering bridge toward a performance garden and I'm not crying for the dead; I'm not scared. I'm not even meditating: I'm just numb. I can't think about everything we lost, not yet.

So I follow orders and pretend I'm okay.

A drop pod waits for us on a sheet filter. Li pops it and withdraws a handheld extractor that looks like a demented rocket launcher. The modified warhead is tipped with green-glowing tubes that remind me of bonespur.

"Looks like a prototype," Ting says on squad channel. She's

monitoring us, of course, and for a moment I'm almost glad she's a technopath.

"Looks like paraframes," Cali says, reaching deeper into the pod for a stack of frames.

"Strap in," Li says. "We've got one shot."

The frames self-assemble at Cali's command and we each grab one. The spindle in my shoulder catches on a strap. Jag winces but I don't feel any pain.

Cali secures my frame.

Li adjusts the extractor.

Then there's a moment. Time freezes and there's a moment when I think: *Stop this, protect the squad. Forget about swooping at a lamprey with a handheld extractor. Just fire a Boaz stream through the paraframes and save the fucking squad.*

The moment passes and we jump off the bridge four stories above the trapped lamprey. The walls and walkways of Belo City flash past me.

"The extractor is more of a sequencer," Ting says on squad channel. "It'll map the lamprey's genome, DNA, RNA, tDNA, and all the—"

I mute her as Cali speeds ahead. Jag and I flank the Sergeant Manager, swooping between cables and banners. Our job is to keep Li alive long enough to fire a single shot into this lamprey's guts, a single probe. I'm not thinking about backblast, I'm not thinking about DNA scans. I'm just following Cali toward the yellow-beige mound that's enveloping the lamprey.

This is just another nightmare, just another day. Just playing capture the crown again—

"It's dissolving!" an unfamiliar voice shouts on squad channel. "Move, move!"

"Who the fuck is that?" Jag asks.

An ID pops onto my suddenly live lens. The voice belongs to a DivCom executive. He sounds panicked as he overrides safeguards to speak directly to us. "It's dissolving! Dee Platoon, make contact now-now-now! We need data, we need that fucking data!"

"Interference abating," Ting reports. "Fire Team L, you are in my signals envelope."

In some deep corner of my mind, I hear Pico laughing at "Fire Team L." Street schematics flash on my lens. I adjust the vector of my descent and Li matches me. Cali shortens her wingspan and drops faster, while Jag sweeps above us, wheeling toward an outcropping for overwatch. She's the only one with enough remaining brane cans—and the sharpshooter rating—to smack away any lamprey cables that threaten us.

Cali lands first, ten yards from the roiling yellowbeige mass surrounding the lamprey. I'm beside her three seconds later. She shucks her paraframe and prowls into position but my frame sticks on my shoulder again, and I'm an unbalanced mess lurching across the ooze-dappled recharge cistern.

The yellowbeige mound gives off waves of heat and chill.

My breath stinks inside my mask.

Without even looking toward the lamprey, Li launches a flechette almost directly upward. A silvery filament stretches between the flechette and her extractor, vanishing toward the rooftops.

"It's a data cord," Ting says in my ear. "The extractor probe is hardwire connected so the other end is plugged into a research craft flying above the enclave, outside the interference, connected to every superprocessor in every corporation in every—"

I flick a blank message at her, not bothering to say *Quiet*, but she understands.

The numbness from my injured shoulder spreads into my arm. My fingers tingle and I brace myself against the charred remains of a post and take aim through tear-blurred eyes.

Sergeant Manager Li kneels twenty feet behind me and Cali, the extractor probe primed. The mound of yellowbeige goo is trembling. I'm trembling too. Li waits for the shot. My lens flickers with orders and blueprints and chatter until Li excludes everything except the four of us—and the lamprey.

And I realize that the post I'm leaning against isn't a post. It's the acid-burned husk of a segment of destroyed CAV.

My mouth tastes like death, but my hand is steady.

I'm ready for this.

A stream of standard liquammo fires from the Orit Gal, sketching an unbroken line across the L-tech mound. They're clearing a path for Li's extractor. Another stream burns down from above and a mottled pink surface bulges through the bubbling yellowbeige goo as the lamprey oozes for freedom.

Take the shot, take the shot.

A lamprey strand unfurls from the impact area. Two strands. Three, four, five. A shifting meaty plate starts to emerge and—

Li takes the shot.

The extractor probe flashes past me with the silvery filament flowing behind. It speeds between shifting plates and strikes a pink node inside the lamprey. The green bonespurlike tubes deploy, burrowing into the lamprey for samples.

My breath catches and my palm tightens on the trigger. The filament shimmers—

The mound explodes.

A gout of slime catches the paraframe I'm strapped into and knocks me sideways. I smack against the CAV segment and fall. My head rings; my vision doubles. I see two recharge cisterns, two tattered ad-banners . . .

Lamprey cables rise from the yellowbeige foam. Shit. *Shit.* I'm on the verge of fainting while that thing is breaking free. I roll to my stomach and brace my Boaz.

"Wait for it," the DivCom exec says, his voice tight. "Almost there. Establishing connec—"

The power dies in the building in front of us.

The windows turn dark one floor at a time.

The lights of the sky bridges and walkways blink off.

The next building dies, and the next one, swallowed by an abyssal darkness. The glow of the uppermost floors fades. Everything is dark except for the yellowbeige bait and the brilliant light of the filament, a pure white crack in a pitch-black world.

Voices crackle in my audio pickup:

"—it's in our systems, it's in our fucking sys—"

"Airgap! Emergency airgap!"

"DROP LINK DROP LINK! Trigger autodestruct!"

Fractal patterns bloom on my lens. Broken shapes strobe and an almost inaudible whine drives needles into my temples. Tears spring to my eyes and I can't tell if I'm really seeing translucent threads wriggling through the air—

"We're not reading *it*," a new voice says. "It's reading *us*."

In the dim glow of the bait, the lamprey emerges from the foam. Its plates swivel and shift on its framework of cords and cables. There's a glint of transparency, like the lamprey is coated in glass—and a pink strand whips at the filament.

Jag fires three times and hits twice.

Foam coats the strand, which twitches and smashes into the cistern underfoot. The grate jerks and lamprey cables lash at Cali.

She bellows and we empty our cans. Pink ooze splatters the ground, and the lamprey feathers into fumes.

CHAPTER 50

A nursurgeon sprays me into thera-sleep on the transport from Belo City. I lose myself in anxious dreams, then wake on a mattress made of starlight and hope. The medical devices around me purr reassuringly, like angels humming a lullaby.

My lens tells me that the spindle damaged my shoulder and I'm concussed. Also, I'm in a hospital room. I lie there and let memory return. I try not to think about Pico and Ridehorse and Elfano, but when sleep finally takes me there are tears on my face.

The next time I wake, it's morning. Turns out that the hospital on Ayko Base is as fancy as the pool. There's a MYRAGE rig, custom fitted for patients, and the vend is packed with delicious gels.

Ting is curled into an extruded cot beside my bed. When I yawn, her gaze shifts to me, and I'm struck with the oddest thought. I want to see her real eyes again, unhidden by her black lenses: I want to see her golden, stemhead pupils.

We talk about Pico for a while. We talk about Ridehorse, and Ting fills me in on the rest of the squad. Shakrabarti is in the next room, growing back his toes. Basdaq is down the hall and expected to make a full recovery. Cali's broken collarbone and the burns on Sergeant Manager Li's calf were outpatient procedures.

The news about M'bari isn't great: the shock round that tapped his head was a vintage neuroweapon and he's in thera-sleep in another wing.

Other news is better. Other news is *miraculous*: Elfano survived.

Apparently there isn't much left of her beyond a head and spinal column, but her suit kept her brain active. In a year or two, sagrado willing, she'll walk again. Maybe she'll even grow back her pointy ears.

"So," I finally ask Ting. "Did we get what we needed?"

She wrinkles her ferrety nose at me. "Well, I don't know what we *needed* exactly, what counts as necessary as opposed to—"

"Did we identify the lamprey, Ting?"

"Oh! Yeah, no. The extractor didn't isolate any genetic material."

"Not *any*?"

She shakes her head. "It's like lampreys weren't bio-forged."

A messy transcription scrolls onto my lens:

—no genetic profile. Zero. None.

Are you saying they're not organic? They're machines?

They're organic and machines. They're remorts.

With zero genetic profile?

Or with unprecedented cellular defenses.

What the fuck are we looking at here? This is like nothing we've seen, this is not like anything any of us has ever seen.

"Wait," I say, skimming the transcription. "Lampreys aren't remorts?"

"Maybe they are." Ting closes one eye thoughtfully. "I mean, if they're based on a SICLE weapon with genetic defenses? That makes sense. Nothing else makes sense. Except maybe they're *not* based on bioweapons with genetic defenses."

"If they're not remorts . . ."

"Yeah," she says. "Boom. It's a whole new world."

"Who is that in the transcription you sent?" I lens.

"C-suite generals, mostly. They're a little panicked. I mean, unnerved or nonplussed. Oh! I wonder if—"

"If you ask if *plussed* is the opposite of *nonplussed*, I'll punch you in the ventricle."

She sticks her tongue out.

"They have to be remorts," I say. "Nothing else makes sense."

"There's nothing like them in the databases. They don't have a genetic signature and, I mean, everyone's dumbfounded. Nobody knows."

"You don't have any personal theories?"

"I can't read them." She makes a religious sign she copied from Ridehorse. "They're all kinds of wrong."

"And what about that blackout? The entire Freehold lost power."

"It wasn't just a blackout. Something—" She pauses. "We made an incision into that lamprey and found *ourselves* on the operating table."

"What does that mean, Ting?"

"We opened a window, but the lamprey looked at *us*."

"Ting! Stop talking shit. What happened?"

"Um, well, we probed the lamprey for genetic tags, right? For tDNA sequences and the rest and—and when we linked to the military processors, to analyze the samples? The lamprey crashed a thousand firewalls and breached a million systems and analyzed *us*."

A chill touches my spine. I don't know what she means, but I know it scares me. "The lamprey hacked the corpo systems?"

"Not really, but pretty much. Do you want to see a transcription of *that*?"

"No, I—"

!SYSTEM INTRUSION ALERT!

!ANOMALY-BASED DEVIATION DETECTED!

!SATURATION SYSTEM INTRUSION ALERT!

!SYSTEM INTRUSION ALERT!

!SATURATION SYSTEM ENCROACHMENT ALERT!

!INTRUSION ALERT!

!INDUCTIVE ANOMALY-BASED DEVIATION FLAGGED!

**ACCESS GRANTED ACCESS GRANTED ACCESS GRANTED
ACCESS GRANTED ACCESS GRANTED ACCESS GRANTED
ACCESS GRANTED ACCESS GRANTED ACCESS GRANTED
ACCESS GRANTED ACCESS GRANTED ACCESS GRANTED
ACCESS GRANTED ACCESS GRANTED ACCESS GRANTED
ACCESS GRANTED**

"Ting, enough!" The scrolling stops. "So the lamprey accessed corpo systems, and that caused the blackout?"

She scrubs her amber hair with her fingers. "Not just corpo systems, though. It hacked vend machines and concert recordings and ratification guides."

"Sagrado," I breathe. "Are they *intelligent*?"

"The corpo's looking into that, she says, and lenses me: "I don't think so. I tracked the hack and it's weird. Random. It grabbed as much trivia and gossip as proprietorial stuff."

I watch one of the medical monitors, my mind whirling around questions I'm not smart enough to ask. Finally, I say, "So what's Javelin thinking now?"

"That they need a corpse."

"A lamprey corpse?"

"The theory is that they don't dissolve if they're dead," Ting says. "Dissolving is like a, a stage in their life cycle. If we kill them, we stop the cycle. And getting a sample didn't work, the probe didn't work. So that's the next step, getting a whole corpse."

"Except nothing short of a hellfrost strike kills these things."

"CAVs might. Enough CAVs. If they send dozens and dozens."

I shiver at the thought of all those dead cry pilots, and Ting changes the subject until my meds put me to sleep.

On my second morning in sick bay, Calil-Du shoves inside my room. Her head is freshly shaved and an evil light glints in her eyes. I expect her to talk about the lamprey, but she says, "The services are tomorrow."

She means the funerals for Pico and Ridehorse. "I know."

"You think it's come as you are?"

"Huh?"

"You're going like *that*?"

I don't know what she means. "Well, I'll get out of bed first. They're releasing me this afternoon."

"And you're planning on rolling up to the funerals in your ugly-ass fatigues?"

We don't have dress uniforms, because we live in the cracks between the services. We're in Javelin but never really left basic. Plus, there *are* no Javelin uniforms, dress or otherwise.

"What?" I ask. "I'll tuck in my shirt."

"No."

"My civilian stuff is—"

"You're wearing this." She lenses me a high-fashion gown that all the stylish Class A men are wearing this season. "And don't whine about the cost. I'm buying."

"Oh, I see now," I tell her. "You think I'm Shakrabarti."

"Muh?" she says.

"If you're looking for a fashionboy, you want Hoppy Two Toes in the next room."

"Please piss me off," Cali says. "I'd love an excuse to dump you on the floor and step on you."

"Well, what are you wearing?"

"Some old rags." She lenses me an image of herself cocooned in what looks like the same high-fashion gown she already showed me. "I've had it for years."

"You clean up good," I say, giving a low whistle. Although actually she does not clean up good. She looks like an executioner at a tea party.

"Asshole," she says, clearly pleased.

"But I'm not wearing that dress."

"Why not?"

"Because it costs more than I've earned in my entire life. Plus, it clashes with my eyes. How about this, Calil-Du? I'll shave my head and we'll go as twins."

So she dumps me on the floor. At least she doesn't step on me.

After the medics kick her out, we argue on our lenses until I agree to wear a kurta she approves of, which is a long golden skirt and a black-and-red smartwired shirt. I don't *only* agree because I'm planning to cannibalize the smartwire into lockpicks. I also agree because Pico would laugh to see me dressed up fancy as a Class B gooddog.

"You hear about the lamprey?" Cali asks, after ordering the kurta.

"That we didn't get any gene markers? Yeah."

"It's not a remort. No genetic information? That's the fucking *opposite* of a remort."

"It's not an alien, Cali."

She lenses me a shrug. "You know what shits me? Pico and Ridehorse died for nothing. We didn't extract DNA, but Li keeps saying that they advanced the mission, that we need to know what *doesn't* work, too. I asked if she knows what *doesn't* get her teeth knocked out."

I check squad channel. "And she enrolled you in a seminar on combat trauma integration."

"It's not combat trauma," she tells me. "I just want to stomp on her intestines."

"That'll prove you're integrated."

"Nah." She shows me an evil grin. "But it'd relieve my stress."

The next day, there's a formal funeral with a hundred people who never met Pico and Ridehorse, which involves solemn speeches and sharp salutes. After the military service, though, a few dozen members of Pico's family arrive via projection. One of Pico's sisters plays a bamboo flute as the children fold origami boats.

I sit with Pico's father, the one who'd been a scorch artist in Burkinabé. He tells me stories about Pico's childhood. I tell him stories about basic until a corporate message flashes on squad channel, reminding us not to discuss proprietorial corporate information such as the existence of a new class of remorts.

"He's a hero," Ting lenses me privately. "He died fighting lampreys, and they'll never know."

"He wouldn't care."

"*I* care! They're saying he died in a training accident. I hate them."

Ridehorse's faith requires a monthlong service at her home. Her family asks us to burn everything she owned and invites us to live with them in the High Atlas enclave. Tingting bursts into tears; she's never been invited anywhere before. Oh, and Ridehorse's family calls her *Annie*, which is short for a nine-syllable name I can't pronounce, and which makes my eyes fill with tears.

Then there's a small service with the squad, which involves sloppy drunks and gales of laughter.

The laughter surprises me.

Ting managed—thankfully, nobody asks how—to collect dozens of loops of Pico and Ridehorse over the past few months. Clips of them screwing around, making jokes, making trouble. We laugh till we cry, till there's no difference between laughter and tears.

Voorhivey—of all people—hijacks a luxury elevator for the funeral, which moves us in endless loops through the building. Cali is drugged out of her bald skull, wearing her horrible dress, stomping her way through a lamentation dance. Shakrabarti sprawls on a swingchair with streamers dangling from his half-healed foot, while Jag is curled on his lap painting jaguar rosettes on his chest. M'bari attends via a hologram. He's deep in conversation with Sergeant Manager Li while I'm on a swing, buzzing on military-spec soft-drugs with Ting pushing me.

"I don't think—" she says, as I swing toward her. "What still bugs me?"

"What," I say, at the top of my arc where she can't hear.

"—what killed them," she says, when I return.

"Huh?" I ask, when she can't hear.

"—nobodyevenknowswhytheydied!" she blurts the next time I'm close. And over the next few swings, she explains. "Lampreys killed them. The worst things since the SICLE War. Maybe even before then. Pico and Ridehorse died fighting a genocide-class weapon. And nobody knows. Their families don't know."

I stop swinging. "We know."

"It's not enough," she says, with a hitch in her voice.

Tears pool in her eyes, so I send her a click that means *tell me*.

Pictures of her mother as a girl immediately bloom around me: she's bulkier than Ting, with the same pointy nose and oddball smile. The collage shifts; her mother ages. Ting's birth is the brightest moment in her mother's life, and seven years later becomes the darkest.

Her mother disappears into a basement so off-grid that there's no MYRAGE connection. The pictures vanish. There's nothing, except Ting's voice: "There's nothing about her on any channel, in any database. Not about *her*. A few dates, sequences, addresses. Nothing that matters. She's gone like she never existed, like her life never happened. Just because she—she got addicted, she sold me to that manufactory—that doesn't mean she's nothing. When we steal memories, we erase people. That won't happen with Pico and Ridehorse. I won't let it."

CHAPTER 51

Anvil Squad is protected from the feverish reaction to the Belo City blackout by virtue of rank. We hear that the executive suites and research units are furiously reevaluating strategies and shifting resources, but nobody bothers the grunts.

Works for me.

M'bari is still recovering, so we're depending on Sergeant Manager Li for gossip. She says there are three primary schools of thought about lampreys:

1. The terrafixing protocol reevolved lampreys from a cyber-warfare intrusion module: a weapon built to infiltrate data labs, bypass signal defenses, and download the contents.

2. Lampreys are the physical forms of weaponized computer viruses, complete with cellular defenses, created when the terrafixing regenned invasive algorithms into corporeal form.

3. Sophisticated patriot groups created lampreys in an attempt to destroy the corporate hegemony. Supporters of this theory point to previous insurgents with impressive capacities, such as the Plaguemaker of Vila Vela.

I'm halfway through physical therapy in the immersion tank when a command-level authorization overrides my lens. Despite being surrounded by calming gel, I feel a jolt of nerves. Is this another deployment? Are we following waves of suicidal CAVs to collect a lamprey corpse?

Except when images brighten on my lens, I'm looking at a dozen models striking poses. Statues? Sims? Some strange MYRAGE event? No. I'm seeing a dozen versions of Shakrabarti, each wearing a different outfit.

"Um," I say.

"Which one do you like best?" Ting asks me, opening another screen with her face. "He keeps asking for my opinion, but I don't know about this stuff."

"I thought you were keeping a low profile."

"I am! That's why I always dress so boring and don't know anything about fashion! He's cute in the little fringy one, don't you think?"

"I mean a low profile with your . . ." I pause a moment too long. "Hacking."

"Oh! Oh, well, I didn't override your lens just to ask you about Shakrabarti."

"No?"

"Course not. I finally got a private link for you. With Rana."

"Right now? A live line? No way."

"Yes way! All the way. Where there's a will way! You ready?"

"Sure, yes," I say. "Thanks. And Tingting?"

"Hm?"

"He looks glossily rakish in that sparkle-suit."

Ting giggles. "What does that mean?"

"No idea."

"I'll tell him!" she says, and shifts the connection.

The various Shakrabartis shatter, and a default bluescreen fuzzes into place. I try to set the immersion tank to private, only to discover that Ting already took care of it.

There's a lag as the link extends into interplanetary space. A haze appears on a field of blue. I opaque my lens. The blue turns black and the haze turns into a million pinpricks of ancient light. Space surrounds me. I feel weightless in the therapeutic gel, and only the faintest trace of the immersion tank peeks from behind the dark sprawling universe.

A Flenser craft drifts into view.

Just one ship, because space is rather large. Even in a massive fleet, the ships aren't visible to each other with the naked eye. The craft floats through the nothingness, spinning slowly. It's cone-shaped and gawky, because one of the great tragedies of the space race was the death of a billion youthful fantasies of cool, stream-lined designs that screamed "interstellar ass-kicker."

Instead, we got cones. Space cones.

Still, as the craft angles closer to my viewpoint, I'm impressed by the curved foametal hull, and the trawler-drive pulling the ship is a marvel of AI engineering. The array rings gyrating along the length of the cone are just goofy, though, like bracelets on a pear.

My perspective shifts through the rings, through the hull, and into the craft. This corridor looks nothing like the triangular one in Dag Bravska; it's claustrophobic and lined with machinery, twice as tall as me but barely as wide.

The hallway vanishes and Rana appears in a transmission chamber. Her skin gleams and her lenses glow green. Her expression is serious, almost stern. Almost *angry*. That's just Rana, though. I know she's happy to see me, even though her lips barely move.

That's okay, my lips move plenty.

She's wearing a billowing suit that looks like white flavorant swirling through a glass of black chai. Flensers don't wear tight uniforms like marines. They wear flowing gowns of programma-ble material that extrude and retract on command to let them in-teract more fully with the cramped environment.

So I say, "You didn't have to get dressed up just for me."

"I'm glad to see," she says, after a lag, "that you still think you're funny."

I laugh, for no reason except that I've missed her voice. "I'm glad to see you're still you."

A hood extrudes from her uniform, like she's pulling a cloak around herself for privacy. "You're lucky your message got through. Ting says you stole an authorization?"

"Oh," I say, not even thinking the word *technopath*. "Yeah, I—I got lucky."

Her gaze sweeps me. "What happened to your shoulder?"

"I caught a spindle."

"You were deployed again? Since Los Anod?"

My happiness curdles. She doesn't know about our losses. "Yeah. Belo City."

"Against a lamprey?" Her green gaze brightens. "Did you get a specimen?"

"There were patriots. It got ugly. We didn't get a sample. At best, we field-tested some gear."

"I wish I were there."

"You're not the only one. We missed you like ozone."

"Oh!" she says, like she's surprised that we remember her.

"We needed a little robotic heartlessness."

She actually smiles. "You're such an asshole."

"Now you sound like Cali. How's the final frontier?"

We talk about the Flensers for a few minutes, about her classes and squadmates, the ship and the vastness. In return, I brag about the elevators of Ayko Base, like I'm the one surrounded by superior tech.

Eventually, though, I drag things back into the gravity well. I tell her about the lamprey defeating an extraction probe and zapping a city grid. "We're deep in the latrine here, Rana. You have any gossip?"

"Almost everything I know, you've probably already heard. They strike in an apparently random pattern, targeting tech and population centers. Nobody knows how, nobody knows why. They self-disassemble after a few hours."

"What set them off in the first place?"

"Nobody knows. One lamprey struck, then two the next month. Nothing for three months, then four within a week. You're still looking for a sample?"

"They want a whole dead lamprey now."

"Since when? They need an intact specimen?"

"That's the theory." I pause. "You said I've heard *almost* everything you know?"

She hesitates. "There's one thing. I . . . I don't think I'll tell you."

"Will it help? If it'll help, tell me."

"It won't help."

"Okay," I say, tightly.

"What? You're hiding something, too."

So I tell her that M'bari is still undergoing tests, and Shakrabarti's waiting for his baby toes to finish growing and Basdaq is weak and wheezing. I tell her about Elfano. I tell her about Pico and Ridehorse. Her face shuts down, which is what she does instead of crying.

I try to comfort her and after a time she says, "Tell them—tell them I'll write Pico's and Ridehorse's names in the stars."

That's a Flenser tradition, sending smoke out an airlock, in commemoration of the dead. "Ridehorse would've liked that. Pico—"

"—would've laughed," she finishes.

We smile at each other for a sad moment, and then a countdown clock appears. 18:63. We don't have much longer.

"Maseo," Rana murmurs.

"I'm right here," I tell her.

"A million miles away. Say my name."

"Sarav."

Her hood shifts around her face. "I'll link you if I hear anything."

"I'll link you even if I hear nothing at all."

Her smile shines, then fades. "The other thing about lampreys? At the highest levels, they're calling this an extinction-class threat. That's why my father pulled me off Earth."

"At least you're safe."

"Safer." She exhales slowly. "You remember Dag Bravska? The hab that exploded?"

"Vividly."

"You were right. A technopath didn't kill Dag Bravska. A lamprey did."

My skin prickles. "They're coming from deep fucking space? What the—"

"No, no! They didn't attack on the way to Earth or anything. But one of them, at least, reached out across ninety million miles . . ."

"So they—are they really a bio-forged computer virus?"

"I don't know. This stuff about a blackout is new to me."

"Reached across ninety million miles," I repeat. "I wish I could do the same."

Her green-lensed eyes crinkle. "I'm Class A and you're a Free-holder. I'm a Flenser and you're a groundhog. I'm me and you're you. We're all wrong for each other."

"At least we have *that* in common."

"I'm coming back," she tells me.

"To me? To us? To Earth?"

She nods. "My father isn't the only one who plays the game. If I score top of my class, they'll let me serve a tour on Earth before—"

The clock flashes, warning us before the link ends. Silence falls. Light from across the solar system glimmers on her cheekbones and sparkles in her eyes. I was wrong the first time I saw her. She's not the brittle, jagged black of onyx; she's the deep, endless black of space.

"Take care of them," she says.

I reach out to touch her face. The image ripples around my fingers, breaking into interference waves. Rana places her projected hand over mine, and I almost feel the warmth of her palm.

CHAPTER 52

Rana isn't the only member of Anvil Squad planning to return. Voorhivey bursts into the barracks the next morning, giddy with excitement. "Ojedonn requested transfer!"

Jag laughs. "He's coming here? When?"

"I don't know." Voorhivey's smile makes him look like a kid. "That's all I heard, I'm not sure. Sarge?" He opens an all-squad channel. "Sergeant Manager? I heard Ojedonn is transferring back to the squad? You don't know him—he's from basic—Kaytu broke his knee in a hallway."

"I broke his back in a bed," Cali says.

A projection appears with Sergeant Manager Li's face. "He's not the only one," she tells us. "I was going to brief you."

"How about Rana?" Cali straightens, like she's about to salute. "Is Rana coming back?"

"She's the CE's daughter?"

"Yeah," Shakrabarti says. "She's in the Flensers now."

"Then she's a long way off," Li says.

"Can you—" Cali ducks her head. "Will you ask her special? I mean, just remind her she can transfer. Just so she knows that . . . you know."

"I'll do that," Li assures her. "I was going to cover this in today's briefing. After the Belo City blackout, Javelin Command put out a request for troops who trained with the Ayko units. For volunteers. Werz and Gazi are coming, too."

"Yin and Yang," Jag says.

Ting giggles. "This is so neat!"

"You didn't know?" I lens her.

"Of course not. I don't monitor *everything*, silly! Only like a tenth of a third of a fraction of a percent of everything. Also, I've been busy."

"Busy with what?"

"Oh," she says, faux innocent. "This and that."

"When're they landing?" Voorhivey asks.

"They're en route already," the sergeant says. "Almost seven thousand troops are rotating into Ayko Base over the next seven days."

"Yeah, but when are they *landing*?"

"Two days," she says, and there's a ragged little cheer.

For the first time since Belo City, I stop thinking about the buildings turning black and my lens crashing. And for the first time, I don't dream about lampreys. Instead, I dream about sitting in the mess hall with Pico and Ridehorse while CAVs roll silently past.

I wake to a training initiative that sharpens our skills in Intensive Paperwork, Tedious Bureaucracy, and Waiting for Former Squadmates to Return. We grumble about the after-action briefings and fitness recertifications and trauma evals . . . and the deployment alarm.

We hate the alarm, because *we're* not being deployed. Other teams roll from Ayko Base, as support for CAVs trying to bag lampreys, but we're low on the rotation.

"The bait's not working anymore," Ting lenses the squad in the middle of the night. "Nobody knows why."

Jagzenka lenses a rude picture. "I'm trying to sleep."

"I'm in treatment," M'bari sends.

"The pattern of lamprey emergence is vacillating, I think," Ting says. "I mean, changing. Except it feels like vacillation. Is there a word that means—"

"Switch it off, fuckhead," Cali lenses her. "Or I will snap your twig neck."

"Sorry! Night, everyone! Have a good treatment, Barleyquan!"

Barleyquan? M'bari's first name is *Barleyquan?*

The next afternoon, Sergeant Manager Li gathers the surviving members of Anvil Squad in the platoon conference room. Calil-Du, Jagzenka, Voorhivey, Ting, Shakrabarti, and me. Apparently M'bari is recovering faster than expected; he joins us on a projection, though Basdaq is otherwise occupied, undergoing a medical procedure.

There are only seven of us here—although our total number will swell to eleven soon, then twelve when Rana arrives—which leaves a lot of empty space in the room. I wonder if the Sergeant Manager is making a point. We've barely started fighting these things, and we've already lost a third of our squad.

"Are they here?" Voorhivey asks, a little too eagerly. "The rest of the squad? Are they here yet?"

The anticipation in his voice bugs me, as does my own excitement. I don't know why, exactly. Maybe I worry that we expect Ojedonn, Werz, and Gazi to fill in for Pico, Ridehorse, and Elfano. Like we're trying to replace our dead friends.

"There's been a delay," Li says.

"What kind of delay?" M'bari's projection asks. "That doesn't sound probable."

"We'll get to that." Sergeant Manager Li talks about various housekeeping issues for twenty minutes and takes a breath like she's getting to the important stuff. "So—"

"What happened in Belo City?" Voorhivey interrupts.

"Whole cities crashed," M'bari says. "Entire enclaves lost power."

"Whatever weapon platform the lampreys are based on," Li says, "they've got cellular defenses and cyberwarfare capacity. That's one theory, at least." She talks about the other theories: weaponized viruses and cutting-edge patriot munitions. "However, we're presuming that the terrafixing is reevolving a prototype bioweapon."

"Do you think they're remorts?" Shakrabarti asks.

Li smiles faintly. "I can't imagine what else they'd be."

"Which isn't exactly a *yes*," Voorhivey says.

Skepticism is so unlike him that we all stare in disbelief and Shakrabarti says, "Our baby is growing up."

"If you want a definite statement," Li says, "here's one. The only way to secure a useful specimen is to kill a lamprey before it can dissolve."

"How?" Jag asks.

"We're support and supply for CAV corps."

Cali grunts. "They're taking us off the front lines?"

"That's correct," Li says. "It's all about the CAVs now."

"Thank the Louvre," Ting whispers.

Li gestures to the screen behind her, which shows a lamprey tearing through a complex of transit pods. "Command distributed this video to impress upon you the seriousness of the situation."

"Because we don't already know they're badass?" Shakrabarti says.

Li gives a shake of her head. "It's not that."

"The delay," M'bari's projection says. "This is why there's a delay with the others getting here."

"Yeah, the lampreys are now targeting—" Li catches herself. "No. They *seem* to be targeting military installations. We're cautioned against ascribing intention to them."

"Hold up!" Cali says. "*They're* targeting *us*?"

"When did that start?" M'bari asks Li. "The, um, apparent targeting?"

"After Belo City," she says. "However, correlation is not causation."

"Yeah," Cali says. "I've got no idea what that means."

"That the targeted attacks might have nothing to do with the blackout," I tell her.

Cali snorts. "And I might have three tits."

"Pretty sure I would've noticed."

She looks around the conference room. "They're coming for us. These fatherfucks hacked us in Belo City and now they're coming for us."

"So the lampreys are attacking military transit stations," Jag says. "And that's why Ojedonn and Werz and Gazi are delayed?"

"That's right," Li says. "But this is nothing new. Remorts have caused delays before."

"Not on purpose," Voorhivey mutters.

"Are they okay?" Tingting asks Li. "Gazi and the others? Are they okay?"

Sergeant Manager Li nods. "They're fine. In other news, quarantine is lifting in a few days, which means—"

"I can talk to my folks!" Jag says.

"In a few days." Li lowers her voice, commanding our full attention. "And the reason the quarantine is lifting is that the embargo failed."

Cali scratches her bald head. "What embargo?"

"The embargo on lamprey-related information in MYRAGE," Li says. "As of this morning, MYRAGE is bursting with scans of lampreys. Including ones from Belo City."

Voorhivey frowns. "Didn't Command censor that?"

"Apparently they missed a game port." The sergeant's lens glimmers with data. "Opium Civil? A player falanx scoped the lamprey and spread the word until half of United North Africa was peering through their port."

I don't react to the words *Opium Civil*; I don't glance at Ting. I don't doubt for a moment that she cracked the embargo after beating the corpos' technopaths and worked through that gamer kid

Loa to spread the news. She wanted people to know what Pico and Ridehorse died fighting. She wanted their families to know.

"So why not drop quarantine *today*?" Jag demands, rubbing a rosette on her neck. "Why wait?"

"Because procedure," Li tells her. "Now, if you don't mind, to the point. With the quarantine ending and our brief reduced to CAV support, you have a choice. This fight is moving into a new phase and Javelin is the tip of the spear."

"Javelin is the tip of the javelin!" Ting says.

Sergeant Major Li quiets her with a look. "The fight is moving into a new phase. You can stick with Javelin or request assignment to one of the branches. If you choose the latter, you'll be placed in the Garda or the Army—"

"Or the marines, right?" Cali asks.

"In theory."

"What about you, Sarge?" I ask. "Are you staying?"

"I was seconded to Javelin to help a squad of untested soldiers face the lamprey threat. Except I don't see any untested soldiers in this room. I don't see any slippers. I see warriors. Yes, I'm staying. This is a fight I believe in. This is a squad I believe in."

I start to say something, then close my mouth.

"Kaytu?" Li asks. "Something to add?"

"No, I just wanted—" I feel myself flush. "I wanted to say something smartass like Pico, but I'm not good at smartass."

"Look on the bright side, prez," Jagzenka tells me, pitching her voice like Pico's. "At least you're good at *dumb*ass."

Cali slugs Jag in the shoulder. "Ha!"

"I don't need a decision now," Li tells us. "There's no rush. You've got till tomorrow."

"I'm glad there's no rush," M'bari says.

"Nobody knows lampreys better than the troops of Ayko Base. We are the tip—" Li glances at Ting. "We're the bleeding edge of the warhead. I won't blame anyone who sticks with their initial career plan, their promotions and bonuses. But this fight? This is a long slog through an acid swamp with nothing on the other side but blood and tears." Her eyes are as intense as her voice is quiet. "And none of you want to miss *that*."

Jagzenka shoots me a look and lenses, "Sarge needs to work on her rousing speeches."

Except we both know she doesn't. *Blood and tears* is music to our ears.

"Questions?" Li asks.

I scratch my bandaged shoulder. "What's the salary?"

"You're so gutter," Cali mutters.

Li lenses the pay schedule.

"Sweet biyo!" Ting blurts.

"Gehenna," I gasp. "That's stockholder pay."

"You're already a stockholder, you splice," Shakrabarti tells me.

"I own one share."

"Check your portfolio again, Kaytu," Li says.

I check, and am struck dumb. I'm worth one hundred and one shares in Shiyogrid. Most Class C shareholders own thousands, and Rana's family probably owns millions, but still . . . one hundred and one shares. That's massive for a roach.

Cali hunches a muscular shoulder. "I've got a question."

"Yes, Private?"

"That guy in Belo City, the patriot commander you talked to? Remember him?"

Li half smiles. "Vaguely."

"Any word on who he is? Or what he's after?"

"Not a peep. And I don't expect one. We're soldiers, Calil-Du; we'll never see the big picture. I'm not sure there *is* one. Belo City—"

Ting pipes up with, "Maybe there's only a lot of little pictures! I mean, like a mosaic!"

"Belo City," Li repeats, "isn't even Shiyogrid turf. It's Unidroit, and no doubt they're already grinding that patriot group into chewable paste."

"Maybe that's what he wanted," M'bari's projection says.

"Maybe it is," Li says, and her flat gaze sweeps the room. "But for once the question is, what do *you* want?"

"To fuck up some lampreys," Cali says. "When do we deploy?"

"Soon," Sergeant Manager Li promises. "As soon as the next generation of firepower is developed and we're recertified for active duty."

"I like the sound of *next generation*," Shakrabarti says.

"I like the sound of *firepower*," Cali says. "They better not screw us with crappy tech."

"We're grunts," the sergeant tells her. "The only thing I *do* know is that they'll screw us. Think it over. What do you want? Stay or leave?"

CHAPTER 53

What do I want? I want to swim.

My shoulder starts stiff but feels better after twenty laps. At forty I find my rhythm—and four laps later, the monitor withdraws permission for continued exercise.

I grab a snack and head for a gazebo in a private corner of a balcony garden. I raise a privacy film and finish working on my black-and-red smartwire lockpicks. While I'm making adjustments, I browse the news on an approved channel. Despite the traces of quarantine that remain, the channel's toppicks strike me as an honest reflection of the current state of MYRAGE.

Panic.

Confusion.

Terror.

The world has discovered lampreys. After the news broke about the attack in Belo City, every hint of a previous sighting received millions of upvotes. Nineteen incidents appear on MYRAGE. At least four hundred thousand casualties, with ten times as many injured and ten times *that* in displacements.

The most inflammatory thing is this: while new remorts, even deadlier than cataphracts, slaughtered entire blocks, the corpos concealed the damage. Everyone understands why. Everyone knows the corpos acted out of concern, because panic only makes things worse. Still, the backlash against the embargo is harsh, and MYRAGE is writhing with questions.

What *are* these remorts? What tech spawned them? What program drives them?

There are no answers.

Conspiracies flourish in the vacuum. Lampreys aren't a new class of remorts, they're an alien invasion! They're bio-forged prototypes developed by a crypto-corporation, living weapons of the now-sentient New Growth, or divine retribution.

I adjust the smartwire, turning things over in my head. The lampreys aren't aliens. Human civilization is surrounded by an impregnable defense against aliens; it's called the speed of light. The New Growth didn't develop self-awareness; there are no secret, hidden crypto-corporations. And I'm pretty sure lampreys aren't supernatural punishment for our sins, though if the Seven Heavens decided to wipe the slate clean, I couldn't really blame them.

This is simple. Lampreys are experimental weapons with uncanny cellular defenses, deployed in the SICLE War and then transformed by the New Growth into something inhuman. Maybe.

Probably. Almost certainly. In the end, I find comfort in not seeing the big picture. I'm with Ting. My vision doesn't extend beyond a single square of the mosaic.

That's okay. I'm a soldier, not a strategist.

When I'm done fashioning my lockpick, the smartwire looks like a braided bracelet and a matching ringset. An *ugly* bracelet and ringset, because I copied the design from a fashion channel that Shakrabarti calls "aggressively bland."

Which happens to be my personal style motto.

I roll my shoulder and decide the lockpick needs a test run. I've popped the lock to the drone maintenance garage twice in the past four days, to stare out the window at the CAV deployment post. I don't know why, but I'm drawn to them.

"You feel a kinship," Ting said into my earbug, the last time I stood at the window watching the CAV post.

I jerked in surprise. "Stop watching me all the time!"

"Okay!" she said. "Sorry! Bye!"

The line went dark. "Tingting?" I asked, after a moment.

"I'm not here," she said. "I'm not monitoring you. I mean, I don't *always* keep tabs on people I care about just in case."

I snorted at the distant Bumblebees. "I don't feel a kinship with them."

"You do, too."

"Why would I—"

"Because you almost paired with your CAV when you were a cry pilot! It interacted with you, didn't it?"

I didn't answer, remembering the CAV's ribbons groping toward me, the sensation of untapped power, my urge to seize the controls.

"I mean," she said, "in that first fight outside the ocean installation place. Against that Ijapa, the submarine remort thingie."

"You watched me?"

"Not at the time! I was busy trying to save my life."

"Which you did by using your . . ." I paused. "You hacked your CAV?"

"I tricked it into bonding with me, at least for a few seconds. Which is what you almost did, even without my trick."

"It didn't feel like bonding," I said.

"Almost means almost," she told me. "CAVs were designed to pair with cry pilots, but they can't, not usually."

"They don't pair with us, Ting. They use our cerebral activity for computing power or something."

"That's what everyone thinks," she said, "but there's deep, buried code in CAVs—not even code, really. There's a protocol for pairing CAVs with the human mind, except they can't."

"Why not?"

She wrinkled her nose. "Who knows? I guess the AIs didn't understand humans."

"So they *can't* pair with us."

"Well, they can, maybe, sort of, in theory. Not easily, though. It's like trying to fit a square peg into a round peg."

"A round hole."

"Oh, no. Pairing is much harder than *that*. You came pretty close, though, because—I don't know. Your brainwaves sort of flat-line sometimes."

"You monitor my brainwaves?" I asked, and didn't mention my cultish terrafixing meditation.

"I monitor your stomach lining," she told me. "How do you do that?"

"Do what, digest?"

"You know what I mean. Suppress your brainwaves."

"I stop using my brain."

She sent me a picture of herself, sticking her tongue out. "Fine! Don't tell me."

"Wait. So you paired to your CAV?"

"Not really. I only tricked it for a minute. Maybe I could pair *you*, if you flatlined first, but probably not. It's like convincing a million fleas to march in, um, consonance or concordance or—"

"Unison," I said. "It's like catching a tsunami in a drinking glass."

She wrinkled her nose. "You're weird. Anyway, I don't know if it's possible, even for me. And without a technopath, forget it. And also, a patrol is coming and they'll find you unless you move."

So I moved, taking care to lock the door behind me with a re-coded meal-chit I'd arranged.

That worked well enough for a simple lock, but my smartwire pick demands a more rigorous challenge. So what the gehenna—that night I break into the CAV post itself.

I clone an all-base permission and wander the grounds until my anti-surveillance loops close. I'm about to pop the exterior gate of the CAV post when three BPs—base police—appear. Before I have a chance to launch into my prepared lies, they open the gate and wave me through.

I catch the lift down to the ninth floor and find a high-security door to the CAV operators station. *Too* high-security. I'm an adequate street burglar, but I can't handle military-grade stuff.

This is a stupid idea anyway. What am I doing? Clinging to my image of myself as a rebel or a Freeholder? Hungering for the hit of adrenaline that comes from breaking the rules? Trying to prove that I'm more than a faceless cog in a corporate military machine?

Maybe I'm just finding reassurance in my old skills. With the lampreys attacking military installations, with old squad members dead and new squad members delayed, I need something to settle my nerves.

I head back toward the supply lift—and spot a door into the CAV bay. Sloppier security than the operators' station, and so what if I *am* just trying to prove I'm not a faceless cog in the corporate machine?

That's a reasonable thing for a faceless cog to try to prove.

When I rub my thumb against my ring, the smartwire unfurls into a tool as fine as a rat's whisker. I direct the head into a film sensor. Twenty seconds later, a tiny decoherence opens. The wire extends through. I feel resistance and current on my fingertips and smile to myself. The lockpick works perfectly; there's no problem with the *pick*.

However, when I slip into the bay, I find someone waiting for me.

The Djembe is standing in the shadows at a line of damaged CAVs.

She's looking directly at me. She's wearing an elegant corporate suit, with her hair in tidy corporate beadwork, and my first impression is that she's small and old and alone. Nothing about her looks commanding . . . but in the gutter, you'd automatically call her *boss*.

For some reason, my heart keeps beating. For some reason, I don't babble excuses or slip away.

Instead I cross the bay to her.

We stand together and watch the strange, looming CAVs self-repair. Alloy ribbons ripple and shrug. Buckled walls shudder, creak, straighten. Flattened shapes smooth and expand.

"There is a limit," the Djembe says.

I'm not sure if she's talking about the CAVs or me. "Yeah?"

"If they're damaged too heavily they never return. You've seen that, I believe?"

"I saw a lamprey shred them into scrap."

"When that happens, we can't even salvage parts."

"Why not?"

She reaches toward a swaying ribbon but doesn't quite touch it. "The CAV repair algorithm is organic in ways we don't understand. Do you know how many CAVs there are?"

"About three hundred."

"Not anymore, Mar Kaytu, not since we've sent them after lampreys." When she turns to me, the light filters through her jacket and I realize she's a high-end holograph. I wonder if she'd been a projection the first time we met, too. "Have you considered my offer?"

"Have you made one?"

She ducks her head. "We are not looking for an agent who is primarily—as I believe you say—a 'hitter.' A trigger-puller. Despite your remarkable numbers in Belo City, we don't need a combat consultant."

"I don't know what our remarka—"

"You're good at forging relationships. You don't crave attention. You think creatively, you understand debts, and you are comfortable inside Freehold blocks."

"I wouldn't say *comfortable*."

"Credible, then." Her mild gaze shifts past me. "What do you know about lampreys?"

A damaged CAV trembles and expands. There's a faint clicking sound, and a murmur of voices carries from an office across the darkened bay.

"Not as much as you," I say.

She inspects my face. "You'd prefer not to take me up on my offer."

"Did you make me an offer or give me an order?"

"A reluctant employee is of limited use to DOPLAR."

"The fight I believe in is here," I tell her. "We've got three soldiers rejoining us and—" And maybe four, maybe Rana. "Let me stay in Javelin."

"To act as a cleanup crew for CAVs?"

"If that's what they need," I say. "What do *you* know about lampreys?"

"My assistant director of research believes they're related to the Gone AIs."

She means the Big Three AIs that ascended, kludged, and crashed. "Related how?"

"Nobody understands the Gone, Mar Kaytu. Some processes they started are still ongoing. Perhaps lampreys are the effects of long-forgotten cause, like flowers blooming over a grave."

"That's not creepy," I say.

She smiles faintly. "What I would like, Mar Kaytu, is—"

"Wait, I'm sorry. You don't think they're remorts?" The full impact of what she's saying strikes me. "You don't think they spawned from the terrafixing because you think they spawned from the dead AIs!"

"That's the assistant director. The *director* tells me they're remorts. What I would like, Mar Kaytu, is for you to leave Javelin and accept assignment with the Garda in the Mosiah enclave."

"What? No, I'm not—"

"However, you won't be in Mosiah long, not after your thefts are discovered."

My head is spinning from the change of subject. "My thefts?"

"Such a disgrace. Your superiors will banish you to the Honeycomb Inside Joyful Freehold. There your continued greed will attract the notice of certain criminal elements—"

"Wait! Stop, stop. The *what* Freehold?"

"Honeycomb Inside Joyful. Commonly known as 'the Joy.' "

"Cute," I say. "You want me to play a corrupt employee to give me cover?"

"Yes."

"To get access inside some Freehold?"

"DOPLAR believes that a patriot group based in the Joy is working with a group of rogue research scientists."

"Rogue scientists? That's something out of a cheesy MYRAGE channel."

"You make a credible criminal, Mar Kaytu. You're well suited for this task—"

"Let me stick with Javelin," I say, a pleading note in my voice. "I trained to face lampreys."

"And it's a fight you believe in. For good reason. But *you* bring no special value to it. The cause is worthy, but your contribution is slight. Now that we're relying on CAVs, it's less than slight. It's negligible."

Every word is true, but abandoning my squad feels like betrayal. "I can't leave them."

"Which is exactly why you must. Do you remember these?"

Reprimands appear on my lens: Kaytu, Maseo ⊘ ⊘ ⊘

"Old news," I tell her.

"Outstanding reprimands remain on your record until resolved," she says. "Yours are not resolved. You are unwilling to sacrifice your squad to achieve mission success."

"I'm not," I say.

She ignores me. "You graduated from Phase Two despite the reprimands for one reason: your Javelin training. However, the time has come to see if you learned your lesson. I pulled a few strings and will test you now."

"Now?" I feel myself tense. "How?"

"By giving you a chance to sacrifice your squad." She raises a placating hand. "Not their lives. You must sacrifice your life with them. Choose to leave them, Kaytu, and prove that you place corporate goals above your own."

I watch the hologram's face. Is she even human? Is she a real person, projecting her real self, or is she a construct, an illusion, a trick? Is this how Corporate Intelligence recruits all its agents? Maybe ten of these holograms are talking to ten potential recruits right now, to learn which of us will jump through the right hoops in the right order.

"What if I say no?" I ask her. "What if I stay in Javelin?"

"You mean, will we discharge you?"

"Yeah."

"No. You make a fine trigger-puller, Kaytu, though that's all you'll ever be if we can't trust you." Her holographic gaze gleams. "Are you here to serve the corporation? To serve the planet and the human race? Or to serve yourself?"

CHAPTER 54

The Djembe is right. I know she's right, but I want to stay with my squad. In honor of Pico and Ridehorse, in support of Elfano. To wait for Rana. To stand with Ting and Cali, for M'bari and Jagzenka and even Voorhivey and Basdaq.

Not only because of the blood on my hands. Also because the thought of Anvil Squad fighting a lamprey without me makes me sick with dread. I can't let them clear patriots from a Freehold apartment without a gutter roach on the team. I can't abandon them in a battlefield, crouching on a ledge waiting for hostile contact.

We're a team. We're together. Maybe we don't see the big picture, but we live or die in the same tiny square of the mosaic.

"You risked a great deal to enlist," the Djembe continues. "You locked yourself in a CAV looking for redemption—or punishment. If you say no to this, you're betraying the reason you enlisted. You're here to serve, Maseo. Honor your contract."

She's right. What I want doesn't matter. You don't join the military like you're picking food off a buffet, a nibble of this and a nibble of that. The chain of command fills your plate, and you eat what's in front of you.

"Can I tell them?" I ask. "My squadmates. Can I explain why I'm leaving?"

"You know the answer to that."

I rub my face. "Shit."

"You'll be notified of your transfer soon," the Djembe tells me. "After you leave Ayko, you'll spend three weeks training for Inventory and Distribution."

"Office work?"

"In theory," she says.

"And in practice?"

"In practice, you still have a great deal to learn." Her projection starts to fade. "No more unsanctioned break-ins, Mar Kaytu. We'll speak again soon."

She vanishes, and I'm left alone with the CAVs.

Emotions surge inside me but I don't want to feel them. I adjust my focus until I'm watching myself from a thousand miles away. I slip into *flow*. My fear and failure aren't real because I'm not real, I'm not myself, I'm simply a ripple in the endless fractal branching of the terrafixing. The breeze on my cheeks, the hum-grunt of the CAVs, the tightness of my throat: they're all fathomless currents in the Edentide.

I'm leaving my squad. Fine. That's the job. You go where they tell you, you do what they say. I know that. And I screwed up in training: I deserved those reprimands. I earned them. I should thank the Djembe for giving me a second chance.

Instead, I walk through the rows of CAVs, between unfurling leaves and twining ribbons. Strolling through alloy mandalas, I can't tell my meditation from my surroundings. Despite being damaged, the CAVs hum with power. I feel it in my spine, like the pounding rhythm of a Freehold dance.

My fingertip runs along a curved alloy shell. I'm saying good-bye to my squad. I'm saying good-bye to the CAVs, too.

Shadows move like snakes. There's the scent of musk and oil. A thousand cry pilots died inside these saddles; a hundred cataphracts felt the killing lash of these ribbons. I press my forehead against a CAV shell and feel the coolness on my skin. A ribbon curls around my left wrist. I'm not frightened. I'm not even alarmed. The touch of alloy feels right on my skin.

I stand there for a long time. I stand there until the world returns.

We spend the next morning on conditioning, and the afternoon in a class covering the structure of corporate joint ventures. Nobody knows why, not even M'bari. The instructors use the rotating deployment of Javelin as a case study of trans-corpo coordination within a wider framework of entrepreneurialism.

"I'm transferring with you," Ting lenses me from her workstation.

"What?"

"To that Garda department in Mosiah."

Which means she eavesdropped on my conversation with the Djembe again. "How?"

"I'll make some adjustments to the assignment schedules."

"Tingting." I lens a warning sign. "If you screw around, they'll find out what you are."

"I want to stay with you."

"You'll be fine. You're good at this. You swat down missiles like . . ." I grope for a pop culture MYRAGE reference. "Like the Eye of Bhima."

"That's not a thing, Maseo."

"You know what I mean. What's the name of the monsoon beast in that *Thoi Tiet* game?"

"You're such an ignorant roach," she says.

"Look who's talking!"

"I'm a well-informed roach."

"Stay close to the Sergeant Manager," I tell her. "She'll look after you."

"She doesn't know me. None of them know me but you." She feeds me audio, and makes her voice small and pathetic. "You're my best friend."

I turn in my seat to glare at her, but she doesn't raise her head. I can't tell if she's serious. I don't know what to think, and for some reason a suspicion rises to the front of my mind. "How old are you, Ting?"

"Nineteen."

"That's what your file says."

She stays silent, which is all kinds of wrong, for Ting.

"Tingting," I say. "Tell me."

"I turned sixteen last month," she says.

"Sagrado, Ting. You're just a kid."

"Don't you pity me," she snaps. "Don't you dare—I'm not—I'm not just a kid. You know that. You're the only one who does."

"I didn't mean—"

She closes our private channel and ignores me. I'm not sure how to make her stay in Javelin instead of trying to join me, but I won't push her. At least not yet.

After class, the squad heads for a third-floor courtyard. We leave the valid cart and lounge around in the unfiltered air. Well, most of us do. M'bari is fully recovered, but some bureaucratic snafu is keeping Basdaq in the hospital. He needs to report for duty before they can release him, but he can't report for duty until after he's released.

I chew on a yeasty tube while Shakrabarti and Voorhivey and Jag play a clunky MYRAGE fami-sim about people playing clunky MYRAGE fami-sims. It's either satire or stupid, I can't tell. Probably both. They open permission for spectators, though, so we cheer and jeer and enjoy the half-screened sunlight.

Ting's still ignoring me, the lying little genefreek. I'm considering pulling her aside when the base channel announces that quarantine is officially over.

Everyone checks their messages. I mostly get channel spam, but Ionesca also sent a five-perspective film about phylogenetic diversity in soda lakes. Jag chatters happily with her parents, and M'bari patiently answers questions from what sounds like a dozen kids. Shakrabarti stands at attention and gives two-word responses to questions I can't hear. Voorhivey is greeted with songs, because his family is in the middle of a festival, while Cali and Ting aren't greeted by anyone at all.

Cali digs into a softbowl with chopsticks, shoving food into her face. Ting hugs her skinny chest and blurs through MYRAGE channels.

Then an announcement flashes across our lenses, and Cali bellows, "Sweet fucking biyo!"

We're third on rotation for deployment supporting a CAV assault. The new gear is ready, the revised strategy is in place, and there's even a motivational annotation: *Secure a lamprey or die trying!* It probably sounds more poetic in the original language.

"Now we just need Ojedonn and Yin/Yang," Voorhivey says.

"There's been another delay," Ting says.

We all look at each other. "Delay as in attack?" I ask.

"I think so."

Basdaq lenses from the treatment ward: "Another transport hub?"

"A power grid, I think. The early reports aren't clear."

"How many casualties?" Voorhivey asks.

"Eighteen thousand and counting but I don't think—I mean, Ojedonn, Gazi, and Werz weren't even in that city. They're just delayed."

"I don't give a shit about eighteen thousand," Cali says. "Long as it's nobody I know."

I'm ashamed to admit that I agree. Sergeant Manager Li claims that nobody thinks lampreys are intelligent, but these things really are focusing on military installations now. Even if they're just obeying some automated defensive protocol, the change in tactics is chilling.

"Nothing we can do," Voorhivey says, "except secure a lamprey—"

"'Or die trying?'" Shakrabarti says. "What kind of splice finds that motivating?"

"I like it," Cali said.

"Asked and answered," M'bari tells Shakrabarti.

Cali is still trying to figure what he means when Sergeant Manager Li summons us to a briefing. There's a pit in my stomach. We're third in line to head into the shit, and I'm transferring away. I'm about to tell the squad that I'm leaving, and I can't admit why.

When we reach the conference room, Sergeant Manager Li projects the weekly stats. She talks us through strategic venture objectives and performance expectations. There's the usual tedium of self-assessment, organizational effectiveness, and core values.

Li closes the projection. "It's that time, colleagues and gentlefolk."

"We heard, Sarge!" Cali growls. "They're sending us out! New ammo, new city, and with a hundred fucking CAVs! These splices think they're gunning for *us*? We're going to fall on the next lamprey like a, um, a . . ."

"A one-legged elephant down a Freehold stairwell?" Ting offers.

"Yeah!" Cali punches Ting happily on the shoulder, hard enough to bruise. "Like *that*!"

Li's gaze sweeps the room. "The question, Private Calil-Du, is who precisely is *we*? In the past few days, two CAV units responded to lampreys. Both failed. Catastrophically."

"Cataclysmically," Ting says.

"Lampreys cut through a dozen CAVs without sustaining more than moderate damage."

"What happened to the support troops?" Shakrabarti asks.

"Ninety-six percent survived."

"That's good."

"Which is why the *new* rules of engagement shift infantry forward," Li says, "into the red zone. We'll support the CAVs at extremely close range."

"That's . . . less good."

"We're gonna drop on them like an anvil," Cali says. "Like an elephant with an anvil. Down a fucking stairwell."

For a moment, even Li stares at her in disbelief. "Well. Now that you are fully apprised of the situation, I need your assignment requests. Are you going to stick with Javelin or return to your Shiyogrid career path? Jagzenka?"

"I'm sticking, prez," Jag says, and the *prez* means *for Pico*.

Li glances at the projection. "Basdaq?"

"If they ever let me out of here," he says from the treatment ward, "I'm with you."

"M'bari?"

"Javelin," he says.

"Calil-Du?"

"You aren't transferring me out of here," Cali says, "until no lamprey is left unfucked."

"Voorhivey?" Li asks.

"My mom's going to kill me," he says. "She was marines. *Her* mom was marines."

"Voorhivey?" Li repeats.

He sighs. "Javelin."

"Ting?"

She makes a little noise in her throat. "Yeah. I mean, me too. I mean, Javelin."

"Shakrabarti?"

"Javelin, Sarge."

"Kaytu?"

I'm trapped between two betrayals. Either I abandon my squad and pass the Djembe's test or I have to face the fact that I'm not a soldier, that I'll never be a soldier. If I stay, I'm making a mockery of the sacrifice of Tokomak Squad—and Pico and Ridehorse. If I stay, I'm calling them fools for fighting for the corporation, fools for dying.

"Garda," I say.

It doesn't go over well.

CHAPTER 55

After I'm released from the infirmary, I head to the gazebo for a little solitude. I'm not sure how I feel. Resigned, mostly. At least that's what I tell myself. Not defeated, not disloyal: resigned.

The bench is cool through my fatigues, but the air is warm and smells of cultivated coral and regenerating seawater. A cascade of reflections glint in the windows facing me. When I raise my head, a flock of passenger pigeons darkens the grids of sky between the buildings of Ayko Base.

Then they're gone, and I'm alone again. Until I'm not.

"Something's fucking with you." M'bari steps into the gazebo from the terraces. "That's the only reason you'd leave the squad." He slides onto the seat beside me. "You grew up in Vila Vela during the insurgency?"

"Yeah."

"Then the refugee camps."

"Yeah."

M'bari falls silent when a squad of Welcome 12 troops strolls past. We watch them file into a lift, then watch the lift angle through the administration building.

"How's your leg?" M'bari asks.

I touch my thigh, feeling the film beneath my pants. The bandage covers a puncture wound from where Cali stabbed me with her chopstick.

"It's fine," I say.

"Cali, huh?"

I snort. "Yeah."

"You're going to miss her."

My throat clenches. "I'm going to miss *you*. I'm going to miss all of you."

"Except Voorhivey."

"Even him."

M'bari tosses me a snack tube. "The Sergeant Manager didn't ask me to talk to you."

"That hadn't occurred to me."

"It should've. You're not stupid."

I pop the tube. It smells like lichennut and citrus. "Where do you get this stuff?"

"You want to stay with the squad," M'bari says, "but something's pulling you away."

"I don't—"

M'bari lenses me a request to shut up. "You can't talk about it."

"There's nothing to talk about."

"Remember the first day in training?" He props his boots on a gazebo bench. "The two of us on dorm overwatch, marching around like toy soldiers."

A smile tugs at my mouth. "I remember looking at you, seeing the wheels turning. I remember thinking, *This one's a planner.*"

"I remember looking at you, too," M'bari tells me. "And I remember thinking, *This one won't leave you behind. This one won't leave* anyone *behind.*"

A flush of shame warms my neck. "I'm sorry."

"Something's fucking with you." He stands and squeezes my shoulder. "I just wanted to tell you that I understand. And that I'll miss you, too."

In barracks that night, Cali tries to pretend I don't exist, but she's incapable of pretense. She keeps scowling at me and swearing under her breath. Jag and Shakrabarti crawl into my bed, eager to convince me to stay.

I don't let myself be convinced. The hurt in Shakrabarti's face shatters my heart, and the disbelief in Jag's crushes the fragments. I'm betraying my friends again, trapped in a nightmarish loop, replaying my worst moments over and over again.

The night feels cold after Shakrabarti and Jag slouch away. I'm left with nobody except myself, just like after the Doom of Vila Vela, but what did I expect? A new family, unbreakable bonds? Brothers and sisters who'll never leave me and a grandmother who—

Ting interrupts my self-pity with a private message. "You need to see this!"

"Go away, Ting."

"Not until you see this!"

I almost blank the channel, then realize that *Ting* will never leave me. Maybe she's an annoying little sister, but she's still my sister. So I say, "I'd rather arm-wrestle a lamprey than watch another one of your cuddle-chans."

"It's not a cuddle-chan!"

"Go away," I tell her. "I'm sleeping."

"You are not."

"Fine," I say. "What is it, then?"

"It's a cuddle-chan."

"Tingting." I roll onto my back. "What do you want?"

"Nothing. I don't know. It's just . . . you keep trying to pay off some debt. You try and try and try, but who are you even paying? There's nobody there but you, Mase. You and—me. And I mean, I guess I worry about you."

"*You* worry about *me*?"

"No," she says. "Shut up. Yes."

"Go away," I tell her, my bleak mood lighter. "I'm watching a cuddle-chan."

I close the link and stare at the ceiling. She's making sense for once. I'm the only one who sees the ledger. I'm the only one who calculates the interest. I can't save Tokomak Squad. I can't save Sergeant-Affiliate Najafi or her squad or her son. I can't save the two thousand two hundred and thirty casualties, killed after Sayti's modified terrafixing protocol struck the orbital Garda HQ.

A war crime.

I'd only been fourteen, but that's no excuse. I still remember Sayti with fondness. With love. What does that say about me? I'm a tangled mess of knots and snarls. And I'm abandoning my squad. Not to pay off my debts, though. The reason I'm leaving is simple: I was raised a patriot but I'm a soldier now.

The new Boazes look just like the old ones. The new brane cans look the same, too. Still, Sergeant Manager Li assures us that the gear is upgraded.

"How are they upgrading our tech to kill a lamprey," Voorhivey asks, "when they need to kill a lamprey to learn how to upgrade our tech?"

"That's above our pay grade," Li tells him.

"We're so screwed," Jag says, rubbing a rosette on her forearm.

"That *is* our pay grade," Li tells her.

Ting wrinkles her nose. "Anyway, we're mostly backup for CAVs."

"Because that worked so well in Belo City," Shakrabarti says.

Cali cracks her neck. "Long as I've got a trigger, I'm happy." She scowls at me over the spray-patch covering her nose. "And a loyal squad."

"I'd settle for one without an impulse control disorder," I tell her.

M'bari drifts between us, and Jag mutters, "Down, orca," to keep Cali from going for my throat.

"What's the fatherfucker still *doing* here?" She spits at my boots. "This isn't a Garda fight. It's a fucking waste of training."

"He's not Garda yet," Li says.

"The update shows Werz due to depart in six hours," Voorhivey reports, changing the subject and not quite looking at me. "And Gazi and Ojedonn are on another transport, three hours later."

The mood lightens, and Sergeant Manager Li leads us to an enclave mock-up for a live weapons training exercise. Impact towers loom overhead, with reinforced skywalks and the shells of dangling railcars.

We trot into position and handshake the other squads, establishing compatibility, before we're hit with pulses designed to mimic the lamprey signal interference. We communicate via paleo buroto, coordinating our disposition in the mock city.

Everything works smoothly, except that instead of getting easygoing chatter from the squad, I'm getting curt professionalism.

Our new crossweave armor is clammy and bulky, though the power-assist is kickass. We're like stripped-down mekas. On common channel, squads bond over complaints about sweating inside the crossweave armor, then share recipes for cooking the fungus growing in your ass-crack. The military is nothing if not refined.

Finally, bright green goo splashes across twenty yards of the street.

"That's the mock-up bait," Sergeant Manager Li says.

"Prettier than the old bait," Ting says, keeping her gaze on the signals sweep.

"I've got anklewraps that color," Shakrabarti says.

Voorhivey peers at him. "Green anklewraps?"

"They're spectrum sensitive," Shakrabarti explains.

"Sweet," Voorhivey tells him. "I once saw a pair of—"

There's a loud crashing, and a fake lamprey bursts through a domed roof. Cali gives a mocking laugh. The lamprey looks perfect, a meaty pink sphere with rotating plates and jutting chains, except there's nothing viscerally disturbing about it. Unlike the real thing, it looks like the result of human design. It's ugly but not upsetting.

The squads open fire in sequence, and six mock CAVs deploy and we win.

"We nailed the baby menace," Jag says.

Shakrabarti snorts. "This is easy when you're playing make-believe."

We run four more training exercises, with increased signal interference each time. We engage the lampreys, we support the CAVs. We secure the corpses. Our coordination gets smoother and our reaction time faster, which is great except these exercises are useless. Our trainers had been right to send us after an assortment of horrors instead of a fake lamprey. The fake ones undermine everything that's terrifying about the real lampreys.

We trot back to barracks in silence. Even Ting is quiet, and Cali is lost in thought. Or in whatever she does instead of thinking.

"I'll talk to command," Li finally tells us, "about a new curriculum."

"Instead of that watery shit," Cali says.

"Nobody else got as close as we did," Voorhivey says. "They don't know better."

Sergeant Manager Li cocks her head.

"What's up, Sarge?" M'bari asks.

"Another delay," she says. "A lamprey hit a switching hub. There were troops."

Jag lenses a ping of alarm. "Are they okay?"

"There's no casualty register yet," Ting tells her. "Ojedonn and Gazi are listed as missing."

"They're okay," Voorhivey says. "They've got to be."

Shakrabarti gives a shaky laugh. "I miss Ridehorse. You know what she'd say?"

"'Even if they're okay now,'" Cali says, doing a remarkably bad impression, "'we're all dead once the lampreys kill us.'"

"That's uncanny," Jag tells her. "It's like Elfano is standing right there."

"What? No!" Cali scowls, honestly offended. "That was *Ridehorse!*"

The ripple of laughter echoes in my empty heart. I'm going to miss them.

CHAPTER 56

That night, an alarm wakes me from unsettled dreams. My lens flashes a Waihi-3 alert, which makes no sense. Ayko Base is under attack? Impossible. Javelin is a joint venture, supported by the entire Cherzo-5. The corpos are united against remorts and lampreys, so—

"Breach, breach, breach," a voice calmly recites through the public address. "We are receiving fire within the perimeter. We are under attack by hostile—"

There's a WHOOM and the scream of static. I'm opening my

locker before I'm fully awake and slapping myself into a quickskin. I grab my unloaded Boaz and lens for updates, for orders, for help. There's no response except a sluggish trickle of data reiterating the Waihi-3 and increasing the casualty rate: 61, 62, 65, 66 . . .

Cali is already strapping into her crossweave armor, like she'd been sleeping in the underlayer. "The fuck is going on?" she barks.

"We need cans," I tell her, shouldering my empty weapon. "Ping the autocart."

Jag shoves off naked from her room, followed by Shakrabarti and a red-faced Voorhivey. "Who's hitting us?" she asks, popping her locker.

"Don't know," I say, then yell, "Ting? *Ting!* What's the status?"

No answer from Ting's room, but M'bari bursts into the common area wearing hospital gear from his latest treatment. "Gallium Quad is under fire. They need backup."

"You have cans?" Cali asks.

"What? No." M'bari looks down at himself. "No, Ting lensed me an alarm and said to warn you."

"Where is she?" I ask.

"No idea."

"This cart's crashed." Cali punches the wall. "It won't dispense."

I kick Ting's door open and find her sitting on her bunk staring at the floor. Blood trickles from her nose and splatters her shirt. I shout her name but she doesn't blink. She's catatonic. What's wrong with her? What did this? Stem or technopathy?

There's no telling, so I throw her over my shoulder—and realize I don't know what I'm doing. What's my plan? To reach Gallium Quad and repel attackers without any ammunition?

Back in the common room, I take a breath. *Slow down. We need ammo. We need a plan—*

"What happened to Ting?" Voorhivey asks, his eyes shaky. "Is she okay?"

"Did she tell you Gallium Quad?" I ask M'bari.

M'bari slaps into a quickskin. "She didn't say anything except to warn you. It's what everyone's yelling: 'Gallium Quad.'"

"Head for the armory," I say. "We're useless without cans."

"Speak for yourself," Voorhivey says, reaching for nonchalance. "My mom took on a remort with a stunstick."

An explosion shakes the building. The lights dim and a window shatters. Screams knife from the darkness. "What about Li?" Jag asks.

"Fuck Li," I say. "She can take care of herself."

"Fuck you," Cali growls at me. "You don't care about the squad. You don't care about anything. Freehold scum."

Jag elbows her. "Focus, orca."

Cali quiets. There's no time for fighting, not right now. Besides, the medics are still pissed at her for stabbing me with the chopstick, and at me for breaking her nose in return.

"Take point," I tell Jag, and flip her my trenchknife.

She catches the handle, extrudes the blade, and leads us into the corridor.

Emergency lights flash in the gloom. Ting jounces on my shoulder, her limp arms dangling. She doesn't weigh anything. Her breathing is steady. She's not losing any blood. Looks to me like she ODed, but she's not an addict, not really.

She's a technopath, which is worse.

There's a crash deeper in the building, then another. I hear a faint *pit-pat-pat*: the sound of Boaz slugs. Is that autonomous fire outside? Are the belly turrets of an Antarmadesha sweeping the rooftops from above?

My lens strobes with conflicting orders and urgent alerts, frantic and distracting: 102 dead. 103 dead, 109 dead . . . I filter the chatter as the gunshots sharpen and—

A Boaz stream slices into the hallway through the wall.

The liquammo opens a gash and an earsplitting thunder of rounds slams at us from the ruined mess hall beyond. A barrage of Boaz rounds chop through a refrigerant unit and rip apart tables and screens. That's corporate gear, that's *our* gear. Who the fuck is attacking us?

Through the gash, the far wall of the mess hall is gone. Just gone. The building opens to the outside, into a night that is alive with hellish screams and the whiny chop of Orit Gal fire. Rounds stitch through the wall, punch into a supply cabinet in the hallway, and Voorhivey jerks and sprawls on the wreckage.

When Shakrabarti rolls him onto his back, Voorhivey's jaw is missing and blood flows from his neck.

"No," Shakrabarti says. "Baby, no."

Someone shrieks and M'bari moves with terrible slowness. He slaps shock-film across Voorhivey's wound and a hailstorm of rounds shreds the wall behind us. Cold air wells around me and freezes the sweat on my face.

Cali helps Shakrabarti lift Voorhivey, and I hold Ting tighter as she jerks and starts to rouse. The world comes in terrified flashes. Jag leads the squad around a corner. She signals us to wait inside a trophy niche while she checks the next intersection.

Casualty rate: 228, 230, 241 . . .

"Who the fuck?" Cali snarls.

"Lampreys," Ting murmurs, still slung over my back.

My stomach drops, and I set her on the floor. "They're here?"

"Voorhivey," Shakrabarti whimpers, looking down at his ruined face. "He just, he just . . ."

"He's alive," Cali says.

I crouch beside Ting. "Lampreys?"

"His grandpa sent churros," Shakrabarti says, in a dull voice. "For the entire squad. They got stuck in quarantine."

"Signal interference," Ting tells me, gesturing weakly. "Coms broke. Yes."

Fear tightens my throat, and my voice sounds scratchy. "Lamprey attack!" I squawk. "It's a—lamprey!"

"I caught a pulse," Ting says aloud, while she lenses. "Tried to stop them with my mind and they broke me."

"We need brane cans," Cali barks, her eyes narrow. "Are there any in the armory?"

"The armory's general issue," M'bari tells her, and then his gaze jerks upward toward the ceiling, toward a crashing stampede on the higher floors. "We need L-tech."

"No way," Jag says, prowling closer and hearing the conversation. "No way. There's a *lamprey*?"

"Where do they keep the new cans?" Cali asks M'bari.

"One of the research wings."

"They won't work," Ting whispers. "The new cans won't work . . ."

"We can't scratch a lamprey," Jagzenka says. "Nothing can."

She's wrong. *One* thing can scratch a lamprey. Except so far CAVs haven't done more than scratch them. I straighten from my crouch and say, "So we run."

"To fight another day," M'bari tells Cali, before she explodes.

"Fuck *another day* with a disembodied dick," she growls.

"Churros with real water," Shakrabarti says, smiling at Voorhivey's limp form in his arms. "White cricketflour and home-made—"

Screams echo from deeper in the corridor. The stomp of booted feet sounds closer, accompanied by frantic shouts. A mob is racing toward us. Jag gestures—and a pink lamprey cable drills through the ceiling into the hallway.

Time freezes.

My heart stops.

The cable branches downward, spreading wide. Pink ligaments brush Voorhivey's helmet and Shakrabarti's shoulder.

When Shakrabarti lifts his hand to his ear, the skin peels away from his arm. There's a flash of red blood and white bone. He screams as his sleeve dissolves.

M'bari lunges for him while flesh sheds from Voorhivey's body in sheets, exposing organs as his flayed corpse flops from Shakrabarti's remaining arm and splats to the floor and I can't take it, I can't take it—

Ting unleashes a shriek that pierces the clamor. Her nosebleed starts again and the trophy niche shatters. She's melting down the circuits around us. My lens turns gray and maintenance bots explode in their housings.

"Ting!" I shake her. "Ting!"

M'bari lunges at Shakrabarti and overrides his quickskin into shock mode. "You're alive!" he shouts. "You're alive."

"Incoming unknowns," Cali announces, through gritted teeth. "Brace for impact."

Screams mix with the tromp of boots, and the mob boils into sight at the intersection.

The first three soldiers whip around the corner—one in PRATO fatigues, one in Shiyogrid, and the third naked. A panicked stampede howls at their heels and they race toward us, shouting, *Run, run, it's coming.*

I yank Ting to her feet and a pink scythe slices through the rearmost soldiers. Blood sprays, screams die. Slimy strands strike through the ceiling: a woman in the middle ranks collapses without any marks on her; a man behind her is dismembered.

The ceiling bulges and the lamprey oozes into sight for a heartbeat before an avalanche of rubble billows down the corridor toward us.

We sprint away.

Jag starts in the lead but Cali outpaces her even though she's carrying Shakrabarti, her long stride powered by the crossweave armor she's wearing. M'bari grabs Ting's other arm and we run with her between us, her feet dragging on the floor.

A dark pink blob splats the wall behind us and burns through.

A wet cable slices the floor and Ting sags in my hand. I think M'bari is hit but he leaps the gap and the strand flicks and vanishes.

A swarm of moskito drones dies in flight and litters the floor. There is nothing but fear and screams and flesh and darkness.

I shove Ting at M'bari and shoulder-check a Unidroit gunner away from the lamprey's strand, but I'm too late and a gout of blood splatters the wall.

Two steps past an open doorway, Cali slams into a vend machine to stop herself, her armored shoulder denting the alloy.

"In there!" She pushes Shakrabarti at Jag. "Inside, inside!"

Jag grunts and swerves into the room with a moaning Shakrabarti. His blood smears the floor. M'bari drags Ting after her and I'm still in the corridor, sprinting to the door.

"Through the window!" Cali bellows at them. "Jump—*jump!*"

I catch a stubborn, stupid look in her eyes as she stands there facing the slaughter: she's going to make a stand. She's going to herd everyone into the room, then wrestle the lamprey with her bare hands.

So I palm her broken nose and drive her backward through the doorway. She's not dying today. No more of my squad is dying today.

Inside the room, Jag drags Shakrabarti backward toward a cracked window. She whips her wrist and an illicit paste grenade—no clue where she got that—splatters the glassine.

When M'bari glances at the door behind me and Cali, his eyes widen in horror.

I don't see the lamprey churning closer, but every cell in my body flares with terror.

Without lensing a single message, M'bari and I act in perfect sync. He shoves Ting at me, grabs Cali's outflung wrist, and yanks her hard toward the window. She's unbalanced and reeling, so she staggers fast across the room.

The window shatters from the paste grenade and Jag pulls Shakrabarti through the jagged hole. M'bari and Cali trip over Shakrabarti's legs and all four of them tumble from sight.

I'm out the window a fraction of a second later, holding Ting to my chest, in freefall.

We're supposed to spin in the air, bellies toward the sky like in the drills, aiming the reinforced rear carapaces of our armor at the ground to take the impact—but we're not wearing armor. We're all in quickskin except Cali, and Ting isn't even wearing that.

We're dead.

Jump, Cali said. *Through the window.*

How did we let *Cali* plan our escape? She couldn't plan an afternoon nap without two missile launchers and a dropship.

The base walls are splattered with pink goo and gunfire is everywhere. The sizzle of assault rifles mixes with the boom of heavy weapons and the *pop*-slurp of rampart guns.

I hug Ting to my chest and watch the sky burn.

CHAPTER 57

Time seems to slow. Ting's amber hair streams upward and she watches me with bright, teary eyes. She smiles and speaks. I can't hear, but the word looks like *Timor*.

Which means she knows my deep, dark secret. She knows my original name. *Timor* was one of Sayti's surnames. I tell myself that I'm only Kaytu now, that my old name doesn't mark me, except of course it marks me. Whatever else I've done, whatever else I've become, I'm still my sayti's grandson.

She turned children into soldiers. She used me as a weapon. I never stopped thinking about one-armed Sergeant Najafi. I never stopped thinking about her son. And now I think about Ting, so fragile in my arms, so terrible and so sweet.

A little late in the day, but I finally have my epiphany as I'm falling to my death.

It's not much, but I realize that there are some lessons I'll never learn. After everything, I still love Sayti. I still miss her. And I'd light the world on fire for Rana, for Ting, for Jag and M'bari and Shakrabarti. Even for Cali. Hell, *especially* for Cali.

They are my people, and I don't care about anything else.

That's a dangerous, small-minded way to live. It's the path of the insurgent, the nationalist; it's the creed of patriots who only care about their own little tribe. That's how the SICLE War started, with a loyal, loving urge that would've destroyed the world if the rational stewardship of the corporations hadn't saved us.

So I'm infantile and coarse, I follow the path of the selfish child. I know that. There's no excuse. Yet my own little tribe is all I have. I'm scared of dying, but at least we're dying together.

We hurtle toward the ground and—

A breakfall rampart expands below us, set to full porosity. I sink into its spongy cushion, too stunned to feel relief, tangled with Ting and M'bari.

Tracer rounds tear through the smoke above us. CAVs launch from the oversized barrels of Bumblebees as we roll off the rampart. More jumpers hit the cushion behind us, and I crawl to the side and help Jag lower Shakrabarti's limp form to the ground.

Unidroit medics pull Shakrabarti into a medipod and my heart booms in time with the *pop*-slurp of rampart fire.

I find myself staring at the source of the sound: two soldiers in CrediMobil fatigues are kneeling beside a filter housing, firing at the ground. They're laying down lifesaving cushions for all the soldiers blindly leaping to their deaths. The woman drops an empty launcher and the man gives her another to fire—*pop*-slurp, *pop*-slurp—and she fires without pause.

She drops the second launcher and the guy feeds her a third.

All around overhead, soldiers leap from windows and balconies, falling to safety if the woman shoots in time . . . and to their death if she doesn't. The ground is littered with bodies. Screams tear the air, orders echo against the walls, and moans waver and fade. Rubbish pukes from shattered windows.

Cali and Jag lead the squad away as the CrediMobil rampart soldier fires again and again. Shards of glassine cascade behind us; some catch the air and slice around us like thrown blades. We duck, dodge, and slide into the cover of an obstacle course trench.

"They took Shakrabarti," Jag says, looking back toward the medipods.

"He's safer with them," I tell her.

"We need rampart guns," M'bari says.

Cali glowers. "We need lamprey cans."

"Did you hear me?" Ting asks me.

"What? Uh. No."

"I said—" She points across the base. "There's *two more*."

Oh! She'd said *two more*, not *Timor*. "Two more lampreys?"

"Fuck me," Cali says. "Three lampreys at once?"

"Never happened before," M'bari says. "We should . . ."

He trails off when a smoking Orit Gal veers wildly overhead, trailing a lamprey strand, then crashes out of sight. A Welcome 12 squad fires an anti-airship barrage at a target we can't see, and twenty yards from them broken CAVs grope unsteadily for the reloading gutter that crosses the grounds.

Beaten CAVs, returning to base.

There's a rumble like thunder, and the building behind the CrediMobil rampart soldiers shudders. The reflection of fire and smoke trembles in a hundred windows. A lamprey is tunneling through the building, heading for the rampart team.

The man glances over his shoulder. He says something to the woman, but she just shrugs and fires—*pop*-slurp—and fires again.

Each pull of the trigger saves lives, and she won't let her own on-rushing death distract her.

"Fuck it," I say, and lens frantic, muddled questions at Ting.

She understands, of course. Ting is good at muddled. "Even if I can pair you," she replies, "I can't protect you."

The building behind the rampart squad cracks open and Cali growls and my lens flickers to life. Casualty rate: 2,602, 2,617, 2,651 . . .

"They're killing us." Horror shines in Jag's eyes. "They're killing us all."

"Without Javelin," M'bari says, "if they wipe out Javelin—what's going to stop them?"

"We are," I say, rising from the trench.

"Gutter roach," Cali snarls.

"Form on me," I say. "I've got an idea."

"W-what kind of idea?" M'bari asks.

I swallow. "A bad one."

"Tell us," Jagzenka says, her voice a rasp.

"We're loading me into a CAV," I tell her. "And seeing if I know how to drive."

"That's suicide," M'bari says. "It's impossible. You can't drive a CAV."

"I came close once before," I say, and don't mention that I've got a technopath this time.

"No way," Jag says. "Even if you could, the lampreys chew through CAVs, you won't last a—"

"Form on Kaytu!" Cali bellows, standing by my side. "Move you lazy fucks, *move!*"

CHAPTER 58

When Cali spots the CAV post through the madness of the base, she powers ahead in her crossweave armor, leaving the rest of us fifty yards behind. Jag and M'bari follow quickly, while I'm slower, supporting Ting in her dazed stupor.

Cali calls to a guy in an up-armored Jitney. She trots beside him and talks for a few seconds. When he frowns, she lunges forward on the balls of her feet and head-butts him.

I absolutely do not feel a sneaking flash of pride.

The guy drops and Cali lenses a request for permission to use the vehicle. That's not a problem: base command is issuing blanket permissions. At this point, they'd give a nutrition consultant permission to fly an Orit Gal.

Three seconds later, Cali is alone in the Jitney, speeding toward the perimeter fence of the CAV post. Driving fast, aiming to crash through.

"Cali, you thick fuck!" I shout, as I drag Ting forward. "You're going to hit the—"

She lenses me an obscene image and smashes the Jitney into the fence at speed. The vehicle pivots, nose down, ass to the sky, engine howling. There's a terrible ripping crumble as the fence sizzles and flattens. Automatic countermeasures pound the Jitney with shock rounds.

Sparks coalesce and shimmer and fade around the wreckage.

"Oh, no," Jag breathes, staring at the charred Jitney. "Oh, orca . . ."

M'bari says, "She popped the gate."

Twenty yards from the point of impact, a gate swings open on bent hinges, sparks crackling across the rings. Of course, the guards would've simply let us in if we'd asked. Except that would've taken time . . . and there are no guards at the gatehouse.

"Bang." Cali pushes unsteadily from the wreckage of the Jitney. "Handled."

Her crossweave armor is in tatters. She peels from the remaining sheets and trots toward us, scratched and bleeding and shining with satisfaction. She's naked except for the underlayer, which is a bright orange mesh, and I feel an upwelling of affection that surprises me.

Jag calls Cali names as we trot into the deployment post. More injured CAVs crawl past us in the re-arming gutter, ribbons severed and bodies scorched. Ting doesn't look much better: I don't know what she's doing with her technopathic brain, but her breath is ragged and her feet are dragging.

On the ninth floor, the door to CAV Operations is still too high-security for me to wire.

"We can't get in here," I say. "I'll pop the lock at the bay—"

M'bari pounds on the door. "Let's try asking, first."

A gray-haired tech with bloodshot eyes flings the door open in a panic. "Are they here? Are they here? Are we evacuating?"

"We need your help," I tell her.

Jag slips past the tech, and then Cali shoves her backward. She and M'bari follow the tech's stumbling retreat and I bring up the rear with Ting.

It's a big room. Screens everywhere. The reek of flop sweat and cutting-edge tech fills the air, along with the thrum of desperate voices and damage reports. The operators' stations—where they remote-control the CAVs—look like saddles without rotating frames.

"Hey!" I call.

Nobody stops. Nobody looks at me.

Six operators are strapped into saddles, remotely guiding CAVs across the base to fight the lampreys. Six more wait for deployable units, wearing matching expressions of unfocused nausea as they witness the destruction of Ayko Base on their lenses. Frantic support staff swarm around projections, all of them on the edge of panic, while two unarmored officers watch from a raised platform.

"Hey!" I repeat.

"LISTEN UP!" Cali yells. "YOU FUCKING FUCKS!"

A ripple of stillness spreads across the frenetic activity. The operators waiting for deployment glance at us briefly. Their harried staff ignores us after a moment, but the rest of the room watches us with varying degrees of surprise and concern.

"We need a CAV decoupled from remote control," I say, leaning Ting against a bank of what I think are orbdata racks. "We're putting our own cry pilot inside."

"On whose authority?" one of the officers asks.

It's a reasonable question, but I just read from my lens: "Three thousand one hundred fifty casualties. Three thousand one hundred seventy. Eighty, ninety—"

"We don't have the time for—"

"Pardon me, san," M'bari interrupts. "Are your CAVs having any effect?"

"Stand down, soldier," the officer barks. "Walk the fuck off my unit."

"Because we saw them in action in Belo City," M'bari says. "Getting crushed."

"You *will* spend the next six years in blinders."

"You have nothing to lose," M'bari says. "We all have nothing to—"

"Get these people out of here!" the other officer roars.

Jag materializes behind the first officer, my trenchknife touching his neck. "We're begging you, san," she says, as gentle as Sergeant Manager Li. "One CAV is all we—"

"Step away!" the other officer says. "Or I will gutterdamn—"

Cali shoots her in the stomach.

The cough of the sidearm is a pressure grenade in the station. A ringing silence fills the air, broken only by the officer's gasping as she slumps against a railing and presses the wound.

A medic sidles toward a supply cabinet, then moves faster at M'bari's nod.

"Three thousand two hundred and forty-two," Cali announces, with a frozen flatness in her voice. "The next time I aim for the head."

"W—what do you need?" one of the staffers asks her.

The officer grunts as the medic films her wound and applies shock patches.

"Two CAVs," Cali says. "With, um—without remote controls."

"We only need one," I say.

Nobody listens to me, though. They're too busy staring at Cali, smeared in blood and wearing crossweave underlayer and looking every inch a deranged killer.

"We're—" The uninjured officer takes a breath and continues in a conversational tone, which is a pretty impressive display of nerve. "We're burning through CAVs at an unsustainable rate. There are under eighty, worldwide, at this point. We can't waste them."

"You *are* wasting them," I tell him.

"Driving a CAV won't work," he says. "They're drones. You want to modify one? Give us a month. Except we don't have a month. We don't have a week."

I privately lens Ting, "Are you ready to pair me?"

She looks unconscious, but replies with a wordless: *!*

"We don't have ten minutes," I tell the officer, throwing the casualty count to an in-room projection.

"With our current strategy approaching critical failure, we need to try something new," M'bari says, his voice professorial. "Standard response isn't enough."

"You!" I point to the gray-haired tech. "Jailbreak a CAV for me."

"Two CAVs," Cali says.

"Me?" the tech asks. "I—I can't."

"Then who can?"

"Nobody?" Her gaze flicks toward a man hunched at a work-station. "Er, nobody."

My lens tells me that the man is a Tech Specialist with a dozen service commendations. I don't care about his skills, though. When he raises his head, I see the gleaming cloisonné on his forehead: brilliant colors and vivid shapes, embedded in the bones of his skull. A gorgeous, segmented, geometric depiction of a CAV.

Yeah. I guess if anyone knows CAVs, it's this guy. "Jailbreak the controls," I tell him. "Cut the remote operator and let the cry pilot drive."

There's a glitter of excitement in his eyes. "It's never been done. Not successfully."

"But you're dying to try."

"No! No, I don't know . . ."

"I survived one trip in a CAV; this time I'm—"

"You were a volunteer?"

"Yeah."

"That won't help. You still can't manually operate a CAV. You'll spin like a—"

"TWO CAVS!" Cali bellows at him, raising her weapon. "NOW!"

The tech snaps into action.

I seriously doubt that even a cloisonnéd freak can decouple CAVs from the remote controls in a matter of minutes, but I know Ting can. I'm positive the tech can't pair me with one, so I'm counting on Ting for that, too. Sure, it's never been done before, but nobody's used a technopath before, either.

That's the only reason I'm dragging the tech into this; I need to draw attention away from Ting and her abilities. This guy's a distraction, not a solution.

Two others techs exchange looks, like they're thinking of making a move. Cali snarls at one of them and Jag gives a twitch. They quiet down. A minute later, the unlinked remote operators are removing softwires attached to their stations, and staffers are prodding at the saddles. Decoupling them from the CAVs . . . I hope.

Meanwhile, the Tech Specialist is furiously plucking at his screens, his cloisonné forehead gleaming. He's such a whirl of focused activity that I start to wonder if he can actually pull this off. Maybe, but my money's still on Ting.

"Cali," I say, edging beside her. "You're not coming."

"Fuck you," she says, with a wolfish grin. "Blaze of glory."

"I need you here," I tell her.

"Was *fuck you* too vague?"

"You think Jag's going to shoot an officer? Because you *know* M'bari won't. They're not damaged enough for this."

"Forget it," she says, a little less firmly. "I'm coming with you."

"If Command hears what we're doing, they'll roll over Jag and M'bari in the blink of an eye. But the entire board of generals could tell you to abort this mission, and what would you do?"

"I'd fuck them all the way off."

"Yeah, you would," I say. "That's why I need you here."

Her jaw clenches, and for a moment I worry she's going to shoot the officer again, just to hear the scream.

"You're such an asshole," she says, which is her way of agreeing.

The remote operators huddle together. The medic treats the injured officer. Cali stalks and mutters while Jag is a lethal statue. M'bari pops a weapon locker and arms himself. And Ting slumps on the floor, looking unconscious.

I'm betting my life—all our lives—that she's not.

A new alert flashes on my lens: someone in the CAV operations station sent up a flare, a plea for help, for base security. Good luck with that, with a thousand alerts blaring and three lampreys laying waste to Ayko Base.

"We're going to hang for this," Jag lenses on the squad channel.

"Only if the lampreys don't kill us first," M'bari says.

"So we'll only hang if we kick their asses?" Cali barks a sudden laugh. "Fair trade."

"Tingting," I lens. "What do I need to make this work?"

"*Me*," she lenses, motionless at the base of the orbdata rack. "And a gutter-ton of luck."

CHAPTER 59

The casualty counter hits six thousand as M'bari and I shove into the CAV deployment bay. A dozen damaged CAVs face three pristine ones. Rows of volunteers are drugged and happy in comfort chairs, but the soldiers tasked with escorting them are defocused and agitated, watching nightmare stats on their lenses.

M'bari and I separate so we won't present a tight target. A few of the soldiers glance at us, eyes flicking over lensed messages. One starts to speak—that's why M'bari is here, to keep them off my back—and then they spin and trot away.

"They think you're relieving them," Ting lenses me, "and I'm two minutes away from a comprehensive breakdown."

"Keep it together," I tell her.

"Two minutes," she repeats. "Start flatlining your brainwaves. So I can pair the connection and not smoosh you."

"Smoosh me? Nobody said anything about smooshing."

"What's wrong with Ting?" Cali asks on-channel. "She's bleeding again."

"She ate a shock round," I lie, crossing toward the CAVs. "She's fine. Tell the operators to open the saddle."

Leaves unfurl at two of the undamaged CAVs—because two is what Cali initially demanded—and I'm halfway inside the closer one before I realize that M'bari is standing there staring at the other CAV like he's looking at his own grave. Which makes a certain amount of sense, considering he's probably dead in the next few minutes.

I guess the same is true of me. I don't say anything, though; I just push into the saddle, imagining fractal blooms in my eyes. Dead doesn't bother me. Death isn't real, there's only the *flow* of life into life, decaying, re-forming. There's nothing to win, nothing to lose. No fear, no joy, no failure—I'm nothing but a swirl of terrafixing telling itself that it's me.

The ribbons braid closed behind me and the interior walls shine white.

I take a breath, soothing my nerves with the calm of Edentide. I ease into the pilot's frame. The open manacles on the armrests rise between me and the joystick-looking ribbons that'll help me fly this thing.

When I rest my wrists inside the manacles to reach the ribbons, they lock around me.

My pulse rockets. "Um . . ."

"Sorry!" Ting's bleeding face appears on a screen. "One sec."

I take another breath, reaching deeper for the meditation, listening for Ionesca's voice, feeling her breath on my face. After a moment, my panic subsides. I'm not quiet, I'm not brave—because I'm not apart from anything, not separate and alone.

Cables squirm and grow into loops at my palms.

The frame shifts, cradling me soft and tight. Not the frame, the *flow*. I'm gone: my body is hollow, my mind is empty, my hope is dead, and my love is unrequited.

The manacles pop open but there's no such thing as free, there's no such thing as bound. My unreal arms reach for the loops. They fit my hands better than my fingers do.

M'bari appears on one of the screens. He's squeezed inside the other CAV, which must've taken Cali-levels of dumb courage. He's trembling as he lowers himself into the saddle, trying to turn himself into a cry pilot—or at least trying to ensure that I don't die alone—but his frame doesn't wrap around him; his CAV remains inert.

On Ting's screen, her body stiffens and she collapses. A CAV station staffer kneels above her with a medkit while Cali scowls in the background.

"You're flatlined," Ting's voice says, though her mouth doesn't move. "I'm pairing you. Can't pair M'bari. He's brain-active and CAVs—permissions—impalpable—" A weak laugh sounds. "If *impalpable* means what I think."

The CAV cables wrap around my hands until I'm not holding them, they're holding me. I'm fraying into fractal threads, and cables grow around me like tree roots around a rock. They extrude across my chest and hips and legs, my neck and forehead. Things get a little intimate, but that's okay, a *flow* doesn't have any personal space.

"CAV Thirteen-Thirteen, this is Tech Specialist Gaaldine," the cloisonné tech's voice says. "I mean, this is Control. You're on, uh, your own recognizance. Operator Thirteen-Thirteen, confirm."

"Confirm," I hear myself say.

The CAV hums around me. "Check your Fita."

"I don't know what that means," I tell the voice. "Pair me."

"I can't! There's no way!"

"Try," I say, shifting slightly in the pilot frame.

The CAV shifts slightly—and golden pinpricks glow in the pure white saddle.

Constellations of stars brighten among the screens and walls, the cables and cords. Branching golden lines take shape between the pinpricks, like lightning bolts or veins.

My breath catches. Ting did it. She paired me.

I don't feel anything except for a fizzing of fear and excitement at the base of my skull, but I'm paired with this CAV.

"He's in control!" another tech blurts. "You did it!"

"I—I did?" the cloisonné tech says. "I did! I wish I knew how."

"Kaytu," M'bari lenses from inside his semiactive CAV. "Are you seeing this?"

I watch the golden threads crisscrossing the saddle. "Yeah."

"On your prox screens."

Oh. Right. I make myself focus as M'bari flashes me semitransparent overlays showing three blue targeting diamonds inside Ayko Base: the three lampreys.

One is tearing through an underground tunnel toward the CAV post, one is pulling down a barracks, and the third is bulging through the building behind the rampart squad.

A hint of confusion penetrates my flowing numbness. How is the lamprey still behind the rampart squad? Is it stalled there? Did it veer away and return? I don't know, I don't care, and I don't wait for the overhead clamp to shunt me into the deployment shaft. A spark of hope kindles in my heart. *Maybe that rampart squad is still alive.*

With a flick of attention, I maximize the targeting diamond and plot a route. And before the jolt of panic can break my calm, I lean forward and shove the control loops.

My CAV slams backward through the bay.

"Shit!" I yelp, my calm shattered. "Wrong way!"

Apparently I'm completely paired, though, because the commands stay responsive despite my spiking brainwaves. The golden lines brighten as I yank the loops toward me and the CAV stops preternaturally quickly—then roars forward.

The CAV ribbons blur, speeding me toward a bank of transmission arrays on the wall. Maybe I should brace myself, but I don't. I lean into the impact, slicing through the wall like alloy through mushmallow.

I burst from the side of the building nine floors from the ground. This time I'm not afraid of falling.

Cali whoops in my ear and M'bari flashes me screens from his CAV—which is still in the bay, not responding to his commands but transmitting me data—and I stab the building wall with my alloy leaves to control the descent. Then I'm soaring or swinging around the corner, I can't tell which; the world is a blur and Cali's whoop is a battlecry and I push forward faster and faster until I launch my CAV from the wall and rocket across the base, ribbons extended to shove and hurtle past a launchway, a sat-array, a skarab deployment housing.

The target lamprey appears on my foremost external screen, churning through a field of ramparts and bodies and the seeded coraloid earth of the island.

The rampart squad is long gone. The rampart squad is long dead. I'll never meet the soldiers who saved our lives, I'll never buy them a tube or shake their hands.

But I'll make these lampreys pay.

My rage is hot for a heartbeat—then turns icy.

I hear myself telling M'bari to plot the movements of the other two lampreys. I hear the cloisonné tech talking about CAV links and signal interference. I hear the sounds of battle all around me as the CAV filters the noise and transmits it into the saddle, maintaining the direction of origin to keep me oriented.

I'm surrounded by rubble and death and speeding at the enemy.

My CAV's ribbons blur like the legs of a mutant remort, pushing, dragging, cutting me closer. The lamprey is three times my size, cables and strands flashing a hundred yards in every direction, spearing into the ground, punching through walls, leaving a trail of pink tar behind.

I drive forward until the lamprey fills my vision—fills my mind. Shifting fleshy plates swarm around a latticework interior. Dripping slime, cutting edges. A faceless, merciless, inhuman *thing*.

My chest clenches, and a pink cable clubs at me, a fast and killing blow.

When I flinch, my CAV hurls itself aside, responding to my reflex.

I dodge the cable, throwing the CAV too far off-course, grinding across a ruined obstacle course and falling into a maze of ditches. Fuck! The controls are too sensitive, or I'm too amped.

Spinning in the gold-tinted frame, I climb from the ditch, grasping for calm, for focus. Trying to shed my fear and anger and turn myself into a weapon, a mindless cutting blade. My CAV thunders across the field, too jerky, too fast. Unstable, unsteady. I'm chopping ramparts to tatters. Part of me is stunned by the sheer power of a CAV—cutting through *ramparts*?—but a bigger part is just stunned.

What if I can't do this? It's too much, it's too big, it's too—

I feel Rana's hand on my shoulder, I see her steady eyes. She expects better than panic. She demands better. Between one breath and the next I tap deeper into the *flow*, and fractal patterns of terrafixing bloom in my mind.

My pulse slows.

My sweat cools.

My shoulders drop.

My hope dies with me, and my fear and shame. Everything falls away except a murderous urge in a killing CAV.

I'm thirty yards away when the lamprey fires strands at me— thinner, longer ones. On my screens, the tips glow but the stems are dull. I've seen what these things do to alloy, and to flesh. If the tips hit me, they'll explode my CAV into a husk.

I pivot slightly in my frame, and the strands miss by three feet.

"Dance, you fatherfuck," Cali growls at the lamprey.

Or maybe at me, I don't know. I don't care, I don't think. I drive forward and spread my wings, slipping ribbons past the glowing tips of the strands—and with a desperate grunt I slice at the stalks behind the tips.

My CAV hacks through ropy pink tar.

The glowing tips splash to the ground in puddles of inert goo. The severed strand retracts, and the lamprey recoils.

The lamprey *retreats*.

A shout sounds in the CAV—from M'bari and Cali and the operators—but I barely hear. I've drawn blood now. I hurt that fucker and I liked it. One thing every patriot hitter knows is this: when your enemy falls to his knees, kick him in the throat.

The golden threads in the saddle throb with my heartbeat.

I feel my lips curl, and I advance faster than the lamprey retreats.

Another fat cable clubs at me and I hit it with a pulse that slows it for a fraction of a second. Just long enough for me to alloystomp another gooey strand with my CAV's shell—sideswiping to avoid the cutting edge.

Then I grab the fat cable in my ribbons and *tug*. I don't think it's possible. These cables seem infinitely expandable. Yet I rip that thing out of the lamprey at the roots.

There's a sound I can't describe, and I use the stump of the cable to pull my CAV at the lamprey and an oilstorm of strands spews at me, like a net thrown at a cockroach.

Except roaches run, roaches scatter.

Not me. Not this time.

CHAPTER 60

M y CAV frame spins and whirls. My ribbons unfurl so fast that sonic booms shake the quad.

I dance through killing pink strands and plates. I'm a whirlwind, a twister. I'm a bladed tornado and I hack the lamprey until it's a dripping heap of fibrous oil and *this* time I hear the shouting.

That time the shouting shakes the world.

Tears pool in my eyes and the cloisonné tech murmurs in my ear. M'bari shoves screens at me, tracking the other two lampreys, and I hear myself say, "I want her name. I want her name."

He doesn't know what I mean. None of them know that I'm talking about that CrediMobil rampart soldier who fired and fired and fired again, utterly calm in the face of her own onrushing death.

Alerts flash before I have a chance to explain.

Images condense on my screens: an underground vault with glowing yellow tanks containing shadowy shapes that look like sea creatures, like M'bari's ass-tat, like L-tech bait; hundreds of civilians crying and soothing children in a bunker; a knotted pink cable slashing at a Bumblebee, then retracting into an access tunnel.

The second lamprey is underground, thrashing closer toward a bunker full of civilians—driving toward the L-tech bait in a vault beyond.

I rise from the smoldering strands of the dead lamprey and lash my CAV toward the shareholders' pavilion, planning on smashing through to the access tunnel.

"Rendezvous with transport," M'bari tells me, sending a route. His words make no sense. "The what?"

"On the rooftop," he says. "Now, Kaytu, confirm-confirm."

I don't know what I'm agreeing to, but M'bari is in my squad, he's in my head; even if he's not here, we're a team. I confirm and climb to the roof, ribbons whirling and slicing, and an Antarmadesha drops from the sky and hovers thirty feet above me.

Oh. That's what I was agreeing to. I launch my CAV upward, and the transport's cargo clamp grabs me like a scraperhook.

I'm swinging through the air. The cloisonné tech sends me a stream of calculations, but I see the lamprey hole before I understand them—a black cavity dripping with slime—and I slash myself free from the clamp and hurtle through the smoke and tracer rounds with the Antarmadesha's momentum behind me.

The CAV lands hard. The gold-flecked saddle buckles toward my shoulder, but my signals stay green.

I fling after the lamprey at whiplash speeds.

My CAV spiders along a tunnel, through shredded layers of exclusion film and a graveyard of anti-assault mines. A swarm of pulse-hardened drones fills the air, pinging off my shell like buckshot.

I reach the lamprey at the mouth of the bunker. Forking pink strands explode inside, slaughtering the civilians—until I stab into the rear of the lamprey like an assassin's blade.

Cali bellows in triumph and calls me a name so foul that it silences the chatter from the CAV operators. M'bari laughs and Jag screams encouragement for the first time, which means her knife isn't at the officer's throat anymore.

"Orca's falling in love with you," Jag tells me. "Two down."

"Ting?" I say. "Ting?"

"She's okay," Jag says. "She's in thera-sleep."

I take a breath. "Where am I?"

"Almost done. The third one's deeper underground."

"Coming at the vault from below you," M'bari says.

"I see it," I say, checking my screens. "What's the best approach?"

"Straight through the dick," Cali snarls. Which, strictly speaking, isn't a lot of help.

M'bari raises maps and schematics around me—I'm still not sure how he's sharing them from his undeployed CAV. The cloisonné tech feeds me walls of data and Jag says, "Go in soft, Kaytu, recon style. This one's ugly."

I'm looking at the same screens and don't see any fresh ugliness, but Jag's got a sharper eye than I do. For the first time since leaving the bay, I feel exposed; I want my squad around me. Or maybe I'm just missing Ting on overwatch, safe in the security of her signals envelope.

There's no time to worry, so I tilt in my frame and move. My CAV scrapes through some kind of ventilation sphincter, and I hunt the third lamprey a half mile into a goo-dripping burrow that it excavated in the seeded coraloid of the island.

I lose contact with the surface three seconds before I splash underwater.

I'm below sea level. I'm in the waterlogged tunnels underneath the vault. The CAV feels sluggish and I'm disoriented by the silent weightlessness.

My screens feed me information that I don't understand, and the calm of my *flow* creaks under the realization that I don't know how CAVs work, not really; I'm operating on guts and guesswork. And while CAVs were clearly built for exactly those two things, I'm surrounded by untapped capacities that I can't imagine, and by critical weakness, too.

Maybe CAVs don't function in whatever fluid's surrounding me. I don't know how much air I have, or how much pressure I can withstand, and I'm still checking my screens when the lamprey explodes from the depths.

No time to focus.

No time to respond.

My CAV jerks; the right-side wall buckles toward me from a nasty hit that cracks my shell. With a surge of panic I corkscrew away from the lamprey.

My frame spins; the control loops curve smoothly in my sweaty palms as the lamprey batters me. I grope for the calm uncaring of meditation, but fluid is pooling inside my saddle, it's rising around me.

When the chill touches my feet, I'm dodging a dozen pink strands, calling on every iota of my self-control. When the cold reaches my knees, I'm cutting my own tunnel away from the lamprey, hacking a path in blind terrified retreat, trying to cling to my meditation. And when the fluid fills the saddle high enough to grab my balls in an icy fist, my mind blanks with panic.

Fear cracks the armor of my calmness.

I'm trapped inside a CAV; I'm trapped in an underwater tunnel fighting an oily beast. I'm drowning in a swimming pool, clenched and—

A pool? An instant before the lamprey's strand slices a hole in my shell, I stop fighting the water and start *swimming*.

Forget about thrashing and frothing, forget about lashing at the lamprey and the tunnel. Forget about my desperation. I'm a weapon, but I'm not a tank, I'm not a Jitney, I'm not a hardened alloy platform.

I'm a dolphin like those catamarans I saw in the ocean months ago, and I knife the CAV through the water. My ribbons are fins and my shell is streamlined muscle, graceful and glossy as an ocean predator.

I've always loved swimming.

I curl between the lamprey's killing cables. I'm a flash of untouchable silver, despite trailing bubbles like guts. Fluid rises to my stomach inside the saddle and I fire a pulse from my CAV. Not just a pulse: a full-bore strobe that stuns me almost as hard as the lamprey.

My vision flickers but I manage to lash forward. I ram my CAV's snout into a curved plate of the lamprey's oily shell. The CAV punches through and with one last gasp I whirl my ribbons and shred that fucker into an oil slick.

Then it's over. It's dead. A floating corpse.

I'm half-drowned and semiconscious, but at least I'm not cold anymore.

The untreated water filling the saddle is acid on my skin.

A plume of my blood wafts across my field of vision.

The golden threads fade to pinpricks, then to a blank whiteness. I'm not paired anymore: I'm finished now, and alone.

I drift in the CAV like a baby in an artificial womb. I remember Ionesca's scarred fingers stroking my arm. I remember Rana standing in the glow of that orbital pod. I remember Ridehorse and Pico, and I smile as screens flicker around me and voices speak. I don't understand a word, but that's okay, I don't mind. My breath is shallow and my mind is unmoored. That's okay, too. Everything's okay.

I'm a little sleepy, that's all.

The CAV jostles when a rescue drone clamps my shell. The world is a meaningless hum except for M'bari's voice. He says my name. He tells me to blink if I can hear him, he tells me to blink. He tells me to blink. He keeps telling me to blink, he won't fucking shut up. He tells me to stay with him.

The tunnel flashes on a wavering screen six inches from my unfocused eyes. M'bari talks nonsense at me until a Tenured Colonel appears on the screen. He's an eyeborg; a web of tech covers the left side of his face from eyeball to ear canal. He talks to me. I can tell, because his mouth is moving. He congratulates me for bagging a lamprey. He mentions *crystalline residue* and *polymorphic specimens*.

I don't understand, but it's not important.

Then I'm on the surface. My saddle ribbons unfurl, releasing me to slide to the puddled floor. Nursurgeons foam spinebraces at me; they prod and spray and I'm suddenly outside my damaged CAV. The daylight surprises me. Maybe it's not daylight; maybe the hangar is brilliant with emergency lights.

I'm lost and dazed until a pattern of jaguar rosettes floats into my vision. I know that pattern. I know the feel and scent of that pattern, and the toughness. The knot in my heart loosens. Jag is trotting beside my stretcher. She's holding my hand hard enough to bruise.

"Shakrabarti?" I gasp to her. "Ting?"

"Still with us," she says.

That's all I need to hear.

CHAPTER 61

Turns out that a full-bore CAV pulse is nonstandard, like everything else about a CAV. The remote operators never trigger them because the effects are unpredictable. For example, a full-bore pulse fired from a leaky CAV in an attempt to kludge an underwater lamprey in the depths of a seeded island might scramble the cry pilot's brain a little.

Just temporarily, nothing serious—but keep it in mind next time you're fighting to the death in a flooded chamber beneath a besieged base.

The toxicities on my skin and in my flesh are excised, the tissue debrided, and the damage repaired. My synapses start firing in the right order again, more or less. The nursurgeons tell me I got off easy. They're right: two days later, when I'm mobile again, mortuary drones are still crawling through the wreckage of Ayko Base.

I'm recovering in a medical carrier that's hovering over the ruins, big enough to block out the sky and full to capacity with casualties. Medipods stream through the air in both directions, like honeyflies from a hive when the lichen force-blooms.

When I realize I'm getting priority treatment, I feel a twist of dread. Not because I don't deserve special treatment, even though I don't. I mean, who knows how many unsung heroes like that Credi-Mobil rampart squad saved lives? I'll still *accept* undeserved benefits, of course: I'm a gutterboy, not a Class A shareholder; I'll take whatever isn't bolted down.

The dread is because I've made myself too visible. I've drawn attention to myself like a search beam at midnight . . . and roaches die in the light.

Forty-seven new messages flash on my lens. Forty-six of them are from officers and executives, with congratulations and commendations. And probably orders, but I hide behind my medical status and don't acknowledge any updated duties.

One message is from Rana. A regular message. Nothing covert, nothing classified. She doesn't even mention trying to get back to Earth. She's just saying hello.

The sound of her unmusical voice joins all my broken places. She chats for a moment, then roller-coasters me through a fast-motion version of one of her "average days." It's a standard template of channel fluff, but it makes me smile. Not because of the herky-jerky experience and the silly zero-gravity sight gags. Because the thought of Rana sending me something so whimsical soothes me better than the narcotic tubes I'm swallowing.

I play through three times before responding with a quick, breezy message. I don't mention lampreys or CAVs. I don't mention Voorhivey's death or Shakrabarti's injury. Not because I'm trying to protect *her*. Rana can take care of herself. What I'm trying to protect is my picture of her, floating happily above me, an unseen star in my personal heaven.

Down on Earth, M'bari visits medical bay and tells me Ting is still in recovery and Cali is in the brig for shooting that officer. He's not worried, though. The officer lived, and the Calil-Du family is wealthy enough to negotiate a proxy sentence or a wergild settlement for any crimes Cali commits, up to and including wiping out an orphanage.

"Don't give her any ideas," I say.

M'bari grins. "And given that we actually *beat* the lampreys? She'll be released with commendations on her braid."

"She'll like that," I say. "How's Shakrabarti?"

"Wishing that he only lost a few toes, but he'll recover."

"Pretty as ever?"

"We can only hope." M'bari takes a breath. "Listen, I tried to come with you. I'm not saying I *wanted* to, but I tried. My CAV wouldn't respond. I didn't just leave you hanging."

I already know that. Ting couldn't work her genefreek magic on M'bari's CAV, and he doesn't know how to zero out his brainwaves in any case.

"Sure," I scoff. "Like you weren't hanging back, calculating the ROI of letting me die."

He nods, playing along. "Corporate policy frowns on risking my Class B life for a Freehold roach."

"Class B? You're not a sniff above C."

"Not yet," he says, taking my hand in both of his. "But after I vest, my whole family's moving up to the bottom of the middle."

I squeeze his fingers. "I never would've made it without you."

"I didn't do anything. I just told you what I was seeing."

"You told me what I *wasn't* seeing."

"Well, you were busy at the time. And uh . . ." He opens a private link and lenses the rest: "You showed the corpos a powerful weapon, Kaytu. They will take a keen interest in you."

The last thing I want is Command focusing on me. "I didn't show them anything."

"You paired with a CAV."

"Not really. I mean, it was all that techie with the cloisonné forehead."

M'bari catches on immediately. "Is that what happened?"

"Yeah."

"I'll tell Jag." He closes the link and speaks aloud. "Our debriefs start in thirty. She's supposed to be meeting me here in—"

"Now," Jag says, stepping through the film.

I stare in horror at Jag's face. "What happened to you?"

"What?" She touches her cheek in alarm. "What?"

"There's panda marks all over you."

She snorts. "Oh! I almost forgot."

"What?"

"This"—she backhands my nose—"is from Cali."

"Ow! Ow! Gutterdammit, Jagzenka. That hurt."

"And this is from me," she says, and kisses me.

"C'mon," M'bari tells her. "We're due to report."

Jag strokes my cheek. "That rampart soldier who saved us? The one you asked about? Her name was Dodovatova. Her squad called her Tova."

"That's a good name," I say.

"Cover your ass," M'bari lenses me as they leave.

I lie there for a while, making sure I know what he means. Nobody cares about my background, not really. Nobody knows about my grandmother—not even the Djembe. Maybe not even Ting. So there's no problem except the CAVs. Command thinks I know how to pair to one. That's not a small thing.

M'bari was warning me about the expectations of overeager

officers, but the real problem is, how do I explain what happened without getting Ting killed? I guess I'll claim I got lucky and I'll push the cloisonné Tech Specialist into the spotlight.

Except what if they notice anomalies? I need Ting to fiddle with the surveillance records. If Command realizes that a technopath messed with the CAVs, they'll vivisect her.

I've been ordered to report to a bridge-level conference room upon discharge. No doubt for a debrief about the CAV-pairing. Strictly speaking, I'm contractually obliged to respond with all due haste, but instead I request information about Ting's location.

She's four floors below me in this labyrinth of a carrier. Ten minutes later, I find her in a medical wing with eighty patients lining the walls, most of them cocooned in treatment film.

Ting looks like a little girl in her pod. She's not in recovery, she's in thera-sleep. She's lacquered with film inside and out. It's breathing for her, pumping for her. Whatever she did to pair me with that CAV is killing her. She pushed her limits for us, and now she's paying the price.

And the medics removed her lenses; her pupils are golden. The sight makes my breath catch. I don't know how to help her, but we've come this far together. I won't leave her behind.

"What's wrong with her?" I ask a passing nursurgeon.

The nursurgeon lenses me a wall of medical jargon without slowing.

I grab her arm a little too hard. "Use little words."

"She's having an idiosyncratic reaction to lamprey contact," the nursurgeon says, jerking her arm away. "The same thing that's wrong with everyone in this ward. We don't know. Some lost consciousness, some lost brain function. Your friend is mimicking stem withdrawal."

"Stem withdrawal?"

"Look at her. The golden pupils? That's a symptom."

"So she . . . you mean she looks like an addict even though she never touched the stuff?"

"I've got four patients covered in crystal welts." The nursurgeon shakes her head and keeps moving. "And you are *not* helping."

The good news is that in the future, Ting's medical file will claim she's not a stemhead, she's just suffering from a strange side effect of lamprey contact.

The bad news is that she doesn't have a future.

She's going through stem withdrawal. When's the last time she dosed herself? She needs stem or she'll convulse like a junkie and die like a technopath.

Her stash is in the base below us. Hidden impossibly away. I'm adequate at picking locks but I'll never find a strip of stem hidden on a military base by a technopath.

So I sit beside her and stroke her arm with my fingertips. I tell her what happened. I tell her I miss her and I study a projection of medicarrier-to-base traffic flow grids. Getting to Ayko Base to search for her stem is easy. Join a volunteer rescue team and I'm there. Of course, I'll need to keep ignoring the summons to the conference room, but in the chaos maybe that'll go unnoticed.

Sure. The service is always happy with what the chaplains

Except what happens once I touch down? I don't even know where to start looking for Ting's stash. Her room? Too obvious. The common areas? Too overwhelming.

While I'm flicking through schematics, one of the columns in my lens blurs. The image turns fuzzy, then clears. Then blurs, then clears, in a familiar rhythm.

When I stop stroking Ting's arm, the blurring stops. I frown and watch the column superimposed over Ting's thera-sleeping face.

I move my fingers again and the data blurs.

Every time I touch her, there's another blur.

"Can you hear me?" I whisper, my finger motionless.

A blur.

"That's a *yes*?"

Another blur.

"I'll take that as a *yes*. Do you need . . ." I don't want to say *stem*, even though if Ting is monitoring this conversation, she's no doubt blocking surveillance. ". . . what I think you need?"

The entire output of my lens blurs wildly.

"Okay, okay! Settle down. Is it in your room?"

No blur. Which I guess means *no*.

"Is it on base?"

A blur. Yes.

"You're going to have to lead me to the right place, one step at a time. Can you do that?"

Another blur.

"Well, *this* is going to be tedious." I squeeze her arm. "If *tedious* means what I think."

CHAPTER 62

catch a cable car to the surface. Rescue and Retrieve is based at the Welcome 12 sports field. Crisis engineers and combat architects bustle around in lens-synced motion, while clouds of moskito-sniffers and EMtechs deploy from bubbledrones.

A few queries hit my lens, requesting my presence at the bridge-level briefing. I blank the messages and head through the managed chaos toward my squad's barracks.

Every time my lens blurs, I pause. I turn until the blurring clears, then head in that direction. I'm just a fleshy lumbering drone, trying to look busy and focused. Nobody bothers me after the first minute—

Until the Djembe flashes an override on my lens.

I don't accept, but that doesn't matter. I can't blank an override. Not hers, at least.

"Mar Kaytu," she says, her face appearing. "You requested a meeting?"

I didn't. I didn't request a meeting and I don't know what's happening. I don't know what she wants, or how she's going to react to my failure to leave Javelin immediately.

However, my lens blurs so I say, "Yes."

"Next time, approach me with a little more subtlety."

"Sorry," I say, wondering how Ting contacted her.

"Not to worry. The coin of my realm is favors, and I suspect that you're about to put yourself deeper in my debt."

"That sounds right," I say, trying to figure what the gehenna is going on. Ting put me in contact with the Djembe. Why? Because she agrees with M'bari, that we're in some kind of danger. "I think I need to cover my ass."

"Let me tell you what *I* think. I think you proved me wrong."

"Oh," I say.

"In the end, your contribution was *not* negligible. Quite the contrary. You saved a lot of lives, Mar Kaytu. More than anyone knows. You killed a lamprey, and—" She pauses. "You killed three."

"Yes, san," I say.

"The research units are humming with activity. They have the specimens they need. For the first time, we have a chance against these things. You did an extraordinary thing."

"Well, um . . ." I follow my lens past a mound of rubble, still scrambling to understand what Ting expects of me. Probably to cover our asses, like M'bari said. "That's the problem. I'm too visible."

"In what way?"

I don't know what I'm saying, I don't know what I'm doing in this conversation and I hear myself blurt, "I mean, whoever's behind the lampreys, what if they track this to me?"

"There is nothing behind remorts except the terrafixing."

"Um, yeah, but . . ." I wince inwardly. "I mean, *if* they're remorts. I heard that maybe they're intelligent."

"Do they seem intelligent to you?"

"No. I don't know. They're not human, I don't know." I take a breath. "My buddy M'bari says I need to cover my ass. He thinks DivCom is going to strap me to a table and run tests until they learn how I paired with a CAV. But I don't know anything. I can't help them. I was just . . . right place, right time."

"Is that what you're afraid of?" she asks. "Being strapped to a table? Or are you frightened that your past will come to light?"

Does she mean Vila Vela? Does she know about Sayti? "I'm afraid of everything, san."

"Your Vila Vela ID is . . . curious."

My heart clenches. "It was a curious time."

"You apparently sprang fully born from the alleys at the age of eleven."

"Maybe *I'm* a remort," I say, trying to hide my fear behind flippancy. "After Sweetwater died, the records went wonky."

The Djembe's virtual face inspects me. I feel her attention like a blade at my neck. "I'm less interested in what you were, Mar Kaytu, than in what you'll become."

"I'd rather—" I clear my throat. "I'd rather not become strapped to a table."

"Mm," she says. "That sounds wasteful."

"Yes, san," I say.

Silence falls as Ting leads me through nonfunctional security film into the pool building. I feel sick about the Djembe rummaging around in my past. I'm not surprised, though. Just scared and ashamed. At least she doesn't know the truth—not yet.

"Tech Specialist Gaaldine is claiming that he paired you with the CAV," she finally says, "despite his inability to replicate the feat. Is that what happened?"

Ah. Ting must've intercepted traffic wondering how I paired with a CAV. I need to shut down that question before anyone even thinks the word *technopath*. The cloisonné tech is the answer; in a moment of inspired genius, he pushed the bounds of the possible.

"Well, this is the guy who decoupled the CAVs." I lens the Djembe a picture of the tech. "He's the one who paired me."

"Yes. That's Tech Specialist Gaaldine."

"I guess he's got a, a special interest in CAVs. Judging from his forehead."

"According to his file, he's an innovative thinker." A gleam shines in the Djembe's eyes. "Though he barely scraped through training on account of all the reprimands."

I don't rise to the bait. "He's the reason we won, san. He's some kind of genius. He's the key, he's the hero. So, um, it makes sense to . . ."

"To increase his visibility, instead of yours!"

"Fair is fair."

"And if *he* ends up strapped to a table?"

"They wouldn't really do that, would they?"

"And risk losing their only edge in this fight? No. Also, shareholders have rights."

"Yeah. Well, that's all I wanted to tell you. That, um—that I'm just an innocent bystander here. I drove, but Gaaldine turned the key."

The Djembe hears something in my voice. "This is not the time to lie, Mar Kaytu."

Shit! She's too smart. She's going to keep digging into this until she reaches Ting. Unless I distract her. "Yeah. Yes. There's more that I'm not telling you."

"Mm. I've learned to expect that."

"I don't know how, but he—Gaaldine pulled off a miracle. He gave me control of a CAV. That's all true. That's the first step."

"The next step is you?" she asks.

"The next step is me," I agree, pausing in a ruined hallway. "I'm a good match with a CAV."

"Why?"

"Because I survived being a cry pilot? I don't know, I just—I understand them."

"What do you understand?"

"That's the wrong word. I *feel* them. We fit."

"What aren't you telling me, Mar Kaytu?"

"Well, um." I take a breath. "I meditate. To clear my mind."

"*You* meditate?"

"Yeah, I learned in the refugee camp." I explain about Ionesca's lessons, though I don't describe the specific cultish method. "I think it helped Gaaldine pair me."

She gives me a thoughtful pause. "There are SICLE techs that synced with dendritic cascades. Illegal now, of course, in these more enlightened times."

"You think CAVs use illegal tech?"

"I think I won't raise that question. We need CAVs more than ever."

"Yes, san," I say.

"I also think that Javelin needs you, Mar Kaytu." The Djembe wields her smile again. "I sound like one of my grandson's channels, but perhaps the *Earth* needs you. I'll pass along the information."

I exhale. "Thanks. And, uh, I can stay with Javelin?"

"For now."

"Good." I manage not to laugh. "Great."

"One day I'll call in your debt."

"One day I'll pay it," I promise.

The connection ends and I find myself standing in the pool building. I'm impressed that Ting—even unconscious—managed to detect trouble and try to keep us safe. I'm also terrified that a technopath can *do* that.

Mostly, though, I'm worried that the Djembe will unearth our secrets. I don't mind so much about mine. Well, my stomach sours at the thought of being exposed as complicit in the Plaguemaker of Vila Vela's war crimes. They'd discharge me and lock me in blinders, but that pales beside what they'd do to Ting. They'd run wires into her brain and turn her into a thing.

My lens blurs twice. I shake myself and mutter, "Okay, okay."

I follow Ting's directions to the overhanging lounge, then into a gloomy alcove lined with vend machines. Despite the wreckage, they're still selling snack nutrition, soft-drugs, MYRAGE gear, lens overlays, n-water. A FrendyPet machine chirps to life while I wait for guidance.

The FrendyPet machine chirps again.

I look at the machine's cheerful animations. "Really? *This* is where you hid it?"

My lens blurs: yes.

So I request a menu of options from FrendyPet, and the blur leads me through a complex series of choices until *bleeeeeep*. The vend extrudes a paw that unclenches to reveal a strip of stem from the case I stole in Los Anod a thousand years ago. They look like barbed thorns: glossy and sharp and menacing despite being no bigger than my pinky nail.

My sleight-of-hand is rusty, but I disappear the strip into my fatigues. I just killed three lampreys, yet here I am, stealing drugs. I guess the saying is true: *You can take the boy out of the gutter . . .*

Another summons appears on my lens, directing me to the conference room. I ignore it; I need to dose Ting first.

The cable car returns me to the belly of the medicarrier and a crash makes a row of vents hiss. I pause for a second, but minor crashes are common. When the vents quiet, I make my way to the ward and sit beside Ting.

She doesn't look any bigger. Or older. Is she even sixteen? Suddenly I'm not so sure. Lying there, she looks like a tired child.

"You ready?" I breathe into her ear.

My lens blurs.

"You saved thousands of people, Tingting. Maybe billions, if the techies learn how to kill these things. But I promise you this: I don't care how many lives you save. You don't have to prove anything, not to me."

Cradling her head, I press stem into the base of her neck. Her flesh parts around the smooth thornlike barb.

"I don't care what you are," I say, feeling a click like the stem is latching onto her vertebra. "Because I know who you are."

When I straighten, my heart is pounding. Ting doesn't move, though. Her breathing doesn't change, her eyes don't shift behind her lids. And I'm out of time: a summons to the briefing flashes *URGENT* on my lens.

I squeeze Ting's hand and leave her there. Small and quiet and limp.

In the hallway outside the medical bay, a squad of soldiers trots around me in tight formation. Most of them are in CrediMobil fatigues, but there's a couple of Shiyogrid and Unidroit grunts, and one each from PRATO and Welcome 12. They move together easily, and I pause for two seconds to watch them.

The *URGENT* message flashes again, and I unpause.

The nearest lift immediately authorizes me for the bridge level. Four women in civilian gear join me on a higher deck. They don't look like civilians, though. I'm still wondering if they're Flensers when we reach the bridge level.

The women stay behind as I ease through the film. I'm almost at the conference room when Ting's voice whispers in my earbug: "I was wrong."

"There's a shock," I lens, after my chest explodes with relief.

"You're not my best friend. You're my brother."

I tell her to knock off the sentimental bullshit and she lenses me a candy-colored kaleidoscope of flying squirrels.

The battlesuited guard outside the conference room eyes me warily. "What're you smiling at, Private?"

"It's private," I tell her, which sends Ting into fits of lensed giggles.

I'm acting the fool, but I don't care. We survived. We killed lampreys and survived. Not all of us, no. I still mourn Pico and Ridehorse and Voorhivey, yet I'm suddenly humming with selfish, greedy life. Despite my meditation, I'm not losing myself in the terrafixing. I'm finding myself in the squad, in the fear and the hurt, the hope and the love. It's all I have. It's all I am.

Death is hard, but life is sweet.

CHAPTER 63

The guard waves me into a plush waiting area. A few people are already waiting, and I recognize one of them, the cloisonné tech—Tech Specialist Gaaldine—who is downloading entire universes inside a cocoon of shimmering screens.

My lens tells me to take a seat . . . and that I've been fined five hundred scrip for Unauthorized Absence, on account of my delay in reporting to the briefing.

"Fuck me," I mutter. "Five *hundred*?"

That's more than I'm worth. What happens when I can't cover the fine? Involuntary internship, probably. I guess asking permission would've been easier than forgiveness after all.

Except when I check my account, there's nineteen thousand eight hundred and seventy-two scrip on my lens, in addition to my 101 shares. Not possible. I check again. The scrip is still there.

Feeling a tingle of excitement, I check my deposit history. Command bonused me twenty thousand scrip for "performance in alignment with the corporate mission statement."

"Twenty thousand scrip!" I lens Ting on the squad channel. "They bonused me twenty thousand! I'm rich!"

"You rock," Jagzenka lenses.

"That's a good chunk of change," M'bari says. "Now ask yourself what it means."

The two of them enter the waiting area, looking stern and professional despite the on-channel chatter. Moving with the quick assurance of soldiers following lensed orders, Jagzenka takes the seat to my left and M'bari the one to my right.

"It means he rocks," Jag lenses, nudging me with her knee. "I only got five thousand."

"I didn't get any!" Ting complains.

"It means they want something," M'bari lenses me. "And they're throwing you a few scrip to keep you happy."

"A few scrip?" I reply. "Twenty thousand. Twenty. Thousand. I'll never work again."

"That's one month's income in a Class B household," Jagzenka tells me, gently. "It's nice, but . . ."

"I spend twice that on my hair every week, roachbait," Cali says on-channel, as a projection of her shimmers into place in front of me.

"Cali!" Ting blurts. "You're free, you're back! Also, you're *bald*. How do you spend money on your hair?"

"That's why the stylist only charges forty small."

"*Small?*" I say, honestly offended. "You call a thousand a 'small'?"

"You're cute when you're stupid." The projection of Cali scratches her neck. "Except wait, no. You can't be cute when you're stupid, because that'd mean you're *always* cute. 'Cause you're always stupid. But you're not always cute, so—"

"We get it," M'bari tells her.

"I missed you, Cali," Ting lenses.

"You saw me three days ago, you splice."

"Are you okay?" Jag asks.

"A couple nights in the brig is nothing," Cali scoffs. "My family wergilded the officer I shot. Everything's cool. I won't say how much they paid, or Kaytu'll start crying."

"I fucking will," I tell her. Twenty thousand *is* a fortune. I don't care what they say.

"I'm on probation is all," Cali continues, "and I got a glowing reference in my file for 'maintaining a proactive approach in a crisis situation.' Proactive. If I'd shot her in the neck they'd think I'm officer material."

"You're not the one who needs to worry about that," Sergeant Manager Li lenses, slipping into the waiting area.

"Huh?" Cali asks.

"They're promoting Kaytu." Li looks to me. "Congratulations, you're a Wing Leader."

"I-I'm not—" I stammer. "They can't—"

"It comes with a pay bump," M'bari assures me, with a quick smile. "San."

"It also comes with expectations," Sergeant Manager Li says. "Kaytu killed a lamprey—"

"He killed *three!*" Cali interrupts.

Sergeant Manager Li ignores her. "—and now every research unit on every continent is working nonstop, reverse engineering the lamprey's arrival vectors."

I frown. "Arrival vectors?"

"To find their point of origin. Their nest. And once they locate it, Kaytu? They'll send you to kill it."

"Me?" I ask. "You mean *us*."

"Same thing." Sergeant Manager Li gestures for everyone to fall in. "Okay, people, we're up. Look lively."

When we push through the security film, the conference room is actually an Operations Theater. There's a raised table in the center, big enough for thirty people. The floor is a maze of workstations and monitors. Dozens of engineers and techs manipulate projections and cluster around workstations, screens streaming with data.

Until we enter. Then there's a lull. A few of the staffers glance at us, a few stand from their desks.

Then the cheering starts.

ACKNOWLEDGMENTS

Many thanks to Caitlin Blasdell, Anne Sowards, Miranda Hill, Megha Jain, Amy J. Schneider, Ross Briscoe, Sage Blackwood, Diana Faujour Skelton, Adana Washington, and Lana Wood Johnson.

KEEP READING FOR AN EXCERPT FROM

BURN CYCLE

COMING SOON FROM ACE

The enemy attacks in the night. Three lampreys—biological weapons of unknown origin—rampage across Ayko Base.

Thousands of soldiers die before a cry pilot rises to defend the besieged base. With his CAV's bladed ribbons whirling, he tears the lampreys apart.

The corporate military withdraws the survivors and relocates Javelin, the anti-lamprey initiative, onto mobile airborne platforms. Soon only a single unit remains in the wreckage of Ayko Base: *Special Weapons Assay and Analysis*.

Where better to evaluate an untested "special weapon" than in a base that's already rubble? Where better to develop the instrument of our retaliation, our revenge? Plus, everything is already on-site: the combat courses, the technicians, the CAVs—and the cry pilot.

Because the special weapon is me.

CHAPTER 1

I spend the morning jogging through abandoned buildings. I'm the only person aboveground in Ayko Base, and my footsteps echo in empty corridors. The evidence of panicked flight is everywhere. In an Executive conference room, the tables are cluttered with abandoned meals, hygiene-sealed by drones after the attack.

A chopstick clatters to the floor when I run past.

My boots thud, my heart pounds. The exertion feels good after days of medical testing and paperwork. My body still responds with the automatic obedience of basic training when my lens directs me leftward at the next juncture.

"Your signals are strong," Ensign Technician Nanty says in my ear. She's in a sub-basement lab across the base, monitoring the LATscan that's clamped to my shoulders and linked to my nervous system. "Proceed at that pace."

"Confirm," I say, swerving around a toxicology station.

A quarter mile along the hallway, an external door unfilms to my right and Nanty says, "Through there."

I lope onto a balcony with a waist-high railing. I'm on the twenty-second story and surrounded by the remains of Ayko Base: dozens of interlinked buildings that rise from the seeded coraloid of one of the New Caspian Islands. The sea breeze is a cool 91 degrees, with a maple-ammonium scent. A flock of white birds swoops around the husk of a decommissioned dreadnought that now serves as a firing range.

A jagged hole gapes in the building to my right, edged by broken glassine. An ugly reminder of the lamprey assault. A weight shifts in my heart—not quite grief, not quite anger—but my lens interrupts, urging me onward.

When I approach the end of the balcony, Ensign Tech Nanty says, "Up and over."

"You mean jump?"

She flashes the route onto my lens and yeah, she means jump.

"Confirm," I say.

I clamp one gloved hand onto a railing and vault over the side. The breeze chills my sweat, and the white birds swirl around a corner and disappear.

This is the third day of a new phase of my testing. The first two days I spent in the lab, sheathed with medical film, poked and prodded like a chunk of dubious vat-meat. Then this morning the techs feathered my blood-brain barrier, clamped the LATscan to my back, and sent me jogging through the ruins to "establish a baseline physiognomic response to engagement with an unsecured, high-affect environment."

I don't understand what that means, but that's okay. I'm not here to understand, I'm here to fight.

Well, and to fling myself off balconies.

After point seven seconds of free fall, a weight thumps my shoulders: that's the remote-operated sailframe linking to my LATscan harness. Wings spread behind me, and my uncontrolled descent curves into an osprey glide.

A moment later, I'm soaring across the base at the mercy of an unseen operator. I'm swooping and banking over the wreckage, catching glimpses of my reflection in the unshattered windows. The rush is better than drugs, but I don't whoop or shout. Because I'm a professional hardass, that's why.

Maybe I laugh a little, though.

"Simmer down," Nanty murmurs in my ear.

The sailframe lowers me to the entrance of the dreadnought combat range. Trash and debris crunch under my boots. "Now what?" I ask.

With a click, the frame detaches and drops to the ground. "Now enter the combat range."

I rub my shoulder and amble forward. The armored doors slide open with a whirr. Inside the dreadnought, my lens adjusts to the shadows and my skin prickles at the feeling of abandoned vacancy.

A pillar of skarab drones orients toward me and an automated voice says, "Unauthorized entry forbidden."

"Yeah," I say, "that's what 'unauthorized' means."

"Unauthorized entry forbidden."

"Wing Leader Maseo Kaytu," I say, and rattle off my Shiyogrid ID.

That's my rank now. Wing Leader. I'm a noncollateralized mission-specific officer, which means that in the field, under specific combat conditions, I'm in charge. Everywhere else, I'm still a grunt. Such as here, where I'm more of a rat in a maze than an officer in a squad.

When the skarab drones disengage, I step into a foyer with a flight of steps leading downward. At the bottom, an autocart offers me a Boaz IV assault rifle and a Vespr sidearm, then ushers me into a shooting gallery that reminds me of basic training. Moskito drones activate. Animated mannequins—animannis— shuffle from storage niches. The walls and ceiling ripple into a depiction of the New Growth, glowing images of fungal trees with gilled trunks and draping filtration moss.

"C'mon," I say. "A firing range?"

"We're comparing your current status to the bio workups from basic," Ensign Technician Nanty lenses me. "This is a two-stage process. First we'll—"

"Document the military potential of a piloted CAV," I continue, because she's told me this a dozen times. "Then we'll get Provisional Approval for a fully funded CAV corps and you'll start pairing cry pilots."

"*If* we get Provisional Approval," she corrects. "And unlock the pairing process."

"Enough chitchat!" Technical Commander Gaaldine interrupts on-channel. "You recognize the weapons, the targets? Surely my intention is clear, Wing Leader?"

"Yessan," I say.

"You are familiar with a firing range. Begin the exercise. Enact! Twelve degrees off-standard, attempt to recalibrate."

The last sentence isn't directed at me. Gaaldine always conducts multiple conversations at once. Still, he's in charge, so I down-strap the Boaz and prowl onto the firing range.

The LATscan pinches my shoulders and a syrupy taste from yesterday's testing lingers in my mouth, but I find myself smiling. This is where I belong. Even though my past—my sins—drove me to enlist, I'm motivated by more than guilt now. The military needs cry pilots. The *world* needs cry pilots. I'm only one small cog in a vast machine, but I'll keep grinding until the corporations authorize a CAV corps.

Then I'll lead them into battle. My past is a minefield but my future is the service.

So that's how I spend my third day as a Trial III test monkey, jogging across an abandoned base, then blasting through a combat course.

Days four through six are even better: the techs tell me to pair with CAVs.

CAV stands for Combatant Activated Vehicle. Decades ago, the corporate military tasked the top-level AIs with designing new weapons. That was long before the AIs ascended into sapience, and even longer before a shadowy faction genocided them.

The military wanted uncrewed drones tough enough to chew through cataphracts, which are bio-forged remorts that nothing else could stop.

Except, to the corpos' dismay, the AIs created "uncrewed drones" that required human occupants. Hence Combatant Activated. The occupants—the cry pilots—didn't operate the vehicles, but CAVs needed to piggyback on the processing power of the human brain to function. My personal theory is that they also draw on human emotion and reflexes.

And frankly, I'd know: I'm the only person who's ever piloted one from the inside.

Not that I'm so special. I didn't earn the distinction, and I don't deserve the praise. I stumbled through an open door, that's all. Any other soldier in the corporate military would've done the same.

When I paired, the corpos learned that a manually piloted CAV is more powerful than a remote-operated one. Geometrically more powerful. They witnessed the birth of a new weapon, the only thing strong enough to kill lampreys. And after a single grunt paired with a CAV, they started calculating the firepower of a dozen, a hundred, a thousand CAVs. An entire army of cry pilots . . . if my test results support the investment.

That's why I'm tucked inside a CAV in the lab, easing my mind into a meditative flow. Fractal starbursts spin behind my eyelids. My pulse slows, my self shrinks. There's a *clunk* in my soul like a vault unlocking. Then golden threads appear in the CAV saddle walls and I'm fully bonded. I needed Ting to pair me the first time, but not anymore. This is all me now, linking the CAV to my brainstem on some subatomic level, until I can't tell where I stop and the machine begins.

Then I disentangle myself and start again. And again and again, feeding the techs data. Blazing a trail. Spending my days pairing inside CAVs and my nights checking on my squad, which is currently stationed on another base.

M'bari suggests that I befriend Tech Commander Gaaldine, to learn more about the approval process. Jag suggests that I spy on the techs, to learn more about the approval process. Cali recommends I break someone's patella, to enjoy more about the approval process. Basdaq tells me I'm doing great: *Keep on keeping on. We're all proud of you.* Sergeant Manager Li assures me that after testing is over, Command will reunite me with the squad. She knows what I need to hear.

Shakrabarti and Ting don't say much because they're still recovering from injuries. Shakrabarti lost half his body during the attack, while Ting lost half her mind while pairing me.

On day seven, the Ayko techs stuff me into the belly of a diagnostic imaging machine for forty-four hours. Not my idea of a good time, but I don't care: I'm part of something I believe in. Something that matters. I'm not proud, exactly—I'm not sure I deserve this—but I'm grateful. The techs can lock me in a machine as long as they need.

We're going to crack this thing.

CHAPTER 2

The next morning, Ensign Tech Nanty lenses me to head into the simulation gym.

"What's on the schedule?" I ask, instead of checking for myself.

"Veridical Cliff," she tells me.

"Sure," I say. "That's clear."

She transfers a file. "Veridical Cliff is—"

"—the most badass CAV operator squad in the Cherzo-5," M'bari lenses.

"Hey!" I smile as I trot into the sim-gym. "What're you doing here?"

"The Ensign Tech invited me onto channel for a few seconds." He pings me a deadpan click. "Just to say that about them being badass."

"You wouldn't believe *me*," Nanty explains. "In any case, Veridical Cliff is here to assist with the final stage of your training."

"Sounds good," I say.

M'bari scrolls through the CAV squad's file, highlighting key passages for my attention, adding annotations too fast for me to track.

"Slow down," I mutter, and Veridical Cliff projects themselves into the simulation gym around me.

I'm from a Freehold, so my home corporation isn't really *mine*. Still, my unofficial home corpo is Shiyogrid. Veridical Cliff, on the other hand, hails from Welcome 12. M'bari tells me that's why pictograms in an imaginary language scroll across their skinprints.

"Huh," I say.

"That's deep corporate culture in Welcome 12," M'bari lenses. "Which is fair enough. They've earned the bragging rights. Between them, these seven operators have killed nineteen cataphracts and hundreds of lesser remorts."

Identical skinprints are a nice touch, but they're also wearing identical scowls. Antagonism frosts the air. I'm not surprised, because M'bari flags this possibility as he vanishes. To Veridical Cliff, I'm an untrained cry pilot who stumbled into a win. I'm a petty criminal, qualified for nothing more than being strapped into a CAV to activate the controls. Throw away the corpse when you're finished and requisition another warm body.

"We're here," the Veridical Cliff captain tells me, "to guide you through the basic CAV combat simulations."

"I know the basics, san," I say. "We could start with more adva—"

"You don't know shit," a stripe-cheeked operator snaps. "Flailing around like a sanitation drone."

"If anyone knows shit," I tell him, "it's a sanitation drone."

Nobody smiles. Well, nobody *else*. I find myself pretty amusing. And pretty glad that M'bari warned that I'd encounter hostility, and explained why: if cry pilots learn to control CAVs, there's no need for remote operators. There's no need for Veridical Cliff.

"Y'know, because they're *sanitation* drones," I explain, into the silence.

"We read your file." The captain frowns. "You assaulted a military recruiter."

"Not really, san. I only broke his nose a little."

"That's assault."

"In my squad, it's a love bite."

"You assaulted a military recruiter," he continues. "And chose to serve as a cry pilot. You survived a CAV deployment. That's how you enlisted. Not by merit."

"By dumb luck," a grizzled-looking operator says.

"My favorite kind," I admit.

"There's nowhere to hide now, Freeholder," the stripe-cheeked operator tells me.

"Nowhere to hide," the grizzled one repeats. "This comes down to skill."

I don't bother responding. The difference between a CAV operator and a cry pilot is the difference between a snakeskin and a snake. I fought inside a CAV, I killed inside a CAV. More important, I *bled* inside a CAV. I almost died. None of these splices know how that feels, and my confidence shades into smugness.

I'll show them what a cry pilot is.

"Make yourself ready," the captain tells me.

When the training simulation engages, a virtual CAV threads into place around me. Screens brighten, cables unspool. The pilot's frame pivots smoothly beneath my weight. I'm impressed: remote operators strap into interfaces to control CAVs from afar, but this one is designed for a cry pilot.

Words flash on my lens—*ACOS 23.4 MODULE BASIC*.

The entrance to a simulated combat course appears in front of my CAV. My scans show a maze of ramparts with a dozen hostiles. Tracking mines blaze to life, assault drones launch, and a spindle barrage fires at my position.

Warheads detonate but I'm already fifty feet away, whipping around a corner. Fast, but not fast enough. Despite my customized interface, this module is designed for remote operators. For squads like Veridical Cliff, who operate drone-CAVs from miles away. The sim is polished and powerful and inadequate. I'm not tapping into my CAV's full potential. The updated code boosts my power, speed, and precision substantially, but in a real CAV I shatter *substantial* into a thousand pieces.

Still, I burn through the timing, then spin to a halt at the exit.

"Nowhere to hide," I say, as my score rises into the highest percentile.

There's no answer from Veridical Cliff. Instead, my lens tells me to begin *ACOS 4.49 MODULE INTERMEDIATE*.

The simulation shifts until I find myself in the terrafixing. A cloudless sky shines around orange mountains. A whitemoss plain stretches beneath me, an uneven carpet of spongy life. Bulbous plants wrapped in diaphanous shrouds flicker into place— and the sim issues orders: *Neutralize incoming remort*.

A swarm of remorted umire assault drones crashes toward me like a tidal wave. An individual umire is the size and shape of my fingernail—and about as dangerous—but I'm not facing an individual umire. I'm facing thousands. Destroying an entire swarm requires pinpoint accuracy. Yet despite my sluggish simulated CAV, when I spin to a halt the remains of the umire swarm drifts around me like falling leaves.

My score hits the top two percent.

The final scenario—*ACOS 3S MODULE EXPERT*—pits a single CAV against a cataphract, the most fearsome remort on the planet.

Or, if lampreys are remorts, the *second* most feared.

Remorts like umires and cataphracts are the reactivated bio-weapons of the SICLE War, a global conflict that almost killed the planet. After the war, the corpos developed the terrafixing to reclaim destroyed biomes and regenerate lost species. Unfortunately, it occasionally repairs—*remorts*—defunct biological weapons as well.

Oops.

A single cataphract is more dangerous than thousands of umires. Hell, a single cataphract is more dangerous than *millions*. Cataphracts are impenetrable assault machines that extrude bio-forged Paladin battlesuits, which shamble into combat like reanimated corpses. Corporate guidelines require deploying no fewer than four remote-operated CAVs against a cataphract. Yet in this exercise I'm alone as a frozen wasteland takes shape around me.

Ice gleams in the moonlight.

Wind howls between my CAV ribbons.

A grooved fore-cab explodes at me through a snowdrift, followed by a sixty-yard cataphract. A segmented serpent with jointed armor, dozens of crushing legs, and arc-ablators capable of blasting holes in my CAV.

At least there aren't any Paladin battlesuits.

Still, the cataphract is awesome and terrifying. I know I'm in a simulation, but I reach for *flow* automatically. The CAV doesn't respond—the program doesn't support pairing—so I leap sideways, slashing with a ribbon.

I miss.

ABOUT THE AUTHOR

Joel Dane is the pseudonym of a full-time writer. As the son of an Army private and an Air Force staff sergeant, he was raised on war stories and interservice rivalry. He's the author of more than twenty books across several genres and has written for film and TV, including a dozen episodes of a Netflix original series. He lives in California and Maine—not at the same time—with his family. Visit him online at joeldane.com.